Marie t
Puppetma
cheek.

"I warr
listen," the man growled low. "You've pulled back one
too many curtains, seen the atrocities behind it, discovered that still more curtains remain." His fist settled
on the head of the blind woman's effigy, a small doll
made in Marie's image. He compressed it until it was flat
on the table. "Don't open that next curtain, Marie. It is
hung for a reason. Trust me, and I will protect you and
your man-giant friend from this killer. If you draw back
that curtain—"

"I'm not afraid," Marie interrupted suddenly, her eyelids red and swollen, "so don't threaten me."

"If you draw back that curtain," he repeated, putting
the puppet into his pocket, "even I cannot save you."

Ravenloft is a netherworld of evil, a place of darkness
that can be reached from any world—escape is a different matter entirely. The unlucky who stumble into the
Dark Domain find themselves trapped in lands filled with
vampires, werebeasts, zombies, and worse.

Each novel in the series is a complete story in itself,
revealing the chilling tales of the beleaguered heroes and
powerful evil lords who populate the Dark Domain.

BOOKS

BOOKS

Carnival
of
Fear

J. Robert King

TSR Inc.

In memory of Frank W. King,
who believed in good jokes, great books,
grandsons, and dreams.

CARNIVAL OF FEAR

First Printing: July 1993
Printed in the United States of America
Library of Congress Catalog Card Number: 92-61093

9 8 7 6 5 4 3 2 1

ISBN: 1-56076-628-X

TSR, Inc.   TSR Ltd.
P.O. Box 756   120 Church End, Cherry Hinton
Lake Geneva, WI 53147   Cambridge CB1 3LB
U.S.A.   United Kingdom

PROLOGUE

Ferin Irongrod stepped back from the massive granite cornerstone and squinted at the letters he had just carved. The crisp cut marks glinted in the afternoon sunlight. The craftsman brushed the stone dust from his pudgy, dwarven fingertips and distractedly slid a stubby chisel into his work-belt.

"Grand Carnival l'Morai, huh?" he muttered. "Grand Carnival . . ." He puffed a bit of rock powder from the serifs of the *M*, spat on the smooth stone surface, and began polishing it with a rag. "More like Grand Freak Show."

A gust of air crossed the grassy knoll where Ferin stood, whipping the heather in strange circles. It was a desolate place for a carnival, made only more so by the plaintive rustle of wind in the canvas tents.

Turning for a moment from the stone, the mason peered out along a sandy path that led to the circus grounds below. The carnival was a weatherworn cluster of tents, caravans, and sideshow booths, spread out across the broad heath. The whole area was hemmed in by a brambly hedgerow, which ran along a briny ditch. Only the wrought-iron gate provided entrance to the carnival, and did so at the cost of a silver lorin.

On Ferin's left stood a triangular district of shanties and caravans where the performers lived. Their hovels emitted thin columns of gray-black smoke, which drifted ghostlike into the sky. A white fence separated these shanties from the booths and boardwalks beyond. Most of the booths were canvas, though some were made of pine planking covered in peeling coats of whitewash. Between these stalls ran sawdust lanes and foot-smoothed boardwalks. Tonight, those avenues would bustle with the folk of l'Morai, but now, they were empty.

Leaning against the stone he'd been chiseling, Ferin squinted at the banners above the stalls. "Freaks Alley," he read, shaking his head as his eyes passed to other banners. "The Amazing Fire-Eater . . . The Three-Legged Woman . . . The Horse-Headed Boy . . . The Feral Folk of Fairy" He winced as he read this final banner: dwarves and elves and halflings were caged curiosities in the human land of l'Morai.

"Admiring my carnival, are we?" The voice, rumbling like thunder, had come from behind the huge stone.

Ferin spun about. "Monsieur Cygne," he whispered, staring at the dark-clothed carnival owner. The man was huge and misshapen, draped in a voluminous black cowl and thick woolen wraps. Beneath the shadow of his deep hood lay a ponderous brow, a hooked nose, and broad, yellow teeth. Ferin averted his eyes and gestured toward the cornerstone. "Admiring, yes. Quite a carnival you have here."

Monsieur Cygne nodded. A shadowy smile formed on his dark face. "Perhaps when your masonry is done, you'll join us. I could use a dwarven sword-swallower. Or you could join the pack of fairies."

Ferin's coal-black eyebrows lowered. "A cage is no place for a dwarf."

"Not for a civilized one perhaps," the dark figure responded, his voice booming, "but our fairy folk are quite wild, I assure you."

Ferin realized then that he had pulled the chisel from

his belt and held it, daggerlike, in his hand. "You don't treat humans that way, wild or not."

"I treat all the freaks that way," Monsieur Cygne replied lightly. He reached his venous hand toward the cornerstone, and, with curving canine nails, began to trace out the lettering on the stone. "Besides, if it weren't for me and my carnival, elves and dwarves— even civilized dwarves—would be hunted down and killed by the people of l'Morai. After all," he added, his teeth grating softly, "freaks *are* freaks."

Ferin nervously watched the man's hand move across the stone. "I've finished the title piece, as you see. Below it, I've etched the starts for your names."

The man's fingers halted on the *M*, and his voice grew cold. "The starts? It must be done tonight."

"I don't plan on staying longer," Ferin muttered, eyeing the afternoon sun.

The carnival owner nodded, his cowled head moving stiffly with his shoulders. "Don't let my presence keep you from your work, my little man."

Ferin bristled, glancing up. Only then did he notice, above the carnival master's broad, picketlike teeth, a deeply cleft scar that split one nostril. Ferin's face flushed, and he averted his eyes again, pretending to look for his mallet. He retrieved it from beside the cornerstone, set his chisel to the granite, and began the *F* of the word "Founders." The chisel bit into the rock, setting the bottom edge of the letter. Ferin sensed the carnival master moving up behind him, hovering close over his shoulder. The man's lungs sawed unevenly. Trying to ignore the onlooker, Ferin finished the top corners of the *F* and began to set the crosspiece.

"Wait! What are you doing?" the man demanded suddenly.

The dwarf clenched his jaw and snorted. He gestured toward the unfinished letter. "What do you mean, what am I doing? I'm carving an *F*."

One of the man's talonlike hands fastened on Ferin's tunic, and his other traced out the etching. "'Founders, André and Juron Cygne'? What is this?"

"If you want your name first, monsieur, you'll need to speak to your brother," Ferin said, his voice quavering.

"*I* am lord of this carnival, dwarf—not my brother," the man hissed. "Mine will be the *only* name on this stone."

"When your brother contracted me—"

The words were choked off in Ferin's throat as knobby hands closed over his windpipe. The dwarf's heart fluttered, and the ground dropped away beneath his feet. He felt himself rising and spinning. He kicked, flailing to break free, but the hands around his neck were like iron. Ferin's eyes bulged; the sky deepened to a purple hue. He rose toward the shadowy cowl, toward the deformed face beneath it, and the smell of rot billowed over him as the man began to speak.

"This isn't a grave marker, Monsieur Dwarf. This is a cornerstone. My brother's name is not to appear on this stone. Do as I say. Remove it." His gashed nostril separated with each word.

Ferin blinked his compliance, blood flushing his face. A cold grin flashed across the shadowy teeth of Monsieur Cygne. Then, slowly, he lowered Ferin to the ground. The dwarf sputtered, drawing a long breath into his lungs. He staggered back against the stone and set his dusty fingers against its cool surface.

"Whatever you want—sir. But I've already started the *F*. The line will be off-center without your brother's name."

"Mortar in the *F* and start again," Cygne barked as he turned away from the dwarf. "It must be done tonight." Without another word, Juron Cygne strode away toward the carnival grounds.

Before the sun set that evening, Ferin had filled the corners and crosspiece of the *F* and finished the lettering. He collected his final payment and, anxiously eyeing the darkness in the east, hurried away along the heath road.

After approving the dwarf's labor, Juron Cygne ascended the dark cornerstone to watch Ferin leave. A knowing smile crept across the carnival lord's lips. You *will* return, he thought, laughing quietly to himself. He would make sure his carnival soon had an exquisite sword-swallower.

On that same stone a few nights later, Juron Cygne lay beneath a black and starless sky. In the distance, some three hundred yards away, patrons were bustling through the carnival gates. The lights of their torches formed a fragile chain along the inky heath road. Dutifully they had come; dutifully they would pay.

Juron listened with satisfaction to the hungry rumble of the crowd, the clink of silver lorins falling into baskets, the cacophony of music and shouts and laughter from the carnival itself. "*My* carnival," Juron whispered to himself, pulling his black hood from his head. A slow smile of satisfaction spread across his lips, and he rolled over to gaze at the river of citizens coursing through the wrought-iron gates.

Their ruddy, ignorant faces beamed in the torchlight as they filed forward, one by one. A burly baker reached into his pocket and dropped a lorin into the basket before him. Dazed, he wandered forward, peering at the barkers lined up just inside the gate.

"Come one! Come all!" cried a narrow man with a striped shirt and a gypsy scarf tied about his brow. "See the twisted freaks of l'Morai—cursed by nature, abhorred by fate—living, breathing creatures, all. Tour the carnival grotesque, and face your deepest fears!"

In a whitewashed booth beside him sat a fat man in a red satin suit. "Fortune awaits. Seek her fickle hand in the Pathway of Chance. Play over a thousand games of skill and luck! Paupers become kings, and kings become paupers!"

"Mighty and ferocious beasts, every one a killer. See them tamed. See them slain! See them battle to the death in the Rings of Combat," came the cries of a third, bearing a pole arm crosswise on his tanned, muscled shoulders.

Juron watched blissfully as the flood of patrons sluiced into the carnival. "All the way from l'Morai they come," he mused to himself, "like cattle into slaughtering pens, wide-eyed and harmless."

Juron's attention shifted downward to a young boy who had wandered near the massive cornerstone. The boy distractedly dragged his fingers across the smooth block of granite. He stepped back and gazed up at the frontpiece, oblivious of the dark creature lying atop it. The child began to read:

"GR—GRAND CAR—CARNIV—CARNIVAL L'MORAI. Found—er—Founder, Juron Cyg—ne—Cygne. Est. 1272." Smiling faintly at his accomplishment, the child reached up to the lettering. His small fingers passed over the filled serifs of the *F*. The cement had shrunk, leaving hollow depressions that resembled the eyes, nose, and mouth of a skull.

"Yes, my lad," Juron said, his voice croaking ravenlike from atop the cornerstone. "This year, 1272, the arena will be built!"

Startled by the sudden voice, the child ran off, howling. Cygne watched him go, his shadowy eyes tracing every step the child took through the sprawling carnival. At last, the boy ducked into the great tent and disappeared.

Sighing, Cygne sat back on the cornerstone. He reached into a deep recess of his cloak, producing a candle and tinderbox. The box opened easily beneath his practiced thumb, and from it he removed a flint and steel. He struck a spark, lit the candle, and, wincing at the sudden light, shielded the small flame with his knobby hand.

"How's my twin brother tonight?" he asked excitedly.

Leaning forward, the carnival master pried a hand-sized plug of granite from the top of the cornerstone. He peered into the hole where the plug had been, down into a dark chamber carved out of the massive stone itself. An acrid odor rose from the cavity, making the flame flare oddly.

Positioning the candle between his fingers, Juron carefully dropped it into the chamber. It fell about four feet before striking the floor, bounced once on end, then dropped to its side. The flame flickered and grew in strength. Its timid light illuminated the remains of seven or eight other candles, their wax lying in hardened puddles on the stone floor and their wicks burned to blackened nubs.

Juron gazed into the chamber. His attention passed from the burned-out candles to the leg of the man who lay naked in the corner of the dark hollow. The man's bones showed through the bruised and papery flesh that covered his body, and veins ran in purple networks across his limbs. His eyes, closed in fitful sleep, were sunken in their sockets, and his lips were dry and cracked. Smiling wryly, Juron noted the candle he'd just dropped lay quite near the man's leg. The flame was already reddening the flesh.

With a rasping cough of pain, the man awoke and pulled his leg back from the fire. His eyes cracked wearily open, then turned to the aperture in the stone above him. "Juron, is that you?" he whispered.

"You are looking more like me every day, Brother," the carnival master responded.

André shook his head and leaned back against the stony wall. "What—what are you doing to me?"

"Don't you remember, André? Was the drug so strong as that?"

"Please, Juron, I'm thirsty."

"Forgive me, Brother," came the cold reply. "There'll be no more water or food for you. You've already fouled the stone enough. It's time for you to die."

"What did I do to deserve this?"

"It's better if I don't tell you," Juron responded simply. "You might pray for absolution." He leaned farther over the opening and drew a glimmering ruby pendant from his robes. "Did you see that I found this?"

The voice from the stone grew frantic. "Give it to me, Juron! Give it to me! It's my birthright."

"You have only death rites to worry about now. Besides, its healing powers work only against disease, not starvation."

"If you're going to kill me, at least let me die wearing my pendant. I beg of you—"

"Did you let me wear it when the Fever disfigured me?"

André's pleading gave way to a feral growl. "Give it to me, or I will curse you, Juron. I will curse you, and your torment will be twice mine."

"Tomorrow, the arena's construction will begin. The first row of stones will be set, my brother, beginning on the cornerstone in which you lie. And then the next row, and the next. . . ."

"I'll scream."

"As you did yesterday and the day before? I think not. This powder will silence you well enough," he said, opening a glass vial.

"I hate you, Juron. All my love has turned to hate."

"At last we are the same," Juron replied as he poured a fine silt from the vial into his brother's cramped tomb.

 **ONE**

Marie pulled a lock of coal-black hair away from her face and tucked it in the blindfold she wore. Then, setting all but one of her daggers on the stool beside her, she held up the remaining blade and readied to throw. The crowd fell silent. With a powerful flick of her wrist, the young woman threw the dagger straight up into the sultry air. The keen knife tumbled end over end as it climbed ever higher. In the stillness, Marie could hear the faint sound of its edge cutting the air. She could also hear, beyond that minute noise, the hush of the arena crowd and the languid flapping of the canvas tent high above.

"You see," she shouted in her elegant stage voice, "juggling is not a matter of eyes, but of instincts."

Shifting her bare feet on the sand beneath her, she judged the dagger had reached the peak of its arc. "You've already seen that I am blind. And for those who do not believe, I wear this blindfold." She raised her hand and held it palm-up before her. "But I need hands, not eyes, to catch a dagger."

The whir of the falling blade was drowned out by the gasp of the crowd. The handle slapped her outspread palm. She winced at the sting, then wrapped her fingers about the handle. Smiling broadly, she said, "Instinct is better than eyes."

The crowd broke into applause as Marie bowed. Reaching to the stool beside her, she picked up two more knives and took a deep breath, readying herself. The arena smelled of stale smoke and sweat: this had to be the largest crowd yet this year. Marie threw the first dagger into the air. The second followed quickly, tumbling easily from her fingers. She caught the first and threw the third. The crowd quieted, and Marie listened to the rhythm of the daggers slipping into and out of her hands.

"The art of juggling is ancient and noble," she said, timing her words with the twirl of the blades. "The Council of l'Morai itself is a crew of jugglers, propelling justice and freedom, law and liberty in their never-ending orbits. I, for one, am glad they are skilled in their throws and catches. Even we, the common folk, are jugglers." She threw one of the daggers higher, then deftly grabbed another blade from the stool and fit it to the rhythm. The audience applauded again.

"Of course none of us—councilor or commoner—are perfect jugglers. We are human. We grow old, and our clockwork hearts lose their steady rhythm." As she spoke the words, Marie began juggling the knives unevenly, rushing some throws and delaying others. "Eventually, our hearts lose a few pulses." She set two knives aside, juggling the remaining two with one hand. "We grow old. In time, the rhythm stops altogether." The two remaining daggers arced up from her hand, then fell, stabbing into the sandy ground at her feet. "And we die. But when the rhythm starts fresh"— she picked up five daggers and began juggling them in a broad circle before her—"we live again."

Suddenly, something fistlike struck Marie's brow. Dazed, she staggered backward, flailing to keep her balance as her foot tangled with the stool legs, spilling the knives from it. The stinging slice of a dagger ran along her calf. Hitting the sand heavily, she drew her leg toward her and placed a sweaty palm on the painful gash.

Only then did she hear the crowd's laughter and smell the rotten apple that had hit her. Holding the wound, she desperately struggled to rise, but her head was spinning.

"How's your rhythm now!" came a shout from the stands.

Forehead furrowed with pain, Marie grimly set her teeth. The crowd was large and nasty, and her calf was already slick and hot with blood. She could feel the sand beneath her growing wet as she turned her face helplessly toward the crowded stands. A moan escaped her lips.

Then, above the crowd's laughter, Marie heard the rustle of gypsy satin and the thud of oversize shoes. "The harlequins," she whispered with relief.

A harlequin came pounding up toward her and shouted, "Bloody good act, Marie! Bloody good!" The resulting applause was joined by the swishing of more pantaloons. A pair of gloved hands fastened over the wound in Marie's calf, and another pair clutched each arm.

One of the gloves lifted away from the gash. "Look! She's caught me red-handed!" the harlequin cried.

Laughter answered from the stony seats of the arena.

Muttering curses on the crowd, the harlequins lifted Marie to their shoulders and began to run from the arena. After every five paces, they hoisted her higher into the air and shouted, "Hey!"

The clamor and din were broken by the deep voice of the carnival master. "Let's hear it for Marie, the amazing blind juggler!" He paused as applause filled the stands. "And now, let me introduce performers with none of the grace or beauty—or blood—of Marie: Prepare yourself for the harlequins of l'Morai!"

As applause heralded their act, the harlequins trundled

Marie from the arena through the stone-walled stage entrance.

"Have you got her then, Anton?" cawed a harlequin as he shifted his grip on Marie. "We've got to set up the bucket brigade."

"It's all right," came Anton's booming voice as he cradled the injured woman against his broad chest. "I'll take her to her caravan."

Marie pushed the harlequin's soiled ruffle away from her face and nodded her thanks.

The barrel-chested man laughed and stepped out across the broad, sandy floor, carrying Marie past a line of yipping dogs and a pair of harlequins on stilts. The roar of the arena lessened as they reached the arched exit and emerged into the night air beyond. "How long's the carnival been on this heath," Anton murmured, "and still they're throwing apples?"

"Four hundred years, my friend," Marie affirmed, "and *rotten* apples, at that." Her pupilless eyes seemed to stare back toward the glowing arena. "The bigger the crowd, the uglier it gets."

"Afraid so, Marie," Anton sighed as his big shoes clomped across the woodchip-strewn ground. "They've outlawed fun amongst themselves, so they come out here for fun at our expense."

"I want to thank you and the brotherhood of fools," Marie said with a tremulous laugh, her hand still clamped over the gash.

"Hey," Anton said in mock incredulity, "us freaks gotta stick together." They had reached the door of her caravan. "Here we are. I'll help you dress the wound, if you need."

"You've been a great help already," Marie said quietly. "I'll be fine. It's only a shallow cut. But you're late for the bucket act," she added with a wan smile. "The Puppetmaster'll have your head on a pike if you don't show."

"Do you think I'd make a good pike-headed man?" Anton asked, laughing, as he lowered her to the ground. "You sure you'll be all right?"

Marie was already on the stoop of her wagon. "I've been hit with worse things. If you see somebody with apple juice on his hands, though, lend him a fist for me." She gestured with her bloody hand.

"At your command!" Anton stomped once in comic salute, then whirled about and marched away.

Marie smiled painfully as he left, then set her sticky fingers on the handle of the door, easing it open. All at once, the sharp smell of blood from her wound sent a wave of nausea over her, and she leaned on the slick knob.

"I'd better stanch this," she said through gritted teeth.

Forcing the door back, she pushed her way into the cramped wagon and headed for the dry sink in the corner. Her hand trembled as she grasped the tin pitcher beside the sink and poured its contents into the basin. After washing her hands she pulled a shabby towel from a nearby chest, bit its hem, and ripped off a thin strip. After soaking the rag in the basin, she dabbed the wound clean and tied the rest of the towel around her calf.

It wasn't the first time she had gotten cut in her act, but always before she had been wounded by accident, and *never* had the audience laughed. Marie braced herself against the dry sink, the cachinnation ringing in her ears. *Laughter and Blood. Laughter and Blood.* It was a line from an old nursery rhyme her father used to read to her. She still had the storybook, shelved with other fairy tales beside her door. But the books were little good to her now: the Fever had taken both her father and her eyes.

Pivoting on her uninjured leg, Marie sat down on a stool beside the dry sink. The seat was warm and wet.

She stood up, brushing the back of her skirt and sniffing her fingers. More blood. "My leg must be bleeding worse than I thought," the young woman mumbled to herself. She reached out to the dry sink, her hand again clenching the crumpled rag. Dizzy, she shook her head, decided to lie down and clean up the blood later.

Marie shuffled across the plank floor toward the bed. Her smooth-soled shoes slipped on the floorboards, and she barely caught her balance on the unlit stove.

The floor was wet.

More blood.

Marie's heart thudded dully in her chest. She sniffed the air and stiffened. Moving to the bed, she cautiously lowered herself to sit, only to find that the bed was also wet. The pounding of her heart grew more insistent. She ran her hand along the bed frame, then drew it back sharply. A warm drop of blood clung to her finger. Dread welled up inside her as she reached toward the center of the narrow cot.

Her hand fell on a leg.

She stood up and whirled about. No sound, except her own, frightened heartbeat. Trembling, Marie extended her hand toward the leg and touched it. It didn't move. She pinched it, twisting the skin. Still no response. The man was dead.

But it wasn't a man: the leg was short and stumpy, the leg of a dwarf. As she nervously leaned over the body, Marie's hand followed the contour of the muscled calf, past a knobby knee, and the coarse, sodden breeches. The clothes grew more blood-soaked as her hand moved upward. She half-expected the still body in her bed to sit up and seize her throat, but then her finger settled on something that dismissed the thought: a sharp, steel edge protruded from the dwarf's stomach . . . a sword tip.

Marie stumbled back from the bed, upsetting a small stack of books on the floor. Her foot slipped on the slick planking, but she caught her balance on the performer's chest beside her bed.

In the moment of silence that followed, she heard breathing. Not from the dwarf, not from her own fear-choked chest, but from someone across the caravan—someone who had watched her come in, had watched her clean and dress her leg, had watched her stumble over to the bed and find the body.

The murderer.

She could feel eyes on her, could sense the killer's brutal smile. Backing away, Marie leaned cautiously toward her bedside stand. Her shaking hand fastened on the top drawer and began to slide it open. She heard a footstep.

Her right hand darted into the drawer and drew out a dagger. She flung it toward the sound. A shout of surprise and pain rang out—a man's voice—and footsteps turned toward the door. Reaching again into the drawer, Marie clutched another dagger, this time by the handle. She lurched toward the intruder as he swung the door inward. The dagger tip dug through the man's clothes and found flesh. Marie dragged the knife downward in a shallow arc across the killer's body, the blade tearing loudly through his clothes. He yelped, stumbling out the door. Marie was right behind him, gripping the doorframe to keep from slipping on the bloody floor. She heard reckless footsteps fade away into the crowded carnival and knew he was gone.

Marie stumbled down the stoop of her caravan and dropped to her knees on the woodchip-covered lane. "Help!" she shouted. "Please help! There's been a murder!"

* * * * *

The man-giant wearily surveyed the line of children that stretched from the front of his booth. The queue that had formed at dusk had only grown longer as the night progressed.

"Me! Pick me, Monsieur Giant!" shouted another dirty child near the front, conspicuously dropping his copper ducre in the wooden chest of coins.

The man-giant turned toward the shrill cry. Torch-light glittered from his sunken eyes and cast shadows over his gaunt face and bare, bony chest. "May Qin-sah grant strength," the man-giant muttered to himself. He knelt before the child. The boy squealed with delight and climbed onto the man-giant's narrow thigh. Clambering up his crossed arms, the boy slid onto the creature's wiry shoulders. The child, in his excitement, released a shrill scream, and the line of waiting children fell back in awe and fear.

Wincing for a moment as the urchin's sharp-nailed toes scrabbled on his bare back, the man-giant began to rise. As he reached his full height—his hips equal to the heads of passers-by—the boy struggled to stand on the freak's shoulders.

"Look at me!" he shouted. "I'm as tall as a tree! I can see everything!" The boy peered excitedly into the next stall, where a fire-eater lowered torches into his mouth. Beyond lay the booth of the fat lady, and farther still, a stage where mangy dogs leaped through ring after flaming ring. The boy laughed, his voice blending with the thumping tune of hurdy-gurdies, the bustling roar of the crowds, the intermittent bursts of applause.

"Whoa!" the boy exclaimed, losing his balance for a moment. He pitched forward, barely catching a hand-hold on the sign in front of the giant's stall: HERMOS, THE AMAZING MAN-GIANT.

Hermos's long arms reached up to steady the boy, and he shifted his feet on the sawdust-strewn floor below. Releasing the sign, the boy looked out again over the broad carnival, with its tents and torches, car-avans and crowds.

Suddenly, a terrified scream broke the rhythm of the raucous carnival sounds. "Help. Please help! There's been a murder!" It came from a dark section of the carnival, fenced off from the roving bands of patrons.

In one swift motion, Hermos shrugged the child from his shoulders and caught the shrieking boy in his arms. He set the boy on the ground, strode to his coin chest, and slammed and locked the lid. Amidst disappointed cries, he waded into the crowd of urchins. They clung to his legs, trying to push him back toward the stall. With a low growl, Hermos gritted his long, white teeth and pulled the clinging children from him. High-stepping beyond their reach, the man-giant plunged into the river of patrons that clogged the boardwalk.

"There's been a murder!"

The shouts came from the Performers Quarter, a cluster of wagons, tents, and shanties where the carnival workers lived. Weaving among patrons who had stopped to hear the screams, Hermos vaulted the six-foot fence that surrounded the quarter. He bolted down the ill-lit lanes, following the cries. At last, rounding an abandoned shack, he caught sight of the woman: the blind juggler, Marie.

His heart leaped. He had seen her pass his stall many times. Once she had even stopped to listen to the excited laughter of the children waiting in line there. He remembered her long hair, black as midnight, and her moon-white eyes. Despite her blindness, she was beautiful. He remembered that plainly.

Hermos rushed out into the commons. He dropped to his knees beside Marie, whose arms and dress and legs were covered in blood. Her whole body shaking with fear, she opened her lips to scream again, but then Hermos was there, his arms wrapped tightly about her.

"You're safe, lady," he blurted, his deep voice sounding thick and clumsy.

She wrapped her arms about his narrow chest. "I

heard him. He—he was still there," she stammered.

"You're safe," Hermos repeated, patting her back with the fingers of his talonlike hand.

A crowd had begun to converge on them now: a limping stable boy, a pair of painted harlequins, Panol and his parasitic twin, a greasy-haired trainer, the goat-faced girl. Their paces slowed as they neared.

"Look at the blood!"

"Marie's dying, isn't she?"

"What's Hermos doing?"

Hermos looked up from blind juggler to the growing crowd. The performers eyed him fearfully, but none reached out to help.

"Oh, my," mumbled a portly man, working his way through the crowd. He pushed his black cape back over narrow shoulders and straightened the red satin surcoat he wore, drawing a string of knotted handkerchiefs from one pocket. He raised the fabric to his mustachioed lip, licked it slightly, and knelt beside Hermos. "Is she quite all right?" the man asked, dabbing Marie's forehead and peering, concerned, into her face.

Hermos averted his eyes from the man's intense gaze. "She was screaming," he said, his voice like a growl.

"There's been a murder!" Marie cried, pulling away from the man-giant.

"A murder?" the black-robed man said distractedly, frowning at the spot of blood on his silk kerchief. "Who?"

"It's Borgo," Marie gasped, burying her blind eyes in her hands, "or I think it is. The body's in my caravan." She waved in the direction of the wagon.

"My word," whispered the man tightly, gazing toward the moonlit vehicle. The caravan was dark, and its door hung uneasily ajar. A nearby lantern glowed warmly across the bright floral patterns painted on the wagon's exterior, but no light shone from within. Rising stiffly to his feet, the robed man said, "Monsieur Giant?"

"Hermos," rumbled the giant.

"Hermos," the man repeated, a smile appearing on his face, "keep her safe. I'll check the caravan." He shot a glance toward Hermos, then Marie. "I'm Morcastle—by the by—magician extraordinaire."

Hermos nodded solemnly as the magician took his first shuffling steps toward the wagon. The crowd's attention shifted from the bloody woman to the open caravan. As Morcastle neared the door, his face went ashen, and his curled black mustache twitched slightly. Stuffing the handkerchiefs into his sleeve, he reached a lamppost, pulled the lantern from it, and raised it toward the entrance. Lifting the hem of his cape as though it were a shield, he stepped up to the caravan and shone the lantern within.

The place was crimson, as though it had been painted with blood. Blood covered the walls and hung in droplets from the ceiling beams. The chest of clothes, the sack of grain, the apples along the windowsill. Everything was soaked in it. Especially the bed.

Morcastle swallowed hard, clutching the edge of his cape over his mouth and nose. His eyes involuntarily closed for a moment, and he steadied himself on the curved doorjamb. "You're fine," he told himself unconvincingly, "you're fine. You don't *have* to look at it." Despite these assurances, his eyes slowly opened.

There was a body on the bed. It was Borgo, the sword-swallowing dwarf, one of the oldest carnival workers. He had been with the carnival for hundreds of years, swallowing swords that were longer than himself. He now lay rigid on the scarlet sheets, his stubby hands clenched and curled up at his sides. His overlarge head was tipped back, and his eyes lay wide open, staring at the massive hilt of a sword that emerged from his mouth. The sword's broad, two-

edged blade ran down through his throat and protruded, bloody, from his stomach. A woman's red
handprint showed on the dwarf's stocking.

Morcastle fell away from the door, dropping to his
knees on the stoop before the wagon. He set the
lantern down beside him and buried his face in his
hands. Other performers approached, whispering fearfully. One picked up the lantern and moved toward the
door. Shaking his head, Morcastle stood and stumbled
back to where Hermos and the blind juggler were.

"I don't believe it," he groaned, his face a green-gray
color. "I don't believe it."

Marie turned her tear-streaked face toward the magician. "The killer was there when I went in. I slashed him
—a long, curving gash in his back."

A cold sweat beaded across the magician's forehead. "Get her out of here, Hermos. Take her to your
tent. Keep her safe. I'll send for a gendarme from
l'Morai."

Hermos, his dark eyes flashing, hesitated, then
reached toward the blind woman. He slipped one arm
behind her back and the other beneath her knees,
intending to pick her up, but Marie pushed away from
him. Hermos withdrew, wringing his hands.

"It's all right. I can walk," she said, rising to her feet.
She added in mild rebuke, "I'm blind, not lame." A brief
smile softened the words. "Besides, I'm going back to
my caravan."

Morcastle stepped in front of her and entreated,
"Please, my dear. That's no place for a lady."

"It's *my* caravan!" she insisted wearily. She brushed
him aside and started forward. "I'll clean up the blood."

Hermos followed closely, hovering like a giant
shadow behind her.

"You can't," Morcastle called after her. The magician
sighed heavily. "It's all ruined."

Marie's pace slackened as she neared the wagon.

Her groping hands found its smooth-painted side, and she felt her way to the door.

"The sheets, the clothes, the bed, the floor," Morcastle said, stepping up behind her, "they're all soaked with it."

Hermos mutely studied the blind woman, and his brow furrowed with concern. She stepped away from the door, drawing the cool night air into her lungs.

Morcastle set a consoling hand on her shoulder. "You can't clean up until the gendarme arrives. Even then, I doubt you will succeed. I imagine you could wash your sheets a hundred times and still not get all the blood out."

"I'm blind," Marie replied. "I can live with stains."

"Come, lady," Hermos mumbled gently, his voice rumbling in his chest.

She pursed her lips and nodded.

*   *   *   *   *

Hermos ducked as he entered the tall tent he called home. With slow, deliberate steps, he led the blind woman in behind him. She clutched his bony hand, and her feet shuffled, halting, on the sandy floor. Despite her blindness, she turned her head as though looking around the room.

"Tight quarters, by the sound of them, and by the stillness," she noted aloud, then sniffed. "But, it smells clean."

Hermos's lips pulled back from his long, white teeth in a nervous smile. Marie had been right on both counts. Despite the high canvas ceiling, the tent walls formed a tight square. When Hermos had assembled his two cots in the tent, he had to lay them diagonally, end-to-end. The cots still stood that way, dividing the already small space. But Hermos didn't mind. He had few possessions, chief of which was a performer's chest, given to him by the Puppetmaster, head of the carnival. It was a simple black box with sturdy steel rims, and an empty hook where a lock might go.

Stepping awkwardly back, Hermos directed Marie toward one of the two cots. Feeling the wooden frame against her knees, she eased herself down to sit. Hermos released her hand and sat down on the adjacent cot. It creaked in complaint beneath his gangly weight.

"You have *two* cots?" Marie asked, astonished.

Hermos nodded slowly, then stopped himself and said, "One for the top, one for the bottom."

Marie smiled—a sweet smile on her smudged features. "You sleep on two cots, just yourself, huh? Couldn't you get the Puppetmaster to commission a bed long enough for you?"

"Didn't think of it," Hermos replied.

Marie nodded. "Not much of a talker?"

He shook his head, peering furtively down toward her. She seemed small and fragile to him and was still covered with blood and shaking fearfully. Swallowing hard, he ventured, "How about you?"

Marie's face became thoughtful. "I don't mind talking. Before the Fever I used to talk a lot, used to read stories to my father. I've still got the books in my caravan."

Swallowing hard in the silence that followed, Hermos asked, "Before the Fever?"

"Yes," Marie said with a slight blush. "We used to read fairy stories together—'The Ear-Tied Hare' and 'The Horse and the Spear'—you know."

The gaunt man shook his head. "I shouldn't ask."

Marie leaned toward Hermos, a quizzical look on her features. "What do you mean?"

"Nobody wants to talk about the Fever," Hermos said flatly.

"Oh, I don't mind," Marie replied. She set her hand on

his knee. "It's the only way I can talk about my father."

"He read to you?" Hermos prompted.

"Yes. And me to him." Her shoulders slumped. "I'm afraid the books might be ruined now, covered in blood."

"I could clean them," Hermos offered. "I could read to you."

"You can read?"

"Yes," the man-giant replied, his voice thick with embarrassment. "I always could."

Marie's expression darkened. "Well, if you can read through blood, we'll be in business." She shook her head in the settling hush. For long moments they sat in uncomfortable quiet before Marie ventured, "What do you do—in your off time, I mean?"

"I sleep and eat," Hermos began. "I mean, I carve . . . things."

"Really?" Marie's face brightened. "Could I hold something you carved?"

Wordlessly, Hermos stood up. He slung one leg over the cots, opened his performer's chest, and reached inside. When he rose again, his hands held a carved wooden horse, about the size of a cat. Its finely sanded surface was stained a satiny brown. "This," he said, leaning toward Marie and placing the horse in her hands. "A horse."

Marie sighed as she ran her hands over the figurine. "It's beautiful." She fingered the bony head, the well-muscled shoulders, the slender legs. "So this is what horses look like. I've touched their muzzles, felt their manes—I've even ridden one. But, even as a child, I never saw one, or if I did, the Fever wiped out my memory as well as my sight. But this, this statue tells me what a horse *is*."

"That's Qin-sah," Hermos said shyly. He reached into the chest and pulled out two more figures, smaller than the first. He handed them to her as well. "The dog is Ru-pah, and the cat is Salore."

Marie laughed delightedly. "These were your pets—before you came to the carnival."

Hermos's face became grave, and he took the horse back from her. "No. These are gods."

"Gods?" Marie responded, the surprise in her voice making her blush. "I'm sorry. I just didn't think anyone in the carnival believed in gods."

Hermos took back the other two sculptures.

"I'm very sorry," Marie repeated, her blind eyes staring sorrowfully up toward him.

"It's all right," Hermos begrudged, closing the statues again in the chest.

"I wish I had gods to believe in," Marie said. "Tell me about them. Who is Qin-sah?"

Hermos swallowed hard. "He's the god for horses."

"Oh," Marie replied, nodding her interest. "And Ru-pah is the god of dogs? And Salore of cats?"

"Yes," Hermos answered. He continued, as though reciting a childish catechism. "And there's one for pigs and cows and chickens and lambs and crows and rats and hares."

"They all have names?"

"Yes." Hermos eyed her narrowly for a moment, then turned toward the chest and began to open it. "I have a carving with all of them." From the black box, he lifted a two-foot-long, triangular block of wood, shaped much like the pediment of a building. "When it's done, it will hang over my doorway." He placed it reverently in Marie's lap.

"Oh," she said when she felt the weight on her legs. Her hands followed the carved moldings around the squat triangle, then moved inward across the forms. Qin-sah, the horse god stood at the center, his flanks muscled and rippling. He was sided by Ru-pah, god of dogs, and Salore, god of cats. Around these three stood figures that Hermos identified as Mu-sah the Pig,

Winare the Cow, Elberith the Chicken, Felune the Lamb, Coa-rah the Crow, and Favius the Rat. At one edge of the pediment, a small, amorphous knot of wood stood out.

Marie ran her fingers over it. "What is this?"

"That's Tidhare, god of rabbits," Hermos replied, then pointed out, embarrassed, "He's not done."

"Are there gods for humans, too?"

Hermos shook his head. "I don't think so. Something happened to them."

Marie's next question came cautiously. "Which god do you pray to?"

"Qin-sah, mostly," Hermos noted, taking the pediment back. "He's strongest. Fastest."

"After tonight, if you don't mind," Marie said, "I'll be praying to Qin-sah myself."

"It's safer that way." Hermos gently lowered the carving into the chest. "You saw him . . . heard him? The killer?"

The smile on Marie's face faded; her lips drew into a grim line. "Yes, I heard him. I hurt him, too. I cut him across the back."

Reaching to a cloak that hung from the center pole of the tent, Hermos laid it over her shoulders. "Were you scared?"

"Yes," Marie replied wearily, drawing the cloak about her. "Well, not at the time. It happened too fast to be scared. But now I am."

"Sorry," Hermos offered, a word that sounded all too ready on his tongue. He rose from the cot and walked toward the tent flap. There he stood, peering into the darksome night. "You knew Borgo."

"Everybody knew Borgo," Marie said, reminiscence touching her face. "He was a carver, like you. A mason really. When I first got here, years ago, he carved me a beautiful little tree out of quartz. And this little tree was so perfect, so intricate that every little leaf stood out on it. He said since I couldn't *see* trees anymore, he wanted to let me feel what they look like."

Marie pushed herself up from the cot and paced toward the giant, standing at the flap. She felt her way along the canvas wall until she reached him, and there she paused. Hermos said nothing, blinking slowly.

"So, what do you do here at the carnival?" she asked.

"I'm tall," he said, simply.

"I know," Marie said with a laugh. "But what do you *do*?"

The man-giant scratched his knobby head. "I lift children so they can see the carnival."

"You lift them to see," Marie repeated absently, crossing her arms over her chest. "How does the carnival look, so high up? Pretty good?"

The man-giant's eyes darkened, and he turned to look out on the carnival. The tent tops and stall roofs glowed with a fiery light as patrons moved in black swarms among them. "Yeah."

Heavy boots thudded along the path that led to the tent. Hermos stepped back as the flap swept to one side. In stepped a gendarme, holding his lantern up before him. The yellow light from the lamp glared brightly in the small tent, casting a giant shadow behind Marie and an even larger one behind Hermos. The latter winced, throwing his arms into the air to shield his eyes. The gendarme gasped when he saw Hermos and dug his feet into the sandy ground.

"Freaks," he muttered beneath his breath.

Marie, lowering herself to sit on one of the cots, said, "Yes, monsieur, a pair of freaks with excellent ears."

His face flushing, the gendarme bowed curtly and set his lantern down on the floor. He smoothed his close-cropped mustache and removed the cap from his head. "Forgive me, madam."

"Might as well not preen," said Morcastle, who had stepped in behind the fidgeting gendarme. The officer finished tugging on his tight surcoat and let his hands fall to his sides. "She's blind," the magician added significantly.

"Blind?" he asked. "Where's your cane?"

"I know this carnival better than anyone," Marie answered civilly. "I don't need a cane."

The gendarme heard none of it, glaring at Morcastle, "She's blind? I thought you said she was the witness."

"I am," Marie replied.

Striding to the cot where Marie sat, the officer barked, "How can you be a witness?"

"By the sound of your voice, you are an inch taller than Morcastle. By your footfalls I'd say you are fourteen stone. I can smell the oil in your hair and could identify your voice out of a hundred," Marie said coolly. "If you were the killer, I would know it."

The gendarme, coloring to a dull shade of scarlet, retrieved a pen and a piece of paper from his pocket. "Tell me about the murder. Where did it happen?"

"In my caravan," the young woman replied calmly. "I came in to dress a cut on my leg and the body was there."

"Whose?" the thin man asked, making scribbling notations on the scrap of paper he held.

"A dwarf," Marie said. "Another freak, like us."

"Borgo the Sword-Swallower," Morcastle interrupted.

The man scratched his head and chuckled. "Sword-swallower, eh? Risky profession. What was the murder weapon?"

"A sword," Morcastle said. He stroked the waxed tips of his mustache and stared at the gendarme, as though in challenge.

The officer looked incredulous. He stopped writing and stowed the quill in a pocket of his surcoat. "A sword?"

"Yes," the magician replied, his voice beginning to waver.

"Let me guess," the gendarme said, crossing his arms over his chest. "The sword went right down his throat. . . ."

"And out his stomach, yes," the magician finished irritably. "But it *wasn't* an accident."

"Oh, no?" the man mocked, clicking his heels together. "How would a sword get down the throat of a sword-swallower?"

Marie stood up and approached the gendarme. "The caravan is filled with blood, and I chased someone out of it. He was taller than average and heavy, perhaps sixteen stone. A laborer, by the smell of him. And aside from my description, there've got to be traces—handprints or footprints."

Stepping toward the open flap of the tent, the gendarme slipped white gloves over his hands. "We shall see."

*　*　*　*　*

Morcastle stood on the stoop of Marie's caravan, holding back a crowd of gawking performers. He watched as the dark-cloaked gendarme moved about within, studying the evidence. Even discounting the blood that covered everything, the place was in shambles. Curtains had been torn from the windows, the stool beside the dry sink lay on its side, the door to the narrow wardrobe hung ajar, tattered clothes had fallen from their hooks on the walls, bed sheets curled in a crumpled heap beside the straw-filled mattress. And, of course, the corpse lay on the bed.

Morcastle looked away from the rigid dwarf, following the eyes of the gendarme. In numerous places along the wall, scarlet handprints showed against the whitewashed wood. Most of the prints were small, though a few were the size of a large man's hand. Looking more intently, Morcastle noticed that every

time a left, man-sized handprint appeared, the index
finger was missing.

Making a mental note of it, Morcastle turned his
attention next to the blood-sodden blankets beside the
bed. There, on one sheet, not far from another bloody
print of the four-fingered hand, he noticed a bootprint,
slightly larger than his own shoe. In the center of the
bootprint rested two small woodchips, apparently
tracked in from the outside. A thin rim of brownish
powder lined the inside edge of the print. As the gendarme moved to another part of the wagon, Morcastle
leaned in through the doorway and touched the powder. It was soft and fine-grained. Like flour.

"Get back!" the gendarme commanded, stomping
his boot where the flour had lain.

Morcastle drew back, watching the powder curl in
puffs about the man's foot. Eyes wide with incredulity,
Morcastle protested, "You've just destroyed—"

"Who are you to tell me what is and isn't evidence?"
the officer snapped. Shaking his head, he bent over the
still body on the bed. The man's nose crinkled as he
tugged on the blood-stiffened clothes of the dwarf. The
body was rigid, hands curled in tight fists at the sides
and eyes wide open. The wide blade had cut the edges
of the dwarf's mouth as it passed down, and a crimson
line snaked from each corner of his lips. The hilt of the
blade was finely crafted and polished, but a strange
series of scratches ran laterally along its lower edge.
The gendarme studied the broad tip of the sword, pro-
truding through the dwarf's stomach. The edges of the
blade were keen, notched in only a few places, even
though the flat of the blade showed a number of scars.

"Sharpened recently," he clucked, making a note on
his paper. Stuffing the scrap into his pocket, he rolled
the rigid body onto its side.

A small, coin-sized circle of skin had been cut from
the base of the dwarf's skull. The cut was precise, not

jagged or hasty or accidental. The officer lowered the body again onto its back. He pulled the paper from his pocket and scrawled a note to himself.

Pivoting on his heel, the gendarme strode from the caravan. "Death by sword ingestion," he noted dryly.

Morcastle watched, dismayed, as the man pushed past him. "What?" he shouted, falling into stride behind the man. "Don't you try to dismiss this. This was murder."

"Freaks trying to be inspectors," the gendarme said disdainfully. He calmly pocketed his paper and quill and continued pacing across the common area.

"How do you explain the ring of skin cut from the back of the skull?"

"Must have hit his head on the bedpost after swallowing that sword." Reaching a gawking stable hand who had been on his way to care for the horses, the officer grabbed a full bucket of water from him. "There was no murder. It was an accident."

"What about the handprints? What about the boot-print? What about the witness?" Morcastle shouted, his flabby jowls reddening.

The gendarme wheeled. "Your supposed witness is *blind* and *female*? Your supposed victim is a sword-swallower who died swallowing a sword? Your supposed murder scene has stood open while a parade of freaks passed through it? What do you expect me to conclude?"

"You don't understand—" Morcastle began, but the words were cut short by a gesture from the gendarme.

"Not another word," he hissed. In two more strides, the gendarme reached the doorway to the caravan. Swinging the full bucket in his arms, he flung the water onto the crimson walls. It splashed loudly, spreading out to soak even the body on the bed. The handprints blurred. Red droplets pattered to the floor and a scarlet tide of water gushed from the door of the caravan. The crowd around stepped back as the ruby liquid began to soak into the woodchips at their feet.

"I suggest you roll your sleeves up," the gendarme growled to the performers gathered about. "You've got some scrubbing to do before the woman can sleep here again."

 **TWO**

"What good is a machine like this without an eager executioner?" Morcastle asked with a laugh, gesturing grandly toward the guillotine beside him. "Surely one of you would like to execute me!"

The audience gazed hungrily at the black iron contraption, shouting and lifting their hands in a flurry of motion. Morcastle was stunned. He didn't want his executioner to be too eager. "Let me see now! Who among you has the sharpest eyes?"

As the shouts redoubled, more patrons drifted from the boardwalk toward the canvas screen that fronted Morcastle's stage. A boy sat by the entrance, his legs wrapped around a small barrel with a slit in its top. "Ducre, ma'am? Ducre, m'sieur?" he asked with weary repetition. Reluctantly, the approaching folk dug into their pockets and purses, squinting to make out the coins in the early dusk. The boy's ragged teeth looked yellow in the lantern light as he smiled mechanically with each contribution. The patrons paid and then wandered, as though mesmerized, past the screen and toward the shiny-bladed guillotine that sat on the stage of planks.

Morcastle smiled fiercely and strutted to the guillotine. He ran his hands along its cold edges. "You need sharp eyes to handle such a deadly device."

Passing behind it, he triggered the blade. It fell abruptly, with the grating hiss of steel on iron. The gleaming blade slid into the top of the neck yoke, slicing a green melon that lay there. The two halves fell cleanly apart as the crowd momentarily recoiled from the stage. Morcastle scooped up each half of the melon and, bowing, presented them to the patrons. "You're assured a clean cut." The red, seedy pulp of the melon halves dripped onto the stained plank floor.

Still more hands went up. Setting down the melon pieces, Morcastle spread his hands in a flourish before him. "All right, we'll play it fair. I shall blindfold myself and walk out through the crowd. The person whom my hand settles on will be the executioner."

Producing a blindfold from his sleeve, Morcastle donned it. Then he folded his arms across his chest. "Executioners—I come!"

He strode to the edge of the stage, stepped off, and began to wade through the crowd. The more insistent volunteers pushed their way toward him, elbowing others out of his reach. But Morcastle continued onward, squinting through the thin fabric toward a meek little girl he had spotted from the stage.

She was a child of seven or eight, dressed in a dirty sackcloth shift. Unfolding his arms, Morcastle reached out and laid his hands on her shoulders. "A *little* executioner!" he cried out in mock amazement. The girl smiled nervously, shrugging her shoulders. Morcastle whipped the mask from his face, took hold of her hand, and shouted, "Let's have a cheer for this little killer."

Applauding, the people in the rows ahead parted to let them through. By the time they reached the stage, the girl's eyes were filled with tears and her smudged face was reddening. "There, there," Morcastle whispered, patting her hand. "It's fine. Yes. You've nothing to fear. It's all pretend." As the crowd settled back toward the front, awaiting the trick, Morcastle soothed the little girl.

"What's your name, child?"

Rubbing tiny fists in her eyes, she mumbled, "Anna."

Morcastle raised his face toward the audience and shouted, "How about an ovation for my lovely assistant, Anna!"

The crowd responded with loud applause, and Anna's face brightened a bit. She shyly peered out toward the people, and a small smile played about her lips. Standing, Morcastle directed her over to the looming black guillotine.

Morcastle knelt beside the guillotine and placed Anna's hand on the broad crank. He began to turn it. "Our little executioner will now rearm the guillotine," Morcastle announced. Anna clenched her jaw and, with struggling heaves, started to crank the blade back into place. As she turned the crank, the steady clink of chains sounded, and the heavy blade rose into the mechanism. While the child labored, Morcastle secretly switched a small lever on the neck yoke. He could feel the iron-and-wood block settle in place over the blade slit. The block would stop the blade and push it back up into its housing.

Shouts and laughter rose up from the stall behind Morcastle's, and he smiled. Gesturing toward the painted tarpaulin backdrop, he said, "You really must see the ventriloquist act of Panol and his mannequin Banol." It wasn't really a ventriloquist act, a fact that Panol and Banol revealed at the end of each show. Though Banol pretended to be a mannequin, he was actually a parasitic twin joined at the stomach to Panol.

A loud clank announced the blade had reached the top of the guillotine. Hearing the sound, Anna's features again clouded, and she recoiled from the metal contraption.

Morcastle gripped her arms and said, "Everything is fine. It's all pretend. Look, if you help me for only a moment, I'll give you some of these!" His nimble fingers slipped into the white cuff of his sleeve and pulled out a bright cluster of daisies. Anna smiled. She reached her stained fingers toward the bouquet, but Morcastle pulled the bundle back. He set it in a notch in the guillotine's frame and said, "You can have those if you do as I say, all right?"

She nodded, peering up toward the wildflowers.

"See that lever on the machine?" Morcastle asked. He pointed to a trigger just within the girl's reach. "When I tell you to, I want you to pull that lever down. But only when I tell you to."

The girl nodded again, snuffling and rubbing her nose.

Facing the audience, Morcastle shouted, "And now, who among you would like to see the demise of the great and wondrous Morcastle the Magician at the hands of this little child?"

The crowd responded with heavy applause. Morcastle bowed dramatically, holding the edges of his satin cape. With a flourish of his hands, he turned toward the guillotine, raised the top section of the collar piece, and lay down on the belly board. Anna watched wide-eyed, her gaze occasionally straying to the flowers on the black iron frame above. Adjusting his position, Morcastle lowered his throat into the round edge of the neck piece and set the top part of the collar down.

The audience had stilled now, but the shouts coming from Panol and Banol's stage had grown loud and angry.

Cold sweat beading across his brow, Morcastle shut out the sounds and directed the girl toward the lever. She approached cautiously, solemnly. Morcastle grew red-faced as he pointed meaningfully toward the trigger. He granted a stiff smile to the pouting girl.

She looked at him with wide, saucerlike eyes. Then, standing on tiptoe, the girl reached her fingertips to the trigger. She braced herself, setting her free hand on the guillotine's iron frame. Her fingers wrapped around the groove where the blade would fall.

Glimpsing this out of the corner of his eye, Morcastle shouted, "Wait! Move your hand!"

Too late. She'd pulled the lever down. With a clank, the blade released. It plunged, shrieking against the iron frame. Screaming, the girl fell back, pulling her fingers away just before the blade passed. The crowd cringed as the flashing steel buried itself in the yoke. Morcastle's hands clutched the frame and his knuckles went white at the heavy thud of impact. The wood-and-iron block in the neck piece had stopped the blade, though it looked to the crowd as though it had passed through.

Even Panol and Banol's crowd was silent.

"Well, were you hoping it would work?" Morcastle asked wryly.

The audience sighed and began to applaud. Morcastle lifted the yoke from his neck and rose from the guillotine. He bowed, sweeping his hands to the side. "So ends the show, my good friends. Guillotines tend to bring an end to things!" As the clapping died away and the crowd began to head for the exit, Morcastle felt a tug on his satin cape. He looked down to see doe-eyed Anna, pointing toward the flowers on the guillotine. Morcastle smiled, patting her on the head. He strode to the black machine, lifted the flowers, and, kneeling, presented them to the little girl.

"I've never had a lovelier executioner," he said with a quick smile as he brushed the tips of his waxed mustache.

Blinking happily, Anna took the flowers and ran from the stage. Morcastle sighed, watching her go. The show had gone well. They must have netted nearly ten lorins, one copper ducre at a time. Producing a silk scarf to mop his brow, the magician did some quick calculations. After the Puppetmaster had his cut and the boy got a pocketful, that ought to leave nearly three lorins for

Morcastle himself. "Not bad," he murmured. "Of course, it ought to be more, seeing as it's my neck."

He knelt beside the guillotine and began to crank the blade into the air again, wondering how Panol and Banol's show had gone. He hadn't ever heard the crowd respond so fiercely to their performance. Most patrons were sickened or strangely fascinated by Panol and his parasitic twin. This crowd, however, had sounded enraged. Enraged then, and silent now. Strange, he thought. Cranking harder, Morcastle raised the blade to the top of the guillotine and locked it in place.

He paced to the painted tarpaulin hung behind his stage, pulled it back, and carefully stepped into the muddy alley that ran between his stage and Panol's. Treading across the lane, he climbed onto the rough planks of Panol's stage and pushed past the backdrop.

No one remained in the stands, nor on the stage itself. In the center of the rough planks, Panol's stool lay on its side next to an overturned prop table. Morcastle stepped out from behind the backdrop and squinted toward the toppled stool. Moving forward, he ran his hand along the rustling tarpaulin.

A spot of blood marked the floor between the stool and the table. Morcastle stepped back, images of Marie's blood-painted caravan flashing through his mind. Again the tarpaulin rustled. The magician's eyes shifted toward it. Just behind the overturned stool, a narrow vertical gash had been cut in the backdrop. A gash large enough for a man to climb through. No wonder the backdrop was luffing so loudly, he thought. Morcastle pushed the slice open.

On the ground below lay a familiar bootprint.

* * * * *

The performers' refectory tent was perhaps the noisiest, darkest, and most frequented place in the carnival.

Its faded canvas roof was stained and sagging from decades of use. Beneath that roof, performers clustered
around tables, their faces marked with greasepaint and
grime and fatigue. The laughter that came from their
lips was harsh, like the laughter of soldiers in battle.

At one such table that evening, Hermos sat alone,
distractedly prodding at his tin plate with a three-
pronged fork. The steam had stopped rising from his
stewed carrots, and they lay now, cold and orange,
beside a thin sliver of mutton. Hermos didn't care. His
dark-ringed eyes lifted from the food to peer across the
crowded refectory tent, to a spot two tables away.
There, beneath the lulling canvas roof, sat the blind
woman. Her coal-black hair and red satin shirt set off
the whiteness of her eyes and her gentle smile.

She was not alone, not like Hermos. A crowd of
young, handsome men hemmed her in: harlequins,
aerialists, stable hands . . . all eagerly clustered about
the beautiful blind woman.

"That's four for four so far," crowed Anton the harlequin, heading the pack of admirers. He lifted his hat
from the tabletop, the coins within it rattling. "The odds
are getting better, boys." He poured the coins into a
drawstring purse at his belt. "I'll give you three to one
odds she can identify any of you freaks by your hands."

Marie smiled faintly at the praise. "Anyone I know,
that is."

"You sure she's blind?" whined a pudgy stabler who
had already lost four ducres.

A short, wiry harlequin named Tor waved his hand
violently in Marie's face. She didn't respond, didn't
blink her blind eyes. Still flipping his hand back and
forth, the harlequin stared up incredulously at the others and scratched his black mop of hair. A leering grin
formed on his lips, and he crossed his eyes. His companions began to laugh.

Marie's hand shot up like a white falcon from the

table and grasped his fingers tightly. "It seems we have a new volunteer, wouldn't you say, Anton?" Marie asked as she tightened her grip.

Tor blushed, trying in vain to free his hand.

"Tell me who it is," Anton said wryly.

"This should be easy," Marie said. "It's a man's hand, but soft, as though he wears gloves all day. Clearly the fellow who belongs to this hand is a lazy lout who's never done an honest day's work. He must a harlequin!"

"She's got you pegged!" hooted a man with a lizard's tongue.

An aerialist in blue tights said, "Glad I didn't bet on this one."

"And," Marie continued, "judging from the sinews of your hand and the shortness of your fingers, I'd say you are short and wiry. I would have guessed Herciol the harlequin, but he left about three weeks ago. Let's see. The coarse hair on the backs of your knuckles means you're probably the son of an ape." She raised her head and winked one blind eye toward the harlequin. "So you must be Tor Vasalbaab."

Tor sighed irritably. "Dead on, Marie." His comrades cheered the guess, slapping Tor on the back and ribbing him with their elbows.

"You need a manicure, Tor."

The harlequin joined the others in laughing as he tried again to pull his hand back. Marie still wouldn't let go. "Grown attached to me, have you, Marie?" Tor asked. "I'd like my hand back."

Marie's lips pursed and a mischievous dimple deepened in her cheek. "Ante up, Tor."

Catcalls and whistles burst out from the crew of performers around Tor. In their midst, Anton shouted, "Better do as she says. Remember, she's also a knife thrower." Marie smiled coldly.

Muttering in feigned anger, Tor set his floppy shoe on

the table and, with his free hand, retrieved a coin from it. He held up the ducre for all to see. "Perhaps I won't pay. Then I can hold this lovely maiden's hand for the rest of eternity."

Marie's jaw clenched. One of Tor's knuckles popped.

"All right, all right," Tor protested, dropping his coin into the hat. Marie let go, his hand now imprinted with the outline of her fingers.

"Who's next? Who's next?" Anton called.

A black-cloaked form loomed up through the crowd and settled like a giant raven on the seat opposite Marie. A palpable hush and darkness surrounded him; the crowd silenced. From a bony hand concealed in his midnight robes, the man flipped a golden reavoire into the awaiting cap.

Marie's voice was suddenly serious. "I don't need to feel your hands to know who you are, Puppetmaster."

"I expect not," came the purred response. The Puppetmaster gestured for the others to disperse. "I'd like to have a word with Marie."

Anton picked up the cap, pocketed the money, and melted into the crowd. In the space of three heartbeats, the others had also left, and Marie and the Puppetmaster sat alone at the table.

"Good," said the Puppetmaster. "We can speak freely." His long, talonlike hands produced a small figurine: a woman with coal-black hair, a red satin chemise, and a black woolen skirt. The figurine's eyes were painted white. Retrieving a wooden block from his pocket, the Puppetmaster placed it on the table. He then positioned the figurine so it was sitting exactly as Marie was.

"I hear from the gendarmerie you had some trouble in your caravan last night," he said softly.

Marie's finger ran along the edge of her plate. "Just a dead body," she said stiffly. "No trouble at all, as far as the gendarmes were concerned."

"Sarcasm," came the husky reply as the Puppetmaster shifted the figurine's hand to mock Marie's movements. "That's what first attracted me to you, my dear. You're smarter, much smarter, than the rest of my performers. That's why you should have known better than to call the gendarmes. You should have known that I look after my own—that I represent the performers' needs before the Council of l'Morai. You should have known the gendarmes care nothing for freaks."

"Yes," Marie said, combing her hair with her fingers. "Next time the council meets, you might mention that the gendarme washed the murder evidence away."

"Precisely," the Puppetmaster said, running the doll's hand across its hair. "So the officer dismissed the murder, did he? Said it was a mere accident?" The Puppetmaster nodded, peering down at the figurine in his hands. "The gendarmes care only about the citizens of l'Morai, about the normals, not the freaks."

"I'll know better next time."

"Indeed, you will. We've got to solve carnival problems ourselves. Borgo was murdered, you know that as well as I . . . and probably by a normal. We'd never get justice going through the gendarmerie or the courts," he said, folding the doll's arms across its chest. "They've got a huge book of laws in l'Morai; you can be imprisoned for frowning at another citizen. But freaks aren't citizens, so murdering a freak isn't a crime to them."

Marie sighed, crossing her arms over her chest. "Are you suggesting we kill a citizen to even the score?"

"No," he replied with a humorless laugh. For the first time he pulled his hands back from the figurine. "I will look into the matter. There will be no more performers murdered."

Marie leaned forward, reaching across the table. "Let me touch your hands, Puppetmaster."

Rapidly brushing the figurine away from her fingertips, the hulking man placed his talonlike hands in hers. Her small, smooth fingers closed over his, and she ran her thumb over his hard and scaly skin. "Good," she said with a nervous smile, "you have all your fingers."

The Puppetmaster withdrew his hands. "And your killer doesn't?"

"Morcastle said he was missing the index finger of his left hand," Marie said simply. "I'm glad you're not."

"What other clues did the gendarme wash away?"

"A bootprint, with flour on the inside edge," Marie replied. "Oh, and I cut a curving scar in his back, from his right shoulder to his left hip." As she traced out the line of the scar across the table, her hand struck the figurine. She clutched it before the Puppetmaster could pull it away. Her expression grew stormy. The Puppetmaster released a dry laugh, and Marie flung the figurine toward him. "Keep your magic for the ignorant, Monsieur Sienne."

The man's hand seized hers. His arm was trembling with anger. "I am lord of this carnival, my dear. Don't cross me."

A pair of hands—narrow and bony—settled heavily on Marie's shoulders. She felt the Puppetmaster's hold on her fingers slacken, and she withdrew her arms. "Who—?"

"I need you, Marie," Hermos broke in. The man-giant shifted his hands under Marie's armpits and lifted her from her seat.

Rising, Marie stepped back against the tall, gaunt man. "I've got to go, monsieur," she said unnecessarily to the Puppetmaster.

"Remember what I said," he growled.

Hermos nodded his farewell to the black-cloaked man, then drew Marie up next to him and began plodding away. She stepped twice for each of his strides and clung to his hand to be sure of her passage. They had almost reached the door when Hermos leaned over her and whispered, "Morcastle's looking for you."

"Why?" Marie asked, breathless. "What's happened?"

"Another murder."

*   *   *   *   *

"As you can see, the tracks lead up to this spot," Morcastle said, gingerly cracking the lantern cover so a triangle of light fell on the muddy ground. Hermos peered at the last bootprint in the trail from Panol and Banol's stage. The tracks had led them to the edge of the carnival, through the hedgerow that surrounded it, across a log that spanned the briny ditch, and into the thick vegetation of the heath beyond.

Beside him, Marie sniffed the air and turned her ear to the wind. "He went out there?" she asked, nodding toward the vast, black heath that stretched before them. "L'Morai's in the other direction. There's nothing out there."

"Nothing but, perhaps, a murderer," Morcastle responded grimly. He eased the cover back over the lantern. In the darkness that settled, he gazed out at the roiling, gray-black heather, which stretched in forbidding clumps to the distant peaks and tarns. Above him, fiercely shining stars dotted the inky sky.

"Do you think we could find him?" Marie wondered aloud.

Morcastle sighed, setting the lantern on the ground. "I couldn't even find Panol and Banol. Perhaps I'm even mistaken about the signs on the stage: the toppled stool, the spot of blood, the torn tarpaulin. But they weren't in their shanty, or the arena, or the refectory tent."

Marie crossed her arms and shook her head. "They may be back in the carnival, or they may be dead. We can't know for certain."

"Maybe the killer has them—on the heath," Hermos

mused, shifting his large feet on the muddy ground. Under his breath he added, "Qin-sah have mercy."

Marie turned her blind eyes up toward him, a sad smile forming on her shadowy face. "You're right, Hermos. We can't just forsake them."

Hermos's hand fastened on the lantern, and he lifted it. "We need to see . . ."

"Wait," exclaimed Morcastle, groping for the lantern. It was already out of his reach. "If you shine that, the Puppetmaster will know we're going out on the heath. What about the prohibition? I've heard he imprisons performers who break the prohibition."

Morcastle was leaping now to grab the lantern, but Hermos pushed the magician away as though he were a child. Raising the hot lamp high into the air, he pulled back the cover. Yellow light spilled across the heath, shining spectrally on the waving grasses and the wrangling shrubs. It cast giant shadows from Morcastle and Marie. Marie's shape stretched to a sharp descent some hundred yards away, while Morcastle's shadow lay like a huge corpse on the tumbled heath.

"There it is," the man-giant muttered, pointing to a track of trampled grass that wound to the drop-off.

Morcastle hissed, "Well, trim that lamp, for mercy's sake! We only need a sliver of light to follow the trail." Hermos complied, lowering the lantern and setting the cover back over it. Morcastle snatched it from the giant's hand and forged down the path.

Releasing the light without squabble, Hermos extended one of his broad hands to Marie. "Let me take you back."

"I brought these to protect us," Marie said, patting a pack of knives at her belt. "*All* of us."

"I will take you back," he said, reaching toward her.

"No." She batted his hand away. "I've every right to go." She started in the direction she had heard Morcastle pass, but her foot caught beneath the root of a gorse bush. Her ankle twisted, and she pitched forward. The man-giant caught her before she hit the ground, lifting her in his gaunt but powerful arms. She squirmed uncomfortably, her face blushing in embarrassment and anger.

"I'd like to carry you," he said quietly.

"Come on, you two," Morcastle snapped impatiently. He cracked the cover of the lantern, and a thin wedge of light shone on the man-giant and the woman he held in his arms.

Hermos looked down toward the blind woman. "May I?"

The frustration fled her face, leaving only the glow of embarrassment. "Yes, of course."

Though the trail was narrow, it was strangely trampled, as though more than one man had passed that way. As the three performers strode out along the track, Morcastle whispered, "Perhaps the killer dragged Panol and Banol. Perhaps that's why the grass is matted."

The man-giant shook his head, blinking slowly. "No heel marks. No blood."

Glancing back toward the carnival to make sure no one would see, Morcastle furtively flashed the lantern on the trail. The man-giant was right. The magician saw no evidence the twins had been dragged over the grass. Morcastle cast a questioning glance toward his companions. "You think the murderer might come back across this path?"

Hermos shrugged, offering no comment. Marie, clinging to the man-giant's arms, didn't answer either.

They followed the trail to a sharp downward slope. Below lay a grassy vale, with a wide, wet basin: a moor winding its way through the lowlands of the heath.

"Looks dangerous," Morcastle observed as he drew up short of the descent. Without responding, Hermos pushed past the magician and plodded down the slope. Morcastle threw his hands out in consternation, but followed anyway.

At the base of the hill, the trail grew uncertain, appearing to enter the marshy slough. The croak and rasp of frogs and crickets filled the air. Hermos halted, and Morcastle came up behind him, nodding solemnly.

"Looks like the trail ends here."

Peering down severely at the magician, Hermos shifted Marie into one of his arms and snatched the lantern with his other hand. He opened it wide, shined the light out over the brushlands, and scanned the bog for sign of the trail. After only a few moments of looking, he spotted some broken reeds. The path began again a stone's throw away, curving around the moor and entering a young wood of thin and stunted trees. "This way," he said, still holding the lantern. He led the way around the rim of the watery trough, Morcastle trotting to keep pace with him.

On the far side of the slough, they entered the wood. Its birch trees rose white and coiled like columns of smoke, and the lantern light flashed spectrally among them. The sounds of frogs and crickets gave way to darker rustlings in the undergrowth.

"We've no idea if this is even the murderer's trail. It could be from a stag or wolf."

"Here it is," Hermos said. "Qin-sah help us." He pulled up short, setting Marie on her feet and hanging the lantern on a nearby tree. Morcastle approached behind him, almost running into the man-giant's legs before he spotted the mound of earth.

The underbrush had been uprooted, and it lay, still green, in a pile on the far side of the mound. Boot marks covered the soil throughout the clearing. It looked as though a hundred men had trampled the ground, and, in a few places, shovel marks cut shallowly into the earth.

"What is it?" Marie asked in a whisper, reaching out to touch one of her companions.

"A grave," replied Morcastle as he approached the mound. "Or at least I believe it is."

The magician shot a worried glance toward Hermos, then looked back at the mound. He set his fingers on the pile of earth. "I wish I had a shovel."

"I brought my daggers," Marie offered as Hermos moved to kneel beside the magician. "They'd make crude spades."

"No," Morcastle snapped, digging his fingers into the ground. He pulled a handful of the rich topsoil from the pile of earth, then said, "Forgive me, my dear. It's just that digging in a grave with daggers seems such . . . sacrilege."

Marie did not respond. She dropped to her knees beside Hermos as he began dragging large swaths of soil from the mound. The performers grew silent as they clawed away more ground, and the black earth worked its way beneath their fingertips. With each swipe of his hands, Morcastle expected his nails to scratch against wet, rubbery flesh. Still he dug, and found only moist soil.

"You'd think it would be a shallow grave," Morcastle said, huffing as he lifted a large rock from the ground.

"If the wolves sniffed out the bodies and dug them up . . . ." Marie began, but the words drew up short. For a moment, the only sound was the ceaseless patter of dirt being tossed from the hole. Swallowing hard, she continued, "If the wolves dug up the bodies, the madman might be caught. . . . Are you quite sure we're alone in this forest?"

His eyes growing wide, Morcastle raised his head and peered out through the young glade. The lantern light illuminated the forest for a short distance in every direction. Morcastle could see only the white-barked trees and the rolling undergrowth. The murderer could easily be hiding only ten feet off, and he wouldn't be able to tell. "Can't say for sure," he replied, gritting his teeth and digging again. "But keep those daggers handy."

Hermos's large, bony hands were sinking like shovels into the soil. As the hole deepened and its base narrowed, Morcastle allowed the man-giant to dig alone. Clumps of moist earth and sprays of sand flew from his fingertips, and rivulets of sweat coursed down his temples. A foot of soil removed—a foot and a half—and still nothing.

Hermos's hands were slowing by the time he finally thrust his fingers down and halted. The man-giant released a quavering moan of dismay, like that of a child. As he pulled the loose earth from the grave, Morcastle leaned forward and peered down into the hole.

A round, childlike face stared up from the ground, a face pinched tight in pain. Dirt rested unnaturally in the corners of the closed eyes and filled the open mouth. Particles of soil clung to the creases between the teeth and packed the gumline. Shaking his head in horror, Hermos brushed more of the dirt away, revealing bloodless cheeks and lips and the wisp of a young man's beard.

"Panol," groaned the man-giant, his lips pulling back in disgust. He glanced for a moment at Morcastle, who sat back on his heels, his hands quivering.

"I can't believe it," Marie said, reaching toward the grave.

The man-giant's huge, soil-encrusted hand clamped over her wrist, but Morcastle said, "No. Let her touch him. Her hands are her eyes." Hermos nodded slowly, releasing her.

Without a word, she crawled forward and felt her way to the hole. Reaching down into it, her fingers came to rest on Panol's knotted brow, then passed over his nose, across the gathered cheek, and to the mouth below. After the briefest pause, she pulled her hand back.

"I half-believed we were deluding ourselves," Marie whispered, "until now."

The man-giant reached out and dug into the soil to the left of Panol's head, his fingers feeling for the face of Banol. He dragged one handful to the surface, then a second, then a third. Reaching down into the grave, he probed the soil again. Surprise, then confusion played over his features, and he jabbed deeper.

"He's not here."

"What?" Morcastle asked.

"Banol's not here."

Marie's voice rang hollowly, "What if . . . what if the murderer separated them?"

Blanching, Morcastle eyed the ground around them. "What do you mean, separated . . . ?" His gaze stopped on another, smaller mound on the other side of a pale beech tree. He tapped Hermos's shoulder and pointed out the second pile of earth, then said to Marie, "You're right. There's another grave, just beyond this tree." He paused a moment, allowing the information to sink in. "I suppose it's a foregone conclusion," he said, clenching his jaw and staring at the smaller mound. "Need we dig him up?"

"Yes," said Marie without hesitation. "Yes, dig him up. They should be buried together."

Morcastle rose and staggered to the other mound. Dropping to his knees, he began to dig.

Marie wiped her brow with the back of her wrist. "What have we got, then?" she muttered in a shaking, tearful voice. "A nine-fingered man, a bootprint with flour on one edge, a crescent-shaped wound. . . . Did you find any other clues on the stage, Morcastle?"

Grunting as he pulled humus from the grave, the magician said, "Well, not as such. Whoever the murderer is, he knows the carnival pretty well. He approached Panol's stage along the performers' alley, behind the backdrop. Then, I suppose, as the crowd left, he cut a swath in the backdrop and pulled them through." Morcastle panted, scooping the last bit of soil from the shallow grave. Wiping his dirty hands on his pantlegs, the magician sat back to survey the corpse. It was Banol, the miniature image of his twin. He lay on his back, packed on all sides with topsoil. He looked like a puppet, his long abdomen as thick as a man's arm and ending in a ragged stump. He had no hips, no legs, no feet. Only the mud-packed gristle where he once was joined to his twin.

Morcastle turned away, sickened. "It's Banol all right. Let me know when the grave's ready," Morcastle said weakly.

The man-giant grunted, clearing the earth from atop Panol's body. "Almost." Panol was whole, except for a muddy ring of flesh on his stomach where his twin had been cut away.

Seeing Hermos nod, Morcastle reached trembling hands toward the severed, parasitic twin. He cradled the creature's narrow body in his hands. Shuddering, he pulled the body free and carried it to the other grave. The man-giant took the corpse and laid it into the well beside his brother. Then, sinking his nails into the loose soil, Hermos began to brush the earth over the bodies.

"Wait," said Marie, latching onto Hermos's arm. "Check the backs of their necks."

The man-giant swung his haunted eyes toward Marie, then bit his lip. Slowly he lifted Banol's body and turned it over. A circle of skin had been cut from the twin's neck. Laying Banol down, Hermos dug around his brother's neck and pivoted the head to the side. Once again, he saw the bloody circle where the skin had been removed. "They've got the marks, too."

"Bury them," the magician blurted, nodding nervously at Hermos. "Bury them now."

The man-giant set to work, muttering prayers to his strange wooden pantheon.

Watching him, Morcastle sat down unsteadily and brushed the dirt from his trouser knees. He saw a tear well up in Marie's eye and streak down her cheek. The magician reached out and pulled her next to him. As she buried her face in his chest, Morcastle looked blankly outward.

"Last night we had a single murder. Now, we've got three," Morcastle said, gazing at the graves. "What are we going to do?"

"Find the murderer," Marie said, clenching her fists. "Find him and convict him. We'll bring the gendarmerie here. They *can't* ignore this."

For a while, no one else spoke, as though Marie had spoken for them all. At last, Morcastle produced a handkerchief from his sleeve and offered it to the blind juggler, saying. "Well, while Hermos gets these two buried, I'll look for some clue as to where our murderer has gone."

Morcastle stood up and staggered away from the clearing, his feet dragging through the uprooted undergrowth. Trudging across the uneven ground, he reached a birch some thirty paces from the clearing. There he stopped, leaning on the tree. His hand rubbed the waxed tips of his mustache as he shook his head. "I'm no gendarme," he murmured to himself, mopping his brow. "Bodies and bones and blood . . ." Pushing away from the tree, he pivoted and set his back against the curving trunk. He peered toward the graves, the lantern casting broad shafts of light through the trees.

His eyebrows knotted in alarm. There, in the lantern light, he could see at least seven other mounds, silhouetted between the birches. The undergrowth had covered them, masking them from view, but they were there all the same. A trickle of sweat ran down Morcastle's temple, and he tried to see how many more mounds lay beyond the lanternlight. As his eyes adjusted to the darkness, the blood ran from his face.

The mounds were everywhere.

"Damnit!" he shouted, clinging to the tree. "Damnit!"

"What is it?" came Marie's voice.

"There are more," Morcastle gasped, beginning to clamber toward them. "The woods are filled with graves."

Hermos stumbled to his feet, and he peered out into the forest. Shaking the dirt from his fingertips, he strode toward Morcastle, confusion written on his features.

"Look there! And here and here!" Morcastle stammered, pointing to the ridged ground.

Hermos's expression became severe. He pivoted, snatched the knife pack from Marie's belt, and plodded into the woods. Reaching one of the mounds, he kicked the underbrush away then dropped to his knees and pulled a knife from the pack. The blade sank easily into the packed ground, loosing a small chunk of soil. Hermos grabbed another blade from the pack and dug with the other hand. After a few more strokes, the dagger struck something hard. Discarding the blade, Hermos sank his fingers into the soil. A putrid smell rose up through the slit left by the knife stroke. The man-giant wrenched a large clod of earth free.

Another body. "Great Qin-sah."

Morcastle stood behind the giant and stared wide-eyed toward the hole. He fell back, his throat constricting. "We need more light," he choked out. He spun about and thrashed back through the underbrush toward Panol and Banol's grave. Standing on tiptoe, he retrieved the lantern, then took Marie on his arm. They walked together to the newly discovered gravesite. By the time they arrived, Hermos had unearthed the body's head.

"Another scar," he muttered, pointing to the worm-eaten skull. On the left side of the face, a brown, fractured cheekbone showed through; on the right side the skin was pulled back in a rictal grin. Hermos rolled the head to one side and lifted a flap of the ragged hair that still clung to the skull. There, very clearly, they could see the spot where a circle of skin had been cut away.

"How long has this been happening?" Morcastle asked.

"How many graves are there?" Marie asked, her blind eyes seeming to search the forest around them.

Morcastle shook his head. "Hundreds."

"Then he must have been killing for years this way," Marie said, her voice cold as iron. "Performers come and go from the carnival all the time. They show up; they disappear. I always thought they'd left for other carnivals. But now I'm starting to think many of them were murdered."

Hermos stood up, panic fluttering across his features. He shook his head and began to kick soil over the shallow grave, mumbling more prayers.

Morcastle said, "Surely the Puppetmaster would have noticed."

"Yes," Marie replied coldly. "Surely he would have."

 **THREE**

Nervously, the man wiped his heavy boots on the woodchips that covered the ground in front of the caravan. He lifted the torch in his hands, and his eyes traced out the huge circus wagon before him. It had once been used to haul animals, back in the days when the carnival had traveled from town to town. Even though the wagon's original paint had been covered by a thick coat of shiny black, the man could still read the embossed lettering on the side. *Exotic Oliphants From Kandrilla.* The thick iron bars of the wagon remained, though walls had been built behind them—windowless black walls. The stout wheels of the caravan, designed to bear the weight of two or three behemoths, had long ago been removed and put to other uses, and the fat axles had rusted to their brackets.

The oliphant wagon was adjoined in back by an equally ominous collection of lean-tos and shacks. The inside of the carnival master's abode must have been a dark and endless catacomb.

Swallowing hard, the man knocked on the ebony door with his right hand. The sound of footsteps came from within the coach, and the door slowly opened. A dark-robed figure, blacker than the black room behind him, peered out. The torchlight reflected in savage flickers from the man's glossy eyes.

"Ah," the Puppetmaster said, his voice heavy on the night air. "It pleases me to greet you, come all the way from the city."

Nodding, the man said, "Yes. They said you wanted to see me."

"Indeed," the Puppetmaster said, swinging the door open and motioning the man inside.

* * * * *

The sun lifted heavily from the horizon as Morcastle and Hermos toiled up the slope toward the carnival. The man-giant guided Marie's steps, whose unseeing face was angled toward the ground. They made their way through tall grasses bristling with dew and smelling of hay—an odor much preferable to the fetid smell of the moor. But none of them noticed the change. Their minds still reeled with the discovery of Panol and Banol, and the forest of graves.

"I just can't believe it," Morcastle said for the third time, his trembling hand mopping the beads of sweat from his forehead.

"The whole thing is unbelievable," Marie replied wearily as she clung to the man-giant.

"There were hundreds of them . . . the graves, I mean," Morcastle replied. "Even if he's been killing one person every night, it would've taken him a year to fill up that wood with bodies."

Marie shook her head. "More than that. Some of those graves had three or four years' growth on them."

"And he's never been caught," Morcastle observed with a shiver. "What does that say for our chances?"

Marie fingered a button on her chemise. "We'll find him. Evil can't endure. It turns in on itself."

Hermos regarded her with a shocked expression. "That is a saying of Qin-sah!"

"The horse god?" Marie murmured. "I thought it was

from a story my father told me: The Ear-Tied Hare."

"I need to read that story," Hermos declared.

The trio reached the top of the rise, a stone's throw from the outskirts of the carnival. A level stretch of heath lay before them.

Morcastle fell in step beside the man-giant. "Evil and good aside, what *are* our chances?"

Marie opened her mouth to reply but stopped short and listened. A low rumble had begun on the distant heath. "What's that noise?" she blurted.

Morcastle turned toward the sound, which came from the direction of the l'Morai road. "Oh, no," he groaned in dismay. The rumble swelled to become the unmistakable sound of horse hooves pounding on packed earth. Shielding his eyes from the morning sun, Morcastle made out a large black form, charging toward them across the dewy grass. A horse and rider, and, judging from the occasional glint of brass buttons on the rider's tunic, it was a gendarme. "The heath patrol. Someone must have told them we'd left the carnival," Morcastle said, cringing. "We're doomed."

"Perhaps not," Marie replied. "Surely they'll waive the trespassing law when we show them the graves."

"Another one," murmured the man-giant, pointing toward the side of the carnival that faced out on the heath. Another rider approached, astride a roan mare at full gallop. Grunting, Hermos stepped in front of Marie. "We'll fight, if we must," he explained.

Morcastle shot a concerned glance at the looming giant, who planted his feet and sank into an imposing crouch. Sighing, the magician tapped his heels together, triggering the spring-loaded dagger in the toe of his boot. He edged the dagger beneath the tenacious grass and conjured a toothy, placating smile as the horses neared.

Both riders were now in view, though the one on the black stallion approached more quickly. He was garbed in a stiff gray jerkin, coarse woolen breeches, and a flapping cape. His left hand held the reins of the steed, and his right hand was clasped over the hilt of his sword. The stallion's broad black hooves cut heavily into the rugged heather as he neared. The horse's pace slowed, and the gendarme pulled his mount to a halt. He swung gracefully from the saddle. The clean-shaven skin of his right cheek was rippled and red, as though he had been burned. His eyes flashed, darting from Morcastle to Hermos to Marie. In two quick strides, the clean-shaven gendarme reached Morcastle. The other gendarme—who wore a tight-trimmed goatee—also dismounted.

The magician dropped to one knee and flourished his hand grandly. "How good it is that the council's men are always on hand when needed!" Morcastle said, rising.

The gendarme drew his sword. Swinging the blade upward, he pointed it at the magician's neck. "What are you freaks doing outside the carnival?"

Struggling to retain his smile, Morcastle replied, "We've discovered a murder, a host of murders, in fact—bodies buried in the woods—and we were on the way to fetch you when you showed up. Come along."

He motioned for them to follow. The gendarme clenched his jaw and kicked Morcastle's foot out from under him. The magician landed in an undignified sprawl on the heath, the dew soaking into his satin cape. He turned over, the smile gone from his lips. The officer moved forward and towered over him, dagger-like teeth showing beneath his thin lip. The man's sword once again hovered above Morcastle's neck. "Been in the woods, too, have you? The heath and the moor weren't enough for you?"

"These freaks look pretty scared, eh, Fassioux?" the other gendarme noted, waving his sword in front of Hermos and Marie.

"Look here, my good man," Morcastle said sternly. "We've just discovered a whole village of graves. You fellows bring this information to your captain and he'll probably promote you to lieutenant. Now get that sword away from my face," Morcastle insisted, pushing the blade away.

Fassioux snarled and planted his sword over the magician's heart, cutting into his surcoat. "You freaks are outside your carnival—you're trespassing, and for a freak that's a capital offense. We could kill you right here—you and the giant. 'Course, we'd have other plans for the woman."

Marie's fist clenched into a tight ball, and she whirled about, aiming her punch in the direction of the gendarme's voice. Her white knuckles struck Fassioux squarely in the jaw. The blow stunned him, knocked his sword loose, and sent him sprawling beside the magician.

Incredulous, Morcastle looked from the prostrate officer to Marie, who wore a wicked smile. Steel flashed behind her: the other gendarme's sword. Morcastle grabbed Marie's hand and yanked her toward him, away from the deadly blade. The sword sliced through the air; its tip caught her shoulder, then swung past. She yelped and plowed into Morcastle, knocking him backward atop Fassioux.

Wailing, Morcastle flipped over and pinned the man beneath him. Fassioux gurgled furiously and struggled to grab his sword, but the magician batted the officer's hands away.

Sudden, sharp pain gripped Morcastle's side, a fist hammering his ribs. He groaned, hurtling sideways and landing on his aching side. Freed, the gendarme scrambled toward the sword. Despite the pain in his chest, Morcastle lurched up from the ground, clutched Fassioux's cape, and hauled backward. Instead of falling, the soldier dropped to one knee and flipped

Morcastle over his shoulder. The sunny sky and windy heath spun unnaturally for a moment before Morcastle's back struck the earth. Breath exploded from his lungs, and the world blackened.

As the darkness closed around him, Morcastle glimpsed a black boot and seized it. It shuddered in his grasp, trying to break free, but he held on tenaciously. The broad heel smashed him in the cheek. Crying out in pain, the magician lost his hold.

Fassioux pulled free with a shout of triumph, and his hand fastened around the hilt of the sword. He yanked on it, but it wouldn't budge. Marie was standing atop it, her slender arms crossed defiantly over her chest. In each of her hands, she held a dagger by the blade.

"You think you're a match for me, woman?" Fassioux asked cynically, rising to a crouch. The soldier smiled and inched toward Marie. "You can't even see where I . . ."

Her wrist moved, and a dagger flashed through the air. With a sickening thud, the knife sank deep in the man's left thigh. He slumped to the ground, clutching it and shouting.

"Left thigh," Marie said coldly. "And I've still got another dagger, and four more in the belt pouch. Let's see, that's enough for your other leg, both arms, your head, and your heart."

Gritting his teeth, the man worked the dagger loose from his thigh. He wiped the blood from its tip and raised it to throw.

"Want another one?" Marie asked, clutching a dagger between her fingertips.

Drawing his arm back, the man rasped in feigned helplessness, "Help! I'm bleeding to death. Help me. Help me!"

"No," Hermos said simply, striking the man soundly on the head. Fassioux's eyes darkened, and he crumpled to the ground. With one step, Hermos reached Marie.

"It's just me," he said.

"I know," Marie sighed, slipping the knives back in her belt holder. "What about the other one?"

"Sleeping," Hermos said, gesturing toward the goateed gendarme, who lay still in the grass, "in the bosom of Tidhare."

A cheer rang out from the carnival grounds, and Hermos glanced up to see a small crowd of performers, clapping and hooting. He smiled nervously, flashing his long white teeth.

As though awakened by the shouts, Morcastle rose dizzily from the ground, his hands clutched about his aching ribs. He managed a halfhearted bow, which brought even more applause. Then, pivoting painfully, he staggered toward his companions. "We've got to get into the carnival before they wake up."

Marie nodded seriously, then gestured toward the motionless Fassioux. "Is he bleeding badly?"

Morcastle glanced irritably toward the gendarme. "Not badly enough. He'll live. But, I suppose I could spare a kerchief." Pulling one from his sleeve, he knelt and tied it over the wound. Then he stumbled to his feet and said, "Let's go home."

Marie asked, "Where did their horses go?"

Morcastle spotted the swish of a black tail amid the crowd of performers. "Looks like they've joined the circus."

*   *   *   *   *

Morcastle unclasped his satin cape, folded it neatly, and set it on the sandy floor beside Hermos's cot. He eased his aching back down onto the cot's creaking frame and stared at the flapping canvas of the high ceiling. "Those gendarmes were pretty unwilling to hear about the murders. Perhaps they committed them, or are protecting someone who did."

Marie sank her fingers into the cool water Hermos had poured into his basin. She cupped her hands, filled them, and pressed the water against her face. Rivulets ran down her weary features. "Perhaps. But the murderer we're dealing with seems a lot smarter than those two fellows were. I think they did what they did because they hate freaks, not because they knew anything."

Hermos handed the blind woman a threadbare towel and, as she bowed her head to pat her face dry, he stared at the back of her neck. His eyes went wide. Tentatively, the man-giant reached out to draw Marie's hair off to one shoulder. Beneath his touch, the blind woman bristled. "What are you doing?"

Hermos leaned forward, touching his narrow fingers to the back of her head. "Something here." He parted the hair, smoothing it to either side. Between the thick strands of black, he glimpsed a pattern on the skin. "Tattoo," he mumbled. "Red tattoo."

Marie lifted her face toward them. "Tattoo? I don't have any tattoos."

"Let me see that!" Morcastle barked nervously, leaping up from the cot. He squinted at the spot Hermos was indicating. There it was: a square red mark, the size of his fingertip. As he meticulously parted and reparted the hair, the tattoo began to take shape in his mind. It had a thin border, which ran around a rearing horse. Looking closer, Morcastle spotted a spear through the horse's back. He shook his head and backed away.

"It *is* a tattoo, Marie," Morcastle said, wringing his hands. "It's above your hairline. I would never have seen it if I didn't know what to look for."

Marie shook her head. "What are you talking about? What is it a tattoo of?"

"A rearing horse, with a spear through its back."

"Barlowe has one," Hermos interrupted.

Morcastle shot a glare his way. "The strong man? Oh, yes. Now I remember seeing it. I thought he got that tattoo after he shaved his head."

"I saw it on two others, too," Hermos said.

Marie clasped the man-giant's hand. "This is insane. Hermos, check Morcastle's neck, and vice versa."

The magician bent his own neck forward, brushing the hair out of the way. "Do I have the same mark?"

Peering for a moment, the man-giant said, "Yes."

"Kneel down—let me check you." The giant dropped to one knee beside the magician. Morcastle's careful fingers probed through the ratty hair. Then, suddenly, he paused.

"Yes, we've all got them. But how? Who tattooed us and when? And why?"

Marie staggered, stepping back and sitting down on one of the cots. "Maybe it's a mark of the plague, the Fever. I was infected. Did either of you have it?"

"Yes," Hermos said, "I was born with it. Right here, at the carnival."

"But I wasn't," Morcastle interjected. "I was thirty-five when I came here—been a traveling magician for twenty years, with hardly food in my stomach and clothes on my back. But I never got the plague."

Marie rubbed her face with her hands. "However we got these tattoos, they must be what the killer's been cutting off of his victims' heads."

"It's sick. Mutilation." Morcastle sat down as well. "We've got a cunning killer loose—cunning and voracious—and no help from the gendarmerie," he mused, shaking his head. The wind languidly flapped the canvas walls of the tent. "What are we going to do?"

"I'll tell you what you're gonna do," came the tinny voice of a short man who strode into the tent. Valor Ceres, the fire-breathing midget, planted his tiny feet firmly, crossed his burly little arms over his chest, and fixed the company with stern eyes. "You're gonna get to the Puppetmaster's place, and now. The gendarmes are combing the carnival for you. If you don't get the

Puppetmaster's protection before they find you, they'll cut your throats."

"Cut our throats?" Morcastle moaned, his hand dropping wearily to the folded cape beside him. "I knew we should have killed those two."

The midget harrumphed, his red eyebrows bristling. "It's not just those two. They got them about twenty others. Hurry up. The Performers Quarter is the first place they'll look."

Marie sat up. "Let's go."

With the fiery-haired Valor in the lead, the three companions stalked through the afternoon carnival, trying to avoid the eyes of the gendarmes. Valor insisted they stay low, especially Hermos, whose head floated above the tops of most of the stalls. They crept from the tight aisles and lanes of the Performers Quarter, through a breach in the fence, and across the sideshow boardwalk. Cutting behind the fat woman's booth, they reached the muddy Freaks Alley, which backed Morcastle's stage. As they moved along the dark lane, Valor peered nervously around corners. More than once, he hissed the three fugitives to a stop, only to motion them forward moments later.

At last they reached the Puppetmaster's caravan, an ominous and rambling structure at the edge of the carnival gardens. Morcastle swallowed hard as he scanned the rows of black iron bars that lined the outside of the wagon. "Are the bars meant to keep us out, or keep him in?"

"Shhhhh!" Valor sputtered angrily, his imperious gaze coming to rest on the magician. The midget pointed toward the caravan with a pudgy finger. "You'd better knock, even though the gendarmerie might be down this aisle any moment. The Puppetmaster don't like people not to knock."

Hermos nodded solemnly, and Marie pressed her lips together. She whispered, "Let's hope the Puppetmaster can work his magic for us."

"It's him or an execution, mark my words," Valor said.

"Thanks for your confidence," Marie said flatly.

Morcastle moved forward, latching onto her arm. "We'd better go." He stepped toward the black, windowless caravan, dragging a reluctant Marie behind him. Hermos followed, scanning the surrounding tents and shanties. All was quiet. The three performers strode to the ebony door, and Morcastle rapped on its frame.

The latch sounded, and the door swung inward. Within the narrow opening, the Puppetmaster hovered, huge and black, wrapped in his thick woolen cloaks. His face was inscrutable beneath the hood, and the ruby pendant he wore swung idly within the folds of his cloak.

"I've been waiting," he said, his voice shaking the dark caravan.

"We've some urgent business," Morcastle blurted. As an afterthought, he bowed awkwardly. "May we come in?"

The Puppetmaster soundlessly drifted back from the door, allowing it to swing open behind him. Steeling his courage, Morcastle stepped across the dark threshold, leading Marie inside. Hermos ducked, nearly bending in half, and shuffled through the portal, pulling the ebony door closed behind him.

Morcastle stared into a narrow, dark hallway. Its walls consisted of tapestries hung from the wooden ceiling, and its floor was the planking of the original circus wagon. The hot, still air within that cramped corridor smelled of dust and old wood. Ahead of them, the hulking Puppetmaster filled the passage, blocking out all light. Morcastle wobbled in the sudden dark and reached his hands out toward the carpeted walls for support. The worn tapestries swayed away from his touch, and Morcastle pitched sideways. Marie, clutching his hand, pulled him back. He nodded mute thanks, forgetting her blindness for a moment, and continued on.

The Puppetmaster rounded the edge of the tapestry to the right, stepping into the room that lay beyond it. Narrow shafts of sunlight knifed from the room's doorway into the hall. Thankful for the light, Morcastle followed the Puppetmaster into the room.

The place was small and cluttered, dark except for the sun's rays that slanted from a high, barred window. Three of the room's walls were made of faded tapestries: one depicting children dancing with a harlequin who had the head of a wolf, another showing dogs fighting in the arena, and a third so dark and dirty that it looked like the mouth of a deep, deep cave.

All four walls were lined with a shadowy collection of junk. In one corner, an embroidered chair sat beside a couch whose back slumped brokenly. The adjacent wall was dominated by a massive black workbench cluttered with saws and chisels and hammers. Next to it lay dusty bolts of fabric and racks of thread. Twisted sticks and thin sheets of copper lay in all the unoccupied corners of the room. And hanging from every wall and littering every corner there were puppets: hand puppets, finger puppets, marionettes, figurines, porcelain dolls, masks, and costumes.

Morcastle blinked. The room was filled with a thousand faces. Then two of the faces moved. The gendarmes.

They were sitting in the darkest corner of the room on a pair of tattered chairs. A chipped teapot rested on a small table between them, and both soldiers balanced saucerless teacups on their laps. They fixed Morcastle with penetrating eyes.

Back-stepping toward the door, Morcastle ran into the massive Puppetmaster, who had slid behind him.

The huge man's long, bony fingers clutched the magician's shoulders.

"You must have a seat for the show," came the Puppetmaster's booming voice. His hands tightened, and he flung Morcastle into a chair the magician hadn't noticed before. "And you must stay for tea."

Sniffing the air, Marie said, "They're here, aren't they?"

The Puppetmaster pivoted on his heel and stalked across the plank floor toward Marie. He leaned over her, whispering, "Yes, they are here."

Marie stood unbending below his gaze, though her lip quivered slightly. "Their blood has an odor," she said flatly.

A long, rheumatic sigh began in the Puppetmaster's robes, and he placed a skeletal hand on the small of her back, urging her forward. "You'll need to sit down as well, my d—"

"I'll help her," interrupted Hermos. "Please." As the carnival master backed away, the man-giant glimpsed the ruby pendant again. A glittering horse appeared in the facets of its surface. "Qin-sah," Hermos muttered in awe as he eased Marie into the seat.

"Quite," replied the black-robed man under his breath, as though the Horse God's name had worked some change inside him. The Puppetmaster paced toward the gendarmes.

Fassioux began to speak, but the Puppetmaster held up his narrow index finger to signal silence. The officer quieted immediately, watching the carnival owner with thinly veiled fear. Maudit Sienne snatched the teapot from the table and filled three more cups with the steaming liquid. Then he drifted toward the performers, like a black thunderhead ready to burst, and delivered a cup to each of them.

The steam rising from the tea was fragrant and smelled of schnapps. Its aroma was sharp and sweet in the hot, musty air of the room.

The Puppetmaster hovered for a moment, half-hidden eyes studying his guests. Then he settled into a dilapidated chair at the far end of the room. His hand dropped over the arm of the chair, coming to rest on a pile of figurines. He caressed the objects with slow affection before selecting two of them. One was a marionette of Punchinello, with a long nose and chin, glowing eyes that peered through a black mask, a star-shaped collar, a hunched back, and colorful clothing. In his tiny hand, Punchinello held a small, wooden knife. The other figure was a hand puppet, black-robed like the Puppetmaster himself, but with a mouse's skull for its head.

Arraying his long fingers about the crosspiece of the marionette, the Puppetmaster lowered it to the floor beside his booted feet. Punchinello bounced unevenly, his wooden shoes clicking on the planks. While the Puppetmaster's veiled features watched Punchinello, he slid the skull-faced puppet on his other hand and began to move the black form about menacingly on the arm of the chair.

"You were saying?" he muttered distractedly to the gendarme.

Fassioux shot a shocked glance toward his partner. Then, setting his teacup on the table, he stood. "These three freaks . . . er . . . performers, are guilty of a capital crime."

"Yes, yes," the Puppetmaster replied, lacing his forefingers beneath the leg threads of the marionette. Punchinello began to kick his legs alternately in a peasant dance. "You said that already. What crime?"

"Assaulting agents of l'Morai and trespassing outside of the carnival. Freaks are, by law, restricted from leaving the carnival, and any who leave may be punished by execution, in case you have forgotten," the gendarme replied, fiddling with a button on his jerkin.

"I know the law, Fassioux," the Puppetmaster intoned, moving the black-cloaked puppet on the arm of the chair as though it were speaking. The puppet shifted, and the black cloak pulled back from its gnarled hands—the dried talons of a chicken. The black-robed puppet now gestured toward Morcastle with the chicken-foot. "So, what have you to say?"

The magician swallowed hard, his eyes growing wide. Before he could speak, however, Marie stood up and said, "This is ludicrous. We were chasing a murderer. We have proof: we found the bodies. We found a whole graveyard of them."

"I shouldn't be surprised." It was the puppet speaking again. "There are lots of dead people in this world. The dead outnumber the living, you know."

"But these are all carnival performers," Marie persisted. "And all were murdered. They have disks of skin cut from the backs of their skulls."

"If you've got a carnival that's over a hundred years old," the marionette seemed to say, his voice high and craggy, "you're going to need a graveyard."

Morcastle rose now, finding his voice. "But, good sir, these people were *murdered*. Panol and—"

"Leave murder investigations to us," interrupted Fassioux as he marched forward. "I demand that these freaks be handed over to me for trial and punishment in l'Morai."

"Sit down, all of you!" the Puppetmaster shouted, suddenly on his feet. Punchinello hung limp at his side, and the black robed puppet had disappeared into his sleeve. As Marie and Morcastle seated themselves, Fassioux staggered backward and sat down beside the tea table. The Puppetmaster strode toward the gendarmes, the boneless marionette dragging across the plank floor beside his thudding boots.

"You demand?" the Puppetmaster repeated, specks of spittle shooting from his hood and falling through the rays of sunlight. "*You* demand? How dare you?" The hulking form had reached the seated man, and his massive boot swung suddenly, striking the gendarme's chair and splintering it beneath him. With a shout, Fassioux fell among the slivers of wood and landed in a sprawl on the floor. The Puppetmaster towered over him and planted a boot on the gendarme's leg to keep him down. "I am the Puppetmaster. The carnival is my kingdom. I *am* the carnival. You are emissaries only."

His face clenched in pain, Fassioux glanced upward. The grimacing Punchinello swung in front of him. The officer snorted derisively, then nodded in compliance. "Understood."

Again Punchinello went slack, crumpling to the planks. The Puppetmaster pivoted, dragging the marionette in a lazy arc around his booted feet. He began to pace the small room, his movements making the tapestry walls billow out slightly. "So, you performers— and I'll take you, Marie, as the voice of the performers—say a murder has taken place. You say hundreds of murders have taken place, enough to fill a graveyard." Spinning about, the enormous man began pacing the other direction. "And you, Gendarme Fassioux, say these three are guilty of trespassing."

Fassioux nodded his assent as Marie said, "I will take you to the bodies."

Ignoring her, the Puppetmaster growled, "We will decide this issue with a trial."

"Exactly!" Fassioux declared, rising from the rubble of his chair.

"Oh, but not a tribunal as you would have it," the carnival owner said, clenching his narrow fingers. "No. We are in my kingdom, in the circus, and folk in my kingdom are judged not by councils and jurors, but by patrons and applause."

"Not the boardwalk trial," Morcastle protested.

"Yes," the Puppetmaster said, halting. "The boardwalk trial. You three will be taken to the boardwalk, where you'll be locked in the stocks. I will post a sign above your heads, proclaiming your supposed crime. Then you may plead your case to the crowd."

Striding to his seat, the Puppetmaster dropped again into the chair. He produced the black-cloaked puppet, pulled it from his hand, and inverted it. Then slowly, deliberately, he lowered Punchinello into the hand-hole of the black puppet. "The crowd will judge you. Every spot of spittle on your faces, every apple core and rotten plum thrown at you, will be a vote of condemnation. Ever copper ducre thrown your way will be a vote of exoneration. If the abuses overmatch the ducres, I will turn you over to the gendarmes for their trial. If, however, the ducres are more plentiful, I will set you free."

*   *   *   *   *

"Ha ha!" shouted a black-haired boy in the mob of children. "Look at the pear wedged behind the blind lady's head!" The youngsters around him peered up blankly and began to giggle. Marie shook her head in the stocks, knocking the pear loose. Seeing the fruit fall, the boy ran up and spit in her face. "Got her, square in the eye!" he shouted, hawking to produce more phlegm.

Before he could launch the spittle, however, he howled in sudden pain. Spinning about, he saw the greasepainted face of a harlequin looming over him. The harlequin's white-gloved hand held a broad, comical shoe, which he had just brought to bear against the boy's backside. In a growling voice, the painted man said, "Get from here now. If I see you again, I'll rip your little ears off."

Spitting on the ground beside the harlequin, the boy dodged another blow and disappeared down the boardwalk. The other children, eyeing the painted man with dismay, fled as well.

The harlequin shook his head, watching them go, then looked about for gendarmes or the Puppetmaster. Seeing neither, he produced a handkerchief from his oversized pocket and wiped Marie's face. She blushed as he did so and bit her lip to force back the tears.

"There, there," the harlequin soothed, his voice gentle now. "We've got to help each other, don't we?"

"It's pointless, Jerome," Morcastle said, turning his hands over in the wooden stocks. He craned his neck against the yoke, trying to see his fellow performer. "Those children couldn't even read, but still they spat in our faces. They think we're just another sideshow attraction."

Jerome stepped back from Marie to read the sign nailed above her head. "Assaulted an agent of l'Morai and trespassed outside the carnival?" The harlequin clucked and shook his head again. "They've got it in for us, they have."

"How many coins are scattered about?" Marie asked quietly.

Jerome sighed, scratching the greasepaint on his face. "Only about four that I can see."

"Before you arrived that boy stole some of them," Morcastle said grimly.

Hermos moaned, the stock collar tight about his neck and his bony face red with blood. The low-slung yoke had forced him to kneel. He ceased his anxious prayers for a moment to ask, "How much garbage?"

"Too much," replied Jerome, sweeping some apple cores and crushed plums together. "I'd better move some of this stuff and wipe your faces, or you'll never be released."

Jerome began to scoot the filthy pile of rubbish away from the stocks, but a shout came from the boardwalk. "Stop there, you. This is a trial. You've no right to remove the verdict."

Jerome spun about, seeing a gray-haired man whose face was covered with scars from a pox. The man stepped from the boardwalk and strode toward them. He wore a cape of red satin over a tailored suit, white ruffled shirt, gray vest, black woolen breeches, and gray stockings. He had a bushy mustache of near-white hair, tapered at its edges, and blue eyes that sparked with strictness. "Away from there, harlequin!"

Jerome stiffened, his gloved hands clenching to fists. As the man approached, Jerome comically dropped his loose shoe on top of the pile of garbage and clumsily tried to slip his foot inside. He laughed a stupid, harlequin laugh as his broad shoe smashed the garbage into the ground. "Just trying to tie my shoe, sir, huh huh!"

"Out of the way," the man sneered, pushing the harlequin aside. Jerome, slipping his shoe in place, rolled head over heels away from the man. Scuttling awkwardly to his feet, the harlequin bowed as though he had a hat and sauntered off into the carnival.

The man brushed his hands distastefully, as though he had touched the garbage himself, then turned toward the three performers. His eyes lingered for long moments on them, his gaze narrowing and lifting to the sign above their heads.

"Assault and trespassing," the man observed aloud. "Serious charges. Have you anything to say to them?"

"We've discovered a murder," Marie said simply.

"A murder?" the man replied with mock amazement. "Now that *is* something worth assaulting gendarmes over."

"Three murders, actually," Morcastle noted, motioning the red-cloaked man toward him. "Two last night and another the night before, Sir—"

"Lord Odieu, council member of l'Morai," the man replied crisply, the crinkly skin of his face drawing back.

"*Councilman!*" Morcastle replied with an ingratiating

smile and a sycophantic wink. "I should have known by your red cape. We are honored by your interest in our investigation of these murders."

"So, tell me about these murders," Lord Odieu said, setting his jaw.

"Last night," Morcastle began, "during my performance, I heard someone abduct two other performers, Panol and Banol, from a stage behind mine. After my performance, I checked their stage and they were gone. The murderer pulled them through a slit in the backdrop and carried them away down Freaks Alley."

"How do you know?" Lord Odieu asked harshly.

"Begging your pardon," Morcastle replied, "but we followed the tracks and found the bodies, buried in a shallow grave."

"I cannot believe this," the councilman said, striding away from Morcastle and knocking over the pile of rubbish with his foot. "Even if you *did* find the bodies, perhaps you three performed the murders yourselves."

"The other murder occurred in my caravan," Marie replied. "I came in to find a performer stabbed through with a long sword. The killer was still there. He barely escaped, and we know what he looks like."

The man laughed outwardly, sinking his hands in the pockets of his breeches. "Am I to believe this? A blind woman knows what the man looks like? Do you have witnesses?"

"Not directly," Morcastle admitted, his head sinking forward.

"Then your stories are badly told lies," the man snapped, spitting on the pile of rubbish and turning to leave.

"He's a heavy man—sixteen stone or so—and tall. He's missing the index finger of his left hand," Marie pursued urgently. "He left no fewer than seven bloody handprints on the walls of my caravan, and we've got a score of witnesses who saw them. He wears heavy boots of identifiable tread—a leather soul with an oddly worn heel. The boot-prints appeared at both murder sites. In my caravan, one of the boots had flour on its inner edge. Furthermore, the murderer has a long knife scar down his back, leading from the right shoulder to the left hip. That's the mark I left when I cut him as he ran from the door."

Lord Odieu halted and he stood, one foot resting on the rugged boardwalk before him, the other still in the sand. His iron-hard expression began to soften. He stepped from the boardwalk.

"I am . . . impressed by your description," he said, approaching Marie. "Do the gendarmes know of all these clues?"

"Yes," Marie replied flatly, her face averted. "The lieutenant who saw my caravan washed it clean before any other gendarmes could arrive. But the twenty witnesses saw."

"This is bad," Lord Odieu said, his face blanching. He leaned against the stocks. "Very bad, indeed."

"What is it?" Morcastle asked, wide-eyed.

The councilman looked up, his aged eyes bleary. "In l'Morai, there is a butcher. Recently, he cleaved the index finger from his hand while gutting a hog." The man paused, the lines around his eyes tightening. "He's a violent man, by all accounts, and is never seen without his heavy boots, which he uses on stray cats and children."

Morcastle fidgeted. A missing finger was not enough to convict a man.

"And," Lord Odieu went on, "when this butcher sells meat, he often coats it in flour to soak up the blood before wrapping it in a meat-sack." Lord Odieu shook his head and approached Morcastle. "How were these murders performed?"

Morcastle nodded stiffly. "All three were killed with blades. One had a sword rammed down his throat and the other two were, well, sliced in half."

"All of them, though," Marie broke in, "had a precise circle of skin cut from the backs of their skulls."

"Just like a butcher might do." Lord Odieu said, his voice cold on the night air. "It must be him."

"If—" Marie said breathlessly, "—if he bears the knife scar, we'll know for certain."

"What is his name?" Morcastle asked.

"Dominick," Lord Odieu replied, loosening the money pouch on his belt. He drew it out, a large bag of coins, and held it up before the three of them. "This should be enough to buy your freedom." Circling around behind the stocks, the council member strapped the bag of coins to Morcastle's belt. Dusting his hands, he said, "It should be safe there until I get back. I'm going to get the Puppetmaster to set you free."

As the red-cloaked man came around to the front of the stocks again, Morcastle smiled and shouted, "Thank you, Lord Odieu! You needn't rush off!"

Spinning about solemnly, the lord said, "Yes, I must. Dominick is at the carnival tonight."

 # FOUR

The heat of the summer evening pressed on the peasant boy as he stood in the torchlit crowd. It seemed the whole town of l'Morai had marched out across the black heath road to the carnival tonight. The boy sighed, shifting from foot to foot as he eyed the hawkers that stood at the carnival's narrow gates.

Tugging the trouser leg of the burly man in front of him, the boy asked, "How much longer, Father?" The man was oblivious. Setting his teeth, the boy tugged again and repeated his question.

The man pivoted, his broad, muscular face swiveling toward the child. He rarely smiled, this bulky man, and his eyes were lightless beneath his puffy lids. He swung his beefy arm toward the boy and clutched the child's shoulder in a bandaged hand. "Just wait," the man growled. Then, releasing the boy's shoulder, he stepped up toward the hawkers.

"Just a ducre for children and a lorin for citizens!" the man at the entrance barked. "The wonders of the world for a ducre or a lorin!"

The man stepped up to the entrance and slipped two huge fingers into the tight purse that hung at his waist. Clenching his jaw, he pulled out a clutch of seven ducres, dwarfed by his pudgy fingertips. He held them up toward the hawker and glared. "This is for me an' the boy!"

"Ducre and a lorin, please, Dominick," the hawker reminded.

"Look," the man said, leaning threateningly over the basket of coins, "you let us in on this. I come here all the time, pay good money inside, too. Let me in, unless you want poison in the next wagon of pork I send out."

Setting his lips together, the man nodded and waved them through. The boy let out a squeal of delight and charged past his father into the crowded forecourt of the carnival.

The brick-paved forecourt was lined with musicians, playing rebecs and lutes and pipes. Some had monkeys scurrying with cups before them, or marionettes hanging from their elbows and dancing jigs on the brick path. Most of the musicians clustered about the ironwork arches that led to the boardwalks, sideshows, and gambling dens. Beyond the leftmost ironwork gate, the granite and limestone arena loomed white against the black sky. A brightly colored canvas awning arched over the arena. It glowed spectrally from the torches and lanterns within.

The wide-eyed peasant boy drifted on tiptoe toward the arena, his ears filling with the applause and excited shouts that rolled over the limestone walls. "Father," he said, his voice lost to the rumble of the crowds, the shouts of the hawkers, and the ever present music. Spinning about, the boy yelled, "Father?"

The man was gone.

* * * * *

"Where could he be?" Morcastle wondered aloud as he roamed Freaks Alley with Marie, Hermos, and Lord Odieu. They moved forward, studying the muddy tracks below them, peering from behind the canvas backdrops, scanning the burgeoning crowds that flooded the walkways.

"He's a big man," Lord Odieu was saying, his fingers clutching at the edges of his red satin cloak. "With a muscular head and face . . . and a missing finger. I heard him say he was coming tonight when I stopped by the butcher shop this afternoon."

"This is pointless," Marie said, leaning against the canvas backdrop of Uri and His Dancing Bears. She shook her head. "Half the town must be here tonight. He could've already killed again."

"Marie is right," said Morcastle. "We need something faster and surer."

Hermos eyed them strangely. "What about Oreaux?"

"Oreaux?" Lord Odieu asked.

"The oracle," Morcastle repeated wistfully. "Now there's an idea."

"A sideshow clairvoyant?" the councilman scoffed. "That's ridiculous. You'll be wasting your time."

"His talents are as true as any of ours," Marie replied flatly. She pulled away from the backdrop where she had been leaning and crossed her arms. "Yes, let's go to Oreaux."

"You go," Lord Odieu huffed, flustered. "I'll keep looking."

Marie, Hermos, and Morcastle were already walking away. Some of the townsfolk recognized the liberated trio, and those who had spit or thrown rotten fruit did so with a measure of fear. Morcastle was heartened by their uneasiness, but he kept Hermos in check on their way to the oracle's pavilion. The blue-striped canvas tent flapped in the wind as they approached. Its angled sides were adorned with clumps of aromatic herbs and strange talismans. At the front of the tent stood one of Oreaux's barkers, a creature much different than those throughout the rest of the carnival.

"Welcome to the tent of Oreaux the Miraculous," said a veiled woman, bowing as Marie, Morcastle, and Hermos approached the pavilion. The woman was dressed in sheer scarves that wrapped her seductive legs and arms in red and green and blue. She had four rings hanging from each ear and a couple of nose-rings in her left nostril. "Within, you will discover the secrets of your lives, your loves, your dreams. Enter for a measly silver lorin."

Marie approached the woman, setting her hands on the velvet rope that hung across the entrance to Oreaux's pavilion. "We haven't a lorin among us. But please, for the brotherhood of performers, let us in to see Oreaux."

Ignoring her, the woman shouted out to the crowd beyond, "Come one, come all, to counsel at the feet of the great Oreaux!"

"There's been a murder—three, in fact," Marie said calmly. As Marie's voice trailed away, Hermos loomed up menacingly behind her. Blinking her painted eyes, the woman unlatched the velvet rope from the post that held it and swung it open.

"Step inside for the great Oracle Oreaux, seer of all worlds, teller of all tales!"

Morcastle bowed curtly and stepped past the woman. He extended a hand to Marie and led her after him, then motioned to Hermos to follow. The door to the tent was overhung with silken veils that draped from the top corner down to the opposite bottom, overlapping in the center. Morcastle pushed the fringed silk out of the way and, stooping, led Marie within. Hermos ducked and hunched his shoulders, sliding through the doorway like a dog through a fence.

The tent within was dark, illuminated by the tepid and continuous glow of brass lamps hanging from the tent poles. The three performers found themselves standing in a narrow hall that ran perpendicular to the doorway. The hall was lined with incense burners, and the area near the ceiling roiled with aromatic smoke.

Another woman, exotically veiled, approached them from the darkness at the end of the hall. She was a young, black-haired beauty with golden eyes, and a wary smile showed through the veil on her features. As she neared, she reached her hand into a basketful of rose petals she carried and cast a handful at their feet. "Welcome. Your destiny awaits."

Bowing, she backed away before them, leaving a trail of petals in her wake. Morcastle followed her down the canvas hallway to where it opened into a moderate-sized room. The walls were adorned with beadwork mosaics, brass trinkets, ivory carvings, and leafy ferns. Veils draped like banners from the pitched roof of the tent, segmenting the room into many translucent compartments. In one compartment, more of the veiled women reclined, their elbows resting on piles of pillows and their feet on ornate rugs. The women had gathered around a short table with a polished ebony top. They spoke furtively with each other, drawing food out of various bowls set about the table.

The veiled woman led the three down the sandy central path of the tent. "Even those of the *brotherhood of performers*," she said, placing emphasis on the phrase, "may not know that Oreaux's true name is Olaal Ab' Haddisha, or that he comes of royal blood from the lines of desert kings. These are but the wives who attend him." The woman graciously nodded toward the short table. "I am Satina. I will interpret the telling of Oreaux."

She rounded an opaque veil, and Morcastle followed. They stepped through a thick curtain of beads into a richly furnished room. The floor was covered by a red and black rug, which was edged with countless pillows. At the end of the room was Oreaux.

He sat in a large black chair. The arms of the chair were hollow boxes into which his forearms and hands were locked. So, too, the legs of the chair ended in boxes that held his feet and ankles. The oracle's head was restrained in a square wooden helmet attached to the back of the chair. A vertical slit in the front of the helm revealed the man's face. He was aged and dark in complexion, with nearly white eyebrows and a long ivory mustache. His eyes lolled dazedly in his head, and a line of drool extended from his lip onto the lower edge of the helm.

Satina stood beside Oreaux, stroking his shoulder and directing the magician and his friends to find seats among the pillows. "Don't let the black chair frighten you," said Satina. "His gift for prophecy came at a price—his sanity. But don't worry, he is quite harmless as long as he remains in the chair."

As Morcastle, Marie, and Hermos seated themselves, the exotic woman continued, "What do you seek, friends? The past, the future, fate, fortune?"

"We seek a murderer," Marie said calmly. The moment her voice sounded in the small room, Oreaux's head turned violently in the box. He sniffed the air, and his eyes made circular sweeps in her direction. His arms began to tremble, and his feet kicked, hammering against the inside of the box.

"The murderer of whom?" Satina asked, ignoring the clamor.

"We know who the man is: Dominick, a butcher from the city. We need to know where he is," Marie elaborated. "We must know quickly."

Nodding, Satina leaned near Oreaux and whispered into a hole in the helm. As she spoke, Oreaux shuddered, spittle sputtering in foamy flecks from his lips. He wrenched, striking his head against the sides of the wooden helm. "Please be still, my dear. Yes, she is a blind girl. Yes, they are performers as are we."

Satina's words drew nothing more than wheezes and grunts from Oreaux. In time, Satina backed away from him and wiped the foam from her head-veil.

"He says that Dominick is here, at this very carnival."

"Yes, we know," Marie replied gently, "but where? We

must find him and stop him."

Again Satina leaned close to her husband, murmuring into his ear. He had not stopped trembling from the previous question, and now he emitted cryptic shouts.

The woman said, "He is stalking through the Performers Quarter, beside the arena."

Hermos started to rise, his eyes wide, but Morcastle motioned him to sit. The magician whispered, "How do we know he is there? Has the oracle even said one word that makes sense?"

Listening for a moment to Oreaux, the woman replied coldly, "Your forward trouser pocket contains a deck of cards, which is missing the four aces. They are hidden in your sleeve, collar, stocking, and breast pocket. The blind juggling woman has seven scars on her right hand, two on her left, one center-thigh, and two on her right shoulder from missing throws. And your man-giant friend—"

"All right, all right," Morcastle protested, waving his hands before him. "I believe you." Turning toward Marie and Hermos, he said, "Let's go capture him."

Oreaux trembled and coughed violently.

"He's not in the Performers Quarter anymore. He's reached the hippo-woman's stall," Satina said.

Rising from his seat, Morcastle asked, "Which way is he headed?'

The man barked out something meaningless, and the woman said, "He is moving toward this tent."

Morcastle's eyes went wide, and he swallowed.

Hermos had also risen. "Here?" the man-giant asked.

"Yes," the woman replied simply. "Oreaux has summoned him."

* * * * *

Morcastle, Marie, and Hermos crouched in Oreaux's crowded trunk room, which was separated from his

sanctuary by a purple veil. Their eyes alternated between the fettered madman in the black box of wood
and the beadwork entrance to the sanctuary. Hermos
stood at the front edge of the veil, peering around it as a
small child might. Behind him, Marie sat amongst a
towering collection of carnival trunks, their tattered
leather sides covered with faded bills posted one atop
another. Morcastle stood at the other end of the bag-
gage room, peering fearfully out. Smoke rising from the
ubiquitous incense burners circulated hypnotically in
the quiet air.

"I feel like an idiot, squatting back here," Morcastle
complained, rubbing his aching legs. "He's not going to
be com—"

Hermos glared at the magician, gesturing for silence.
Directing his gaze back down the hallway, Hermos
murmured another prayer to Qin-sah, god of horses.
The words had just concluded when he spotted movement.

Satina was leading a stocky man down the aisle,
throwing rose petals before him. The man was mesmerized, his eyes wide and glassy. Running a meaty hand
over his balding head, he absently pushed the woman
out of the way, spilling her rose petals on the sandy
floor, and strode past her toward Oreaux.

The butcher muttered flatly, "Where's the oracle?"

"Dominick," Morcastle mouthed to the man-giant.

Rounding the corner that led to Oreaux's sanctuary,
the butcher caught sight of the oracle imprisoned in his
throne of black wood. Oreaux was quivering, his feet
shuddering in the wooden box that held them. His eyes
spun in panicked circles in his head.

Blinking dully, Dominick crossed muscled arms over
his chest and stepped toward the seer. The butcher's
face was expressionless, except for a momentary
twinge when he bumped the bandaged stump of his
index finger.

"You are the oracle?" he slurred, his expressionless eyes pinning Oreaux.

Under the weight of that gaze Oreaux spasmed again.

The butcher smiled vacuously, and the dim glow of an oil lamp glinted off a silver tooth in his mouth. "I came to see you," he said stupidly. A look of confusion scrolled across his features as though he suddenly wondered why he had come.

Satina slipped soundlessly between the looming butcher and Oreaux. With averted eyes, she motioned for the butcher to be seated among the pillows. "Please, sir, recline for a moment as the oracle prepares himself to speak." Her thin hand settled on his and she drew him, stiffly, to the ground.

The butcher's brows were knotted in confusion, but he dropped among the pillows. "How did I get here?" he wondered aloud.

Patting his hand gently, the woman retreated to the oracle's side. Her voice was throaty and soothing. "You've come to learn your fortune, like everyone."

Dominick nodded blankly. Then his eyes darkened. He began to stand again, saying, "I haven't time for—"

"Stay, sir," Satina urged, running her hand seductively along her thigh. "You can learn what luck you'll have this evening."

Watching her fingers glide along her leg, the butcher again nodded, seating himself numbly back onto the pillows. "What luck I'll have this evening?"

"Yes—how you will do," the woman replied, her voice quavering and her smile looking strained. "But first we must learn of your past."

She set her slender hand on the box that encased Oreaux's forearm. Her lips murmured into the ear hole of the wooden helm. Oreaux shuddered once as she spoke, then sat still, his glazed eyes wide and locked on the butcher. He whispered unintelligible words to her. Satina listened, watching his lips and nodding.

The butcher leaned forward with a look of concern, "What's he saying?"

Without pulling her ear away, Satina whispered, "You are a man of blood and slaughter."

" 'Course," Dominick replied, rubbing his balding head. "I'm a butcher."

"More than that," Satina said, nodding as Oreaux mumbled to her. "You kill humans, too."

"Yeah. Occasionally, when I'm a city guard," the butcher said, still dazed. "What's wrong with that?"

Oreaux had begun to convulse again, and gagged and garbled shouts emerged from his lips. Satina drew back as the oracle spasmed and sprayed, hissing like a caged serpent.

"He sees knives and blood," Satina said, her voice rising in fear. "Many kills. Hundreds . . . or thousands."

"Enough!" the butcher growled, stomping his broad, booted foot on the rug. Satina paused, shaking and staring fearfully at him. A brutal smile cracked his face and, rubbing his hands together, he said, "What about tonight? How will I do?"

"Not very well, I'm afraid," came a man's narrow voice. Morcastle stepped from behind the purple veil and flipped his satin cape defiantly. He now stood between Satina and the butcher.

Dominick jolted, startled, his fat hands clenching into fists. He struggled to his feet, only then seeing the man-giant who had appeared to block the other end of the room.

Morcastle said, "You, Monsieur Dominick, are under arrest for the murder of Panol, Banol, Borgo, and a hundred other carnival workers."

The butcher glared incredulously back and forth between the two men as Satina moved out of harm's way. Again he flashed an uneasy smile, his silver tooth gleaming. "This is some kind of joke, right?"

"I'm afraid not." The voice was a woman's this time,

but it did not come from the retreating Satina. Looking about, Dominick saw through a purple veil the dark and ghostly form of Marie, almost indistinguishable among the trunks and crates around her. She moved into the light, her young and beautiful face contrasting with her white eyes. In her hands, she held a brace of gleaming daggers.

"We found your handprints," said the magician, taking a cautious step toward the man. "Missing the index finger. We found your bootprints and your precision knife work on the backs of your victims' skulls."

"What are you talking about?" the man bellowed.

"I think you know," Morcastle said, taking another step forward. "The confirming proof will be the scar on your back."

Before the butcher could move, Hermos's strong, narrow fingers grasped the back of his collar. With a loud rending, the tattered chemise ripped straight down Dominick's back. Hermos released the two ends of the shirt, his sunken eyes growing grave. A long, fresh scar cut from the man's right shoulder to his left hip.

"He's got the—" Hermos's words were cut short by the butcher's fist, which rammed like a sledgehammer into his stomach. With a groan, Hermos fell, reeling back into the beadwork entrance.

Morcastle leaped on the butcher's back, wrapping a line of knotted kerchiefs around his neck. Twisting the scarves tightly, the magician watched as the man's head reddened with exertion. The butcher abruptly pitched forward. Morcastle tumbled over the meaty shoulder and through the air. He landed flat on his back and gasped. Dominick laughed.

Turning toward the laughter, Marie ripped the purple veil down and threw one of her knives toward the butcher. The dagger struck, burying deep in the man's thigh-sized arm. His laughter gave way to groans as he grabbed the knife's black hilt to pull it forth. Before he could dislodge it, though, another set of arms wrapped about him.

Hermos tackled the butcher. Clenching his jaw, the man-giant fastened a headlock on Dominick and cinched it tight. A silver tooth flashed. Dominick roared, and his teeth clamped down on the man-giant's arm, biting through the skin. Hermos shouted in pain, his arm going limp. He rolled, knocking the butcher loose.

Dominick scrabbled backward and yanked the knife from his arm. Snorting like a bull, he charged Hermos and drove the blade into the man-giant's stomach. With a quivering gasp, Hermos rolled away, clutching the hilt of the dagger. Dominick rose and laughed through bloodied teeth. He vaulted toward Oreaux, planted his enormous boot on the oracle's thin chest, and knocked the black throne over backward. Shuddering and screaming, Oreaux tipped over. The back of the chair struck the ground and cracked. Dominick ran for the tent wall. Reaching it, he lifted the tarp and slipped out into the crowded circus.

Glaring toward the flapping tent wall, Morcastle rushed to the bleeding man-giant and knelt down beside him. Satina latched onto Marie's arms and led her toward Hermos as well. The other veiled ladies, seeing that the butcher was gone, descended on the scene in a fluttering flock, their hushed voices murmuring back and forth in an exotic and musical language.

"Back, ladies! Back!" Morcastle snapped in frustration as he wrapped a torn sash around the wound and then gripped the knife blade still sunk into Hermos's stomach. The magician drew the knife gently, cleanly forth. He held one hand atop the sash, now growing warm with blood, and gestured the crowd back with the other hand.

Hermos's long, narrow fingers clasped the magician's hand, and the man-giant stared at him with solemn, sober eyes. "Go catch him," Hermos said.

"What? Don't be a fool," Morcastle said, glancing at the rumpled tent wall where the butcher had exited. "You're wounded."

Marie's slim hand settled on the magician's shoulder. "I can tend him, Morcastle. Go."

The magician looked at his companions, concern and fear mixing on his features. He pressed his lips together, rose, and headed for the spot where Dominick had made his escape. Wrapping his fingers around the base of the thick canvas, Morcastle lifted the tent side, ducked under, and disappeared into the carnival beyond.

He emerged onto a crowded boardwalk, a wide and steady river of patrons flowing past him. The butcher was nowhere in sight. Morcastle set his jaw and pushed through the crowd, his eyes darting to each side. There was a gawky farmer, a scarred mercenary, a rotund council member, a sticky-faced girl. . . .

"Damn," Morcastle spat as an embarrassing sense of relief spread through him. Reaching the opposite side of the walkway, Morcastle stepped up on a broken crate, lifted his head above the crowd, and gazed down the boardwalk.

There, in the river of patrons, lay a long, wide gap, like the wake of a boat. Squinting, Morcastle looked to the head of the gap. Dominick was there. The muscles of his shirtless back pumped as he ran, and the crescent knife wound from his shoulder to his hip showed red with the exertion.

Morcastle opened his mouth to shout, but his breath caught short. The heavy throbbing of his heart beat out one damning word.

"Murder . . . murder . . . murder . . ."

Morcastle blinked. Dominick was almost out of sight now. Best to let him flee.

"Murder . . . murder . . . murder . . ."

His lungs filled with the steamy night air, and he

shouted, "Murderer! Stop him! Dominick the butcher is a murderer!"

The crowd around Morcastle stilled, then pulled back from him. The patrons gawked at the shouting magician, shock and fear on their faces.

Morcastle stepped from the box and pushed his way across the boardwalk. "Stop the butcher! Stop the murderer Dominick." The crowd recoiled from him, clearing a lane as Morcastle began to run. "Help me," he implored, growing breathless. "Stop that man—that murderer!"

Only empty, fearful stares answered him, a grim gauntlet he was running.

Ahead, the butcher had almost reached the lower end of the Performers Quarter—Tent Town, where the carnival's newest performers dwelt. The perfect place to hide. The perfect place for another murder.

Pointing toward him, Morcastle screamed out angrily, "Stop him! Doesn't anyone care?" His aching feet slowed and stopped on the boardwalk. Doubling over, he set his hands on his knees and drew deep, raking breaths into his lungs.

Someone tapped him on the shoulder. It was Arkoo the Leopard Boy: his hands and feet were nubby and clawed like a leopard's and his lean, youthful body was covered in orange and black fur. Arkoo's cleft lip drew back as he smoothed a whisker with his pawlike hand. "What's happening?" he murmured excitedly.

A pained smile formed on Morcastle's face. "Can you run, child?"

"Faster than an arrow," Arkoo said proudly, scratching the planking with his thick-clawed toes.

"Run, then, and catch that shirtless man up there," Morcastle said as he pointed toward the retreating butcher.

Arkoo nodded excitedly, making a clicking sound between his teeth. Then, dropping to all fours, he dashed away down the boardwalk. His clawed toes and fingers scratched deeply into the worn planks, propelling him past rows of startled patrons. As they drew back from him, gasping and shielding their faces, Arkoo released a laughing snarl.

Ahead, the fleeing man rounded the fence of Tent Town and disappeared into the maze of canvas beyond. Arkoo growled, quickening his pace. He roared like wildfire past the patrons, his orange, spotted skin undulating like flame. In four bounds, he reached the fence that surrounded the Performers Quarter. Clamping his jagged teeth together, the feline boy pivoted and leaped. He rose with quiet grace, arcing above the screaming patrons, above the whitewashed fence. He landed on skidding claws in a sandy alley between two tents.

The alley was empty. Arkoo's eyes narrowed, but his slitted pupils widened just perceptibly. He sniffed the air, smelling sand and smoke, fish, dung, canvas, straw—the perpetual bouquet of carnival scents. But, lying atop them all was a distinct combination of odors: sweat, blood, anxiety.

The man the leopard boy was chasing had come this way, and, by the smell of it, was still nearby. Rising on his back legs, Arkoo padded down the alley. He paused, turning his ear to the wind. The screams of the crowd had silenced, leaving only a fearful hush behind him, a fearful hush and the distant murmur of the carnival. But another sound was there, deceptively interlaced with these others. Quick, cautious footsteps. The footsteps of a large man.

Arkoo flexed his legs and shot down the alley, past the flapping tents, to a tree-sized lantern post that stood at the far end. He leaped for the wooden pole and sank his claws in amongst the tattered remains of bills once posted there. Strengthening his hold, Arkoo lurched upward. His claws released from the wood and dug in higher

up. The broad lantern at the top of the post pitched precariously with each jarring jump.

Rising above the canvas rooftops, Arkoo scanned the
carnival around him. He spotted furtive movement
beside a gray-and-white striped tent some fifty feet
from the post. A muscled arm swung back for a moment, then disappeared into the tent.

Arkoo hurled himself from the post, soaring like a bat
to the ground. His feet fell into rhythm, carrying him
toward the gray and white tent. In six easy bounds, he
reached the canvas wall. Planting his rear feet in the
sand, he vaulted onto the tent. The tall center pole
cracked and snapped. The canvas roof buckled, yanking stay cords from the sandy soil. As the leopard boy
descended atop the billowing tent, a man's shout came
from within, punctuated by the crash and shatter of
glassware.

The leopard boy glimpsed a form struggling beneath
the canvas. Scrambling across the cloth, Arkoo landed
atop the form, knocking him to the ground within the
collapsing tent. The man shrieked, trying to roll over,
but Arkoo sank his claws through the canvas, pinning
the burly man to the ground.

"Stay still," he snarled, panting.

*   *   *   *   *

"This way," the Puppetmaster said, making a vague,
sweeping gesture with his black-clothed arm. The hulking carnival owner glared at the two gendarmes, then
stomped through the gate of Tent Town. His broad
boots left heavy tracks in the sand.

Captain Moldau, the taller and older of the two gendarmes, regarded the Puppetmaster dubiously before
following him through the ratty fence. He eyed the
crowd that filled Tent Town and the torches glowing
among the ropes and canvas. The captain tapped his

partner's shoulder and motioned toward the mob. "This one's not gonna be pretty."

Lieutenant Ransen nodded, patting the club looped onto his leather belt. He fell in step beside Moldau, rubbing his young face with a cold, trembling hand.

Three tents on the outskirts of the Performers Quarter had been trampled down by the crowd, and one accidentally set ablaze. The grubby, torch-bearing performers eyed the gendarmes suspiciously as the Puppetmaster led them toward the center of the crowd. Lieutenant Ransen tried to ignore them: the bearded woman, the man with three legs, the armless acrobat, the goat-headed boy. . . .

"Here they are," the Puppetmaster growled, gesturing toward a circle of the performers.

A blind woman, a leopard boy, and a cheap-suited magician held Dominick the butcher to the ground.

Ransen unlooped his club and approached the three. "Get off him, you freaks!"

"Wait," snapped the blind woman angrily, stepping between the lieutenant and the others. "That man is a murderer."

"Nonsense," said the captain, crossing his hands over his chest, "that's Dominick the butcher."

"Butcher indeed," said the magician, struggling to keep the man down. "He has committed three murders here on the carnival grounds. We have evidence to convict him."

"What evidence? Let's see it," Lieutenant Ransen demanded curtly.

"He killed Borgo the Sword-Swallower in my caravan," the blind woman began, "leaving a number of bloody handprints without the index finger. The gendarme on the scene tried to wash them away, but they still show faintly."

"And the bootprints here and at the other murder site match this man's boots."

The lieutenant leaned over, peering at the sole of his foot. "They also match mine pretty well."

"We can show you a whole graveyard in the woods below the carnival. He's killed over a hundred of us, one by one so that no one would notice—so that we would think they had just moved on," Marie said.

"How do we know you're not making this up?" the captain asked with a laugh.

"We'll show you the graveyard, and the handprints—"

"They came to me," the Puppetmaster rumbled suddenly. "They came this morning with this news. I believe them, lieutenant, and Lord Odieu does as well. I suggest you do the same."

Ransen's eyes narrowed as he studied the performers' faces. "These are serious charges. You'll have to come with us to l'Morai to state them in full. It'll take a council hearing to convict him."

The blind woman's features hardened. "When do we leave?"

"Tonight."

 **FIVE**

Hermos lay on the floor of the healer's caravan, watching the hypnotic sway of lanterns above his head. His toes reached to one end of the stuffy wagon, and his head touched the other. On both sides, shuffling feet hemmed him in. Heads hovered over his still form, heads of crouching people, their eyes trained on him.

It was the first time he had ever looked *up* at any of them.

The healer herself prattled about with gritty powders and pungent salves. The drooping, silken sleeves of her shirt swiped back and forth across the man-giant's face as she worked.

"Give him some air," she croaked, oblivious to the position of her sleeve. "Back up, you folk. Give him some air!"

She dumped a thick, mustardy concoction on his chest and began to rub it in. Those who hadn't backed up before did so now. Hermos winced, his nostrils flaring and his nose crinkling. He peered suspiciously toward the woman, his bony hands clutching bloody linen over the knife wound in his stomach.

"Don't worry, Hermos. The salve drives out the spirits," the healer said with a toothy leer.

"I thought it might come to this," came a wry voice from the crowded doorway to the caravan.

The gawkers lining the wagon looked in shock toward the woman standing at the door. Marie the Blind Juggler stood there with Morcastle at her side. Despite her sightless eyes, white as boiled eggs, Marie knew exactly what was going on. She pressed toward the man-giant, pushing the milling people out of her way. Her nose led her to the salve-besmeared Hermos, beside whom she dropped to her knees. "What's this stuff?" she asked, holding her hands out to the sides.

"Salve," Hermos blurted, "for the spirits."

Marie shook her head and smiled. "Salve?" She leaned forward, scraping the pasty concoction from Hermos's chest and flinging it to the floor. In a conspiratorial whisper she said, "Mighty Qin-sah! I wish we had a real healer."

"I *am* a real healer," the bent old woman protested.

Marie felt along the bandage on the man-giant's knife wound. It was loose and fouled with salve. "We'll have to rewrap this." She wiped the smelly salve from her hands onto her tattered skirt and began to remove the bandage.

Morcastle knelt down beside her. "Wait. I've got something that'll really drive out the spirits." The magician lifted the wraps from the wound. "Hmmm. The cut is deep." Producing a thin metal flask from his coat pocket, the magician poured a capful of brownish liquid from it. "Take hold, man, and keep your tongue away from your teeth. This'll sting a bit."

In each hand, Hermos clutched the ankle of one of his attendants. Morcastle, setting his jaw, poured the liquid onto the wound. The man-giant cried out as he gripped the ankles.

Morcastle drew back, holding the cloths over the wound. As Hermos's thrashing slowed, the magician shot a concerned look at Marie. "He shouldn't go anywhere, I'm afraid," he said as he gently rebandaged the wound.

Marie blinked, setting her hands on Hermos's shoulders. "He's right, Hermos. But don't you worry. We'll convict that butcher."

The man-giant's brow furrowed. "Where are you going?"

"Arkoo caught the murderer," Morcastle replied, his eyes gleaming. "You know, Arkoo the Leopard Boy. We're going to l'Morai to testify against Dominick. Don't worry, he won't get loose again."

Marie smiled and patted Hermos's shoulder. "You'd better rest, but you'd do well to get out of this witch doctor's hut and into your own tent."

Beside her, Morcastle gained his feet, groaning all the while, then extended his hand to help Marie up. They pushed toward the door.

Before Marie passed through, she said, "Wish us luck, Hermos."

"I do," Hermos said before his face was eclipsed by the fervid motions of the healer.

"I wish you luck, too," Marie muttered.

Morcastle gave a strong yank on her arm, pulling her down the two wooden steps in front of the caravan and into the cold night air. Marie, half-stumbling, ran into the stock-still form of the magician. "Why'd you pull me? He didn't hear what—"

"Marie, there's someone here to see us," Morcastle interrupted, his voice cold and edged with apprehension. He stroked the waxed tip of his mustache as he stared at the stranger. The man wore a fine surcoat of gray wool over a white, ruffled shirt, black knickers, gray stockings, and shoes of black leather. His face betrayed his youth, with wide, bright eyes, a hawklike nose, and a rumpled mouth. Sweeping outward with his thin hand, he snatched Marie's fingers. Then he dropped to one knee, doffed his plumed hat, and kissed her hand.

"Good evening," he said, his voice nasal. "I'm L'Aris, page to the Council of l'Morai and jurisconsult to accusers, such as yourselves. When the gendarmes returned with word of Dominick's arrest, the council sent me. I place myself in your service," he finished, rising gracefully.

Marie drew her hand back and pulled Morcastle toward her. "Good to make your acquaintance, sir. But my friend and I must hurry on. The gendarme's phaeton is waiting." She took a step past the jurist, leading Morcastle after her.

L'Aris's eyes fastened quizzically on the young woman as she walked away with the magician. For a moment, he stood and stared in their direction, then he stomped after them, trotting to catch up.

"Pardon me, mademoiselle. I'm here to represent you, not convict you," L'Aris insisted, gesturing at the carnival around them.

Marie spun, her tattered skirt fluttering in a broad circle around her thin legs. A puff of sawdust rose beneath her foot. "Thank you for your offer, sir, but I thought perhaps the Puppetmaster would counsel us."

Amusement filled the young man's eyes. "The Puppetmaster? He's one of the council members. Only in extreme cases does—"

"Then we will argue our own case," Marie said politely.

The young man's face reddened, and he averted his gaze. "*You* aren't on trial here, mademoiselle. Dominick the butcher is."

"Let me be blunt with you, Jurist L'Aris," Marie said. "Jurisconsults like yourself have a reputation of favoring citizens over freaks."

"You have no chance without me," the lean jurist said, folding his gloved hands over his chest.

Morcastle shot a concerned glance at his companion and pulled her aside. "He may be our only hope. We can't expect to plead our own case and win. And we've got to convict this monster."

Marie's expression was distant, as though she were listening to some faraway voice. "There's something about them, Morcastle—about jurisconsults, I mean. Something my father told me, but I can't remember it." Then, with slow and measured words, she asked the jurist, "What will you do for us?"

Uncrossing his arms, L'Aris said, "I will interview you, for one, getting the full story and learning about every possible shred of evidence against Dominick. I'll also counsel you on what to say and what not to say. I'll search for, gather, and present evidence based on the interviews. Then, I'll argue the case for you, before the council."

"Answer one more question," Marie said quietly. "Do you, Jurist L'Aris, consider us freaks?"

Now the young man's face blanched. His lip pulled back from his teeth. "Yes," he replied quietly. "I suppose I do. I suppose I always have. But without me, you don't stand a chance of even being heard."

Marie's lips drew into a thin, grim line. She replied, "At least you're honest." She motioned for him to follow her. "Let's go."

* * * * *

The open-air carriage labored over the pitch black heath. The sky above it was clogged with thick clouds, which blotted out the stars and hung with tangible weight over the blasted ground. Only the fender lanterns shed any light on the heath road, casting angular shadows beneath the puffing horses. The phaeton had left the glow and clamor of the carnival behind, and the lamps of l'Morai valley were still five miles away. Blackness filled the heath in between. Blackness and the cold winds.

Morcastle drew his thin cape about him, watching his breath curl in ghostly clouds from his mouth. Beside him sat Marie, her slender body quivering in the cold. About her shoulders, she wore the jurist's satin cape, which did little to shut out the cold.

As they rode along, L'Aris squinted at a bit of paper on a silver tray he balanced on his lap. He'd been writing on the paper the whole while, asking questions of Marie and Morcastle, lifting the page occasionally to better see its contents. Who was murdered? How? Where are the bodies? Who was the first witness to the scene? Who was the first gendarme? Why do you suspect Dominick?

The questions rattled on and on through the night, reconstructing the horrible evening when Marie entered her blood-washed caravan and found the body there. And when L'Aris had learned enough of that incident, he asked about the abduction and murder of Panol and Banol, the mounded graves on the heath, and the chase through the carnival.

At last L'Aris asked the question that jarred both Marie and Morcastle awake. "What will you do if Dominick accuses you?"

"Accuses us?" Morcastle asked, his eyes turning from the dark sky and flashing beneath their neatly trimmed eyebrows. "What do you mean, accuses *us*?"

"Anything can happen before the council," the young man replied coolly, brushing a bit of dew from the collar of his coat. "I've heard of accusations reversing on accusers, of public executions on the courtroom floor, even of the council turning in on itself. The Council of l'Morai is a volatile place."

"But how could Dominick accuse us?" Morcastle pressed. "We've done nothing."

"You are the only ones who've been gathering evidence," L'Aris replied. He rubbed his fingertips together. "Worse yet, the first murder occurred in Marie's caravan. Perhaps, he'll argue, you've concocted this whole thing: trumped up evidence, fed clues to the Puppetmaster, sent him to l'Morai to hunt up a likely suspect, had him chop Dominick's finger off, draw a scar across his back . . ."

"This is preposterous," Morcastle blurted indignantly.

"Preposterous or not, it may be Dominick's defense," the young jurist said with a shrug.

"We've answered enough of your questions," Marie broke in. She huddled closer to Morcastle. "Now you answer one of ours. What else could happen at the trial?"

With a brief, guarded smile, the jurist leaned back on the seat of the open coach and folded his arms. "There will be two trials: the arraignment and the actual trial. The arraignment takes place tonight, as soon as we arrive. There the accusers—you two—present your claims to the court and file a grievance. You need provide no physical evidence or extensive testimony tonight. If the council finds your accusations worth pursuing, you and the prisoner will await trial. At that point, the accused is assumed guilty and must assemble evidence and testimony to prove otherwise. I will gather the evidence and witnesses for our side. Then, we'll hold the trial—present evidence, examine and cross-examine witnesses. And the people will decide."

"The people?" Marie asked.

"Yes," L'Aris said. "The council only adjudicates. It's a vote of the people that brings a verdict."

"Wait," Morcastle said, inching forward on the seat, "we're coming to something."

L'Aris folded the piece of paper and slipped it into his pocket as he looked beyond the carriage. From the deep shadows, two large stone peaks loomed up on either side of the road, black and enormous in the night. The high road headed between them, then curved to the right. After they passed the rock formations, a wide valley opened on the left of the carriage. The valley walls and floor shimmered with light.

"We're coming down off the high heath," L'Aris said. "On your left is l'Morai. It fills this valley and the next. I assume you've never been to l'Morai."

"Yes," replied Morcastle distractedly. "I haven't. Marie was born in l'Morai, but after the Fever blinded her and killed her father . . ." He paused. "I'm sorry, Marie."

"It's all right," she responded quietly. "What do you see, Morcastle?"

Blushing in the night, he leaned to the left side of the phaeton and peered over. The steep-sloped face below them was illuminated with a hundred flickering lights, which fanned into a broad valley and rose up the face of the opposite mountain. "It's all lit up. There must be a thousand houses and shops." The warm glow from the windows shimmered across the rocky sides of the valley. "I can see where the road goes. It switches back and forth on the mountainside until it gets down to the bottom."

"There's a river there," Marie murmured, her ear toward the valley.

Morcastle nodded, hearing the sound now as well. The distant rush and plummet of a wide, white-water river rose to the magician's ear. He thought he could see the snaking flood and the four or five bridges that arched over it. On the other side of the river, more lanterns dotted the slope, and Morcastle could distinguish the thin roads that passed among the buildings.

"It's beautiful," the magician noted offhandedly.

"Yes," Marie said. "I wish I could remember where Father's shop was. I was so young. I don't even know what it looked like, or what he did, for that matter. But I remember feeling safe there."

"Perhaps we could find it together," Morcastle suggested.

"Unfortunately," L'Aris interrupted, "you won't be able to roam the city by yourselves. I guess now is as

good a time as any to tell you the rules: While in
l'Morai, you must obey me in all things; you must
remain with me except when in your quarters; you
mustn't speak to or touch any villager but me, even if
spoken to—"

"We must not breathe unless breathed upon," Morcastle supplied.

Ignoring the comment, L'Aris continued, "You are
visitors, so you won't be held to the strict moral code of
l'Morai. But any citizen you offend could have you up
on charges in an instant, so deal with me only. You leave
the citizens alone; they will leave you alone. Understand?"

"Yes," Marie said quietly. "As long as it's mutual."

The phaeton reached a tight switchback. The driver
snapped a small whip and clicked at the horses, turning
them hard to the left. As the carriage rounded the corner, L'Aris said dryly, "Yes. It is very mutual."

The new road was steeper than the previous one, and
the grassy ruts gave way to sun-hardened mud. They
passed occasional cabins and terraced farms as they
traveled. Eventually, the houses along the roadside
became so close together they formed a solid wall.
Smoke curled up from the rows and rows of chimneys,
sometimes sending sparks like tiny meteors to spin in
the chill air and settle out on the roofs of slate or thatch.

Beyond the row houses, they reached a merchant
district. After passing four pubs, three inns, a candle-
maker, blacksmith, stable, tinsmith, limner, glassblower, and countless other shops, the carriage reached
the base of the valley.

The rushing roar of the river pounded in their ears as
the coachman steered them toward an arched bridge.
On the other side of the bridge, a massive, round building sat, overhanging the sluicing waters. The building's
stone walls were ringed by angled columns of marble
that slanted toward a fat, domed roof. The black sky

itself seemed to rest on the roof, compressing and bending the columns outward.

"What *is* that thing?" Morcastle shouted over the pounding roar as they topped the arched bridge. He pointed to the edifice.

L'Aris answered, "That's the Council Hall."

"Looks more like a fortress than a Council Hall," Morcastle noted.

"It is," L'Aris replied. "Before the village was here, that building guarded the bridge over the Vinrouge River. A trading village was settled around it, then came farmers on the heath, a college, a library . . . and, of course, your carnival."

The carriage shifted backward, the horses pulling in their traces as they started up a new road. At the end of the cobbled lane, the Council Hall loomed in the night.

"Remember, first it's the arraignment. Tell the council what you told me," L'Aris said. "I'll provide the legal language as needed. Oh, and be ready to testify as soon as we get inside. Dominick's already there."

*   *   *   *   *

The council chamber was cavernous. It was laid out in a heptagon, its seven outer walls masoned in gray-black marble. In each corner, a lantern glowed sullenly, casting long shadows over the mildewed stone. Archways opened in the walls, leading to dark halls beyond. Water dripped in one such passage.

Within the outer heptagon stood a ring of huge granite drums. They supported the groin vaults of the gallery as well as girding the ribbed dome that arched over the central section of the council chamber. Each of the dome's seven sections contained a dark fresco of peeling paint.

The main floor of the council chamber was lined with benches that converged on a large, round dais. On either side of the dais sat two tables, each surrounded by high-backed chairs and oak railings. Behind the dais, the wall was segmented into twenty-some arched niches, their interiors black and, apparently, empty.

Morcastle guided Marie into the chamber, feeling her hand shiver in his. She whispered, "I can feel how large it is. Large and dank."

Moving toward the center aisle of the chamber, Morcastle tugged on Marie's hand. "It's all right, come inside."

"What do you see?" Marie asked, stepping away from the thick oak doors at the front of the council chamber. The worn leather soles of her shoes scraped uneasily across the stone floor.

"Not much," the magician whispered. "It's pretty dark." He strained his eyes to see across the chamber. "It's like a cave," he said, "a big cavern, with columns and lanterns. There are benches and some tables and a dais."

The magician felt a tap on his shoulder, and L'Aris gestured them toward the dais. "Please move forward. We're late."

Morcastle stepped into the aisle between the benches, drawing Marie behind him.

At the far end of the chamber, a failing lantern cast light over two panels of the fresco. The one on the left showed a man leaving a prison cell, his jailor bowing graciously toward him and a bright, haloed sun shining in the heavens. The panel on the right showed the same man, transfigured and hovering over a crowd of adoring peasant folk. He held his hands out to either side. Dark cords of power emanated from his head and spread out to the people below.

"Beautiful," Morcastle whispered.

L'Aris touched his shoulder, urging him forward. "Let's go. They're waiting on us."

"Who are?" Morcastle asked distractedly, his eyes

still tracing the lines of the vault.

"*They* are," L'Aris replied, pointing to the far end of the council chamber.

There, amongst a forest of chairs and angular rails of oak, sat the butcher, Dominick. Beside him stood a man with an imposing build. Instead of a tattered peasant chemise, however, he wore a silken surcoat, a ruffled shirt, a woolen jacket, and tailored trousers. His clothes made L'Aris's attire look like farm rags.

"I wondered if you'd been eaten by wolves," the man said, standing up. His booming voice resounded through the chamber. "Or if your witnesses had reconsidered their implausible account."

"You always hope as much, don't you, Brucin?" asked L'Aris jovially. "It's the only way you can win a trial." As he spoke, the lean jurist directed Morcastle and Marie toward the high-backed chairs at the front of the hall. L'Aris added with theatrical flair, "Please forgive any lateness on our part. One of the witnesses had been stabbed through by your patron."

"Wait a moment," protested Brucin. "The trial's not even begun yet, and already you make unfounded accusations. Don't listen to him, my lords. It's just another one of L'Aris's famous breaches of etiquette."

"Breaches?" L'Aris cried with dramatic indignation. "And who's to talk . . . ?"

As the jurists continued their banter, Morcastle's eyes studied the arched niches that fronted the chamber. They were black, as though each opened on a long tunnel. But the niches weren't empty. There were eyes in them, staring out, watching with silent, patient interest. In the dark movement of black on black, Morcastle saw a hand wrap about the arm of a chair.

"Enough!" came a voice from one of the niches. "Bad enough that you drag us from our beds in the second watch of the night. Now you've got to delay us with posturing. None of us came here for your theatrics. Bring forward the accusers, and let's get this unpleasant business done with."

"I couldn't agree more!" Brucin replied, shooting an indignant glare toward L'Aris. The lean jurist didn't notice it, however, having taken Marie's hands.

She pulled back. "Let Morcastle speak first."

"No," L'Aris whispered with a dismissing gesture. "You're more direct, more honest. And your blindness and femininity might help us gain the council members' sympathy."

Marie's eyes narrowed, but she stood up and followed the jurist to a granite lectern on the dais. L'Aris positioned her hands on a large, black stone embedded in the top of the lectern. "Keep your hands on this. It's a logolith, a word-stone. It'll glow to indicate whether you are speaking the truth or not."

Marie nodded, cold sweat dotting her palms.

A nasal, feminine voice emerged from one of the side niches. "Provide your full name, relevant lineage, and family trade."

Coughing to clear the mildewy air from her lungs, Marie said, "I am Marie. I do not know what my last name is. I have no known lineage or family. The Fever plague blinded me and killed my parents. I appeared, a beggar, on the carnival's doorstep one evening. My trade is juggling."

The logolith glowed white, the color of truth.

"A performer," blurted a man from the council.

"What do you juggle?" came a different female voice.

"Daggers."

"A juggler of daggers," muttered a man in one of the niches, "accusing the butcher. Should be interesting."

"What accusation do you bring to this court today, Marie?" intoned the first woman.

Blinking, Marie said, "I accuse Dominick the butcher of stabbing my friend Hermos and killing Borgo the Sword-Swallower, Panol and his parasitic twin Banol, and countless other members of Carnival l'Morai."

The word-stone glowed red, the color of hatred.

"Assault and murder, my lords," L'Aris interjected.

A deep, disembodied voice with a lisp said, "You have heard these statements against you, Dominick. How do you respond?"

"She's a lunatic, a freak," Dominick said, spittle on his meaty lips.

Brucin rose beside him, placing a hand on his shoulder. "We deny all accusations. This blind woman surely is not a valid witness as to identity. She cannot even see those of whom she speaks."

"She is a valid witness," interjected L'Aris, standing now. "You saw how the stone glowed white. She's telling the truth."

"White is also the color of strong passion," Brucin barked. "Whores are passionate, yes, but truthful?"

The logolith became blood red under Marie's hands. "How dare you—"

"I too have witnessed his crimes," Morcastle interposed nervously, "and my eyes are as good as anyone's."

"Excuse the intrusion, noble councilors," L'Aris said with a smooth smile. "This is Morcastle the Magician, who chased down the murderer in the carnival."

"My client is no murderer," Brucin blustered, pounding his fist on the oak table before him, "and already the accusers lie: it was not Monsieur Morcastle who chased Monsieur Dominick, but rather a beast-boy— half-cat, half-human. Will you believe the protests of a blind woman, a beast-boy, and a con artist? Monsieur Morcastle, after all, makes his money through deception of the senses!"

"Brucin speaks convincingly," came the rasping voice of a crone. "What evidence will you freaks present in the trial against Dominick the butcher?"

Marie rallied herself, and the swirling scarlet in the logolith gave way to ivory, then white. "At the site of

Borgo's murder, the butcher left several handprints that showed he had a missing index finger."

"Which hand?" Brucin challenged.

Marie's knuckles whitened, and the logolith clouded for a moment. "I . . . I honestly do not remember, though I believe it was the left."

"My patron's missing finger is on the right hand."

"Furthermore," Marie continued, "I surprised the butcher at the murder scene and cut him across the back as he fled, a long gash from right shoulder to left hip." She could feel the white heat of the word-stone.

"Please turn about, Monsieur Butcher," said the flat voice of the first woman, "and show your back."

Dominick sat wordless, his arms crossed, until Brucin gestured for him to stand. Sullenly, the muscular man rose. He shuffled about and raised the tattered shirt from his back.

There it was, the crimson, crescent scar.

Silence fell over the council. In the stillness, L'Aris stepped forward and said, "If necessary, I shall take council members to the wood outside the carnival, where over a hundred performers have been buried, each bearing the same peculiar cut marks Dominick made on Borgo, Panol, and Banol."

"May I interject something?" Brucin asked, sarcasm edging his words. "Rarely has this council considered the cases of carnival . . . performers. Traditionally, the Puppetmaster has handled the governance of his carnival, and the council has governed l'Morai. I move that we dismiss this case, placing it in the noble judgment of the Puppetmaster."

"Wait a moment," L'Aris interrupted.

"You are out of order, Jurist L'Aris," came a grating response from one of the council members. "We must consider Jurist Brucin's proposal."

As L'Aris sat back down, the council began discussing the call for dismissal.

"He's right about the laws."

"Perhaps this is all a scheme."

"We've got to protect citizens first and freaks second."

"Of course the carnival has a graveyard; it's been there for hundreds of years."

Morcastle listened unhappily to the statements traded back and forth among the council members, and Marie withdrew from the lectern, groping for her seat among the high-backed chairs.

In time, the discussions among the councilors quieted, and a man with a booming voice spoke. "In light of the grim truths the honorable Jurist Brucin brings to our attention, I must inform you that—"

"Hold, please," came a deeper voice. "I've held my tongue because this trial involves two of my own folk. But I can be silent no longer."

Morcastle's face went white as he studied the hulking figure that rose in one of the side niches, and Marie lifted a hand to her mouth.

"Yes, you know me, don't you, my children?" the man continued, stepping from the niche and descending a shallow ring of stairs. The man lumbered into the flickering lamplight, his thick, black wraps flapping gently.

"I am Maudit Sienne, Puppetmaster of the Carnival l'Morai and councilor to this city of justice. This morning, these two performers and a third came to me with their concerns. Rather than listen, I set them in the stocks. I should have heard them out. By law, the greatest punishment I can mete out is imprisonment. But, if Dominick is guilty of murdering performers in my circus, he should hang in a crow's cage until dead. Perhaps one freak's life is not commensurate to one citizen's life. But what of two? What of ten? What of one hundred? Hear this trial, or I shall move my carnival to a city that knows of justice. And all of you know what that would do to l'Morai the Beautiful."

"Yes," came the voice of Lord Odieu from one of the niches, "I concur. We must take this matter seriously."

Again the councilors fell to whisperings and mutterings. The Puppetmaster made some semblance of a bow and withdrew into the shadows as the discussions swelled.

L'Aris whispered to Marie and Morcastle, "Now we must wait and hope. The Puppetmaster may have saved us. But," he paused, listening to the buzz of speech behind him, "many citizens consider him the greatest freak of all."

Morcastle shook his head and cast a glance toward the defense table.

Brucin eyed them hostilely and muttered something to Dominick. Before he had finished what he was saying, the councilman with the resonant voice began to speak. "How long, honorable Jurist L'Aris, would you need to gather your evidence and witnesses?"

L'Aris rose and bowed toward the dark niches. "There is such an abundance of damning evidence that I would need merely one day to gather it—that is, if two of my lords are at liberty to accompany me to the carnival."

"Most certainly," replied the disembodied voice. "And you, Brucin?"

"I'll need no more time than the accusers. Many of Dominick's friends—hearty citizens all—saw the good butcher in town at the times when it is claimed the murders took place."

"Then," resumed the booming voice, "tomorrow at dusk, the trial begins."

* * * * *

L'Aris held Marie's shaking hand as she ducked through the stony portal. Morcastle followed afterward, clutching his satin cape to keep it off the watery stone of the threshold. A sleepy guard impatiently motioned them through the gateway, then swung the thick iron door closed and turned a fat key in the lock.

"Your cell is up here," the guard said, pointing toward a line of iron-barred rooms.

"Again," L'Aris said apologetically, "forgive me for these accommodations. Typically, accusers may remain in their own homes before a trial, but—"

"—But freaks aren't allowed to run free in the city," Marie finished bitterly. "We might attack people—or entertain them."

L'Aris laughed nervously. "Of course, they'll have separate cells, won't they?" he asked their escort.

Marie broke in before the guard could respond. "Don't put me alone in this place. I'll need someone with eyes to kill the centipedes for me."

Morcastle shot a worried look toward Marie, his eyes glistening in the wan torchlight. "Centipedes? Here, below the Council Hall?"

The guard fit another broad key into the lock of a cage. The mechanism ground and clattered, and the ancient door swung open. Waving his torch into the small cell, the guard said, "All right. Inside now."

Morcastle stepped across the threshold. The walls of the cell were hewn from the thick granite of the cliff face, and its front was lined with iron bars the width of a man's arm. On the left, a narrow wooden bed hung, anchored to the wall with thick chains. Water and latrine buckets sat in the far left corner of the cell, and a pile of straw lay in the right. Two sets of shackles hung on one wall.

Morcastle took Marie's hand and led her into the cell. "It's all right. Clean enough, and dry."

"And cold," said Marie, biting her lip.

"Could you bring them a set of blankets, monsieur?" L'Aris asked the guard.

The young soldier cast an irritated glance at him. "I'll

have to see." He swung the metal door closed behind the two performers and turned the key in the rusty lock. "Got to get back to my post," he muttered.

L'Aris stood by the bars, peering into the cell. "I apologize—"

Marie interrupted, "At least we're safe from the murderer."

"I'll be back tomorrow evening. I'll have a section of the sheet with the bloody handprint and a plaster casting of the boot print behind Panol's stage, if it's still there. And I'll also record the testimony of your mangiant friend and the two councilors who will have seen the graves." The guard nudged him and motioned toward the door. Before leaving, L'Aris said, "Don't worry. We'll convict him."

Morcastle nodded, despite the lines of worry across his lips. He watched as L'Aris withdrew from the cell, taking the torchlight with him. Morcastle stood, the angular shadows of the bars sweeping over him in nauseating arcs before the light disappeared entirely. Hearing the clank of the key in the cellblock door, Morcastle withdrew to the wooden bed. He reached out for Marie's hand and drew her over to sit beside him.

"Well," the magician said in a hush, "we've made our accusations. Now we can only hope for enough evidence to prove them." The words sounded stale in the dank cell.

Marie buried her face in her hands. "I'm just tired and cold," she said.

Morcastle stood up, slipped the cape from his shoulders, and placed it around Marie. "Keep it. I've a shirt surcoat to keep me warm."

Marie knocked on the hard, wooden bed. "How are we supposed to sleep on this? There's only room for one, with no blankets, no mattress, no pillow. . . ."

"You sleep now," Morcastle said. "I'll sleep tomorrow. Use my cape as a blanket; I can bring over some straw for a mattress and pillow. It looks clean enough." The magician rose from the bed and shuffled blindly across the cell to the opposite wall. He picked up a clump of straw and carried it to the wooden bed. There, he made a small pile and patted it with his hand.

"There you are. Lie down and sleep."

Marie rolled onto her side and rested her head on the straw. "Thank you," she said. Morcastle smiled grimly. He brushed the chaff from his hands and paced to the bars, groping so as not to run into them. As he reached the front of the cell, he heard the faint clink of the final jail door being closed. Marie's regular breaths rose and fell in the utter darkness behind him. Soon, she fell asleep.

Silence. Silence, but for an occasional drop of water falling into a pool in some other section of the jail.

Then Morcastle heard the voice.

It was faint and liquid. At first he thought he had imagined it, but the words continued to sound. It was Dominick, muttering in his cell down the long hallway. Unmistakably Dominick. He was murmuring to himself, the words almost becoming a chant.

"I'm going to kill you freaks. I'm going to get free, and I'm going to kill you."

 **SIX**

Morning sunlight slanted in through the high, narrow windows of the prison and warmed the sleepless face of Morcastle the Amazing. His eyes were red and anxious, swollen from lack of sleep and from the dark, dark night.

He had sat for long hours with hands clamped over his ears, trying to block Dominick's threats from his mind. Still they echoed. Morcastle directed his thoughts to many other things—card tricks, finger traps, audiences, traveling shows. But all his memories and speculations led back to Marie, to how fragile she was, how in need of protection. And Morcastle knew that inside, he was more fragile than she.

Marie turned over on the wooden bed. She moaned and stretched her stiff muscles. "It must be morning," she said, touching her leg where a patch of sunlight struck it.

Morcastle cast a fevered glance toward her, then stood up and began pacing.

Swinging her legs down onto the floor, Marie stretched again. "It wasn't very restful," she said absently, "but at least it passed the time. Did you manage any sleep, Morcastle?"

The magician paused. He'd not spoken all night, and his voice was raspy. "Too busy hunting centipedes."

Marie rose from the bed and patted the straw pillow with her hand. "Lie down. The trial doesn't resume until tonight."

The magician strode to the wooden pallet and dropped down onto it. "Last night did wonders for my resolve. I'd kill Dominick with my bare hands right now, just to return to my caravan and my own bed."

Marie leaned over him, her hands settling on his shoulders. She kissed his forehead as a mother might, then guided him down onto the makeshift pillow. "Rest now. I'm going to need you tonight."

Morcastle rolled onto his side, setting his head on the pile of straw. Marie removed the magician's cape from her shoulders and laid it over him. "Sleep well," she said, but he didn't hear her. Already he had slipped away into darkness and dreams.

*   *   *   *   *

There was a man in his dream, a man who had the face of Father and the voice of Mother. The face and the voice said, "If ever I catch you fiddling about with those books again, my boy, I'll give you to the council and sell chestnuts at your hanging."

But Morcastle did fiddle, did open the magic books and learn the spells they held. The arcane phrases fell easily from his lips and struck dark lines in the air, like symbols on a page. The lines lengthened and thickened and joined until they formed a dreary cellar laboratory, fetid like the jail cell where he lay. It was a subterranean space, hemmed in by rock walls that held a hundred faces. High along one wall hung a window that smiled nervously. The winter sun rolled tonguelike across that window, licking the secret laboratory within, touching upon the flasks and vials, jars and tables, books and fears and secrets it held.

And Morcastle the Magician, too.

But one night, one terrible night, the sun vanished from the window like a swallowed wafer, and lanterns glowed in the cobwebbed rafters. In the pool of light beneath the lanterns, Morcastle sat, poring over a magic book. He held a quill that was a tiny woman's leg and dipped the toe into a pot of black ink. The nail scrawled words from right to left across the book's pages. Then stopped.

There had been a noise. That's why he had stopped writing.

Morcastle peered up from the manuscript, and the woman's leg began kicking fearfully in his hand. He looked past the dusty jars of bat-wing and newt-eye, past the spinning armillary sphere, past the water reservoir, the kiln, the rack of dancing aprons. There, in the darkly smiling window, he glimpsed eyes.

"Must be Father," he murmured in his sleep, knowing vaguely Marie had heard him, "come to sell his chestnuts."

The eyes disappeared from the smiling window, and footsteps pounded on his front stoop. The scent of roasted chestnuts filled the air. And Morcastle knew.

He slammed the book closed. The wet ink on the pages blotted into bats that flew from the book and were caught in the cobwebs. He lifted the book from its stand. Already, the *lub-dub* of Father's boot was cracking the ribs of the door. Morcastle hurried to a big red **X** on the sandy floor. He brushed the sand away from a wooden hatch and opened the compartment beneath. Lowering the book onto a tongue within, he closed the hatch and smoothed the sand over it.

The door above gave way. With shouts and a flutter of torchlight, Father leaped into the lab and splintered into five or ten gendarmes. They were like bees pouring from a bottle. Morcastle stepped back from the secret hatch, his nose turning to wax and running hotly down his face. The guardsmen welled, black as ink, in the cellar, their lightless tide rising to Morcastle's neck. A small boy floated among them, a boy with a beard and bleeding palms. He flung an accusing finger at Morcastle.

"That's him!" the boy declared angrily, his voice the voice of Mother. "That's the warlock!"

The gendarmes released a harmonic chorus of belches and had a good laugh about it. Then they grabbed Morcastle by the arms and smashed his precious glass and crockery with rabbits they pulled from their hats. One toppled a lantern, which cracked, pouring lamp oil across the floor. The oil lit instantly, and fire raced out through the laboratory. The flames leaped up onto tables and shelves and cabinets, taking the form of Father's face and roaring with Mother's voice. Morcastle cried out, but already the uniformed men were carrying him toward the stairs. He saw the armillary sphere engulfed in flames, the planets blackening with soot, melting.

*   *   *   *   *

Morcastle lurched awake, his eyes filled with light from the burning torch L'Aris held. The jurist was leaning over the bed, his face solemn as he studied the disheveled magician. "Wake up, Morcastle. Trial time has arrived."

Morcastle pushed off the now bedraggled satin cape and struggled to sit up. His legs felt leaden and cramped, as though his bones were made of rusted iron. He ran a hand through his hair and rubbed his weary face. The straw had left red lines on his cheeks.

L'Aris took Marie's hand. "I've gathered all the evidence and testimony we'll need. Let's just hope Brucin hasn't any surprises."

"Surprises?" Marie asked.

"Yes, surprises," the lean man replied simply. "After I

went to the graveyard with a couple council members, Brucin visited it too. He had three councilors with him."

A resounding chime filled the air. Then came a second and a third, each a different pitch and each reverberating in the stony jail. Morcastle clamped his hands over his ears and stood up.

"What is that infernal racket?"

"The Council Chimes," L'Aris said, "the Chimes of l'Morai. They call the citizens to the hall for trials."

Morcastle's eyes registered his shock. "The whole town's going to be there?"

"Yes, they will," L'Aris replied, swinging open the groaning door of the cell. "Which is why we should be going."

* * * * *

Morcastle heard little of the opening comments. He was distracted by his lingering dreams and by the domed vault that seemed to spin like a great wheel above him. Tonight, the fresco panels on the ceiling were lit by a hundred lanterns, not just one. And they horrified him. The first panel, over the doors in back of the hall, showed a pillow-faced scholar being arrested by a pack of gendarmes. The panels on the left side of the dome displayed the scholar in an arraignment and trial that led to his exoneration. The final scene, above the dais in front of the hall, showed the old man leaving prison before a bowing jailor and a sympathetic crowd.

The panels on the right, however, depicted a different arraignment and trial—and verdict. The final fresco on that side was an execution scene. What Morcastle had mistaken the night before as rays of power streaming from the man's head were, in fact, ropes around his neck. He was lifted up on a post, and the people thronging below pulled on a multitude of nooses.

Morcastle's heart was racing again, and Dominick's

chant murmured through his mind. He blinked and gripped the arms of his high-backed chair. Concentrate, he told himself, or you'll end up on that post.

"In conclusion," L'Aris intoned from the dais, "I ask why have we been so blind to the violence of this man? Why did it take so long to realize a man who relishes slaying defenseless cattle would find killing humans at least as exhilarating? Those among you with children, those among you who remember when l'Morai's streets were safe and friendly, hear these words I speak. L'Morai will not be safe until this man, this murderer, Dominick the butcher, has been convicted and punished for his crimes against the people."

Reaching the lectern in the center of the podium, L'Aris dropped his voice and said, "You will be asked to listen to two unfortunates describe the crimes of Dominick. Please judge them not, but hear what they say." L'Aris bowed dramatically before the gathered throng. Murmurs and unsettled whispers circulated among the crowd, and a few spectators clapped conspicuously. The thin jurist straightened and strode to his seat.

Brucin now stepped imperiously onto the dais. He slid a meaty thumb along the waistline of his trousers and leveled his stormy gaze.

"Elegant and forceful rhetoric from my esteemed colleague," Brucin said, gesturing toward the accusers' table. "But only rhetoric, and nothing more. None of what L'Aris said touches in the least on the truth.

"The truth is this!" Brucin shouted with a sudden stomp of his booted foot. "The accusation of murder has been leveled, not by citizens of l'Morai, not by folk whose history and disposition are known to us. No. The accusers in this trial are carnival workers, 'freaks from the heath' as one lord calls them." The reference garnered laughter from the crowd, and Brucin smiled fatly.

"Indeed, consider the fact that these performers make their money not by honest toil and sweat, but by startling our eyes with grotesqueries, tricks, and *shams*. Consider, too, the abnormality—nay, the freakishness—of these folk. All of you have been to the carnival. All of you know the peculiarity of the performers there.

"And who do they turn their accusations against but Dominick? Dominick, who was born here in l'Morai, raised beside our hearth fires, tutored and apprenticed by his father, Cisioux—may he rest in peace.

"In light of these facts, and in disregard of L'Aris's rhetoric, I ask the honorable council and the citizens of l'Morai to bring forth a Writ of Innocence for this man, our friend." Brucin's voice faded away as applause swelled through the chamber.

A man spoke from among the shadowed council members. "Bring forth your first witness, jurist of the accusers."

Rising, L'Aris bowed to the council and cried, "First, I call Marie the Juggler to testify." He took hold of Marie's hand. Biting her lip, she rose from the high-backed chair. L'Aris led her to the lectern on the dais and set her hands on the logolith. It began to glow a mixture of crimson and purple.

He whispered through clenched teeth, "Look scared, if you can."

A humorless smile spread across her face. "Not a problem."

"Now I want to do a bit of reconstruction," L'Aris said to the crowd. "As I ask questions of this lovely woman, picture in your mind what must have happened on the night when Borgo the Sword-Swallower died. Picture in your mind who"—here he gestured toward Dominick—"must have been responsible. Let me introduce you to this beautiful young woman, Marie, whose caravan was violated and bloodied by the murderer's hand. Tell us, Marie, what happened the night you found the murderer in your caravan?"

Marie swallowed hard. The logolith faded from scarlet to ivory to white. "Well, you see, I juggle knives. . . ."

*   *   *   *   *

Borgo the sword-swallowing dwarf stood outside the arena, listening to the roar and applause from the stands within. "Marie certainly does draw the crowds," he murmured admiringly to himself. His puffy eyebrows bristled, casting a shadow over his bearded face. "Always tough to follow a crowd-pleaser."

Nervously he turned away from the arena entrance, his stubby fingers settling on the sword hilt at his side. He drew the sword forth and held it up before him. Torchlight from the nearby Performers Quarter glinted off the sword's keen edges. The blade was as long from tip to hilt as he was tall. Lowering the sword, Borgo slid it into its scabbard. "Wonder if Marie could juggle one of these."

Another cry of delight erupted within. Borgo strode to the wall of the arena and leaned against it. He folded his arms, waiting to hear the final trumpets and the harlequin interlude.

Movement caught his eye, movement in the Performers Quarter. An unfamiliar man slipped among the caravans. Peering about suspiciously, the man stalked up to the stoop of one of the wagons. There in the lantern light he stood, dark and burly, a barrel-shaped torso with a fleshy, balding head and meaty hands. The man turned, seeming to stare straight at the watching dwarf, then with a quick twist of the handle, the intruder opened the door and slipped inside.

"What's this business, then?" Borgo whispered self-importantly. He listened again to the crowd in the arena: Marie's act still had some minutes before it finished. "Best go see," Borgo said to himself, his hand loose on the hilt of his sword.

He stepped away from the wall and cautiously strode along the woodchip path to the caravan the man had entered—Marie's caravan. "Fellow's up to no good." Eyeing the small wagon, Borgo decided to leave the weighty sword sheathed in favor of a dagger he kept strapped to his belt. *Not even a mouthful*, he said of the dagger during his nightly performances.

Borgo reached the caravan and set his hand on the doorknob. The door swung open. Beyond lay darkness, illuminated only by the lantern light that shone through the veiled windows. *The blind girl has little need for light*, Borgo thought. *Me neither, thanks to these dwarven eyes of mine.*

He gazed into the darksome caravan. His night vision found no immediate sign of the intruder, so Borgo stepped into the wagon. His shadow fell, long and shifting, across the furnishings of the caravan. The bed and stool were empty. . . .

The slice of steel sounded beside Borgo. He started, lashing out with his dagger, reaching for his sword. . . .

It was gone.

A footstep thumped on the caravan floor. Borgo wheeled, jostling the table. Light flashed on the edges of his own sword, descending toward him. Descending. Borgo screamed, and the blade sank violently home down his throat. He fell to the bed as the door slammed closed behind him.

*   *   *   *   *

"I feel compelled to remind the council," Brucin intoned, pacing across the dais in front of Marie, "we did not so much hear Marie's version of the story, but L'Aris's reconstruction. Now, my dear, let's hear the truth. You returned from the arena to find a dead body and a murderer in your caravan. Is this a correct statement?"

"Yes," Marie said.

Brucin theatrically drew a silken handkerchief from his coat pocket and held it up before Marie. "Jurist L'Aris also presented this bit of rag, with a very faint bloody stain on it showing a handprint with a thumb and only three fingers. Did it indeed come from your caravan, as he said?"

"Yes, it did," Marie replied.

"Wrong," Brucin said blandly, dropping the kerchief onto Marie's shoulder. "Wrong, wrong, wrong. The cloth you identified is *my* handkerchief." He pulled his other hand from behind his back and held up the ragged square of linen L'Aris had presented earlier. "This, my dear, is the rag of which you spoke." Dangling the cloth by its frayed corner, Brucin said, "How blind are you, Marie, my dear?"

"I can *hear* that you're about twenty stone. I can *hear* you scratch your scaly chin."

"How blind are you?" Brucin roared.

"Utterly!" Marie snapped.

"I see," Brucin said as he paced away. "So, you never saw the alleged handprints on your bed, on the walls, on the ceiling? You never saw the alleged bootprint, with flour along its edge? You never saw the face of the man who supposedly assailed you?"

"Of course not!" Marie snapped. "But I marked him with a knife gouge, from—"

"Correct me if I am wrong," Brucin interrupted angrily, "but only last night you told the council your murderer is missing the index finger of his left hand, while Dominick is missing that of his right."

"What about the scar on his back?"

"Come now!" Brucin growled. "The gendarmes said you did not mention the scar until Dominick had been captured. Indeed, they indicated you said nothing at all until you had your suspect in hand. No wonder he so fully matches your descriptions! You built them around my patron!"

Marie gritted her teeth and said, "What about the bloody handprint on my bed sheets?"

"If tales are true," Brucin replied with fierce levity, "gendarmes could find all manner of handprints on the bed sheets of women such as you." The statement brought derisive laughter from the crowd, laughter that filled the dome and echoed through the stony hall. Brucin drew his kerchief from Marie's shoulder and said, "No more questions. You're excused."

Marie gritted her teeth. "Just hope he doesn't decide to kill anyone *you* love." Pushing away his guiding hand, she strode to the edge of the dais and stepped down toward the chairs.

Brucin backed away, brushing his hands clean as he watched her go. He dabbed his forehead with the kerchief, folded it neatly, and deposited it in a stiff pocket of his vest.

A woman's voice arose from the council. "L'Aris, bring forth your next witness."

The jurist stood and bowed. His face looked pallid in the jaundiced lantern light. "I call Monsieur Morcastle."

He gestured toward the magician, who rose and approached the dais. Morcastle felt strangely vulnerable without his black satin cape, which was so stained with dirt and rumpled from the long night that he had left it in the cell. Reaching the lectern, the magician set his hand on the logolith, which turned a sickly green. Giggles circulated through the chamber.

"People of l'Morai, open your mind's-eyes once again to see the murderer commit his next crime," L'Aris began, gesturing toward Dominick. "Prepare with me to reconstruct the events of Panol and Banol's murder. Monsieur Morcastle, tell us of that terrible night."

Morcastle coughed once and began. "The first thing I remember was putting my head in the guillotine. . . ."

* * * * *

Panol sat atop a stool on the whitewashed stage and waited for the roar of the crowd to die down. He gazed dully at his parasitic twin. Banol was decked out to look like a ventriloquist's dummy: his small, doll-like body was dressed in a miniature tabard that matched his brother's. Banol even had false cloth legs sewn to the bottom of his tabard. The outfit was working. No one in the packed audience seemed to realize that Banol wasn't a mannequin—that he was really a flesh and blood being, joined to his brother at the stomach. But they would soon find out.

"Duh," Panol blustered as the laughter died away, "whadda you mean I dress dirty?"

"Look! You've got bird droppings on your shirt," crooned Banol. He pulled back his false legs and revealed a white splotch on his partner's tabard.

Panol clutched a dirty cap to his head and stared down at the spot. The shock on his face elicited a howl from the crowd. Panol pointed to the offending blotch. "This is a tabard, not a shirt."

Banol snickered. "That's what I said: Ta-bird took a shirt on you!" The throng roared.

Panol turned an uncomprehending face toward them. "Wonder why the bird picked me?" He removed the cap from his bowed head, revealing a red bull's-eye painted on his bald spot.

"Why the bird picked you?" Banol echoed innocently. He produced a paintbrush tipped in red paint. "I haven't the slightest!"

Tossing the brush away, Banol leaned for a closer look at the stained cloth. He hawked and spit on the tabard: another white, foamy spot appeared beside the first. "You've been hit by another bird. Look!"

Panol blinked. He lifted the tabard toward his face and sniffed the spots.

"Hey," Panol declared, "this stuff smells like garlic. Why would a bird eat garlic?"

Banol shrugged sheepishly. "Maybe to keep the bats away?"

Panol dropped the tabard and stared severely at his partner. "Birds don't eat garlic! But *you* do! *You* eat garlic all the time!"

"You eat crow all the time," Banol pointed out fearfully. "Maybe that's why you're such a target for the birds."

"Maybe . . . maybe *nothing*!" Panol barked, grabbing his partner about the neck and shaking him. "Maybe you spit on me!"

"Spit on you?" Banol replied with a squeak of mock fear. "Why would I spit on you? I loathe you very much!"

"Maybe," Panol replied, considering for a moment. "But still, you spit on me!"

"Perhaps I expectorate too much from you," Banol jabbered.

"I think you do!" Panol shouted, the muscles of his face clenching and his fingers tightening around the narrow neck of his partner.

"Wait!" Banol gagged. "How could I spit on you? I'm only a dummy, a mannequin. Dummies can't spit!"

A confused look appeared on Panol's face and his grip around Banol's bony neck slackened. "I guess you're right, little chum."

" 'Course I'm right," Banol quipped indignantly, straightening his rumpled tabard. "I'm just made out of wood. Whatever I do, you make me do."

Panol nodded stupidly and said, "Yep."

"So . . . *you* made me spit on you!" Banol shouted triumphantly. "I guess that makes *you* the dummy after all!"

"Wait," Panol protested, angry again. "I ain't the dummy! Look. I gots the legs!" He sat back on the stool and kicked his legs thrice in the air.

"Oh, yeah?" challenged Banol, leaning back as his

partner had just done. "Maybe I got the legs, too." His false cloth legs didn't move, but Panol's real ones did, kicking again.

Panol snorted, fuming, and crossed both arms over his chest. "Hey, hows come you can still move when I gots my puppet arm up here on my belly?"

The crowd's laughter stilled, and a child in the front row covered his gaping mouth. Banol continued the ludicrous dance of his partner's legs.

Panol huffed. He threw the tabard back over his shoulder and began unbuttoning the soiled chemise beneath. "We'll see who's really got the legs!" he declared angrily.

The dance stopped. "Don't do that!" Banol shouted in dramatic fear. "Better not do that!" He tried to bat his partner's hands from the buttons, but the pudgy fingers continued their work.

The tails of the shirt parted, revealing a stout and hairless stomach. Panol pulled back the hem.

A woman leaning on the stage screamed.

There, plain in the lantern light, the crowd saw the rumpled ring of flesh where Banol's torso fused with the abdomen of Panol.

"He's not a dummy!" shouted a man in the crowd. "They're deformed!"

A roar of disgust, shock, and anger moved through the crowd. Three boys along the outer edge of the group began throwing handfuls of mud at the stage. Others, taking their cue from the boys, picked up small rocks.

Panol, accustomed to such responses, lurched up from the stool to make a quick escape. He stepped back, shielding his cowering twin with one massive arm.

The canvas backdrop behind him tore, and a burly hand reached through the opening, seizing Panol's leg. He fell to the stage, toppling the stool behind him. The hand dragged him across the rough boards. Panol screamed, scrabbling for a hold, but was pulled through the torn backdrop into Freaks Alley beyond.

Flailing in the sudden darkness, Panol glimpsed a huge black form against the starry sky. Then the butt of the dagger fell, smashing him in the brow. He slumped, unconscious.

And Banol was left to scream.

*   *   *   *   *

"More spurious conjecture and construction from L'Aris," Brucin objected.

Morcastle released a weak moan and said, "It's not conj—"

"A toppled stool and a bootprint," Brucin interrupted, incredulous. He shook his head as he walked past Morcastle. "You are saying my patron—this longstanding friend and citizen of l'Morai—committed murder, because you found a toppled stool and a bootprint?"

"Yes, but—"

"And, according to your story, Panol and Banol were taken before a throng of witnesses, but not a single one will corroborate your story?"

Morcastle smiled and mopped the sweat from his brow. "They probably thought it was part of the act. Besides, we found the bodies—"

"*You* found the bodies!" Brucin declared, whirling around and leveling a finger toward the magician. "You and that blind woman! Before anyone else knew the performers were even missing, you were at their grave. How do you explain that?"

"Why would I lie?" Morcastle blurted desperately. The green of the logolith deepened. "Why would I accuse Dominick?"

"Fear," Brucin said, his voice echoing through the room. "That's what the green stone means. Fear. You fear the citizens of l'Morai, and Marie hates them. All you freaks fear us and hate us because we are everything you wish you were."

Morcastle had left the lectern. "I have nothing more to say."

Brucin shook his head. He glowered at the magician as the man retreated to his chair at the accusers' table. "Fear."

SEVEN

"Esteemed and honorable members of the council," Brucin began as Morcastle retired like a whipped dog to his seat, "I have arrayed not *two* witnesses, as the estimable Jurist L'Aris has, but *ten* witnesses, each prepared to testify at length as to my patron's whereabouts and innocence."

He set his boot heel down on the granite dais and pivoted to face the throng. "But, unlike L'Aris, I have no wish to waste the time of the good folk of l'Morai when Dominick's innocence is so clear." This statement brought heavy applause from the crowd, and a few citizens near the back edged toward the doors. "The accusers have proved nothing but that they have tainted blood and gypsy souls." Again, the clapping resounded.

"If, therefore," Brucin continued, "the council will entertain a motion to dismiss this matter, I will forgo the testimony of these witnesses."

The councilors began to confer amongst themselves.

Morcastle, sitting beside Marie, already knew what their answer would be. The council would not listen to freaks. Morcastle cast a killing glare toward Dominick, who sat placidly across the aisle. The butcher smiled and winked in the direction of Marie. His teeth parted and a fat tongue emerged, running over his meaty lips and leaving a sheen. Morcastle looked away.

I'm going to kill you two freaks. . . .

The resonant voice of a council member sounded above the murmur in the room. "We will entertain the movement for dismissal after each side presents its closing comments." The crowd responded with impatient murmurs. "First we shall hear from the accusers."

"If I may, noble councilors," Brucin interjected. He still stood on the dais. "I would deliver my comments now, to save us all some time."

"Proceed."

Brucin clasped his hands behind his back and began to speak. "I have little need for closing comment. The accusations come from freaks, whose job it is to deceive our senses. One of them is blind, the other a con artist. One hates us, as the logolith has shown, and the other fears us. Both have brought faulty circumstantial evidence to bear against Dominick, who is known and respected by us all."

He slipped his thick hands into the pockets of his waistcoat. "But, just so the people might know the full truth, I call on council member Leonid Klee to speak for me. He accompanied me to the so-called graveyard where the accusers claim my patron buried his victims." Backing off the dais, Brucin gestured toward one of the niches in the ancient wall. "Councilor Klee, tell them what we found."

Morcastle stared at the niche, his eyes straining to make out the figure veiled in darkness. He could see nothing. When Klee began to speak, however, Morcastle realized he had officiated the whole trial.

"Thank you, Jurist Brucin. Yes. I have seen the supposed graveyard. I went there in search of the bodies claimed to be buried there. We found no graves—only bones and remains scattered across the ground. They weren't the bones of humans, but of animals, all of them. We searched for two hours and didn't find a single grave, let alone a single human's remains. Just those of bears and goats and wolves and lambs."

The chamber filled with the buzz of speculation. Mor-castle turned, tight-lipped, to Marie and L'Aris. The jurist whispered, "It's over. I may as well decline my closing comments."

Before L'Aris could stop her, Marie pushed away from the table and circled toward the dais. Seeing the lone woman walking to the front of the Council Hall, the audience quieted. A few folk snickered as she found her stumbling way up onto the granite stage.

The voice of Leonid Klee silenced the crowd. "Do you plan to deliver closing remarks for the accusers?"

"Yes," Marie responded. She reached the lectern and set her hands on the logolith. It flared red, then became lightning-white. "The accusations tonight have not come from us—they have come from Jurist Brucin. He does not indicate why the butcher is innocent, but why we are guilty. Councilman Klee and Jurist Brucin tell you the heath is filled with animal bones. I tell you, those folk in the forest are not animals. They may have been deformed. They may have been grotesque and horrible and repugnant to the men I just mentioned. But beyond the differences in bone and muscle and sinew, those folk are the same as you.

"We are not animals. We are not monsters. Our souls are the same as yours. And when a man such as Dom-inick kills one of us, he is a murderer. If any of you has during this trial known the slightest pang of empathy for Borgo or Panol or Banol, I beg of you, convict this man. You have seen his bloody handprint on my sheet. You have heard the atrocities he has performed time and again. Unless you would welcome his knife at your own neck, I beg you to find him guilty. Thank you."

Marie's hands left the logolith, which immediately went dark, and she shuffled back toward the accusers' table. L'Aris met her halfway, taking hold of her arm and guiding her. As they returned to their seats, the deep voice of Leonid Klee sounded. "The council will consider the call for dismissal."

L'Aris leaned toward the seated Marie and patted her shoulder. "I hope they heard you, my dear."

The council did not deliberate for long.

"All listen now to hear the verdict of the twelve Councilors of l'Morai concerning the dismissal of Dominick the Butcher," came the thin voice of a council page. The crowd quieted, and Morcastle dropped his gaze from the fresco. "Those who say *aye* call for dismissal, while those who say *nay* call for continuance."

"Aye," cried a councilwoman on the far left of the wall.

"Aye," called the man seated in the next niche.

"Aye," declare the third in line.

"Aye."

"That's four for dismissal," the page called out.

"Nay," came the unmistakable voice of the Puppet-master.

"Nay," said the voice of Lord Odieu.

"Nay."

"Aye," Councilor Klee called out.

"Five of eight for dismissal," the page announced.

"Nay" . . . "Nay" . . . "Nay" . . .

"Six of eleven for continuance," the page noted.

"Aye," came the final vote.

"Six for dismissal, six for continuance," the page tallied. "A tied vote. I defer in this matter to the council master, Monsieur Leonid Klee."

Marie's grip tightened on the arms of her high-backed chair, and Morcastle slumped, shielding his eyes with a weary hand.

"A tied vote," Klee said, musing. His resonant voice quieted the murmuring crowd. "I, too, recognize the eloquence of Marie the Blind Juggler, but the fact remains that a citizen of our fair city has been accused by foreigners. The Grand Charter of l'Morai does not even account for such accusations. Therefore, unless some citizen among you can provide testimony or evidence to support these unlikely claims, I cannot allow the continuance of this travesty."

His words were met only by the creaking vault.

"None offers further testimony," Monsieur Klee said, an edge of pleasure in his voice.

Marie stood up and, facing the crowd, shouted, "Don't be afraid! There must be one of you who'll speak of this man's depravity!"

L'Aris pulled her to her chair as Klee's voice rang out, "Silence! If the abstention of the citizenry had not ended this trial, your outburst has!"

"Wait!" came the thin cry of a child. The call had come from the central aisle, and those sitting along it whirled about to see a small blond boy walking toward the front of the hall. He was shaking.

The boy's pure, high voice rang out. "It's true. Everything they said is true." He rolled a tattered sleeve back from his arm, showing a deep purple bruise on his shoulder. "He beats me all the time. He's threatened to sell me to the circus, and then hunt me down and kill me."

"It's the butcher's son!" whispered a man along the aisle.

Dominick was already on his feet, and he shouted, "Boy, you're gonna regret this."

Marie also stood up. "Speak out, all of you. Don't listen to his threats!"

"The boy speaks the truth," shouted a tinsmith from the crowd. "Dominick's shop is annexed to mine, and I hear that boy screaming all the time. For eight years Dominick's been beating him."

Dominick's son dashed fearfully past his father and set his hands on the logolith. Its white light was blinding. "My father is evil."

The pronouncement brought a roar of accusations

from the crowd. "I found a handprint missing the index finger," a farmer called out, "on my shed. I saw then my shovel and pick were missing. Next day, they were back, and had blood on 'em."

"He once threatened me with a cleaver."

"I heard he skins cats and hangs 'em to sell as rabbits."

"He's uncommon cruel in his butcherin'."

As the clamor of accusations mounted up, Marie began to smile. She slid into the high-backed chair, listening as the sharp cries filled the vault above. Morcastle, too, was smiling. He watched Dominick, who stood now at the opposite table, the muscles of his balding head clenched and his skin red as blood. Despite Brucin's warnings, Dominick faced the crowd like an angry bull, his small eyes searching for each accuser. When the cries became too many to track, Dominick glanced toward Morcastle and Marie. The magician wore a toothy smile, winked, and wet his lips mockingly.

"Hold now!" Councilor Klee shouted, trying to quell the crowd. "Hold now! We cannot and will not try a man in mob fashion!" The crowd quieted, and the shouted accusations stilled entirely. "Most of what you are presenting is rumor and gossip, circumstantial and anecdotal. I will admit none of it to this trial unless the accusers step forward and present their names, lines, and labors for the scribe's record."

Numerous shouts of "I will!" interrupted the council master. The page who had served during the council vote appeared at the front of the chamber, holding up his hands in a gesture for silence. Monsieur Klee continued, "Those with accusations—and those with exonerations, line up along the center aisle. One by one you will announce yourself and provide your testimony, and a scribe will record it." Citizens flooded into the center aisle.

A rotund scribe carrying a large book beneath his robed arm appeared from the dark recesses near the front of the chamber. Two page boys accompanied him, one bearing a small desk and the other a low stool. The scribe motioned the boys to set up the desk and stool at the front edge of the dais as he opened the book and withdrew a blotter. The scribe seated himself before the desk and prepared to record.

The line forming in the aisle already reached halfway to the doors. The scribe nodded to the wall of councilors behind him, and the voice of Leonid Klee rose again.

"Let us begin without further delay. The first of you in line—step forward, identify yourself, and provide your testimony."

A lanky farmer sauntered up to the desk. He drew the hat from his head and began rolling it in nervous circles between his clutching hands.

"Name, line, and occupation," the scribe said.

"I'm Francois of the Verdermeir line, farmer by trade."

Scribbling on the page before him, the scribe nodded. "And your testimony?"

"Dominick comes out and butchers my cows and sheep. 'Course, that's the business arrangement, and all, but I always noticed, he butchers 'em slow. Seems to enjoy the pain and fear. Uses a sledge and hits 'em as many as five times before they drop dead."

"Next," the scribe said, still writing.

A stout woman stomped forward. "Antoinette from the Londau kin, though I married a Merrion. Have ten children. Monsieur Dominick's not done any murders to me, but he's never been kind to me or my children. I believe the boy and these others and the freaks. I believe he's guilty."

Marie listened to the first fifty witnesses, each bringing forward his petty accusations and suspicions. Only one person spoke in Dominick's behalf, and only two had any evidence that regarded a possible murder. Still they came, tireless and determined, each telling a grim tale, or saying "I have no personal quarrel with Dominick, but believe him guilty of crimes against the citizens."

In time, a weary Leonid Klee put an end to the testimonies and called for a shouted vote.

"All those who hold Dominick guilty of the crimes of murder, theft, adultery, cruelty, depravity, greed, and the others mentioned here, give answer by shouting *aye*."

The cry was deafening.

"And those of you who believe this man innocent of all these crimes, give answer by shouting *nay*."

No one spoke.

*   *   *   *   *

Marie, Morcastle, and L'Aris walked together down the jail corridor.

"I still can't believe it," Morcastle said, clapping L'Aris on the back. "I was just hoping we'd get out of there without being lynched ourselves, but now we've won!"

Marie laughed. "One moment, they were calling us foreigners and freaks, and the next moment, they're carrying us on their shoulders and calling us heroes."

"You must remember," said L'Aris happily as he drew the cell keys from his pocket, "the citizens are fickle. It was your speech and the boy's testimony that swung them to vote for Dominick's guilt. And once a few swung, they all did."

The jurist halted before the cell where Marie and Morcastle had stayed and slipped the key into the door. With a grind and a clank, the iron gate swung open and L'Aris gestured Morcastle inside. "Fetch your cape. A phaeton is waiting for you out on the streets."

Nodding, Morcastle started in, but Marie pulled up short. She latched on to the bars of the cell and said, "I can't bear to go back in there."

The magician said, "Don't worry, Marie. It was Dominick who got sentenced, not us."

Marie leaned back against the bars and addressed L'Aris. "What does that sentence mean, 'the living death'?"

L'Aris shook his head, watching Morcastle dust off his cape. "It's . . . it's the mandatory sentence for any serious crime. Basically, it amounts to exile. If a citizen is so warped as to perform such heinous crimes, l'Morai rids itself of that person's corrupting influence."

"That's it?" Marie asked, anger entering her voice. "Exile? What if he comes to the heath again? L'Morai will be safe, but not the carnival."

"No, it's not like that," L'Aris assured, setting a hand on her shoulder. "Before the council exiles him, they . . . they make assurances he won't be harming anyone again."

"What do you mean, assurances?" Marie asked. "Shackles and chains? Or do they hobble him, or cut off his hands or something?"

"Something," L'Aris said as Morcastle emerged.

"I'm certainly grateful to Dominick's son," the magician noted cheerily. "I had visions of us spending the rest of our lives in this cell."

"Yes," L'Aris replied, happy to change the subject. "We all owe a great debt of gratitude to the boy." He pulled a rumpled white rag from his breast pocket and shook it out in front of them. The rag had been cut from Marie's bed linen and showed the faint handprint of the murderer. "Aside from the boy, this was our clearest bit of physical evidence, and it wasn't nearly enough to sway the crowd and the council."

Morcastle snatched the rag from L'Aris and kissed it. He held it up to the light, shaking his head. "The print is so faint the council could hardly see it." He turned the cloth over in his hands. A quizzical look crossed his brow. "Why is the stain darker on the other side?"

"Something about the blood soaking in—" L'Aris began as he made an unsuccessful grab at the rag.

"No, wait." Morcastle guarded the cloth from the jurist. He gazed at the darker print, a very clear blood-stain showing the missing index finger. "This must be the correct side. If so, the murderer was missing the *left* index finger. But Dominick's stump is on his right hand, not his left."

Incredulous, Marie said, "You mean that wasn't Dom-inick's handprint in my caravan?"

L'Aris swung the creaking door closed and slipped the key into the lock. "It's not a very good piece of evi-dence."

"But, if this really *was* made by the murderer, Dom-inick might not be guilty," Marie insisted. "This evi-dence might have saved him, not condemned him. We've got to tell someone! We've got to suspend his sentence until we can sort this out."

L'Aris's face was suddenly serious. "We can't stop it, Marie. What are you worried about? It was the people of l'Morai who convicted him, not you. His own *son* testi-fied against him." He latched on to her elbow and began walking from the cell.

Marie pulled away and cried out, "But, what if he's innocent?"

"It doesn't matter, Marie," L'Aris responded gently. "The people believe Dominick to be a murderer. And, if the people believe it, then Dominick *is* a murderer. Even the logolith says we're right."

"But the logolith can't tell truth from passion," Marie persisted. "You said so yourself."

"If you believe something passionately enough," L'Aris replied, "it is the truth."

"But—"

"Enough! You push this, Marie, and you and Morcastle will end up with your heads on the block," L'Aris shouted.

Morcastle took her arm. His hand was cold and clammy. "Marie, let's go."

Marie's lip trembled and tears were forming in her eyes, but she said nothing.

They followed L'Aris down the prison passage, their shoes making watery sounds on the stone. Silent though they were, the former prisoners looked anything but victorious. Marie's face was drawn into a tight scowl. The magician, on the other hand, was pallid, his features sprinkled with beads of sweat. The long, dank corridor led to a guard, to whom L'Aris handed the keys.

Passing the guard, the trio continued on without speaking, rising up a broad staircase of stone. At the top sat another guard, this one fat and half-awake. Leaning lethargically, he opened the doors for them. L'Aris stepped through, drawing Marie after him. Morcastle followed.

The curved passageway above led alongside the council chamber. L'Aris leaned toward Marie, "Don't mention the handprint to anyone. If the court overturns their ruling, you and Morcastle would be accused of perjury, or worse."

Morcastle hovered behind them, ears attentive to every word.

"You jurists have earned your reputation," Marie replied.

L'Aris shook his head, sighing irritably.

Morcastle eyed the two nervously. As they passed a dark doorway, the magician's ears caught the sound of wailing voices. He softened his tread to listen. The clamor came from the council chamber. It sounded like a wolf pack howling, or perhaps like those strange hyenas the Puppetmaster used in the blood sports. It was a chorus of voices—laughing, howling, snarling, growling, screaming.

"What is that?" Morcastle murmured, distracted.

Wheeling about, L'Aris replied, "That's why we cannot mention the handprint. That's the sound of Dominick's sentence. It's already begun." As the young jurist turned about, Morcastle's steps slowed. He eyed the wall of the council chamber, noting the many alcoves and crevasses in the stone.

Marie and L'Aris rounded a corner, heading toward the main doors of the Council Hall. They passed through a final vault and came to the gate guard. The soldier snapped to attention. His young voice carried crisply to them through the clattering hall.

"Good evening, Jurist L'Aris. Congratulations on your victory tonight."

"Thank you, Ruesin," L'Aris said civilly, nodding toward the young man as the jurist and Marie exited.

"Have you separate travel arrangements for the magician?" the guard asked, eyeing Marie.

"No," L'Aris responded with irritation. "They'll both ride the same coach back to the carnival."

"Where is he, then, sir?"

L'Aris halted and whirled around. Morcastle was nowhere to be seen.

* * * * *

Morcastle brushed his sagging mustache and drew back into the wall niche were he stood. As near as he could guess, he'd found his way into one of the council members' alcoves, located in the wall some five feet from the floor. The height of the alcove gave a clear view of the dark council chamber below.

The floor brimmed with townsfolk of l'Morai, many of them bearing torches, flails, and swords. They milled in thick clumps, their voices filling the hall with a dizzying clamor. Occasional shouts and hoots rose and mixed with the uneasy rumble of shifting feet. The crowd's attention was focused to the rear of the Council Hall, where torches and swords flashed unevenly in the dusky air.

A throng of forty or fifty people near the back doors suddenly broke into a run. As quickly as the charge began, it halted, circling around a spot on the floor. Morcastle strained to see what could be causing the commotion. The people were stabbing at something with blades and torches. A cry of triumph rang out and spread in waves through the chamber. Two of the swordsmen fell back from the disturbance and toppled a bench. Through the open space, a beast charged. As it broke from the circle of its attackers, Morcastle could finally see what it was.

Dominick.

He had been stripped of his clothes and fitted with a metal collar that glowed a sickly red. His bare skin was covered with scars and bruises and filth. As he scrambled away from his tormentors, he drew a dagger from a wound in his stomach. A fiery trail of light snaked down from the glowing collar and passed over the wound, sealing it.

With a fierce, bestial roar, Dominick leaped at a woman, slashing down with the dagger. Before the blade could fall, though, the iron rods of a farmer's flail struck him across the forearm. The crack of bone was answered by another joyful shout from the crowd, and the dagger dropped, spinning, to the floor. As Dominick toppled forward, a flash of fiery light arced from the collar to his fractured arm and healed it. The crowd again converged, their shovels and picks descending hungrily on the prone figure.

Rolling and screaming, Dominick struggled to break free. His scarred, misshapen hands swung about in a vain attempt to ward off blows. The broad blade of an

axe glanced across his meaty shoulder, severing muscles down to the bone. He roared from the pain, seized
the haft of the axe, and pulled its wielder forward
beneath the blows of the villagers. Wrenching the axe
free, the butcher swung the blade to clear a path. The
villagers fell back from him in fear. The axe blade
hewed a man in half and sliced the arm off a woman.
Flaming light issued from the red collar and danced
across Dominick's wounds, sealing each of them.

In five thunderous strides, the burly man reached the
doors to the chamber. He swung the axe, notching out
a large chunk of the wood. The doors heaved but held.
Before he could pull the axe free, the crowd had again
surrounded him, running swords through his back and
into his heart. As the blood sprayed forth, the light
again arced from the collar, healing the wounds with
the blades still embedded.

Morcastle fell from the niche, his head spinning. He
could bear no more; he had to escape. Stumbling
through the dark passage, he groped for the doorway
that led out. Sudden pain lanced across his forehead.
He reeled and the smell of blood filled his nose. Falling
to all fours, he crawled across the stony floor and felt
his way along the wall. At last his fingers found the
wooden door. He opened it and crawled through. Closing the door behind him, he tried to rise, but the hallway
pitched to one side. He fell, and his mind drifted away
into darkness.

 **EIGHT**

"Bring him in here, Hermos," Marie said, opening the door of her dark caravan.

The man-giant stooped, dropped to one knee, and lifted the limp form of Morcastle through the dark doorway. "What happened?"

Marie cleared a spot on the floorboards of the caravan, moving a basket of tea out of the way. "He hit his head. At least that's what I assume from the knot on his brow. We found him in the hall."

The man-giant, now inside the caravan, slid Morcastle into the space cleared for him. He pulled a cloak from a hook on the wall and bunched it like a pillow beneath the magician's head. "He'll be all right?"

Marie smiled and nodded gently. "Yes. He'll be all right."

Hermos drew his gangly legs inside the wagon and swung the door closed. The place was suddenly dark. Wan light from the street lantern outside sifted through the curtains that veiled the windows. The man-giant squinted, trying to make out Marie's form as she lit a small stove and set a pot of water on it to boil. She opened a cabinet and rummaged within.

"You're pretty quiet, Hermos. Is there something wrong—something aside from the murder and the trial and everything else?"

"It's dark," the man-giant replied simply.

Marie paused and laughed. "Sorry. I've got a lamp, but don't often light it."

An odd rattling of metal sounded, then Hermos felt a sharp pain in his chest. He moaned, and his hand reflexively clutched the small tin tinderbox that had hit him.

"Sorry again," Marie said. "I'd forgotten you couldn't catch what you couldn't see."

Hermos clutched the brass lantern that hung, swaying, from the painted rafters of the ceiling, and lit it. "What happened . . . at the trial?"

Marie's rummaging ceased for a moment. "We won. Sort of."

"Sort of?" Hermos echoed.

With a crinkle of dried leaves, Marie drew a couple small portions of spices from bags in the cabinet. She straightened her back and crumpled the aromatics into a wooden bowl. "We won. We got our conviction. But I'm afraid we were wrong, Hermos." She paused, her voice quavering. "We've made a terrible mistake."

The man-giant blanched but said nothing.

"Dominick was innocent," Marie continued.

Hermos sat back against the bed and stared blankly at the magician lying across from him. "Innocent?"

"Yes." The blind woman's hands hovered above the bowl. "The real murderer threw off our suspicion by making Dominick look guilty. The murderer must have—" The words caught short. Hermos stared at the blind woman, the skin along his back prickling with fear. "The murderer must've cut Dominick across the back . . . must have cut his finger off to make him look guilty." Marie brushed the last leaves from her hands and faced Hermos. "Only he cut the finger from the wrong hand."

"So, Dominick went free?" Hermos asked.

"No, he didn't," Marie said. "We found out after they

had sentenced him. Nobody knows, but us." She lifted the steaming kettle from the stove and poured it into the bowl. Aromatic mists rose, twisting, into the air of the caravan, and the pungent steam spread out along the rafters. Hermos watched it curl among the darksome shadows of the ceiling, then descend in a thick sheet over him. The powerful fragrance made his eyes burn and his nose run.

It had the same effect on Morcastle.

"What's happening? Where am I?" he muttered, trying to sit up. His eyes fluttered closed again. He slumped back onto the cloak and hit his head against the wall. With a groan, he rubbed the knot on the back of his head.

"You're awake," Marie noted unnecessarily. She strained the contents of the bowl through a piece of cheesecloth, wrapped the bundle, and brought it to Morcastle. "There, there," Marie said. She tested the heat with her fingertips, then applied the poultice to his head. "You're in my caravan with me and Hermos."

The man-giant leaned over him and nodded, his dark eyes fixed worriedly on Morcastle.

The magician blinked twice. His hand clutched the poultice on his forehead and dragged it away. "How did I get here?"

"You hit your head on something as we left the Council Hall," Marie replied as she lifted the poultice back into place. "You need to keep this on your head."

Morcastle grunted and pulled the hot pack away again. "I had the most . . . peculiar nightmare." A wan smile crossed his face as Marie repositioned the poultice. "I dreamed about Dominick, that he was being tortured."

"A pretty accurate dream," Marie said.

"What do you mean?"

"We *did* convict him. And he *was* innocent," she pressed.

"Yes, yes," Morcastle replied, clamping his eyes shut. "I feel horrible about it. That must be why I dreamed what I dreamed."

Hermos asked, "Who was torturing him . . . in your dream?"

"I don't know," Morcastle responded. "It seemed as if everyone was. They were stabbing him and clubbing him. It was a huge crowd, like everybody who saw the trial was there."

Marie sat back on her feet. "Was I there?"

"No," Morcastle recalled, shaking his head. "I'd left you and L'Aris to find out what the sound was and . . ." He stopped speaking, a tiny line of regret folding along one corner of his mouth. "This wasn't a dream."

"What?" Marie asked. Her voice was low as though she had expected the statement.

"It wasn't a dream," Morcastle repeated. He sat up, gripping her arms. "It was *real*. The crowd was torturing him. The people of l'Morai were cutting him and bruising him, but he wouldn't die. They had some kind of magic collar on him. It would heal him—close up the wounds. They could have tortured him for hours."

"I can't believe this," Marie said. She stood up, her hands still wet from the poultice, and wandered to the sink. Her sightless eyes seemed to stare out past the caravan's walls. "I can't believe this. He was innocent."

"I tell you, it's true," Morcastle said.

"That's what 'the living death' must really mean," Marie whispered. "L'Aris said it meant exile. But it must mean torture with that . . . that collar."

Morcastle lay back against the cloak, his chin quivering. The man-giant, who still knelt over him, had his eyes closed and was mumbling a prayer. Morcastle looked up to Marie. "We're as bad as the murderer, now. We've killed an innocent."

Hermos's eyes opened slowly. "We didn't mean to."

"Maybe he isn't dead," Marie said, pivoting to face

them. "You said the collar was healing him. Maybe he's still alive in some dungeon somewhere. We could exonerate him—get him out of whatever torture machine he's strapped to."

"Yes," Morcastle replied, a fragile hope entering his voice. "We've got to make this right. We can turn this around." Color began to return to his face, and he stroked his crumpled mustache. "But the cloth isn't enough to do it. You heard L'Aris: the people believe Dominick is guilty, and the cloth won't be enough to sway them. The only way to convince the people Dominick is innocent is to find the real murderer."

Marie approached the other two. Her face was reddened by tears, but her lips hardened with determination. "You're right. But if the people think we were mistaken before, they'll have no reason to believe us now."

"We need the Puppetmaster," Hermos noted quietly.

The other two turned toward the man-giant, unspoken agreement on their faces. Marie said, "The phaeton driver said the Puppetmaster would be staying in l'Morai until the day after tomorrow. I'll meet with him as soon as he comes back."

"Until then, we'll need to be careful," Morcastle cautioned. "There's still a murderer out there, and we're the only ones who know."

"The only ones," Hermos agreed.

* * * * *

The lean man retreated from the backdrop of Morcastle's stage and hid in the darkness of Freaks Alley. His eyes gleamed with reflected torchlight as he surveyed the plank platform. The magician was late this night after the great trial. The shadowy figure folded a metallic object and slid it into his pocket as the crowd out front began to murmur with excitement. Morcastle was here.

The magician stepped up onto the planks and bowed grandly, sweeping his hands in a flourish.

"You must pardon my lateness," Morcastle shouted, "but I was detained last evening on an errand of justice and have slept the day away."

Rising from his bow, the magician paced across the stage to the prop guillotine. It stood, cold and gleaming, in the center of the planks. "And, having seen the way justice is handled in l'Morai, I know what short tempers you townsfolk have. No mere slap on the wrist can discipline a late performer such as myself! No! Such folk should be hanged, or skewered, or roasted, or . . . guillotined!"

The crowd roared with applause. Bowing once again, Morcastle lifted a trembling finger to smooth the curls of his mustache.

The man in the shadows watched, his eye twitching spasmodically.

Straightening again, Morcastle spread his arms wide and declared, "Yes, I know how justice works in l'Morai. The guillotine blade separates the innocent from the guilty . . . and the guilty from their heads!" Again the hoots and shouts arose. Morcastle stilled them with a gesture. "But tonight, this blade will prove me innocent, for I will drop it upon my own neck, yet walk away whole." Stepping up to the guillotine, Morcastle set his thumb to the cutting edge and plucked it. The glistening steel rang lightly, and its tone carried through the hushed crowd.

The shadowy figure behind the backdrop fastened his fingers on the implement in his pocket. His knuckles went white.

"Lest anyone here think this blade dull," Morcastle continued, "I have here a solid melon that will attest to its keenness." Morcastle reached into a box along the stage edge and produced a bulbous green melon. He held it high, then passed the fruit to a grimy farmer who stood along the stage front. "Investigate this melon, good sir, and tell me and these gathered citizens—is it not round and ripe and perfectly whole?"

The stern farmer studied the fruit carefully, his bulging eye following the venous contours of its rind. After turning the melon over numerous times, the man nodded and handed the fruit back to Morcastle. "Looks as solid as your head," the man noted dryly.

Ignoring the bursts of laughter, Morcastle wheeled about, strode to the guillotine, and placed the melon in the yoke. Then, wordlessly, he tripped the trigger. With a shooshing scrape, the blade dropped into the yoke. A profound thud sounded as the keen edge reached the bottom of its path. In the silence that followed, the melon halves dropped to either side, one slice rolling back onto the breastboard, and the other falling into a basket beneath. The front row of patrons recoiled as juice from the melon spattered them.

Morcastle smiled wickedly, watching them wipe the juice from their faces. "You might want to back up," he said, motioning them away. "Next time it may be blood."

The crowd shifted, the faint of heart pulling back while the younger patrons pushed forward. Morcastle circled to the back of the guillotine and began to noisily crank the blade back to the top of the frame. As the glistening edge lurched up above the yoke, he turned the switch on the guillotine's frame. The noise of the eager crowd drowned out the hollow thump made by the block settling into place in the yoke.

The man in the shadows smiled.

With a clank, the blade locked in place at the top of the guillotine. Morcastle brushed the dust from his hands and lowered himself to sit on the breastboard. "You must understand, I usually perform this trick at the end of my act—losing my head makes it difficult to carry out the sleight of hand later on."

This joke was greeted by a deadly hush in the crowd. Smiling uneasily, Morcastle lowered himself to lie prone on the breastboard. He lifted the yoke and slipped his head through, feeling the blood fill the swelling veins in his temples. The yoke dropped into place behind his neck.

"Here, now, is the trial," Morcastle said stiffly, gritting his teeth. "If the blade finds me guilty, these boys crowded up beside the basket will go home looking like beets." He paused, his waxed mustache rising in the hint of a smile. "I shall trigger it on the count of three." He raised one gloved hand, holding three fingers aloft, and set the other hand on the blade lever.

"Count with me now. One . . . two . . . three!"

His fingers tightened on the trigger. The blade dislodged and dropped, whistling in its descent. Morcastle's eyes went wide: the rope to the block switch had been cut.

Then came the hollow thud.

*   *   *   *   *

Marie awoke with a start, panting and clutching the rumpled bed sheet to her bare chest. The back of her skull ached, and hairs prickled along her spine.

Someone was in the caravan.

She lunged for the bag of juggling daggers at her bedside, but her hand came up short. Sinewy fingers fastened around her wrist. She swung her free fist toward the intruder, but another huge hand fastened over hers.

"Help!" Marie screamed shrilly, trying to yank loose.

"Wait," came the low, breathy voice of Hermos.

Marie could feel her face flush as she pulled her hands away and drew the blanket up over her. "What are you doing in here?"

"I knocked," he replied simply. "You didn't answer."

"What are you doing here?" she repeated irritably, wriggling down into the spare covers.

"Come with me," he replied, backing clumsily away from the bed. "Something important."

The thick chorus of crickets came to Marie through the caravan windows, and she drew a trembling hand through her disheveled hair. Had any other man entered her caravan while she slept, she would have stabbed him, friend or no. But Hermos was different. He was like a little child.

"Night already," Marie noted, shaking her head.

"Yeah," Hermos replied thickly, his voice muffled as he peered out the window. "You got to come out."

Sniffing, Marie motioned the man-giant toward the door. "Go outside. I'll get dressed and come with you."

Hermos grunted gently, opened the door, and stepped out into the chill night air.

*   *   *   *   *

The boy saw it all from his vantage atop the crate pile. The guillotine blade dropped swiftly, flashing in the fiery torchlight. It slid down the frame into the yoke at its base. Then came the dull crunch of metal passing through muscle and sinew and bone. The boy flinched as the blade-stop slammed into the yoke. He turned his water-blue eyes away as the head toppled forward and dropped with a thump into the basket below. The front row of patrons recoiled with a gasp as a crimson spray blanketed them.

A moment of shocked silence followed.

Then, like a splintering ice floe, the crowd shifted and buckled, drifting back in stunned clumps. Parents closed their eyes and shielded their children's faces; patrons broke into howling moans; children screamed in terror.

But the boy's eyes were wide and clear. He watched as, stumbling back from the stage, a fat man with a red cummerbund trod over a fallen child. He watched as a screaming woman rushed toward the crowded lane beyond, pushing and clawing others out of her path. He saw the tide of people surging away from the bloody spectacle and colliding with a swell of patrons drifting in from the lane, curious to see what amusement had inspired such shrieks from the crowd.

One man even emerged from Freaks Alley, a cruel and greedy smile draping his lips.

Whistles began to sound in the distance. Someone had told the gendarmes. The boy peered out over the carnival, brushing the filthy blond hair from his eyes and squinting to see the officers. The gendarmes were still far off, their whistles mingling with the screams of a washerwoman. The boy looked back again toward the crowd: a ring of locals encircled the guillotine, gawking at the lifeless form on the breastboard, prodding into the basket with a stick.

A new agitation drew the boy's eyes. The crowd before the stage parted as a gangly man-giant forced his way through, carrying a blind woman. He reached the stage and dropped to his knees, and the woman slid from his arms to stand in the sand. The giant clasped his narrow, mantislike hands together and began to moan. "Great Qin-sah, kind Ru-pah, wise Salore . . ." He rocked back and forth, murmuring deeply, "not Morcastle . . . not Morcastle . . . oh, lowly Tidhare . . . not Morcastle." An odd quivering spread through him and he fell, face first, onto the sawdust-strewn ground.

The woman held her hands out before her and staggered toward the stage. She felt her way forward until her hands rested on the spattered planks, then set a knee on the wood and climbed up.

The boy's eyes narrowed, studying the woman as she pushed through the crowd of gawkers to the guillotine frame. He recognized that woman—the blind woman from the trial. Sliding off the top crate, he clambered down to the audience pit. He wriggled past a wall of onlookers and ran, dodging, through the crowd. In moments, he reached the stage, vaulted onto it, and nudged his way toward the guillotine. Elbowing a tall priest out of the way, the boy glimpsed the full tableau.

Blood covered everything: the black frame, the wooden yoke, the breastboard, the plank floor, the spectators, the canvas backdrop. Someone had even cranked the blade partway out of the yoke, as though hoping to reconnect the head somehow. The body lay prone upon the breastboard, one hand draping from the platform and the other clutching the side of the guillotine. Blood rimmed the stumpy neck and spattered the shoulders; it pooled upon the board and dripped from the dangling hand. No one touched the bloody form. No one but the blind woman.

She had pushed through the crowd and reached the guillotine itself. Her ragged skirt rested against the edge of the breastboard, wicking blood into its tattered fabric. Her small white hands tugged on the dead man's satin cape and vest. Tears streamed unabashedly from her empty eyes.

"Morcastle. Morcastle," she repeated, stunned. The crowd of citizens pressed about her, gazing into her tear-filled face. She pushed them angrily back, knocking a man and his wife from the stage. "Get out of here, you monsters! You're the ones who did this to him. You're doing it to all of us!"

The man-giant approached, parting the swarm of patrons to reach the blind woman. He set his hands on her shoulders, his sunken eyes burning with fear and anger as he saw the body. His voice rose quiet and powerful over the murmuring crowd, like the sound of distant thunder.

"Come, Marie," he said sadly.

The blind woman shook her head, clutching more tightly to the blood-soaked garments.

"The killer's still loose," the man-giant whispered, "prob'ly watching us now."

Marie raised her head and shouted, a shrill scream that quieted the crowd, "You hear that, killer? We know you're out there! We'll find you before you find us! We'll kill you before you kill us!"

The boy glimpsed the backdrop man—the narrow man with the twisted smile—as he edged away from the stage.

The crowd churned in sudden turmoil, and a loud chorus of whistles announced that the gendarmes had arrived. The officers bustled through the throng, pushing patrons aside in their race toward the stage. Like a baying group of hounds, they charged to the front, clawing their way up onto the planks and rushing to surround the spattered corpse.

"Back, back—all of you!" shouted a portly officer, his chins wobbling as he blew his whistle. Two others grasped patrons by the shoulders and urged them off the stage. The sanguinary crowd reluctantly melted back, leaving Marie, the man-giant, and the boy near the still form.

The paunchy officer stomped over to Marie and shouted, "I said get back!"

"But," the man-giant blurted, "he's our friend."

The gendarme's stubby fingers tried to pry Marie's hands from the dead man's clothes. "What happened here?"

"He's been murdered," Marie snapped, "obviously."

"We weren't here," the man-giant added.

"Then how do you know he was murdered?" the officer pressed, his teeth clenched.

"The guillotine's been tampered with," Marie replied angrily.

"How does she know?" the gendarme spat at Hermos.

Baring her teeth as she held on, Marie said, "Morcastle was too cautious to let this happen."

"Let go of the body," the officer demanded, removing a sap from his belt, "or I'll have to remove you."

"No," Hermos said, fastening a long, bony hand over the officer's head and pushing him out of reach of Marie.

As the man-giant and the gendarme struggled, the boy's attention shifted to the basket, where a lean, black-haired officer was kneeling. Creeping closer, the boy saw the crimson head, facedown beside a halved melon. The gendarme's fingers were searching through the hair at the back of the man's skull. After a few moments of digging, the man's hands stilled.

There were two tattoos, one black and one red.

The man sighed heavily. He produced a small knife from his vest pocket and cut around the tattoos. Scanning the crowd for watchful eyes, he palmed the bloody clump and slipped it into one of his pockets.

Then, standing, he declared, "There was no murder here. Just a faulty contraption." He kicked the guillotine, and the half-raised blade plummeted into the yoke.

"There you have it," shouted the portly gendarme as he wrenched his head from the man-giant's grip. "An accident! Now move along, or, so help me, I'll lock you both away!"

The third officer, a short, blond-haired man, knelt beside the boy and said, "Come along, lad. We need you to move from here."

"Not till they do," the boy responded, crossing his arms over his chest and setting his small jaw.

"Don't be hard," soothed the officer. "They're friends of this fellow here. They get special privilege."

The boy didn't respond, bracing himself in a defiant stance.

A light of recognition broke over the officer's face. "Oh, I recognize you! You're the son of the butcher!"

*   *   *   *   *

One corner of the refectory tent was cordoned off for
the Puppetmaster's private use. It was surrounded by
canvas draperies that ran from ceiling to floor. Two oil
lamps hung from a tilting pole in the center of the
space, shedding insufficient light on the scarred oaken
table and the pallet beneath. The corner would have
been brighter if opened to the morning sunlight, but the
light of day was repulsive to the Puppetmaster, who
now sat at the table, picking through his morning meal.
And, he told himself, the darkness wouldn't bother
Marie.

The curtain pulled back, and Marie's lovely face
stared blindly into the alcove. "Good morning, Puppetmaster. I need your help." Her voice was shaking with
fear and grief.

"Yes," the man uttered, the sound barely audible
from his voluminous robes. He distractedly picked up
the doll of Marie that sat before him on the table, and he
turned it in one knobby hand. "I knew you needed my
help. You know it now, too."

Marie slid through the gap in the canvas, groped
toward the table, and sat down opposite the Puppetmaster. "I know you've been back from l'Morai for only
an hour or so, but there's terrible news—"

"Morcastle is dead," the Puppetmaster supplied.
"Yes, I know." He adjusted the doll's legs so it could
stand on the table, then placed it just within Marie's
reach. The lamps above cast a swaying shadow beneath the fragile puppet. "It seems you have convicted
the wrong killer, wouldn't you agree?"

The blind woman blushed. It was perhaps the first
time the Puppetmaster had seen shame on her pale
features. "We've got to catch this killer," she said.
"We've got to exonerate Dominick."

The Puppetmaster set his curved index finger in front

of the doll and flicked it over. The effigy toppled toward Marie, its beautiful, blind face striking the tabletop without blinking. "You are wrong, my dear. *You* need to do *nothing*. In fact, you had *better* do nothing. I thought I had made that clear to you before. I told you I would catch this killer for you."

"But the murders continued," Marie protested. "Now even Morcastle is dead."

"You can't expect justice from the Council of l'Morai. I told you that. You are more loathsome to them than any murderer."

Marie's shade of red deepened, but now in anger rather than shame. "What were we supposed to do? We thought we had caught the murderer."

"You should have killed him on the spot," the Puppetmaster replied. "Even if he had been innocent, his death would've helped settle the score. Death for death."

"Then we would have been murderers ourselves," Marie snapped.

"Look what happened instead." The Puppetmaster drew the doll back, bending its legs at the knees and folding its hands together. He positioned it before him, as though it were kneeling in prayer. "I told you to let me handle justice within the circus. I told you to leave well enough alone. And now, an innocent man has been convicted. The killer is licensed to continue his slaughter. And a third-rate magician is dead."

Marie turned away, but not before the Puppetmaster glimpsed the tear that streaked down her cheek.

"I warned you to stop your meddling, but you didn't listen," the man growled. "You've pulled back one too many curtains, seen the atrocities behind it, and discovered that still more curtains remain." His fist settled on the head of the effigy, and he compressed it until it was flat on the table. "Don't open that next curtain, Marie. It is hung for a reason. Trust me, and I will protect you and your man-giant friend from this killer. If you draw back that curtain—"

"I'm not afraid," Marie interrupted suddenly, her eyelids red and swollen, "so don't threaten me."

"If you draw back that curtain," he repeated, putting the puppet into his pocket, "even I cannot save you."

 **NINE**

Marie listened to the shovels biting into the spongy heath. One was a wooden shovel with steel teeth: it made a thunking sound as it sank into the ground, then a watery gurgle as the soil was pulled up and mounded. The other shovel had an entirely metal blade, and it produced a metallic scrape as it dug. Marie could tell, too, that both gravediggers were fat men: even before they had begun to dig, their breaths were loud in the hot heath air.

Aside from the sound of the shovels, though, the moorland below the carnival was silent. Not a sound came from the hundreds of carnival workers standing around Marie. She had gathered them, hoping to make public the Puppetmaster's private burial of Morcastle. But it was as if they weren't there. There were to be no eulogies read, no songs sung, no mourners present to witness the body's entombment. Only the two fat grave-diggers, the Puppetmaster, and the slender birch trees of the heath's edge. Until Marie had puzzled it out.

Even now, the throng of carnival workers stood hushed. The winds, too, were still today. Only the steady, rhythmic slice of the shovel blades, the spray of the pitched earth, and the restless, muted footfalls of the Puppetmaster broke the quiet.

Marie reached out to Hermos, who stood beside her

like one of the birches. Her hand clasped his large, bony fingers. She felt the concern in his sunken eyes, but she said nothing. She wanted to scream, but said nothing. Morcastle's murder had gone unpunished, and almost unnoticed. Even with all the witnesses Marie had gathered, his grave would be unmarked—another mound in a broad field of the dead.

Marie felt as though the world should crumble and break into pieces under its own weight. And yet, voiceless, tolerant—enduring—the forest stood and watched.

"We ought to mark this spot," Marie murmured to Hermos.

He squeezed her hand and responded with a rumbling whisper, "I could not forget it."

The man-giant cast a sad look toward Marie, then looked at the grave site. The diggers had nearly completed the hole, a narrow gash three feet deep. After they broke through the sinewy roots of the heath floor, each doffed his tunic, baring ripples of filthy, stained flesh. The Puppetmaster loomed over them the entire time, his face buried in the shadows of his cowl despite the horrible heat.

Beside his feet, on a makeshift litter, Morcastle lay. His head was tucked beneath one arm to keep it from rolling off. His clothes were bloody, muddy and disheveled. The stench carried thick through the hot air, and flies buzzed in dense swarms about the man.

"Deep enough," the Puppetmaster growled, catching the shoulder of one of the diggers.

Looking up gratefully toward him, the diggers stepped from the grave and stood their shovels in the mounds of loosened earth. Then, stretching their backs and arms, they moved to the head and foot of the litter. With a groan, they hoisted the body up and bore it to the shallow grave. Nodding to each other, they tipped the body and let it drop prone into the moist ground. Stiff though it was, the body fell askew into the hole.

"Great Qin-sah," Hermos began.

"Yes, Hermos," Marie said, "now is time to pray."

"Carry Morcastle to safety," Hermos continued. "Your back is strong."

The workmen had begun to shovel dirt onto the corpse. Hermos released Marie's hand and strode forward. "Turn him over," he growled, but the shovels kept tossing dirt on the tumbled form. Reaching the grave, Hermos pushed the diggers back and knelt down beside the body. A tear barely had time to streak down his long, gaunt cheek before the muscular diggers seized Hermos's shoulders to fling him back. In one swift motion, Hermos struck one of the diggers in the face with his elbow and tripped the other one, who landed flat on his back. Hermos turned back to the grave, but the Puppetmaster loomed over him. The man-giant's expression hardened, and he stood to his full height, staring down at the Puppetmaster.

"Turn him over," growled Hermos.

The gravediggers rose, lifting the shovels to use them as bludgeons.

"Turn him over," the Puppetmaster commanded to the diggers, "and put his head back on his shoulders."

Hermos stepped back from the grave as the reluctant diggers knelt down to turn the body. The man-giant, retreating to Marie's side, added, "Give him a gravestone, too."

The Puppetmaster, glowering beneath his robes, muttered, "We shall see. . . . We shall see."

*   *   *   *   *

Word of Morcastle's murder and his ignominious burial spread through the rest of Carnival l'Morai that day. By evening, extra lamps were posted in the buzzing Performers Quarter, and doors to dressing caravans were tightly locked. Despite the normal flow of patrons, the boardwalks and sideshows were quiet. Watchful workers stalked the carnival, their belts bulging with unaccustomed daggers.

The refectory tent was the single noisy place in the carnival, burgeoning with performers who sought refuge in its lights and crowds and thousand eyes. What laughter came from the packed tables was loud and edged in anger, as though the performers could use sheer volume to keep the killer at bay.

Everywhere, in the refectory and on the boardwalk, fear hung in the air like thin smoke. And, as though summoned by that very fear, the next horror arose.

"He's down here," the man-giant said. He gestured toward the sideshow and shot a nervous, sidelong glance toward Marie. Although she clung to his hand and strode beside him, she fell farther behind with each step. Hermos studied her determined little face and clenched his jaw, curbing the impulse to sweep her up and carry her like a child down the sawdust-strewn path.

"Only a little farther," he blurted for the fourth time.

Marie shook her head and muttered breathlessly, "You drag; I'll follow."

Hermos nodded. They rounded a crowded corner of the carnival, and forced their way through the milling throng. Beyond lay a lamplit lane of shops and stalls: a clairvoyant, an ale master, a tattooist, a salve-seller, a confectioner. . . . They reached the sideshows, a series of stalls set behind a wall of canvas. The inmates of the show were depicted in vivid paints on the canvas wall: the leopard boy, the calf-headed woman, the midget circus, the dwarves of Helms Deep, the goiter man. . . .

"He's in here," Hermos said, bypassing the hawker who fronted the sideshow. They wormed around a dozen patron-crowded stalls before Hermos came to a stop.

"What is it?" Marie asked. "*Who* is it?"

"It's him," Hermos replied, staring at the man on display before him. "The butcher, Dominick."

Marie's hand tightened on the man-giant's arm. "He's escaped?"

"No," Hermos replied. "He's one of us now."

Dominick sat before them on a crate, but he was no longer the cocky, fearless monster that had stabbed Hermos in the seer's tent. He was not the nine-fingered killer who had slain Panol and Banol, and Borgo the Sword-Swallower.

Dominick had changed. Gleaming metal blades jutted from his body everywhere. From the crown of his shoulders down to his bruised and inward-turning feet, the butcher's naked body prickled with blades—long razors, jag-toothed saws, blocky cleavers, curved knives, glistening shears, stilettos. . . . Hundreds of them emerged from his skin, as though an army inside him were cutting its way out.

"Fabulous Karrick, the Man of a Thousand Knives . . ." shouted a runty hawker. The man stood on a ragged crate and gestured toward the butcher. "The only man in the world who can grow knives out of his very body. . . ."

Marie winced, as though struck across the face by a fist, and she clutched Hermos's hand.

"Yes, indeed!" the barker continued. "Watch and see, folks, as the knives grow through his very skin. . . ."

Each blade was nested in an oozing wound in Dominick's flesh. Apparently the steel had slowly grown from the inside out, cutting its way out of the skin like teeth cutting through gums. Some of the blades protruded very little; others were almost complete—blade, hilt, and guard, hanging from a healing wound. But all of them moved outward with a gradual force, cutting the skin as they went.

"Knives as good as any butcher's," the hawker continued. He approached the dazed Dominick. Clasping his fingers on the flat of a boning knife, the runty man grunted and heaved. With a small snap and a rumbling, sucking sound, the knife—handle and all—pulled free from its place in Dominick's body. Dominick shuddered, his eyes rolling crazily in his meaty face.

Holding the crimson blade high, the little man smiled and shouted, "A knife that'll cut through gristle and bone, even the mighty thighbone." For effect, he brought the knife down as though to slice his own thigh, then wiped the blood off on an already crimson tunic. Holding the gleaming steel aloft again, the man shouted, "Ten lorin and a ducre for a mighty blade indeed!"

Hermos backed away with Marie in tow.

"What could have transformed him like this?" she wondered aloud.

Hermos shook his head, his eyes fixed to the atrocity before him. A blue-black, charred ring surrounded the butcher's neck. Narrow trails of gray-black skin led from the ring, down across Dominick's chest, and up his chin.

"The collar. The one Morcastle said," Hermos observed in a hushed voice. "It burned him."

Marie's expression hardened. "The collar must have done this with its magic."

"Wherever they cut him," Hermos added, "the knives grow."

"Does he even remember who he is?" Marie wondered, her voice trembling. "Can he even speak?"

Hearing Marie's voice, the hawker left a group of unwilling buyers and approached the blind woman. He held the knife up before him. "I'm sure he'll get better, Marie. He was pretty dazed when they brought him in here. Boy, what a find he was! By the way, wouldn't you like to buy this lovely boning blade?"

Hermos led Marie from the stall and lifted her in his arms. She was oblivious to him, oblivious to the patrons clogging the aisle all about them. Her pupilless eyes were wide and white like those of a rabbit in a trap.

Hermos emerged from the sideshow walkway onto the main lane. "Don't worry, Marie," he said as he made his way through the throng. "He can't hurt you now."

Marie was chewing her lip. "It's not that," she said with a nervous smile. She shook her head, and her chin began to tremble. "It's not that at all. Don't you see, Hermos?"

The man-giant stared into her egglike eyes.

As though she could sense his attention, Marie turned her face away and said, "He's become one of us. That was his real sentence, not the torture itself. He was a murderer, so they sentenced him to become one of us—to become an exile."

"I'll protect you—"

"That's not it!" Marie insisted, her voice urgent. She pushed against his chest and slid from his arms to the ground. Placing fists on her hips, she raised her reddening face toward the man-giant. "This has to have happened before. They tortured Dominick, then dumped him on us. I wonder how many other criminals live here among us. I wonder if the murderer is a carnival performer, himself."

Hermos staggered as the words sank in. He stared, dumbfounded, at her. A finely attired gentryman walked nervously past them and ushered his family by, and a filthy flock of orphans passed in a cloud of dust.

"Maybe if we can prove Dominick is innocent, can prove who really *is* guilty," Marie continued, "the magical sentence could be reversed. That wasn't his handprint in my caravan. It was the wrong hand. Someone cut his finger off. Someone cut the scar into his back. We've got to find who did that."

Hermos's eyes darkened as he studied her face. "How?"

Marie's expression grew grim. "I don't know. It could have been anyone. The real killer might have been in the crowd outside my caravan when I talked to the gendarmes. He might have been one of the gendarmes. He could be the Puppetmaster for all we know. The murderer knows what clues we were looking for. And"— she almost couldn't say it—"if he knew every clue we were searching for, he knows right now everything we've just discovered."

"Great Qin-sah. We'll never track him down," Hermos moaned.

"Yes, we will," Marie responded, sudden hope entering her voice. "We'll try to find out who it is after the carnival closes, in the hours before morning."

*   *   *   *   *

The night had been long. Very long, and filled with faces and faces and faces. Their voices still echoed in his head. Loudly. But he knew they were no longer there. This was not the same place—not the place with all the faces. That place was loud and lamplit and sandy and starry, and it had a thousand faces and two thousand eyes. But this place was not that way. It was quiet and dark and covered with canvas, and it had only one face and two eyes.

But a thousand knives.

They were all sticking into and out of him. They grew out of wounds all across his body. If he walked, knives from one leg would cut into the other. So they carried him in a cart, carried him like a load of apples. They dumped him at the other place, and then later at this place. Both times he'd hollered; both times the blades stuck into him and into the ground. He was rooted by them like a thornbush. He'd tried to pull free from the knives. Only a couple broke loose and remained in the ground. Most were joined, steel to bone.

It seemed a strange state. The people who pulled him up and set him in the chair did not have knives sticking from them. The faces and faces and faces did not have knives sticking from them. And he had thought how good it would be to not have knives sticking from him.

But he couldn't remember being that way. He couldn't even remember his name, though he thought he ought to have one. He couldn't remember a time without the knives, without the nakedness.

And so he sat, on a prickly mound of hay, in the second place, the canvas place. He could feel the knives in his back embed themselves in the thick-packed straw. He could feel them growing, inching their way through the flesh. And he wondered vaguely if any would have dropped off before they came for him again. At one point, beneath the blackness of the canvas tent, he thrashed about across the hay, hoping to break the blades loose, hoping they would not grow again. But only one knife snapped off, and the pain of it, and the rushing gout of blood, and the bit of bone that clung to the half-formed steel handle were unbearable.

So now he waited. Patient. Wide-eyed. Sweating. Biting back the pain of the broken knife. Feeling fear wrap him like a cold wind. And he wondered if the darkness would ever go away. That was when the two others came.

They were like shadows on the blackness. They emerged through a seam in the canvas and stalked inward. One was tall and gaunt, like the swaying shadow of a tree. The other was small and lithe. Their voices were hushed, sibilant as they moved, one to each side. These were not the ones with the cart. They smelled like fear and desperation.

The knife-man sat still, holding his breath. Only his eyes moved, following them in the pithy dark. He hoped they did not see him, hoped they'd come for someone else. But they drew warily near him, and began to whisper.

"Aer niw wron fiirsig," came the voice of the small one, a woman. The knife-man bit his lip, a tear of terror streaking down his cheek. She prodded him, her fingers touching his neck, which ached with fire. The other creature loomed forward, peering where the woman had prodded.

Bristling, the knife-man shook violently and shouted them back. The vague realization surfaced in his mind that what he shouted made no sense to him. But the two others drew back momentarily, and the gaunt one circled, surveying from a distance.

"Doyoo rimeeber yore naam iss domeeneek?" the woman asked.

The knife-man trembled, sweat dropping from his forehead onto a blade that emerged from his chest. The last word, *domeeneek*, echoed in his head. It had snagged on some familiar memory, like a wind-tumbled rag catching on an outcrop of wood . . . domeeneek, domeeneek, domeeneek. . . . At the sound of the word, a peculiar dread welled up in him. Again he shivered.

"Presarve, o gotts," the knife-man muttered, the nonsense words providing comfort.

The woman sighed, and the other eased.

"Goot," she said, patting his hand with her delicate fingers, "goot. Thaarstil sumtheeng left inim."

Her hand settled on his right arm, and she began tracing the painful knob on his hand.

"Whoo cuttoff yore feenger?"

The knife-man's brow furrowed, and he peered at the bloody stump where his index finger had been.

"Whoo cuttoff yore feenger?" the woman repeated.

Still the words were senseless. They rattled emptily against the murmuring echo of "domeeneek . . . domeeneek . . . domeeneek."

The woman shook her head and released his hand. For long moments, she sat staring at him, and the knife-man set his hands over his face. She murmured to the other. Then she bent down to get something from the floor. She straightened, and the object she held in her hand gleamed and glittered.

It was the knife that had broken from his back. The bone-chip knife.

The knife-man gasped as the woman approached. Her small, strong fingers fastened on his injured hand and pulled it from his face. Gripping his hand tightly, she gestured with the blade at the injured nub. The flashing steel sliced through the air. She shouted.

"Whoo?"

The knife-man remembered another blade flashing across his hand. It cut through the finger that had been there. Cut brutally through flesh and bone.

"Whoo?"

It was a man's hands that had held his fingers in place, a man's hands that had forced the blade through the crunching sinew. The hands were deformed, skewed and quivering, but powerful all the same. He remembered feeling their strength and their tremor. Remembered how slick they became when the knife had cut almost through. There had been ropes about his arms and feet, ropes about his chest. He'd kicked and struggled to escape, but could not. And the knife cut through. And the finger fell to the floor.

"Who?"

The hands had emerged from thick woolen robes. The knife-man remembered kicking against the ropes and the chair where he was bound, struggling to break free. And the man towered before him. Black robes looming in the black and cluttered room. He could feel the man's eyes boring into him, could feel them but could not see them. A massive cowl covered the man's features. Then, he remembered the low, shuddering

laugh as the man did his work. Forming out of that
laugh, a name emerged in the knife-man's mind. He
muttered it once, twice, struggling with its strange
sound on his tongue.

"Polemasser . . . Pullepmatser . . . Puppetmaster."

TEN

It was a typical night, as carnival nights go. Chill, midnight winds descended from the mountain peaks about the carnival and channeled down the packed boardwalks. The cries of hawkers rang on the night air, along with shouts and laughter from the growing throng.

But Hermos's stall stood dark and empty, as did Marie's caravan. The two performers lurked behind the rubbish piles in the carnival gardens, watching the Puppetmaster's caravan. He habitually took a midnight walk, and the moon was past midnight.

"What should we look for inside?" Hermos asked.

"Something to prove the Puppetmaster is the murderer," Marie whispered. She gagged for a moment on the rank air of the rubbish piles.

"There he is," Hermos said as he ducked behind the shattered remains of a caravan.

Marie dropped behind a fly-infested mound of rubbish and hissed, "What's he doing?"

"He's leaving."

The black-cowled man stepped through the doorway of his sprawling quarters and stopped. He sniffed the cold air and, with one hoary hand, drew his robes tight around him. Then he strode out toward the Performers Quarter.

Hermos watched for another few moments. "He's gone."

"Let's go then," Marie replied, stepping around the rubbish pile. Hermos took her hand and led her at a loping stride to the Puppetmaster's black hovel.

It was ugly and enormous. The front section, once a giant, wheeled cage for "Exotic Oliphants," now rested on its axles. Behind the decrepit caravan crowded a number of lean-tos constructed of wire, rubble, old fencing, and stage planks. Other coaches had also been haphazardly joined to the back of the cage by a network of slanting ramps and causeways. It was like the black nest of a mud dauber.

Hermos reached the door and swung it open. Cool, fetid air billowed out and swept over the pair. Hermos waved a hand before his nose while Marie stepped inside.

She moved into the long hall that lay beyond the door, remembering when she had first ventured there, after the deaths of Panol and Banol. Her hands reached out to touch the tapestry walls, and she paced toward the end of the hall. "Do you remember anything important in the puppet room, where we were before?" Marie asked with a whisper.

Hermos came through the door behind her and ducked to avoid the rough, wooden ceiling. "No."

"I didn't expect he would've ushered us into a place where his secrets might be hidden." She passed the puppet room and came to a doorway on the other side. "What do you see in here, Hermos?"

The man-giant peered into the opening. "A bed . . . cloaks hanging on the wall . . . pillows and sheets."

"Hmm," Marie responded. "We'll come back here, but let's explore the rest first. Why don't you go ahead of me."

He did so. The passage grew darker until it halted and dropped away. A short set of ramshackle stairs led down to a room with a low ceiling and a dirt floor. Hermos half-crawled through the small anteroom toward a semicircular wall of poorly mortared stone. There, three doors stood. Two were closed and locked, but the third, a shabby door covered in fading white- wash, stood open. Hermos moved toward it.

Pushing back the door, he glimpsed a long, narrow room filled with books. Some sat on teetering shelves and others formed towers on the floor. A squat window ran just beneath the cobweb-laced ceiling and admitted yellow light from the street lantern outside. The glow dimly lit an enormous stonework fireplace, which dom- inated the right wall of the room. Hermos stepped across the battered threshold, the dust and mold of the room whirling up in thick clouds around him.

"Not been here for months," Hermos muttered to Marie, who held to the fingers of one huge hand. "Noth- ing in—" He paused, noting a trail across the clay floor. A line of footprints stretched from the door to a book- stand at the opposite end of the room. Across that path, the dust had been trampled into the floor, and the cob- webs broken.

Hermos followed the trail to a broad bookstand beneath the windows. The stand held a massive tome, its leather binding peeling about the corners and stained with time. Hermos kneeled down beside the bookrest and began to thumb through the tome. Its ragged-cut pages were segmented by a set of thick, leather-and- wood dividers, each with a small, sturdy lock attached to it. Running his fingertips along the descending line of locks, Hermos counted thirteen that had been fastened already. The last three locks were open.

Hermos folded his arms and stared for a moment at the dark book. He reached out and opened the book past the thirteenth lock. The page that fell open was filled with small, frenetic scribbles in eight narrow columns. The paper was ancient and brittle, and it crackled beneath his touch. The entries looked like those of a diary, leading off with years and days. The man-giant flipped to the next page. It was the same. He turned another page and another. All were crowded with the cramped handwriting. If this were a diary, the murders would appear on the final page. After flipping two-score pages, Hermos reached the last sheet with writing on it; only five of the eight columns were filled. His hands fastened around the tome and he lifted it into the light.

1693, 13 Drossilmont, Fellsday (Death) Ranwen Feronne 'Morcastle the Magician' dead by beheading. Q14 killed, tattoo warranted. Grove burial witnessed by performers due to Francis Ciantioux 'Hermos the Man-Giant' and Yvette Martinique 'Marie the Blind Juggler.'

"Did you find something?" came Marie's voice behind him.

Hermos, startled, spun about. He held the book to his chest. "A . . . a book," he stammered.

Marie shook her head sarcastically. "A blind woman and an illiterate find a book. We're getting nowhere fast."

Hermos stared at her for a moment, then murmured softly, "I can read, remember?"

Marie's eyebrows raised. "Oh, yes, the fairy tales."

Hermos leaned the book away from his chest and stared down into it. "The fairy tales."

"Well," Marie responded, rubbing her hands together, "what does this tale say?"

Hermos muttered, "Dates and names. It says about Morcastle."

"*What* about Morcastle."

"How he died, was buried," Hermos replied sullenly. He read to her the entry on Morcastle, pausing to sound out names and longer words.

As he read, Marie's expression grew stunned with disbelief. "'Q14 killed, tattoo warranted'?" she echoed dazedly. "What could that mean?"

Hermos shrugged and peered out the high windows.

"Skim backward a few entries. See what it says about Borgo, and Panol and Banol." After long moments, the man-giant found the passage and read:

"*1693, 9 Drossilmont, Heathday (Death) Ferin Iron-grod 'Borgo the Sword-Swallowing Dwarf' dead by sword-stab. P33 killed, tattoo warranted. Grove burial.*

"*1693, 10 Drossilmont, Moorday (Death) Jean-Claude Uberon 'Panol and Banol the Parasitic Twins' dead by dismemberment. T5 killed, tattoo warranted. Grove bur-ial.*

"*1693, 11 Drossilmont, Winday (Arrest) Dominick d'Louve arrested for P33/T5 murders. Yvette Martinique 'Marie the Blind Juggler,' and Ranwen Feronne 'Mor-castle the Magician' accompany gendarmerie for accu-sation.*

"*1693, 12 Drossilmont, Doorday (Trial) Dominick d'Louve wrongly convicted of P33/T5 murders, be-comes 'Karrick the Man of a Thousand Knives.' Arrives 14 Drossilmont.*"

Marie stomped her foot on the floor. "The Puppet-master's known everything as it happened. But none of it proves his guilt. If we could figure out what the letters and numbers stand for, and what 'tattoo warranted' means, I bet we'd have our proof."

Hermos flipped back a few pages, his fingers skim-ming along the list of years. When he reached 1687, he slowed. At last, Hermos's finger came to rest over one entry:

"*1687, 27 Venremont, Moorday (Trial) Francis Cian-tioux convicted of disobedience to parents. Became 'Hermos the Man-Giant.' Arrives 29 Venremont.*"

Marie placed her cold hand on his arm. "He did it to you, too. He did it to you."

The man-giant studied her face, his eyes narrowing. "Francis Ciantioux?" The name sounded strangely familiar in his throat.

"He did it to you," Marie repeated. She released his

hand and clutched one corner of the book. "Am I in there?"

Stunned, the man-giant began to page through the crinkling paper. He skimmed the dates, the names, his long fingers quickly flipping the pages.

"It would be before 1680. I was here when I was nine-teen," Marie noted.

Hermos came to a locked section. "Stops at 1684. Rest is locked."

"I know I'm in there—just like you are," Marie said, shaking her head. "But I'd always thought I'd grown up here at the carnival."

"Me, too."

"I bet that's what the Fever was. I bet I've forgotten my past, just like Dominick—like Karrick the Man of a Thousand Knives," Marie realized. A tiny moan emerged from her lips, and when she spoke again her voice was husky with fear. "It's not just Dominick. It's me, too. And you, Hermos. And all of us."

"I hid from my parents."

"I wonder if I could—" she began "—I wonder if they took my eyes away in that trial." She fell to her knees on the clay floor and buried her face in her hands. "I wonder what I did to deserve this."

Hermos folded the book to his side and knelt beside her. He laid a quivering hand on her back and strained to see her face. Rivulets of sweat rolled down his gaunt features as he tried to speak. At first, only an inarticulate whimper emerged.

"What do we do?"

Marie remained silent, shaking her head and cradling her face in her hands.

A sound came at the door.

"I warned you, Marie," came the booming voice of the Puppetmaster.

Dashing the tears from her eyes Marie stood up, her delicate fingers clutching the tattered edges of her skirt.

Hermos also stood, looming protectively over his companion. The Puppetmaster stepped across the threshold, his woolen cloak rustling against the doorjamb as he passed.

"Curiosity . . ." he rasped, rubbing his thumbs on the tips of his fingers. "The deadliest sin. In the city of l'Morai, it is a capital offense."

Marie spoke, the words little more than a whisper. "You are a killer, Puppetmaster."

"And if I were," the man asked, a darksome smile forming beneath his hood, "what would you do?"

Hermos interposed himself between Marie and the Puppetmaster. "We must go," the man-giant said. He pushed Marie toward the doorway.

Marie resisted. "I'll convict you."

"By whom? The Council of l'Morai?"

"I'll kill you myself, if I have to."

Hermos's hand tightened on her arm. "We must go."

The Puppetmaster blocked their path. "I told you not to open that curtain, Marie. Now even I cannot stop what will happen."

"I want my eyes back, damn you! You've stolen everything from me," Marie shouted. "We've paged through your logbook, your journal. We know about the trials and the tortures you've been party to. We know you've been changing citizens of l'Morai into freaks. I know how you made *me* into a freak."

"So you think I am guilty," the man replied in a voice that mixed a growl and a laugh. His skeletal hands idly fingered the ruby pendant about his neck, and Hermos once again noted the glistening emblem of Qin-sah. But only now did he see the spear that protruded from the horse's back.

"You tortured Hermos, you tortured *me*."

The Puppetmaster hissed, drawing air through a fissure between his teeth. "There's a bigger book than the one you've seen, you know. It has no names in it, but it has *everyone's* name in it. It condemns us all. The *Statutes of l'Morai*. They make it a sin to speak, to breathe, to piss, to be. That's where everyone's name is written."

Marie grabbed the Puppetmaster's cloak. "Look at me," she shouted. "Look at me, damnit. You know I can't look at you. I want my eyes back, Monsieur Puppetmaster. I want my world back. That's what you've stolen from me!"

"And the lambs want their mutton back, Marie, and the pigs want their pork," the Puppetmaster replied evenly. He pried her hands loose. "We all want it back, every damn piece of it, don't we, blind Marie? But the pigs can't have it back, and neither can the freaks."

Marie gritted her teeth and tried to push past him. "There won't be any more freaks, any more murders, Monsieur Puppetmaster. I'm going to stop you."

Maudit Sienne laughed loudly and seized Marie's arm. Whirling her about, his clawed hands forced her into a twisting dance, and he began to sing a bawdy tavern song:

I spoke to a blind lass one day in the tall grass.
I told her I loved her. She said that her lover
Had told her I'm ugly as death.

I then met her tall lad, whose temperament was bad.
He told me "'Tis not wise to flirt with her blind eyes.
Improper affections bring death."

I scoffed: she could not see! I forced her to bed me,
For which her tall laddy proclaimed me a baddie,
And gouged my eyes till they ran red.
So now I'm blind, ugly, and dead.

As the man sang, he backed Marie toward a corner of the library. Hermos tried to push his way between them.

But, without missing a note of his song, the Puppetmaster brutally shoved Hermos back against the man-
tel. The man-giant's back struck the fireplace, knocking
the wind from him. He crumpled to the floor, clutching
his side and gasping.

Marie, meanwhile, groped about for some weapon,
but her hands settled only on musty, rotting books.
Backed against a rocking shelf, her nails scraped over
the ancient spines, trying to work one loose.

The shouted song stopped. The Puppetmaster leaned
over her, putrid breath spilling down from his thick,
woolen wraps.

"Did you like that song?"

Marie refused to avert her face. She clenched her jaw
and said, "No. Not in the least."

The man neither moved nor spoke. "Then you had
better leave, *now*."

He pushed her away. Marie stumbled and held her
hands outward to find Hermos. He was rising from the
floor and gasping. "You're going to—" Marie began, her
voice quavering "—you're going to let us go?"

"Yes," the Puppetmaster replied. "I needn't kill you.
You've already killed yourselves."

Clinging to Hermos, Marie motioned toward the door.
The man-giant hurried across the clay floor. The
Puppetmaster made no move to stop them. But the
tuneless song began again:

And gouged my eyes till they ran red.
So now I'm blind, ugly, and dead.

*   *   *   *   *

"What are we going to do?" Marie was saying as she
closed the final window of her caravan. A shiver ran
over her skin, whether from the cold night or from fear
of the Puppetmaster, she didn't know. "He's guilty,

that's clear enough. But we can't take him to trial."

Hermos shifted his weight, trying to get comfortable sitting on the floor. "His pendant had Qin-sah," the man-giant said morosely.

"Yes, you told me," Marie replied.

"Qin-sah with a spear in his back. Like the tattoo."

Marie rubbed the spot on the back of her skull. "He must have been the one who branded us. All of us. He made us freaks, and branded us with his damned pendant. That's what the tattoo must mean. It shows we're all freaks."

"I'm afraid."

Marie drifted to the door, her hand dropping once again to its secured lock. She said absently, "Who can we turn to? Certainly not the gendarmes, the council, the citizens."

Hermos nodded. He pulled one of the two pillows from Marie's small bed and compressed it into a wedge between his back and the wall. Then, with a small groan, he lifted his long legs and shifted them across the cramped floor.

Hearing the shuffling noises, Marie asked, "Are you sure you'll be able to sleep here tonight?"

The man-giant looked up toward her, his sunken eyes small and expressionless. "It's safer," he said simply.

"Yes," Marie replied with a grim shrug. "Tents don't lock." She moved to her bed, careful not to step on Hermos's feet or trip over his legs. "Whatever else we do, we've got to survive the night. And we're more likely to do that together than apart."

"We'll see," Hermos responded gloomily.

"I'll take first guard," Marie volunteered, struggling to marshal her spirits. "They'd have to make quite a noise to break in here."

"Can't sleep."

"Hmmmm," Marie considered. "You've been saying

you could read me a story. Why don't you read one now? It's been a while since anyone's read to me."

Hermos shifted, rolling to one side and studying the spines of the shelved books.

"My favorite book of fairy tales is on the end," Marie said, a weary smile on her lips. "It has a leather cover with raised letters—"

"I found it," Hermos said. He pulled the book from the shelf and opened its crackling, aged spine. The pages were ragged-cut, filled with margin traceries and illuminations.

"If I remember right," Marie mused, "those fairy tales are morality stories, meant to teach the Statutes of l'Morai to children."

Hermos turned to the first page. There he found a picture of a rabbit, which reminded him of Tidhare, god of rabbits. But this rabbit's ears, stretched and torn and bloodied, rested in a tight knot atop his head. Hermos's attention drifted to the large capital that began the text, and he began to read aloud:

The Ear-Tied Hare

'Twas after the fire killed Farmer and Wife,
The animals met in their stalls.
They thought to take stock of their own loss of life
And plan who would rule their halls.

So Quince the Draft Horse said, "I'm strongest by far."
But Rooter the Dog said, "I'm smartest for war."
Then Stalker the Cat, in the rafters and dust,
Said, "I am the hunter, so I should rule us."
And Mucker the Pig and then Winker the Cow,
And Egger the Chick and the Lamb, Fleecy, now
Cried, "We are the ones who fed Farmer and Wife."
The Crow and the Rat next defended their life.
But poor Lop-Eared Hare had had nothing to say.

Then Quince shouted, "Quiet! We must decide this
By judging our worth on the farm.
And in this fair fashion we'll fill out the lists
So none of us comes to great harm."

So Stalker, from rafters above all the rest,
Said, "I have the vantage to judge for the best.
Lord Quince, you are tops, for you do the work
That all of the rest of us willingly shirk.
Then Rooter and I, companions to men,
Should rule over Pig and the Cow, Lamb, and Hen.
But next come these four, who'd each give its life
To set a fine table for Farmer and Wife.
And Raptor the Crow, and Fang the Brown Rat
Are last—the crumb-pickers, drinkers of fat."
The poor Lop-Eared Hare had had nothing to say.

"Your plan sounds quite fine," said Quince the Draft
    Horse,
His hooves stomping loudly, indeed.
The others, who noted his threat, said, "Of course."
Each one of them quickly agreed.

But, least of all these, the poor Lop-Eared Hare
Did not speak a word, did not voice a prayer,
And in his sad silence, became nought to them
But straw on the stall floor, but mud in the pen.
The others stomped past him like he wasn't there.
He skittered away; they stepped on his ears.
But never a cry came from Lop-Ear the Least,
For he was the silent one, dumb among beasts.
The poor Lop-Eared Hare had had nothing to say.

Beneath the sharp hooves, his ears stretched out long,
And from deep-scratched claw-marks they tore.
These kicks and abuses and other grave wrongs,
The Lop-Eared Hare patiently bore.

Till one horrid day, most horrid that year,
When Quince in a prancing pace stepped on his ear,
And poor Lop-Eared Bunny released his first squeal,
Which made the proud Quince rear and whicker and
    wheel;
His hooves struck the rafters and Stalker did fall;
Then Quince swung his hindquarters, smashing the
    stall;
And Rooter received a mild cut on one ear;
And Pig, Cow, and Lamb shrieked and bolted in fear:
The poor Lop-Eared Hare now had something to say.

So Quince called a caucus where they all agreed
That Lop-Ear should not speak again.
They filled his small mouth with a white cotton-weed
And knotted his ears with a rein.

The poor Ear-Tied Hare then had nothing to say,
And down in the straw and the mud he did lay,
Where, silent and deaf, he awaited their paws,
Their hooves and their merciless, razor-sharp claws.
And though his companions meant no harm to him,
They paced and they pranced there in vanity's whim
Atop the poor Lop-Ear, whose fleece-muffled cries
Were too weak to mark the sad moment he died.
The poor Ear-Tied Hare had had nothing to say.

Hermos looked up from the book, a dull pounding filling his ears. "I know this story."

Marie rose to check the door again. "I told you about it. It's very common."

"It scares me," Hermos said, his throat constricting around the words. "I know it from . . . from before."

The door was still locked. Marie edged back to the bed. "Can you remember? Can you remember what you were doing when you heard it, Francis?"

Hermos shook his head. "Don't want to remember."

"It's all right," Marie soothed. "It's all right. I shouldn't have suggested fairy stories for tonight. Tales to frighten children."

The man-giant nodded abjectly, but trembled. Nothing Marie could say would comfort him. He was beyond words now. She dropped down from the bed and wrapped a motherly arm about him. "It's all right. Sleep. I will guard us both." She held him, deep into the night, and listened for telltale clicks at the windows or doors. At last, he fell into a fitful and exhausted sleep in her embrace, like a giant, mourning child.

"Dream good dreams," she whispered.

But by his shaking, she knew he did not.

*   *   *   *   *

"Francis, where are you?" It was Mother, he knew, for her voice was always Fear. Father was Rage and Mother was Fear.

The boy held his breath, squeezed his pounding heart in blood-red hands. Mother's shrill voice stalked nearer, a yellowish wraith in the alley. Gritting his teeth, Francis pulled his polished leather shoe farther into the crate where he hid. The box was breathing, and its breath was rank like Father's cheese shop. The smell of Pain.

"Francis, you're being naughty," Mother cawed, no longer a wraith. She was a crow, scrabbling on the brick alleyway. "Naughty boys get beaten."

The bruise on Francis's neck was spreading down toward his heart, like fingers of a blue hand.

A fly buzzed into the crate, a fly with his father's face. It landed on his nose, and the boy knew if he dared to brush it away, his father would know where he was.

"Come out now, Francis," Mother demanded, her talons sinking into the bricks and her beak—as large as Francis himself—pecking stupidly upon the crate, "and you won't get beat as bad."

The boy had to restrain himself from snorting: the fly would have heard him. He always got beat the same, till he was unconscious and bleeding. Better later than sooner.

"Damnit!" roared a new voice. Rage stood at the end of the alleyway. "Has he gone off and hid again?" Through the slits in the crate, the boy could see Father —a giant mouth with wiggling teeth like those of a snake. The mouth fell forward, sinking fangs into the street, dragging itself toward the pile of crates. Father's tongue snapped horribly, a leather belt in a brawny man's hands. "Last time he'll cross me!" laughed Rage. "I sent Paul for the gendarmes. They said they'd bring the dogs."

Francis swallowed hard, and a line of sweat swept the fly down his shirt where he crushed it against his blue heart.

"The dogs?" the woman repeated, a note of fear ringing in her voice. "The gendarmes will take him from us, you know."

"Aw, let 'em have 'im," the Father-Rage-Mouth blustered, swinging his belt-tongue wildly and letting the heavy buckle smash through a cheese crate near Francis. "No good in the store . . . reads all day, scrawny and weak and disobedient." Francis knew the book Rage meant, the fairy stories, the book about the Ear-Tied Hare. He hoped Quince's shoe wouldn't crush him flat.

Another crash sounded as the venomous buckle smashed through a second crate. "If they don't haul 'im off, I'll kill 'im myself."

"You've been drinking," Fear entreated as she drew a fat worm from a vein in her talon. "I don't want no gendarmes, no dogs. Beat the boy later."

"Now!" he roared, pushing her back onto the crates. She fell, heavily, onto the box where Francis was hiding. The wood cracked and then shattered, bringing the

giant crow down atop him. Francis released a muffled
shriek and tried to scramble free of the broken frame,
but it clutched him with iron-nail claws. The belt
buckle, whirring as it cut through the air, sank like a
barbed harpoon into his back.

"No, Quince!" he screamed. The buckle was like a
prancing hoof on him.

He screamed again as the second blow fell. And the
third and fourth. "It's me! Ear-Tied—Tied Hare . . . Tidhare!"

Over his own shrieks, he heard the dogs.

The dogs were barking in the Council Hall, and he
was there among them. Their sound filled the soaring
vault above—the vault filled with pictures. Bandaged
and weary, the boy sat in a high-backed chair, whose
arms gripped him tightly. The gauze on his jaw was tied
atop his head, like rabbit ears.

The boy, Francis, now had a name, too—Oblivious,
or was it Oblivion? Didn't matter. He swung his legs
back and forth, his toes inches off the floor. A tall and
serious man sat beside him, a man whose head was a
salmon, and his parents sat on the other side of the
room. Their eyes were black and sunken and itchy, surrounded by rings.

They were not bad parents. Not when they were
sober. They didn't understand books and stories
because they were Fear and Rage. They didn't understand. That was all. And now Oblivion felt sorry the
gendarmes had even come, felt sorry the dogs had
swarmed over him and stopped the beating. Green
tears fell from his cheeks and planted black roses in the
stone floor.

The niches in front of the hall also had black rose-
bushes in them—the Councilors of l'Morai.

"All rise and give heed," came the voice from the
biggest bush. Benches and chairs scraped as the people stood. Oblivion saw the salmon-headed man nod,

and he slipped from his chair and stood amongst the black thorns.

"So begins the trial of Francis Ciantioux, standing accused now of heinous disobedience to his parents, most recently by hiding from just punishment. The accusers stand now to your left and my right—Phillipe and Margorie Ciantioux, makers of cheese, parents of the disobedient child. In the adjudication of this matter, let all citizens of l'Morai draw near in good faith, those with knowledge of this child's deeds and misdeeds to testify, and those without to bring fair and impartial judgment unto this case."

"Guilty," rang out the shout of the crowd.

"Let it so be written," gurgled the salmon-headed man. "And let it be decreed that Francis Ciantioux shall be transformed into a man-giant, that he may never, ever, ever, ever hide again."

 **ELEVEN**

Marie didn't awaken Hermos for the second watch. Someone had come that night and made sure she didn't.

The young woman awoke to a throbbing ache in her head. She shifted, trying to push herself up from the bed, but her arms wouldn't respond. They were numb. She struggled to turn from her stomach to her back, but something constrained her feet. Her ankles had lost feeling beneath the ragged hemp rope that bound them. Only then did Marie realize she lay not on the sheets of her bed, but on the foot-smoothed planks of a floor.

"Hermos?" she murmured fearfully. The deadened sound of her voice assured her she was still in her caravan, and the whiff of old incense and straw bedding confirmed it. She also smelled the man-giant. "Hermos?" she repeated more insistently.

A prolonged groan came from the corner.

Marie managed to sit up. "Hermos!"

The man-giant lurched, moaning irritably.

"What're these?" he grunted, struggling against the cords that bound him.

"Somebody's tied us up," Marie spat, rolling to her knees. "Look around to see if anyone's in here with us."

Hermos's lean arms went slack behind him as he looked up, blinking. No one else was in the caravan. It looked strangely untouched, just as it had looked when he'd drifted into a fitful sleep the night before. Even the door was locked. Now, though, the morning sun shone dimly through the windows.

"Nobody's here. The door is still locked."

Marie grunted, preoccupied with getting to her feet. From a kneeling position, she placed her head on the seat of a tall stool and pushed herself up from the floor. With short, hopping steps, she brought her bound feet up beneath her and stood, her legs braced against Hermos's huge form. The brief smile of success gave way to a scowl as she sorely wriggled her fingers. "Pins and needles," she growled. Tugging one last time on the bindings behind her, she said, "Move your legs; I need to get past."

"Where are you going?" Hermos blurted, drawing his legs painfully up toward him.

Marie began hopping toward the bed. "I've got a set of daggers beneath the mattress." Reaching the bed, she stooped and groped along the wooden bed frame. "Aha!" she cried out, gritting her teeth and pulling a bundle of daggers forth.

"Who did this?" Hermos wondered aloud, peering angrily at the ropes that bound his swollen feet.

"You said the door is locked. Windows, too, I take it," Marie said. She sat down on the bed and stiffly worked a knife from the pack. "It was somebody with a key—and with sleep powder. Somebody like the Puppetmaster."

"Yes," Hermos mused, eyes watching the door fearfully.

Marie gritted her teeth and managed to slide the knife into the ropes around her wrists.

"Why didn't he just kill us?" the man-giant moaned.

"Why?" Marie snapped, grimacing as the ropes bit deeper into her wrists. "I don't know why. We've got four murders in one fortnight, and not a single reason why. We've got a man whose finger was cut off, and his back scarred just to make him look guilty. I'm scared, Hermos. How are we going to get out of this one?"

Hermos arched his back, pushing himself higher against the wall. He leaned his head beside one of the windows and peered out. Beyond the sill lay the Performers Quarter and the rambling promenades, and beyond these, the wide and golden heath, glimmering in the morning sun.

"We have to escape," Hermos muttered distractedly.

Marie stopped cutting the ropes, the deep creases in her face softening. "Yes," she breathed wearily. "Yes. We've got to escape."

"Where?"

"I don't know," Marie replied as she sawed at the ropes. "Away. Far away, out of the gendarmes' reach. If they catch us off the carnival grounds again, they'll kill us on the spot."

Hermos asked, "But how can we get them all away?"

"All?" Marie asked.

"The carnival . . . all away."

"We can't," Marie said. "It's got to be just you and me."

"The murders won't stop."

The knife finally cut through the cord. Marie pulled her sleep-stiffened arms free from the uncoiling ropes. With a groan, she flexed her wrists, twisting them in slow circles.

"Yes, you're right. The murders won't stop." Wringing her hands, she leaned over to cut the ropes from her feet.

Hermos watched as her long, black hair fell in a shimmering wave from her shoulders and cascaded over her head.

"Guess it'd be wrong of us to just run away from all this," Marie continued as she finished slicing through the rope and pulled it from her bruised ankles. "After

all, we're the only ones who know. Whoever tied us up
wanted to scare us silent, or scare us into running. We
can't let him do that."

Sighing again, she turned her ankles in stiff circles,
kicking the rope fragments away. Hermos watched her,
his large, white teeth raking his lower lip. Marie stood
and shuffled toward the man-giant. She dropped to one
knee beside him and set the knife down on the floor.

"Where are your hands?"

"Behind me," Hermos replied, shifting away from the
wall. His eyes never lifted from her pallid face.

Marie leaned toward him, setting her hands on his
shoulders and feeling her way down to his bound wrists.
She ran her fingers once or twice over the knotted
ropes, searching for a safe spot to begin cutting. Finding one, she picked up the dagger again, set it to the
ropes, and began to slice.

Hermos sat quietly as she worked, her light breaths
wafting over his shoulder. At last, the rope gave way.
He pulled his aching arms from behind him, feeling the
painful pulse of blood reentering his fingers.

Marie shifted back onto her legs and patted his high,
bony knee. "Let your hands rest. I'll cut your feet free."

Hermos drew his feet up near her. He watched as
Marie placed her hands on the knots about his ankles.
The man-giant's face darkened. A black circle about
the size of a ducre showed faintly through the hairline
on the back of her head. Beside it rested the red tattoo
they had found before. Hermos latched onto her shoulders with his trembling hands. He pulled her to him,
pressing her head against his narrow chest.

"What are you doing?" Marie protested as she struggled to break free.

"Be still," Hermos commanded in a quiet, rumbling
voice that filled the caravan. His thin fingers swept her
hair from the back of her neck, and he peered into her
hairline.

It *was* a tattoo. A second tattoo.

Drawing the hair back from the mark, Hermos could see the pattern plainly. It was dark, black circle with fiery edges like a sun. Within the sun stood a single figure: a heathland hare with its ears knotted.

"Let me go," Marie insisted, pushing away. She sat back out of his reach, her face red with anger and embarrassment. "Don't ever do that again."

Hermos studied her and reached back to feel his own neck. His fingertip settled on a sore spot.

"We've been tattooed," he said flatly, "again."

Marie's pupilless eyes went wide, and her hand shot to the back of her neck. "Again? What does it look like?"

"It's black," Hermos muttered, his chin beginning to tremble. "A hare with tied ears."

"Oh, no," Marie gasped, dropping back and bracing herself against the floor. "The Ear-Tied Hare."

"Tidhare," Hermos whispered, fear ringing in his voice. "Marked for death."

Marie was shaking. "The killer must have drugged us and then tattooed us."

"We must escape," Hermos said again suddenly, stomping his still-bound feet on the floor. "Cut me loose!"

Marie groped for a safe spot to cut. As she set her knife to the hemp, she said, "Yes, we must escape. All of us."

*   *   *   *   *

As the blind woman finished her impassioned speech, the midget Valor ecstatically nodded his fiery red mop of hair. He turned from Marie and the man-giant to his fellow midgets. The twenty diminutive performers had gathered in the supply shed among shovels and barrels of wine to hear Marie's "urgent news."

Other than Valor, though, they were unimpressed. Big Boy and the Clatch looked particularly dour, sitting beside each other on a rolled tarpaulin. Big Boy's fat face held a smug frown, and he crossed his arms dubiously over a red cummerbund he always wore. On a clear day, performers could spot that cummerbund from across the carnival. Next to Big Boy sat his emaciated lackey the Clatch, who had weepy eyes and no lips to speak of. The Clatch mimicked his friend's doubtful posture.

"Come on now!" Valor implored, stepping away from Marie and balling his child-sized hands into fists. "Worley, I know *you* were at Morcastle's funeral. You seen the mounds where they'd buried the bodies."

"Ya—Ya—Ya . . . yeah," replied a long-nosed midget, sitting atop a high pile of crates. He swept a green cap from his head and bowed furtively toward Marie. "B—Begging your p—p—pardon, milady, but I seen . . . I seen hu—hu-hundreds of mounds, but notta s—, notta single b—body."

"What're those mounds gonna *be* out there but graves!" Valor shouted, exasperated. He had long been a secret admirer of Marie's, and the doubt of his comrades made him blush with shame. He stomped his foot once and roared, "They were even trying to bury Morcastle in a secret grave, though he was murdered right before your eyes!"

" 'Twasn't murder, but a accident," blurted Big Boy with a confrontational glare. The Clatch nodded and added, significantly, "Yeah."

"The fourth *accident* in a fortnight?" Marie challenged. "And the heath is full of a couple hundred more accidents? I tell you, the Puppetmaster's been killing us, one at a time. And he's been at it forever."

"Why don't you just leave the carnival?" a midget named Boris chimed in. He leaned back, running stubby fingers through his long, black beard.

"That's just it," Valor replied. "Nobody ever leaves here alive. Remember Fats and Monsieur R? Remember Billy and the Goat-Man? They didn't leave here on their own, like the Puppetmaster's pretended all these years. They're out there under the heath grass right now."

"How do you know?" Big Boy pressed. The Clatch nodded in agreement.

"There's been a sign up on Panol and Banol's stage that says 'Gone to New Carnival,'" Marie replied evenly. "And they put that sign up *after* we found their bodies out on the heath."

"But you're saying that not only is the Puppetmaster killing us off," Big Boy began, his voice edged with derision, "but that he made us into freaks. You're saying we're all from the city—we all used to be tall, and normal. And *you* used to *see*, Marie? And *you* used to be *short*, man-giant?" The Clatch laughed aloud as his friend finished.

Marie's features hardened. "We saw your name in the book, too, Big Boy."

A palpable wave of shock swept through the crowd. Hermos cast Marie a sidelong glance. The blind woman nudged him gently.

Big Boy's face grew red with nervous embarrassment. "*My* name?" he replied. "Right! And what was I called when I lived in l'Morai?"

"Your name was Pierre Remroit. You were a fishmonger who shortchanged your customers," Marie replied without a pause.

Big Boy opened his mouth to speak, but nothing came forth.

"And if you each check the back of your companions' heads, you'll find the tattoo of a rearing horse that has been speared," Marie pursued. "That's the mark on the Puppetmaster's pendant, the mark you got when he turned you into a freak."

Marie's words met with mutterings and the patter of

feet as the midgets shifted about to check each other's necks. The mumbling gave way to a series of gasps and moans. Dread spread palpably through the shanty.

Big Boy slid off the rolled tarpaulin, followed by the Clatch, and paced toward Marie and Hermos. Spreading his small, scarred hands, he said, "What do we do?"

Marie smiled grimly. "First, we spread the news to all the performers. Then, we need to stockpile weapons for tonight."

*   *   *   *   *

Edeve giggled delightedly between bites of dried fruit, which she held in her small, sticky hands. The evening arena show had been great so far. Now, in the center ring, her favorite act was setting up: the harlequins. Edeve elbowed her blond-haired brother, who sat beside her on the arena's limestone bench.

"Look, Marcus! They got sa-woards!"

The harlequins were going to war.

Marcus smiled stupidly at her and mocked his sister's childish voice. "I know." He shoved her sideways, almost tipping the girl into the aisle beside her.

Edeve struggled to right herself. Once she did, she turned a darkened face toward her brother, balled her hand into a sticky fist, and punched him in the shoulder.

Marcus rubbed the spot, whimpering in feigned pain, and then said, "Just watch the show, stupid."

The harlequins had begun marching out into the sandy arena. Ten came from the entrance near Edeve, and ten more from the opposite entrance. They carried ludicrously long pole arms, whose blunt ends bent and wobbled as they marched along. Fat swords hung from their belts, and small, scarred bucklers from their arms. Edeve giggled as she spotted one buckler with a smoking hole blown in it. The last harlequin carried no armor or weapons. He patted out a dour rhythm on a drum strapped to his waist.

The harlequin general marched out beyond the rest, and began stepping backward. He lifted a floppy glove to his eyes to survey his soldiers. "Red Noses, sound off!"

The whole company released a resounding, "Here!"

Across the arena, a shout came from the second company, "Blue Ruffs, sound off!"

The company of harlequins let out a long, harsh raspberry.

Edeve laughed, prodding another date into her brimming mouth. As the Red Noses passed by, Edeve noticed their heads weren't real: they were painted balls of wood strapped atop the harlequins' real heads, which were hidden in their shirts. Looking closely, she spotted eyeholes in their silk shirts. She also saw that each soldier had a false arm. Edeve almost nudged Marcus to point this out, but remembered she was still mad at him.

The Red Nose platoon made its way to one end of the large, center circle of the arena. There, they lined up and stood at attention. Across the arena, the platoon of Blue Ruffs assembled in similar fashion. Edeve laughed as one red-haired harlequin sat down in the sand while his comrades stood. The general, noting the breach of etiquette, hustled over to him and knocked him backward.

The entrances to the arena suddenly pounded with rushing feet. Edeve saw harlequin cavalries ride in from the wings. She counted ten riders, each mounted on a harlequin horse: two men in a costume. A number of the mock horses, galloping proudly toward the center ring, tripped in the uneven sand, spilling their riders to the ground. Edeve laughed so loud she swallowed a half-chewed date. She grimaced and gave her big brother a whack for good measure.

One of the horses, a piebald mare, broke apart into front and back halves. The forequarters spun dizzily on the ground. The hindquarters raced around the arena, trying to join themselves to anyone who stood about: the peanut man, the dung scoopers, a pregnant woman. . . . The forequarters got up and ran pell-mell toward their other half, but before the two could be joined, the hindquarters connected themselves to the backside of a mule. The ass let out a distressed bray and kicked, sending the horse's rear flying through the air.

The laughter in the tent was deafening as workers dragged the motionless backside out of the arena. Dejected, the forequarters trotted to where the Red Nose cavalry was lining up in front of the infantry. The piebald horse head stepped in line, and its rider mounted it, piggyback.

The drummers played a loud, thundering cadence, and the crowd quieted in anticipation. Then, in one voice, the harlequins on the opposite side of the arena shouted, "Down with the Red Noses!"

"Down with the Blue Ruffs!" came the return shout from the harlequins near Edeve. She nodded her solemn agreement.

The Blue Ruffs chimed out, "You harlequins would run from a mouse!"

"You mice would run from us harlequins!" the Red Noses chorused.

"Kill the harlequins!" shouted the Blue Ruffs. Their line of cavalry broke into an ungainly charge.

The Red Noses shouted, "Kill the mice!"

As the horses converged, their riders tilted the long, drooping lances they bore. One of the lances dipped too low, digging its tip into the ground. With a stunned whoop, the rider flew off his saddle, and his horse ripped in half.

Shouting silly slogans, the lines of cavalry met. Next came a snapping crash of lances and a series of comic groans. Some of the cavalrymen fell from their mounts, their false heads brutally popping off. Their necks sprayed crimson blood from pig bladders filled with the stuff.

The crowd cheered. Edeve slipped excitedly from her seat.

The riders who were still mounted spun in chaotic circles, seeking their opponents. With a unison, "Ah, ha!" they discovered their enemies and charged the center-point of the battlefield. The resultant collision sent all the horses reeling. Simultaneously, the mounts separated and dropped their riders, and they all fell down.

Again the crowd applauded, shouts of "Red Noses," beginning in the stands around Edeve. The cries of the crowd were quickly replaced by angry shouts from the harlequin infantry, who charged.

Hearing the shouts, the bodies on the battlefield—riders and horses alike—sat bolt upright. They shrieked, scrambled to their feet, and ran to the edges of the arena. A lone pair of forequarters, dazed, stumbled about on the head- and arm-strewn battlefield as the troops converged.

Again, the air filled with the crash and crack of lances meeting shields. In the center of the battle, three or four soldiers lost their wooden heads, which flew in high, tumbling arcs beneath the canvas roof. Spouts of pig's blood shot like geysers from the vacated necks. Edeve applauded as a Red Nose infantryman struck off his opponent's arm, bringing forth the same red gush.

One by one, the harlequins threw the battered and splintered pole arms down and unsheathed their mammoth swords. More fake arms and heads flew, their owners occasionally fighting on until someone pointed out their missing member. One of the headless Blue Ruffs cut off a Red Nose's head and struggled to set it on his own empty shoulders. But the crimson spray of blood from his neck ceased before he could cap it off, and he crumpled to the ground.

The cavalry, assembling itself again on the outskirts of the battle, made another charge. The din of battle redoubled as they joined the bloody fray, and Edeve watched, enraptured. All across the battlefield, harlequins slipped and fell on the blood-slick piles of arms and heads and bodies. Edeve cheered as a Red Nose slew a cavalryman, and then cleft the enemy horse in two. The rider hit the ground in the same instant as both halves of the horse.

At last, only two harlequins remained, swinging their swords in weary, halfhearted swipes at each other.

"Die, you foolish Blue Ruff!" cried one of the soldiers, batting his sword in a ridiculously slow sweep.

"I'm not the Blue Ruff!" the other rejoined. He began to spin like a top, his blade cutting circles in the air around him. "I'm the Red Nose!"

The other harlequin, studying his opponent's tactic, lifted his sword so their blades struck lazily each time his enemy turned. "*I'm* the Red Nose, idiot!"

The spinning harlequin slowed and staggered to a stop. His head bobbed in dizzy circles. "Yeah! You've got a red nose! Three of 'em, even!"

"And you've got one, too!" the other responded, exhausted. "And one plus too makes three! We both have three red noses."

"If we both have three red noses, why are we fighting?" they asked each other in unison.

They traded incredulous glances and peered up at the crowd. For a moment, they broke into laughter. Then each fell, exhausted, into the other's arms. Their heads popped from their fake shoulders, and pig's blood sprayed over the whole, lifeless field.

The arena grew silent. The crowd expectantly scanned the still forms. Then, slowly, the audience broke into applause and uneasy laughter. Edeve wriggled her way back up onto the cold seat and clapped her sticky hands together twice.

The harlequin war was over.

As the applause died down, a woman ran out into the center of the blood-soaked arena. In one hand, she carried a brightly burning torch. She neared the battle site and slowed, her feet confidently picking out the path to the arena's center pole. Setting her torch into a bracket on the pole, the woman bowed to the still-applauding crowd.

"I am Marie the Blind Juggler!" she proclaimed.

The ovation swelled anew, and the tattered and bloodstained harlequins began to pick themselves up from the sandy floor.

"That's right!" Marie shouted to them over the applause. "Drag your worthless bodies off this plot of land. This is a carnival arena, not a graveyard! But leave your heads and limbs. After all, I've got a juggling act to do."

Casting suspicious glances her way, the headless harlequins sullenly shuffled toward the arena exits. Edeve ignored the bloody clowns. Her eyes were intent on the blind woman in the limb-strewn sand.

Marie stepped lightly through the battlefield, picking up three of the slick, wooden heads. She began to juggle them in looping circles around her.

"Warfare is a real juggling act," she called out with a wry smile. "Each general is trying to get a head of the other." The audience groaned in response to the pun. Marie held out one hand, shifting the heads into a circular pattern sustained by the other hand. Shaking her free finger at the crowd, she said, "Don't worry, they get worse."

Leaning over quickly, Marie grabbed an arm that lay next to her foot. She tossed it into the air, and it joined the tumbling arc of the heads. "Of course, the side with superior arms almost always wins. And for the prisoners of the other side . . . the heads will roll!" With that, she tossed the three heads out to tumble across the battlefield. She caught the fake arm, however, and flipped it so her hand grasped its hand. "How do you do?" she asked in a deep, manlike voice.

As the crowd laughed and applauded, she gathered together three arms and began juggling them. "Now, almost all generals are handy at killing off their own soldiers. Occasionally they even finger a specific fighter to be the one who dies." She flipped one of the arms up toward her forehead, catching it there and balancing it on its wooden fingertip. A sigh of amazement swept through the crowd, followed by more applause.

Tipping the appendage back into the juggling pattern, she said, "Some men execute their own lieutenants"—she held up a left hand—"and some execute their right-hand men"—she held up a right hand. "Generals can do that, you see, even in times of peace. But as soon as you start killing someone else's soldiers, that's when a war starts." She flung the arms wide, and they soared out, landing in the sandy border of the arena.

"That's what's been happening here, at Carnival l'Morai." The blind woman's voice had grown deadly serious. Edeve felt a chill rush down her spine. "Someone has been killing off our people. Perhaps a solitary maniac, perhaps an army of maniacs. But over the past years, an army's worth of our folk have died. By definition, he has started a war."

Marie walked over to the pole and pulled the torch from its bracket. It turned out to be not a single torch, but six thin ones. Planting the butt ends of three of them in the sand, Marie began juggling the other three. The flaming brands tumbled in hypnotic circles about her head, leaving thin trails of black smoke that twisted and rose into the air.

"Of course, the problem with any war is the bodies left on the battlefield. What do you do with them? You can't just juggle them the way I've been doing, because your hands get covered with blood. And, eventually, the bodies will fall to earth."

Marie switched the tumbling brands to one hand. Stooping quickly, she snatched up the other three burning brands and flung them into the air. The twirling paths of the new torches merged with those of the old. All six of the flaming brands rose into high arcs, looping near the canvas ceiling. The crowd broke into appreciative applause, and a smile cut across Marie's face.

"Maybe you can bury some of them, but if you've got too many bodies, the ground fills up."

Edeve watched the mesmerizing whirl of the torches. A few of them had gone out as they spun. Marie continued to keep them aloft, her pretty, blind face twitching with the effort.

Cracking another smile, Marie said, "But if you burn them, you've got nothing left except ashes and bones . . . ashes and bones. You've buried the dead in the sky. That's what's so wonderful about the sky: it goes on forever. You could bury a whole nation there, and they would be gone—gone without a trace. One thousand, one million, six million . . . how many could you burn away without a trace?"

Marcus shouted out, "Your torches are going out!"

Edeve blushed and whispered, "Now *you* shut up."

"Are they going out?" Marie asked. "Thank you, young sir, for letting me know."

Marcus smirked at his little sister. Edeve ignored him, sliding once again off the bench and craning to see.

Between catches and throws, Marie snatched a small oilskin from her belt and threw it up into the air along with the torches. The crowd responded with an awe-filled, "Ooooh!"

Edeve murmured, "That's seven things she's juggling."

As Marie caught the tumbling skin and threw it again into the air, she said, "I brought this skin of oil just in case my torches went out."

The next time the oilskin fell into her waiting hand, she squeezed a bit of its contents into her mouth and dropped the skin onto the ground. Then, leaning back, Marie sprayed the liquid in a fine mist from her mouth. As soon as the shooting vapor struck the first torch, it burst into flame. A column of fire twice as tall as Marie erupted with a roar above her head, engulfing the torches. Moments later, the flame dissipated.

Now all the torches burned.

Edeve squealed with a delighted cry, and the audience applauded heartily.

Marie smiled and shouted, "You liked that?"

The crowd responded with a jumbled yes.

Marie shook her head. "What was that you said?"

The people responded in a ragged unison, "Yes!"

Marie cried at the top of her lungs, "What did you say?"

"*Yes!*"

Marie flung all but one of the torches out away from her. Each curved like a flickering meteor and dropped, harmless, into the bloody sand. Stooping to pick up the oilskin, Marie said, "Quite an efficient way to clear the dead from a battlefield, wouldn't you say?"

"Yes!"

"I thought so too," Marie replied quietly. She emptied the skin into her mouth and drew a long breath in through her nose. Holding the final torch above her lips, she sprayed out a dense cloud, which erupted into a roaring pillar of fire.

The flaming specter rose up to the luffing canvas high above and curled evilly beneath it. The cloud of fire billowed out along the seams of the tent, where its orange-red glow lingered. Suddenly, the tent roof burst into flames. In one spot, the aged canopy was instantly consumed. Stars shown through the flaming, yawning hole, and winds rushed out into the night sky. The air fueled the fire, and it spread out toward the stands.

"The pyre is lit. Flee while you can, people of l'Morai!"

*   *   *   *   *

Marie rushed toward the arena exit. Her ears were filled with the roar of fire, which spread in deadly waves across the tent canopy. The sound of the flames was redoubled by the shrill screams and heavy stomps of the panicked crowd. The people were pouring from the stands.

Marie held her trembling hands out before her. She could easily be crushed—or murdered—in the stampede. A small hand latched on to hers, and a thin, welcoming voice cut through the din.

"Great show, Marie," said Valor happily, drawing her into step behind him. "You really brought down the house."

Holding tight to his hand, Marie ran nervously behind him. Amid the shouts and footfalls, she had to fight the impulse to duck and shy back. "Is everything in place?"

"Yes," Valor replied, growing serious. "We've set up gauntlets beyond the arena to channel people out of the carnival. I've also got a brute squad combing the sideshows and tents and caravans. We'll have every damned citizen out of this place before moonrise."

Marie nodded with satisfaction as Valor guided her into the high-arched exit. When she spoke again, her voice reverberated from the stone walls. "So, all the performers are with us?"

"Yeah," Valor replied, skirting around a cluster of arguing harlequins. "We just now told the harlequins. Their resolve is being carried mostly by the rest of us. Everybody else has been in since sundown. It's the tattoos that've convinced 'em all. Everybody thought it was just the strongman and a couple others who had them."

As they stepped from the corridor, cold night air washed over Marie: heath air. It was aromatic, filled with cries and the frenetic stomp of the fleeing citizens. "How much longer before they're all out?"

Valor paused, eyeing the main road, thickly lined on both sides with an army of performers bearing torches. In the fiery light, Valor could make out the glint of shovels and axes and the fearful faces of the fleeing mob. "A quarter-hour at most."

"Where's Hermos?"

Valor directed Marie down a side path. "He's with the performers at the Puppetmaster's. They're having trouble rousting the old bastard from his hovel."

"Take me there," Marie said quickly, "then go round up more skins of flame oil."

"Five or six?"

"Thirty or forty."

* * * * *

"Great Qin-sah." Hermos plodded in a wide, frustrated arc around the Puppetmaster's black caravan. He eyed the restless crowd of performers that surrounded the dwelling. Despite all their threats and jeers and chants, the Puppetmaster had not emerged from his hovel. The doors were barred, the windows empty.

Except for the bodies. A few impatient performers had decided to break in. After smashing the thick carnival glass, the performers had tried to scramble through. A moment later, they slumped dead across the sills. The rest of the mob drew back, knowing some sort of evil magic warded the caravan.

The Puppetmaster wasn't coming out, and those who were going in were ending up dead.

"What's the news?" came Marie's voice as her small hand fit into the man-giant's.

Hermos turned, a faint smile on his brooding features. Beyond Marie, the red-haired midget Valor slipped away through the crowd.

"Not going well," the man-giant rumbled.

Marie nodded. "Valor said the Puppetmaster wouldn't come out."

"Three killed already, going in," Hermos observed heavily.

"What?" Marie asked, lifting her stunned face up toward him. "*Three*? Whether he was a murderer before or not, he is one now."

Tugging Hermos after her, Marie edged through the crowd. The performers parted to let them pass.

"What's the plan, Marie?" a lithe acrobat shouted, hopeful. Murmurs of interest spread through the mob.

Marie replied sharply. "To drive out the normals, and chain the Puppetmaster. As to specifics . . . I'm making it up as I go." Humorless chuckles passed through the crowd around her.

Marie pressed on until she reached the narrow gap that stood between the mob and the Puppetmaster's hovel. She let go of Hermos's hand and cupped her fingers about her mouth.

"Come out, Puppetmaster," she shouted, her voice edged with anger. "The performers of Carnival l'Morai hereby accuse you of crimes against us. Come out, and we'll grant you a fair trial, much as those in l'Morai would."

The rioters hushed, waiting for a sound from the hovel. None came.

"Last chance," Marie called. "Trial by freaks, or trial by fire!"

She counted ten heartbeats. Still no answer.

Marie felt a tap at her elbow. "I've rounded up about fifty of the skins, milady," Valor said, latching on to her hand and setting it around the neck of a burgeoning sack.

Marie smiled. She reached into the sack and lifted three of the skins. With a loud and angry laugh, she threw them onto the rooftop of the hovel. They burst on impact, and oil ran down the building's planks. Taking a fourth skin from the bag, Marie opened it and began spraying its contents along the wall.

"Hand the rest out, Valor," Marie instructed as she sprayed the wall. "Tell everyone to do the same with the oil." The red-haired midget nodded and began circulating among the crowd. Meanwhile, Marie hurled the now-emptied skin onto the ground and shouted, "Which do you fear more, Puppetmaster—the people or the pyre?"

Setting a hand on her ear to listen for a response, Marie heard only the sound of oilskins beginning to burst on the rooftop. She shrugged, brushed her hands clean, and headed back into the crowd.

"Burn the place to the ground."

 **TWELVE**

With a triumphant shout, Valor snatched another torch from a harlequin and tossed it atop the Puppetmaster's hovel. The black walls of the ramshackle dwelling already glowed with dancing flames, and an inky column of smoke rose dense and hot into the starry heavens. Peering up at the pillar of soot, the midget clapped his hands together with glee and skipped in a merry circle about the legs of a female acrobat standing nearby.

"Down with the normals. Up with the freaks!" Valor shouted in a loud, singsong voice. The crackling pops of the wood and the gradual roar of the blaze provided a haunting counterpoint to the chant. Laughing, Valor snatched the acrobat's hand and cried out, "Come on! Surely you can get the roll of it!"

The acrobat pulled her hand back and ran it through her dark brown hair. Behind the dark mask she wore, her eyes were wide with fear.

"Come on!" Valor goaded, grabbing her other hand. "The tyrant is dead! Long live the freaks!"

Uncertain at first, the acrobat took a few cautious steps, careful to keep her white tights clear of the dust. Frowning at the woman's reluctance, Valor whacked her on the backside. "Step into it!"

"Oh, silk be damned," the acrobat blurted. She

began to whirl in a circle with the midget as a cloud of
dust rose about her feet. Her dark hair spun in loops,
and a wicked smile crossed her face.

"Down with the normals! Up with the freaks!" she
proclaimed as they spun. The crowd around them
pulled back, clearing room for them to turn. A harlot
and the dog-faced boy at the edge of the group began
to clap to the rhythm of the chant. Beside them, a
bearded lady and the stick-legged man began skipping
and swinging precariously.

"Down with the normals! Up with the freaks!"

The cry spread in waves. The performers grabbed
partners and twirled to the shouts. In their midst, the fire
became a holocaust, sending burning sheets of fabric
and wood in red-hot spirals around the silvery moon.
The debris broke into ash and tumbled like gray snow,
covering the ground around the dancers. Faster they
spun, their macabre ballet filling the grounds around
the burning building.

A man with a stoma in his neck shouted the chant in
a gurgling, throaty roar. A young woman slipped out of
her stained chemise and ran naked through the riotous
throng. The tumblers were leaping in rhythm from
hands to feet to elbows to knees. The snake-man, who
had two pythons instead of arms, curled them in wild,
hypnotic circles and wrapped women in them, running
the hissing snake heads through their hair. Even Karrick, the Man of a Thousand Knives, was there. His
mind had returned to him, even though his memory
had not. And tonight, amid the intoxicating chant of the
crowd, in the mesmerizing whirl and dance, Karrick was
embracing his fellow freaks.

The smoke rose now like a coiling, black god, oblit-
erating all the stars. The house had become a furnace,
moaning and humming as the wood gave itself up to
the air. And, always, the quickening chant of the revelers overtopped the roar of the flames. As the pitch and

sway of the dance grew more frenetic, the old slogan compacted and the shouts redoubled.

"Kill the normals! Kill the normals!"

Letting go of the acrobat's arm, Valor slowed and stopped. His heart was pounding loudly. He peered, dumbfounded, at the spinning throng, their words echoing in his ears. Even Big Boy and the Clatch had joined the ecstatic dance. A sneering cluster of grubby boys clapped their hands in a quickening rhythm, shouting to change the chant again.

"Kill, kill, kill . . ."

But the new chant had no time to spread.

A window casing, mantled in blood-red flame, burst out into the smoldering night. Through the gaping hole, a broad mass of fire belched forth. The performers near the window screamed as the blast pelted them with hot shards of glass, and the dancers stumbled to a halt. The crowd fell back, gaping. Amid showers of descending ash, something was solidifying out of the writhing flames, something that stalked with heavy steps toward them.

The Puppetmaster.

His enormous form was wreathed in fire, and blazing swaths of wool draped from his horrible, blistering arms. He was like a great, enormous ape—black and muscular and fierce and unstoppable. Amber flames licked the malformed features of his face, revealed now beneath a smoldering hood: a tall and dented forehead, skewed eyes, a half-rotted nose, a curled harelip, and a shattered chin covered in burned mats of hair. Every line of his body was rimmed in fire, and, as Valor watched in horror, the skin blistered and blackened beneath the flames.

But the Puppetmaster was heedless. He strode to a crane-necked man and seized him by the throat, snapping his head from its shoulders. In the same, relentless motion, the Puppetmaster's other arm swung in a flaming arc about the naked woman, and he drew her into the thick, fire-soaked folds of his robe. She thrashed, screaming, struggling against the coarse fabric, which broke away in blackened sheets and adhered, sizzling, to her skin.

Valor pushed his way forward, stunned. He had no idea what he might do, but he knew he must do something. Drawing a dagger from his waistband, the midget released an angry growl and vaulted toward the burning Puppetmaster. His foot struck the flaming arm loose. The woman fell free. Valor's dagger sank into the burning mass that was the Puppetmaster's shoulder.

A huge fist buried itself in Valor's stomach. He felt the impact more than the fire, smelled the acrid smoke from his own hair. He was falling. Pain exploded through his right elbow. He couldn't breathe. The Puppetmaster loomed over him like a tree in a forest fire, pitching and shuddering and shrieking with the flames. His ponderous arm swung down to finish the midget.

The fist struck the earth just behind Valor. Someone had yanked him out of the way, and was kicking sand and dust onto his flaming body.

With a roar of white rage, the Puppetmaster hurtled forward, stepping on a dog that had stumbled, panicked, into his path. The poor creature's yelp was cut short by a loud snapping sound and the dull wheeze of air from its dead body. The Puppetmaster strode on, the crowd falling away before him. He reached back over his shoulder and clasped a flaming sheet of wool. His fingers tightened, his broad arm wrenched the fabric from his shoulder, and he flung it atop the cowering crowd.

"I am a freak, like you!" he bellowed, his voice admixed with the demonic wail of the fire. "And I'll be a freak after you're all buried!" He broke free from the crowd and ran, burning, out toward the open heath.

Valor dropped his head back to the ground as the performers gathered around him, studying his wounds. The chants were gone, replaced by fearful mutterings and cries, barely audible against the loud fury of the fire.

"Not deep burns," Valor heard one of the performers say.

"Shattered his elbow," another observed.

"The girl's lots worse."

". . . need a sling, some water."

Then Valor spotted the man-giant, staring sadly down at him. Hermos's emberlike eyes looked strangely deep against the sky of pitch. A moment later, Marie's lovely face appeared beside his, her features hard with anger and concentration.

"We'll tend him, Hermos," she said, her voice high and thin against the roaring blaze. "Take thirty of the brute squad. Hunt down the Puppetmaster."

Hermos's face became quizzical, and he pointed toward the burning man, disappearing over the horizon. "Won't the Puppetmaster die?"

Marie's sightless eyes narrowed to thin slits. "I'm beginning to wonder if he can."

* * * * *

"Come out, come out, wherever you are!" growled Felix excitedly as he reached one gnarled hand over his hunched back to scratch his shoulder blade. "Just us here freaks from the brute squad," he muttered. He idly swung the iron rod he held.

The hunchback's lip drew into a purple-skinned scowl as he scanned the deserted boardwalk. All the stages so far had been empty, aside from carelessly strewn props and bits of debris. The canvas backdrops fluttered casually in the stiff nighttime wind. In the distance, the prolonged clamor of shouts assured Felix he was outside the real action. Suited him just as well. Either way, the smoke and the shouts meant freedom to him—freedom from the sideshows and the arena blood sports.

Felix took another step, the severed chain about his ankle rattling on the boardwalk beneath him. He bounced the iron rod in his scabrous hand. "Come on out," he coaxed in a rattling voice. "The show's definitely over."

In the fat woman's stall he spotted the slow rise and fall of a sheet that lay oddly crumpled near the back of the stage. Spitting onto his hands for better grip, Felix stepped from the boardwalk and padded across the sandy ground. The stage's two low steps creaked as Felix climbed up them. He smiled crookedly, and a lascivious gleam entered his glossy eyes. There was someone under the sheet.

Felix stepped across the complaining plank stage, his eyes fastening on a long, leg-shaped fold in the fabric. He raised the bar over his head; his muscles tensed.

He swung.

The creature leaped away, half-entangled in the sheet. Felix's iron bar struck the stage where the leg once had been and cracked through its top planks. Scrambling away from the hunchback, the form freed itself from the sheet and threw it to the ground. It was a boy, an orphan by the look of his dingy clothes. The waif shot Felix a startled, angry look, whimpered once, almost inaudibly, and flung himself through a gap in the backdrop.

Felix groaned in anger as he worked to wrench the bar from the splintered wood. Between heaves, he could hear the boy's retreating footfalls.

"You got one?" came a deep voice from the adjacent sideshow lane.

Gritting his uneven teeth, Felix yanked the bar free. He stood up, straightening as best he could despite the

hump on his back. "Nope. Flushed him out's all. A kid.
Run off down the alley."

A heavy-browed face emerged from behind the
backdrop, followed by a rotund body. The man's head
bristled with thick, wet hair, like the barbed whiskers of
a catfish. "Awww. A kid? That's it?"

"Nobody's left on *this* street," Felix said by way of
apology. Flexing his arms spasmodically, he rammed
the rod through the plank floor again. "Nobody no
more."

The man fit a meaty hand into the waistband of his
trousers and spat on the ground. "Don't get sore. Look.
I hear some of the guys got themselves a real treat, better than no kid, nohow. Better than no empty sideshow,
neither."

"Where?" Felix asked, struggling again to pull the rod
from the stage. "Where are you talking about?"

"Come on," the man replied with an awkward wave
of his hand. He disappeared around the backdrop.

With a roaring groan, Felix pulled the bar loose and
ambled after him. The man didn't slow, hurrying down
the alley toward the outer rim of the carnival. As he
pursued the man, Felix stared back at the blazing
arena. The canvas and its wooden framework were ribboned with flame, glowing skeletal above the solid rock
walls. In the shadow of the arena, another fire raged, its
bright, high flames sending up a thick pall of smoke. All
about the fire, a thick crowd gathered, churning and
boiling like some chaotic brew. The shrieks and howls
and chants of the crowd merged with the moaning
holocaust.

"Come on," the heavy-browed man reiterated, tapping Felix on the shoulder. "You're gonna love this."

Turning about, Felix blinked his eyes, stunned by the
sudden darkness of the heath beyond. He blinked
again; the dancing revelers still moved across his vision
like jittering gray specters. The man rounded a corner

in front of Felix, who followed, then drew up short.

Five gendarmes stood in the stocks, surrounded by a ring of club-toting brutes. The officers' faces were bruised and bloodied. Two of them slumped, either dead or unconscious.

"Hey, fellows," the man with the catfish whiskers shouted, "I brought another one to the festivities."

A burly ogre stepped back from the stocks, set the tip of his mammoth club down between his feet and growled. "Well, looky here. If it ain't the crooked little hunchback."

"Hello, Kougan," Felix said sullenly, his twisted shoulders twinging with remembered pain.

"Felix and me used to be chained together, didn't we, Felix?" the ogre explained with a snorting laugh. His shadowy comrades echoed the laughter. "Felix always had his lump there, but one time when he got particular annoying t' me, I made a mountain of his molehill."

Felix shrugged and turned away from the group. "I got to finish cleaning out the sideshow."

"You said it was empty already," reminded the man who brought him. Felix waved him off and began hobbling away.

"Wait," Kougan bellowed, imperious. He lifted his massive club from the ground and pointed it at Felix. "You ain't gonna leave all the dirty business to us, are ya?"

Felix muttered, "I got no business here. It ain't a fair fight. You're as bad as them."

Kougan released a deep grunt as he flung the club toward the hunchback's legs. It spun once in midair, then struck the ground with a spray of dirt and slammed into the back of Felix's knees. His legs folded, and he fell to the dusty ground.

The ogre leaped forward and loomed over him. "Get up, you little worm. I already killed two o' these here officers: simple as holdin' his head 'tween my two fingers'n twistin'. Be glad I never done that t' you! Now you gotta kill one yourself."

A wall of brutes formed around Felix as the ogre spoke. Sighing deeply, the hunchback rose to his elbows and said, "But I never killed nobody before. I broke some legs, sure, but never killed nobody."

Laughing brutally, Kougan yanked Felix to his feet and pushed him forward. "Now's your chance."

The ring of performers edged him closer to the stocks where the five men stood. Three still shuddered, their wounds dripping blood onto the soil.

"Oh, please," one begged. "Please, I have a family."

"Shut up," shouted the one beside him. "It does no good to beg. They're monsters. They've no mercy. They should've been burned alive years ago."

The crowd of brutes laughed at this, a few of them mocking the man with his own words. Felix stopped before the stocks, his legs trembling beneath him. Kougan pounded up beside the fearful hunchback, gripped the hair of the third man and pulled upward, revealing his face to the crowd. His cheeks were battered and his lips split and bloody. Despite the ogre's tight grip on his hair, the man gazed at the dark crowd with strange calm.

"One of 'em begs us, another one curses us," Kougan seethed. "What's the third stack o' dung got to say?"

The officer made no response.

Kougan jiggled his captive's head angrily and cried, "Tell me, or I'll kill you now myself!"

The man pressed his bloodied lips together for a moment, then spoke with supreme calm. "You'll kill me no matter what I say."

"Aren't you 'fraid t' die?" the ogre snarled.

The man swallowed, struggling to close his drying eyes. "No. Not when it is like this to live."

Kougan released the man, stepped away from the stocks, and barked, "Kill him, Felix."

"Wh—what with?" the hunchback stammered fearfully.

The ogre whirled, "Your hands, what else?"

"I can't do it," Felix moaned, his eyes fastened to the crown of the man's head. "He's got no way to fight. He's—"

"You've got to the count o' three," Kougan warned, hefting his club high overhead. "One . . . Two . . ."

"But—"

"Three."

The club fell. It struck the hunchback's twisted collarbone with a dull crunch. The bent man crumpled to the ground, slumping amidst a cloud of dust.

"Pick him up and stand clear," the ogre demanded. The group of brutes converged on the fallen hunchback, lifted him again to his feet, and backed away. Felix reeled, the arm beneath his crushed collarbone hanging limp, its fingers swelling.

The ogre raised the club again. "One . . . Two . . ."

"Wait, I can't ki—"

The wooden mass smashed into the other collarbone. Felix flipped over sideways and struck his head against the ground. There he lay in a crumpled heap, peering toward the down-turned faces in the stocks. The second officer spit on Felix as the brutes came and lifted him up again. Felix gritted his teeth against the throbbing, fragmented pain in his shoulders. Before he knew what had happened, the bloody ground was again beneath his feet, and the brutes were backing away.

"One . . . Two . . ."

Seeing a triangular glint of metal at the belt of one of the brutes, Felix lunged for it.

"Three."

The club struck the ground just behind Felix, sending a quake through the soil. The ogre groaned and pitched forward. Felix's gnarled fingers wrapped around the gleaming knife. In one clumsy motion, he spun about and drew the blade across the stooping ogre's neck.

Kougan gasped, the air rushing in foamy gulps through his severed throat. Blood sprayed the prisoners and the stocks, hissing between the ogre's clenching fingers. He shuddered once, dropped to one knee, then collapsed in a heap over the screaming hunchback.

*   *   *   *   *

Hermos's breaths swirled out white-hot beneath the descending moon. He struggled to quiet his lungs and hush the insistent drumming of his heart as he stepped through a stand of slender birch trees.

Still no sign of the Puppetmaster.

Lifting his torch high, Hermos shot a quick glance to his left. About a stone's throw away, Big Boy and the Clatch were searching another section of forest. As though sensing the man-giant's gaze, Big Boy shook his head solemnly and took another step forward. The Clatch followed, making a similar motion.

Hermos snorted grimly. His lips pursed as he squinted to make out the line of torches past the midgets, a string of lights that extended into the dim reaches of the forest.

"Still all here," he murmured to himself. Scanning ahead of him for a moment, Hermos took another step and peered down the line to his right. The searchers on that side, too, had found nothing. "Maybe he's gone."

When the flaming Puppetmaster had descended from the carnival grounds, he doused himself in a watery slough in the moorlands. His muddy track then led east, toward the forest. Hermos and the others had followed the trail until only Arkoo the Leopard Boy could trace it. Eventually, even he had lost the scent. Hermos had then arranged them in a line, one torch per searcher, and sent them fanning out through the forest. They'd swept from the tarn on the far southern tip of the wood to the rim of Valley l'Morai in the north. Still no sign.

Hermos sighed angrily, lifting his torch once again and studying the woods around him. The fiery light cast shifting shadows into the deep forest. Hermos stalked forward, his feet rising on yet another unmarked grave. A chill ran through him. In the brief moment he stood atop the spot, the man-giant glimpsed the mounds that spread out all around him, like gooseflesh across the forest floor. The graves seemed to stretch on forever.

The torchbearers to his left were gathering in a cluster. Hermos cupped a hand to his mouth and shouted, "Find something?" The noise of his cry routed a flock of sleepy birds, whose fast-beating wings slapped frantically in the forest canopy.

One of the searchers motioned Hermos over.

The man-giant's heart leaped. They *had* found something. He gestured for the searchers to his right to follow, then struck out through the thickening woods toward the gathering of torches.

As he reached the gathering—a small group of searchers standing on a ridge of humus—he noticed their slumped shoulders and narrowed eyes.

"What is it?" Hermos asked.

"Nothing," said Big Boy, crossing his arms over his chest. "That's just it! Nothing! We've been out here all night and not found a single clue." The Clatch harrumphed his agreement.

Hermos's eyes darkened, and he studied the other searchers.

A man with a small, third arm beneath his left armpit spoke up, "It's getting near dawn, Hermos." He nodded in the direction the sun would rise and pointed toward the rose-tinged black of the sky above. "The carnival will be needing all the warriors they can get, come dawn. The gendarmes are sure to pay a call."

Hermos was incredulous. He released a long, angry

sigh and set a fist on his hip. "We're supposed to bring him back!"

Big Boy threw his hands in the air. "So what if he got away? He's probably dead already! Nobody could survive after getting burned that bad."

"Nobody 'cept the Puppetmaster," interjected the leopard boy, who only now joined the group, curling into a miserable heap against a nearby fern. "They say he never dies. If he's Juron Cygne—and *I* for one think he *is*—the cornerstone of the arena says he's at least four hundred years old."

Nodding, Hermos said, "So we must catch him."

"I don't know if we can catch him . . . at least not tonight," the boy replied with a yawn, rolling over and stretching his back with a feline whine. "I've lost the scent, and no one else can find him either."

Hermos shook his head, fuming. "And you?"

The rotund man whom Hermos stared at looked up with sudden shock. He pulled the collar back from his red, swollen neck. "Whether we *should* go on or not, I just *can't*. I'm worn to the bone."

Hermos flashed the fat man a dubious glare, but the searchers clustered behind him nodded in agreement.

One performer, the man with the stoma in his throat, growled out, "Maybe the Puppetmaster's gone back to the carnival while we were gone."

"No," Hermos insisted. "We've searched the—"

"We're going," Big Boy declared preemptively, stomping off in the direction of the carnival, "and that's final."

Hermos staggered back, watching, dumbfounded, as his companions one by one fell in line behind the marching midget. Setting his jaw, Hermos snatched an extra torch from one of them and snorted. Before the ridge had even emptied, the man-giant lifted his two torches high and struck out on his own path, heading deeper into the woods. He refused to look back. In but a few heartbeats, the others had marched out of sight and out of earshot.

Muttering prayers to his gods, Hermos pressed along warily. His eyes strained to check every knoll and gully in the landscape about him. As he strode deeper into the woods, the forest floor slowly rose, and he found himself mopping his sweaty brow with an equally sweaty arm. In time, the trees thinned, and boulders began to supplant the thistle brakes. Occasionally, Hermos's ears popped, and he wondered at the sensation, straining all the more to hear the sounds around him.

The man with three arms had been right about the dawn's approach. Just as Hermos cleared the timberline and entered a high meadow, the great, blazing orb of the sun lifted, enormous and soundless, from the rugged mountains on the horizon. Walking through the meadow toward the sunrise, Hermos reached a cliff.

"Great Qin-sah."

The morning landscape stretched out below him. The mountains rankled, dark and misty beneath the drowsy sun. Their massive folds of blue-black rock reached out to the eastern corners of the world.

Hermos's throat tightened, and he blinked his wide, aching eyes. The smoldering torches fell from his trembling hands and, though he had not intended it, he dropped down to sit on the boulder beneath him. The cold, hard stone felt reassuring against his skin. He could not remember ever seeing the world beyond the carnival. It was beautiful and wide . . . fearfully so.

As Hermos caught his breath, he noted, in the valley below him, the tiny rooftops of houses and shops. They spread out to fill the gorge in the mountain range beyond. From this height, the houses looked like clumps of clinging lichen on a dark stone.

L'Morai.

"He's down there," Hermos muttered. He peered at

the commotion in one of the streets. Citizens were lining up, their brilliant red cloaks shining in the sun. As Hermos's gaze wandered along a few more streets, he saw a tide of red-cloaked townsfolk rolling toward a bridge. Atop the bridge, which arched a raging, turgid river, stood rows upon rows of the men in crimson jackets. And more columns formed as he watched, metal glittering amongst them.

These were not mere citizens. They were soldiers. And they were massing for war.

*   *   *   *   *

Marie sighed as she felt the warm morning sunlight on her face. She eased her grip on the woolen blanket bundled about her shoulders. The night of terrors was over. Despite the gradual heat of the rising sun, the air at the rim of the amphitheater where she sat was still cold as the night. "Cold, even with all the fires," Marie mused as she brushed charred wood from the arena's stone rail.

"What was that?" Valor asked dully, yawning and stretching, awakened by her words. He shifted, sitting up beside Marie on the cold bench of stone.

"Nothing," Marie dismissed, inhaling in the ash-heavy air. "It's a fine morning."

Valor nodded with a wry smile and prodded at the splint on his arm. "We survived the night. I guess that makes it a fine morning."

Marie sighed solemnly and her voice grew chill. "What do you see in the carnival this morning?"

The midget eyed her quizzically for a moment, then slid from the bench and stepped to the rubble-strewn rail. At first, he saw only the blood-red sun lifting from the horizon. Shading his eyes, he noted the carnival grounds spread out below. They were in ruins. Smoke still rose in twisting black tendrils from a number of smoldering fires. The largest mound of charred wood and half-melted metal was the Puppetmaster's hovel, but many other booths and shanties had burned in the evening of riots.

"The carnival is in ruins. Shacks and caravans and tents and hovels are smoking wrecks. The freaks have started fires to keep warm, and they huddle about them, laughing." He paused, his voice growing philosophical. "They're laughing, Marie. We may look and smell like vagabonds, but at least we're free. Looks like a whole new order," Valor finished.

"Any gendarmes or citizens about?" Marie asked, her hands tightening once again on the blanket she clutched.

Valor studied the trash-strewn carnival below and muttered, "No. Not a single one."

"Good," Marie said, her back and shoulders easing. "The guards are still at their posts?"

Again came the wry smile. "Well, yes. They've started small fires. Most of the guardposts've got a bunch of folk gathered around. But, suffice it to say, nobody's sneaked through." The midget folded his arms and snorted.

"What is it?" Marie asked.

He tossed her another scrutinizing look, then settled back onto the bench. "The place really *is* in ruins, Marie. You should see it. The people look like . . . garbage . . . like animals dressed in clothes."

"I know," Marie responded heavily, her sightless eyes devoid of expression. "But not for long."

The midget blinked slowly, his eyes wide and disillusioned. "What do we do now?"

"I've been thinking about that all night," Marie replied as she rose, stiffly, from the stone bench. She leaned back against the blackened arena rail. The dawn winds blew through her black hair, separating the tangled clumps. For a long while, she said nothing. Her face was placid and her features fixed. She seemed a statue, gazing into the arena with unseeing eyes.

At last, she spoke. "To stay free, free of the Puppetmaster, free of the gendarmes, free of the l'Morai laws that make our kind, we must raise our own army—a strong and well-trained group of fighters to defend our gates and protect our citizens." She paused. "That's what we've got to become now—citizens, not performing freaks."

Valor's face was lined with skepticism. "But we'll have no money if we don't perform, if the crowds don't line up to see us. We'll starve."

"Nonsense," Marie replied, her voice soft and faraway. "We've got livestock here and all the provisions of the refectory and the supply shed. We've got enough grain to plant the heath. We've got enough cattle and lambs to raise our own herds. There's already a blacksmith here, and a tin-maker, and workers of leather and iron and wax—woodcutters, stablers, glassblowers. . . . We could string together the largest merchant caravan ever to course the heath road, going to whatever villages we can find. After all, we've got the caravans."

"No more shows, no more acts?" Valor muttered, stunned.

"We've got to be real people now, Valor, not puppets," Marie said, her tone growing harsh. "We can't demean ourselves by putting our freakishness on display for gawking foreigners. Those who wish to perform can do so during our own feast days. We'll keep our music and our dance, keep our actors and poets. But we'll have no more farces or burlesque shows. At least not for anyone but ourselves."

Valor scratched his head and said, "It sounds wonderful, sure. But it'll never work. Do you really think you can make a city out of us?"

"Come on, Valor," Marie sighed, patting his shoulder. "We threw out the Puppetmaster and the patrons last night, tasks most would've thought impossible. We can make us a city, too."

Crossing his healthy arm over the splinted one, Valor said, "Destroying a city is easier than building one."

The capricious curl in the blind woman's lips slid away, and her sightless eyes seemed to bore right through Valor. She faced the morning sun. "Are you well enough to walk?"

"Yes," Valor said, dropping to his feet. "Unless you want me to walk on my hands."

"Go find the trumpeters and bring them up here," she replied without hesitation. "I want them to summon the citizens to the arena. It's time we inform them of their destiny."

* * * * *

Valor scanned the gathered performers, black and ratty in the gray stands of the amphitheater. His throat tightened just looking at the impassive crowd, and he was glad Marie couldn't see them. Otherwise, she might not have done so well.

Marie's impassioned voice rang out from the center of the amphitheater, her words echoing across the silent stands of limestone. Not one performer among the motley assortment had moved, or even offered praise or blame. As far as Marie could tell, she might have been addressing an empty canyon of stone.

Except for the eyes.

She could feel the eyes, hooked into her, drawing her toward them. Fifteen hundred eyes. And, unlike Marie's past arena performances, the crowd today was deathly still.

"By now, we all have told and been told the stories of our origins, how once we were citizens of l'Morai and were turned into freaks. I heard your voices as I spent a sleepless night upon the arena wall. I heard what you were saying to each other. I heard how you felt: shock, anger, fear, resentment. These passions have taken hold of all of us. These passions sparked the fire that brought down our oppressors. These passions kept us awake through the long, dark night, waiting and hoping for a new dawn."

Marie turned toward the sunlight and held her hand out. "The dawn has come. I felt it on my face this morning and rejoiced. Most of you saw the sunrise yourselves. How jealous I am of you—for you will say to your grandchildren and your great-grandchildren, 'I saw the sunrise on the day of our freedom.' And now, that powerful sun will warm our cold hearts, banish the passions of darkness that wrought our chaotic escape, and kindle in us a new passion.

"From this moment forward, the word freak shall no longer be a term of derision, a weapon of our enemies. If we are the freaks, than to be a freak is to be free! Freaks are no longer the dispossessed, the unloved, the unlovable. We, the freaks, now possess our own destinies, now embrace one another. By virtue of our freedom and our choice, we will stand together against the folk of l'Morai. We will work together, eat together, fight together . . . and together we will forge a new society, a just and good society. From this moment forward, we must take up the torch of hope and freedom and justice—a beacon the folk of l'Morai dropped long ago— and hold it high to illuminate the world."

Her echoing cry met with modest applause, the sound reverberating through the arena like the patter of summer rain.

"No longer will we bear names of ridicule, or struggle under the yoke of hatred. Now, we will call each other citizen and equal. No longer will we be forced to bare our bodies and souls to the gawking eyes of others. Now, we will work hand in hand at honest toils, strengthening our backs and whetting our minds for knowledge.

No longer will we live in fear of a murderer, of a monster roaming our streets and slaying our folk. Now we will guard each other from the murderers without, we will cherish the lives of our fellow citizens, for we remember at what great cost they were bought!"

The ovation now was strong, girded up by happy shouts.

"Ours will be a city without oppressors, without injustices, without murders. A starving woman will need no money to feed herself and her children. An injured man will not be relegated to the ditches and the rats that live there. A fearful child will not have only one set of parents to comfort it, but the whole community of the free."

Marie paused, and, rather than the expected ovation, angry shouts rang out—angry shouts and the jingling of massive chains.

"Clear the way," came the growling cry of a brute squad member. "We caught this here murderer—Felix the hunchback. He done slain Kougan the ogre, and we wants justice."

THIRTEEN

The shouts of the brute squad reverberated through the auditorium, past rows of shocked performers. Marie's voice caught in her throat, and her face went very white. The front row of carnival workers began to stand, leaning forward to gawk at the grim procession.

The group of captors was led by a stocky man with a heavy brow and an anvil-like jaw. He held aloft a guttering torch in one hand and a broad jangling chain in the other. As he walked, he shouted, "Behold Felix, the murderer of Carnival l'Morai. Behold the murderer!"

The chain the man held draped back to a weary, trudging hunchback. The hunchback's shoulders, black with bruises, bore an oxen yoke. His shirt had been ripped away from his neck and dangled now about his knees. He staggered forward, nearly stumbling under the weight he bore.

The captors to either side of the hunchback yanked on the yoke to pull him upright. The chain drew taut about the prisoner's neck for a moment, and he stumbled, gasping for air. The brute behind him, a younger man, braced the prisoner's armpit and helped him gain his balance. As the chain loosened about the hunchback's neck, he released a weary sigh, which echoed, plaintive and pathetic, through the shocked arena.

Before the cry could die away, the man at the head of

the procession cried out, "Behold, the slayer of Carnival l'Morai!"

"Kougan was just an ogre," came the shrill shout of a man in the crowd. "What's wrong about killing—"

" 'Just an ogre'?" an angry roar interrupted. The people in the stands turned about to see a hulking, gray creature rise up beside one of the aisles. His arms were each as great in girth as an entire man, and his tiny eyes peered suspiciously about. "We're citizens now! The blind woman said there'd be no more murders. Here's one right now!"

A carnival pleasure maid stood up, tossing a coal-smudged silken veil over her shoulder. "I seen the way Kougan treated Felix—an' all the rest of us, for that matter. He had it comin', if you ask me. 'Twas kill or be killed."

The gray ogre pointed a blunt finger in the woman's direction. "You always hated ogres."

"Let him go!" came the man's shrill voice again. He stood up. It was Mort, the hostler—a cranky old expert with horses and cattle. "What right have you to chain up another citizen? What right have you to take one of my yokes?"

More freaks stood up to speak, their voices mixing with the protests of the brutes in the procession.

Marie gritted her teeth and released a sudden, insistent shout that squelched all of the voices. "Quiet! Quiet, all of you! This isn't the time for a trial. And, in *our* city, people won't be tried by angry mobs! This is just what I would have expected from citizens of l'Morai, but you folk should be better than that." Marie waved her hand in the direction of the halted procession. "Unchain him and take him under guard to his quarters. Sit with him there—and don't lay a hand on him until we can set up a proper trial!"

The head captor dropped the chain to his side, stomped once on the sandy ground, and shouted,

"You're not even going to lock him away in a cage? What if he tries to kill us? I tell you, we have here the killer of Morcastle and Borgo and Panol and Banol, and a thousand others. It's not the Puppetmaster, who you killed to take control. It's this hunchbacked monster!" he cried and yanked twice on the chain.

"Only a fair trial will tell," Marie answered, her voice cold and commanding. She wore a calm, regal expression, but her hands were balled in white-knuckled fists.

"What right have *you* to hold trials against *us*?" the harlot screamed out in anger. "What right have any of us over any others?"

"Don't you see?" Marie implored. "We're not talking about rights. We're talking about survival. We've got to cling to one another, otherwise we'll end up killing each other. Then we'll all be murderers. We can become monsters and animals, as the people of l'Morai believe us to be, or we can become citizens ourselves. It is our choice," she said, raising her hands toward the multitude. "If one of us dies, we are all diminished and endangered."

As though he hadn't heard a word she spoke, the brute with the heavy brow asked angrily, "So which is it? The cage for the murderer, or freedom?"

"Neither, yet," Marie responded, exasperated. "Our new city hasn't even been founded, and you're talking about executions? We have greater matters to tend to."

"Greater matters than murder?" the ogre in the stands called out furiously, pounding his enormous feet on the stone aisle.

"Yes!" Marie shouted. "One murder is terrible. But if you continue with this, you will kill us all."

"Words!" the ogre bellowed belligerently. "All who want the murderer to die, follow me!" He took a broad, ambling step down the stairs, heading for the sandy arena floor far below.

The crowd was on its feet. Some performers pressed

toward the ogre; others tried to head him off; still others drew back in fear.

"Wait!" Marie cried, though her voice was lost to the thronging clamor of the mob.

"All those to defend Felix, follow me!" cried Mort of the stables, standing atop his stone seat and waving his arms. A great mass of the crowd split off and shifted toward him. Mort gestured for them to follow and lurched down the benches toward the arena center.

The stands were churning with freaks, clambering and shouting, pushing and fleeing. Fights erupted, dragging in even the few who were still seated.

Marie shouted out again, "Wait!" but could hardly hear her own voice over the roaring crowd.

Freaks were now dropping from the first row of seats down to the sandy floor, some hanging, some leaping and rolling. The brute heading the procession pulled on Felix's chain, trying to drag him toward the stairway where the gray ogre descended. Felix dug in his heels, even though it tightened the yoke about his throat. The youth behind him struggled to unfasten the throttling chain.

The gray ogre vaulted from the stands, and in two loping leaps reached the shuddering prisoner. The ogre's massive hand balled into a fist and swung, thrumming past the chains and guards. His knuckles smashed Felix full in the chest. The crack of ribs sounded, and the hunchback tumbled backward, his yoke tracing odd curves in the air as he flew. The chain ripped itself from the fat-browed captor, who cried out in alarm and pain. Laughing blackly, the gray ogre sprang after his prey. He clenched his fists for another strike as the tide of freaks converged on him. His arm lurched back like a metal siege weapon preparing to strike. His muscles bundled like springs.

He shrieked as a burning pain spread across his muscled midsection. Reeling backward, the ogre peered down. Mort had thrust a jagged, burning timber into his stomach. The blackened wood had penetrated little, but burns formed red ribbons on his stomach. Seizing the unburned end of the log, the ogre rammed the narrow hostler out of the way.

One pounding step brought the monstrous creature again to where the hunchback lay, tangled in chains and the unwieldy yoke. The ogre drew his foot back to kick the little twisted man, aiming up into the opposite stands.

Marie appeared before him.

Arching his back and spinning, the ogre narrowly missed smashing her with his tree-trunk leg. His off-balance kick brought him crashing to his back amid scurrying carnival workers. The blunt thud of impact knocked his breath out as clouds of sand whirled in a circle around him. Before he could lift his aching body, he realized that the blind woman was standing on his chest. Her face was red as blood, her expression livid.

"He's dead! He's dead already! You snapped his neck when you hit him the first time! Isn't that enough for you?" She lifted her face toward the crowd that had gathered. "Isn't that enough for all of you? We've got our execution out of the way, haven't we? We've got a body for our cornerstone now, don't we? We can build our city now. Thank you, Felix the Hunchback, for being our sacrifice. Let's hope your blood blesses rather than curses this soil."

"There will be more blood," came a dull, deep voice from the hushed crowd. It was Hermos. The man-giant approached Marie and, without raising his voice, said, "An army is massing in l'Morai."

* * * * *

"No—tighter," Hermos blurted. He picked up one of the makeshift spears leaning against the arena's inner wall. The still-hot head of iron wobbled at the end of its shaft. Hermos cast a dubious glance down at the group of boys clustered there. With one hand, he undid the knot that held the spearhead in place and stripped off the leather band. Shaking it out to unravel it, he began relacing the head, wrapping it in a crisscross fashion. Finishing, he threaded the end beneath the leather band and cinched it down tight. He then shook the spear back and forth. The spearhead remained solid and straight.

"See?" he asked his young crowd, who all nodded sullenly. Hermos placed the spear back against the wall. "Restrap these."

"Hermos!" came a shout from the arena stands. It was Valor, motioning to him with his good hand. "Marie wants to see you."

Hermos nodded, taking one last look at the weaponry that lined the arena wall. They had a few real weapons: bows and crossbows, swords and maces. But many others had been cobbled together beneath the hot midday sun. They had constructed slings and bolas from tack and harness, clubs and quarterstaves from the wood they could salvage in the carnival, and chain flails from every link they could scrounge. Most of all, though, the freaks were armed with weaponlike tools: hammers, sickles, axes, flails, pitchforks, hoes, billhooks, picks, shovels, branding irons, shepherd's crooks, and the like. The whole inner wall of the arena bristled with them. A pair of boys carrying skins of poison and small brushes were circulating among the weapons, painting their edges with the black concoction.

Grunting in grim satisfaction, Hermos started up the stairs into the stands. He rose six steps at a stride, passing workers who struggled to hoist a massive iron kettle up the long flight of stone stairs. Hermos noted three other kettles on the rim of the arena, set in place above three of the four entrances. Each rested on a rickety frame of iron bars, salvaged from the wreckage of the Puppetmaster's hovel. Stacks of firewood lay beside the kettles and lines of buckets led up to them. Even now, down below, the gray ogre and other muscular workers were moving giant water troughs to the base of the bucket lines. Hermos nodded appreciatively: the water for the animals would also fill the siege kettles.

He reached the top row of the arena and walked along it to where Marie sat. Valor was there, too, standing beside the rail, his splinted arm resting on it.

"How does it look?" Marie asked Hermos as he halted to sit on the rail.

"Good," Hermos said simply.

Marie smiled, shaking her head and laughing mildly. "I'm glad to hear such a concise report." She placed her white, trembling hand on his knee and said, "If I'd wanted an in-depth account, I would have asked someone else." Marie sighed. "Besides, Valor has already told me the details." Her blind eyes seemed to scan the distance. "How soon do you think they will attack?"

Hermos's eyes darkened. He glanced out across the high heath and the mountains beyond. "Tomorrow night, for sure. Maybe tonight."

The smile on Marie's face faded, and she began to bite at her lip. "Tonight, perhaps?"

"Perhaps."

Crossing her arms over her chest, Marie said to Valor, "Go and spread the word to stop stockpiling stones and rubble for throwing off the walls. First, let's seal the entrances with a rubblework wall."

The midget's face was red beneath the sun, and his eyes drew to squinting slits. "We may run out of mortar before we run out of rubble."

Marie nodded. "Send out the scavengers to find more. They've worked miracles so far." As the midget rose to deliver her messages, Marie added, "And get all the livestock in before they seal off the entrances.

Afterward, everything gets lifted in by platform and pulley."

Valor nodded. "I'll make sure it happens."

As he left, Marie turned to the man-giant. A wry, almost angry grimace crossed her lips. She shook her head. "You got any gods in your pantheon who'll listen to us now, to the freaks?"

"Yes," Hermos replied. "Tidhare."

Marie clutched the stone seat. "He's sort of a freak, too, isn't he? Yes, he'll listen. I think Qin-sah has abandoned us."

"Don't say that," Hermos replied. His sunken eyes studied the distant horizon. "Qin-sah's ears are sharp."

"Well," Marie said, blushing slightly, "whomever you pray to, pray the armies don't attack tonight. The rubble-work walls will still be half-soft."

"Yes," Hermos noted, his eyes straying to the work crews at the entrances. The meaty scent of stew rose up for a moment on the wind, and Hermos eyed the steaming kettles in the center of the arena.

Marie smacked her forehead. "I should have told him to make sure the workers eat. They've got to have strength left for the battle."

"They'll eat," Hermos said. He slipped from the rail and seated himself beside the blind woman. She seemed small and fragile next to his looming frame. She was no longer the orator, the general of the freakish nation, but only the blind juggler. Hermos set his arm around her. She stiffened for a moment. Then, releasing a tiny sigh, leaned against his tall, gaunt frame.

"Do you think, Hermos, that Tidhare can hear us?" she asked, her voice small against the heath wind. "Or, do you think the other gods have already tied his ears and stuffed his mouth?"

Hermos shuddered slightly, his expression blank and somber. He drew her to his side. A shrill neigh rose up from a frightened horse in the stable below.

Marie continued, "Perhaps Qin-sah will save us, if only for the horses' sake."

"Shush," Hermos said, setting a finger to her lips.

Laughing humorlessly, Marie stood up and sloughed off the man-giant's arm. She approached the rail and set her slender hands onto the charred rubble there. The wide heath and the triangular mountaintops beyond reflected in her white and sightless eyes.

"How long has it been, Hermos? A fortnight? A month? I can't remember when this whole thing began. What have we gotten ourselves into? We chased a murderer and caught a war. In the name of escape I've led everyone to doom. And my dream city is built on a grave. It was the war that saved us, you know; it was the approaching armies that kept us from killing each other. Maybe we need the Puppetmaster after all: its better to have him kill us one by one than break into factions and kill ourselves."

Hermos stood and hovered behind Marie, his arms reaching out to comfort her. A chill wind swept between them, lifting Marie's black hair from her shoulders. A pang flared through Hermos's giant heart: Marie looked like a china doll, pale and fragile and beautiful.

A harlequin in filthy tights approached them. "Marie, we can't get anyone to work the well."

She whirled about, her face fierce and iron-hard. "Damnit. The boiling water's what'll guard the rubble walls long enough for them to set. Doesn't anyone want to survive the night!"

* * * * *

As evening came, the sandy floor of the arena bustled with activity. The odor of sweat and fear filled the air, mixed with smoke and harsh laughter and crude jokes. On one side of the arena, a painted harlot served supper. Minstrels and harlequins sat beside freaks and hawkers; an ogre and a dwarf ate from the same bowl; two harlots told bawdy jokes to the midget contingent. Marie's army was eating, singing, juggling, telling stories, wringing harsh, defiant guffaws from their anxious fellows.

On the opposite side of the arena lay a broad field of cots and beds and mats, where at least two hundred of the performers lay bundled in fitful sleep. Their ghosty breath rose white from them, whirling into the cold night air.

Only the horses and sheep were under cover, two or three per stall in the crowded stable beneath the stone seats. They champed and stomped, slurping from the troughs that lined the walls and gorging themselves on piles of hay. Their stink poured out into the arena at large, and, consequently, the entrance to the stables enjoyed clear passage.

Nearby, lanterns beamed over long tables. There, Marie and a group of amateur generals pored over hastily drawn maps and battle plans. A steady stream of scouts and messengers, most of them children or members of the midget coalition, brought news from the heath road, the mountainside, and the moorlands below.

"Still no sign of movement on the road," croaked a midget messenger to Marie.

She nodded toward him, then granted him a fleeting, appreciative smile. "That's good news. I want to get some screens and shelters set up down here before the arrows start flying. Have you gotten a glimpse of the army?"

"No," the midget replied, snapping the response with a militaristic relish. "All reports indicate, though, that they're still gathering and drilling outside the Council Hall."

"Now's the hour they should be attacking," Marie mused aloud. "The night gets shorter from here on out.

They'd not be drilling if they intended to attack tonight."
Marie's expression hardened, "You've got damn sharp
eyes."

"Damn sharp," the midget repeated proudly.

"See if you can get any closer to that council chamber—or if you can't, find someone who can. I want to
know how many archers they've got, and how many
pikemen. I want to know if they're bringing a ram, or
ladders, or grapples."

"You want me to get close enough to hear their
plans?"

"If you can," Marie said grimly. "But don't take any
foolish risks. We need every warrior we've got when the
armies march on us, and we don't want their discovery
of spies to trigger them to march any sooner."

The midget grabbed hold of her hand and shook it
vigorously. "I'll tell you what gods they're praying to."

Marie smiled and allowed herself a laugh as the messenger charged away into the bustling arena. Hearing
his footfalls retreat toward the pulley platform, Marie
said to her generals, "How far is the gate from the
arena?"

A round-faced glassblower in a greasy smock leaned
on the maps. He pointed toward the round arena and
the roughly sketched gate along the heath road. "Just
over three hundred yards, if I paced it right."

"Just out of bow range," Marie noted flatly. "Any way
we can defend it?"

"No point," said another general, a square-jawed
hypnotist. "The ditch along the heath road will prevent
them from crossing except at the gate, 'less they throw
planks over it. Anyway, the south, east, and north sides
of the carnival are open to the heath. Only a hedgerow
stands between the heath and the carnival. We can't
defend from the hedge, nor the gate, neither."

"So, the arena's our best hope," Marie said with a
nod. "Thank Tidhare it's limestone and granite."

"Tidhare?" asked the glassblower.

"God of the Freaks," Marie explained without pause. "Deaf and dumb and deformed like us."

The hypnotist blinked solemnly. "Praise be to Tidhare."

*   *   *   *   *

Marie sat drowsily at the table, her limp hands resting on a crinkly pile of the maps her generals had sketched through the night. The sun was going down again, and the cold shadows of evening had already welled up and engulfed her. She shivered. She wished she had a blanket, but was too exhausted to find one.

The ceaseless thunder of her heart had slowed, quieting to a dull rumble. Likewise, the frenetic clamor of the freaks had eased as each performer found his or her place in Marie's army. They had spent two days preparing for the war; panic had given way to patience.

During the day, the midget scout Marie had sent indicated that workers could scavenge the carnival grounds for planks and wooden frames. They did so, lifting them via pulley to the top of the wall. There, other workers assembled them into boxy redoubts where the archers could fire and reload their crossbows without fear of being hit by arrows. They also set up small barracks, a mess hut, a shelter for the well, and tunnels to protect the bucket lines from missiles. The food was stockpiled; the water was drawn; the performer-soldiers rested.

They were ready for war.

Marie felt the tug of a small hand on hers, and the voice of Valor spoke. "You should get some sleep. Everything is prepared."

Marie shook her head grimly. "We're not prepared. We've been granted a day's reprieve from our sentence, thanks be to all-gracious Tidhare—" she added with gentle sarcasm "—but the sentence will come down all the same."

Valor looked about, his eyes fuming. "Listen to yourself. You need rest. If somebody else said what you just said, you'd slap his face, knock him over, preach about freedom and responsibility. Do I have to do the same to you? I'd rather slap you than let you go on like this."

"Save your sentiments," Marie said irritably. "The sun is setting. We both know that's the most likely time for an attack."

"You've forced everyone else to lie down for at least two hours today, whether they could sleep or not. And though some of them griped, just like you, they all felt rested and hopeful because of it," Valor said, lifting his hand to slap her. "What kind of example are you setting? If anyone else acted this way, we wouldn't have an army!"

Marie waved him off and rose. "All right, all right. I'm going to bed."

Valor smiled, leading her toward the barracks.

A scout in tattered robes approached them. "The army of l'Morai marches," was all he said.

Marie drew her hand away from Valor, and her weary face grew stern. Whirling about, she stepped onto the chair where she had been sitting, and then onto the tabletop.

"To arms! To arms!" she shouted through cupped hands, her clear, impassioned voice ringing through the arena. "The army of l'Morai is on the march. This is our night of liberation!"

* * * * *

The noise of running feet and barked orders and sloshing buckets had dissipated by the time they heard the drums of l'Morai. On the moaning heath road they came—distant and dark, children of the deepening night. The sentries shifted and mumbled prayers to their new god, Tidhare.

Marie had withdrawn all the scouts and messengers when she learned the force was marching. She wanted everyone within the walls before the attack. But with scouts inside, no one knew the march formation of the approaching army. No one knew who led them, or when and where they planned to attack. They only knew that the siege army numbered at least two thousand, with five hundred archers. Marie's midget scout, sent out one final time to the city, had never returned.

The drums sounded again.

The rhythmic beat was nearer now, mixed with the distant, heavy tread of booted feet. Marie stepped to the rim of the arena and listened. The rattling cadence echoed from the gorge walls on the heath road. "Still about a mile off," she murmured aloud, running her hand through her black hair. "At least a score of drummers."

"What?" a guard who stood near her asked. His makeshift breastplate and greaves rattled dully as he edged toward the supreme commander.

Marie shook her head. "At least twenty drummers. My guess is that they wouldn't waste that many men to drums unless they had five hundred warriors."

"Yes," the young man groaned quietly, a hand straying up to his fire-scarred features.

"Don't listen to the drums, soldier," Marie commanded suddenly. "The drums'll unnerve you, hypnotize you with the rhythm, fill your head with marching feet and shouted commands. Shut them out."

The man snapped to attention.

A mild smile played about Marie's lips.

The drums sounded again, louder, without the echoes of stone walls. The heath wind carried to them the stomp of feet and the toil of wagon wheels.

"Look down the road, soldier, and tell me what you see."

The soldier turned away from the commander and gazed down the highroad. He muttered, his voice quavering, "There'd been a kind of fiery glow a while back, and now I can see the torches individually."

"How many?" Marie asked.

The soldier replied. "They stretch out from about a quarter-mile down to the gorge. I'd guess about twenty, so far."

"Does every warrior have a torch?"

"No," the young man replied, straining his eyes toward the road, "too far apart for that. One in every ten, maybe."

"Two hundred men so far," Marie mused aloud. "If the scouts were right, that means another three hundred will be coming through that gorge. Who's leading them up?"

"A pack of drummers. Looks like about ten at the head, and another ten or so back a quarter-mile. In front of the drummers, there's a dark form walking. Probably the general, but I can't quite make him out."

Marie stiffened. The guardsman cast a concerned eye on her, but she said, "Wait till they reach the gate. We'll see then."

Nodding, the guard faced the string of lights along the heath road. All the guards were watching, their young faces blanched, their feet shuffling on the ash-strewn parapets. No one could distinguish who led the army, but everyone saw now what made the toiling noises. A giant ram.

The massive siege weapon rolled heavily down the road, borne on four sets of wheels, and drawn by six stout war-horses. The shaft of the ram was a great tree, some ten feet in diameter, and its massive head was gleaming steel, reflecting the golden tongues of flame all about it. The ram moved along in the midst of the marching men, a ridged segment of the snaking army. As it drew nearer, the guards on the arena wall gasped and pulled back, staggered by what they saw.

The steel head of the ram bore the face of Marie.

Her lovely, well-turned features, her long hair, her glowing, sightless eyes.

"It's you," the young guard murmured to the commander. "The ram has your face." He stared at her impassive, iron-hard features, looking for incredulity and fear. But Marie was silent and still. Only the slow clench of her jaw betrayed any emotion. The guard looked back to the road as she spoke.

"Forget the ram. Who's leading the army?"

The army had just reached the gates of the carnival, and suddenly, the identity of the black-garbed general was clear.

The Puppetmaster. Despite the burns, despite the knives, despite the pursuit through the forest, the man lived. He didn't so much walk as propel himself forward with spasmodic jerks and surges. Black woolen bindings wrapped him, swinging with each shambling step, and, beneath them, white gauzy bandages covered his body.

"It's the Puppetmaster," the young guard whispered, his throat bone dry.

"I expected as much," Marie replied quietly.

The Puppetmaster waved the drummers behind him to a halt. The army pulled up short, marching in place. Then, trudging forward, the Puppetmaster reached the closed and barred iron gate of the carnival. It was the first time those gates had been closed in decades. He fastened his hands on the wrought iron, and his arm and shoulder muscles began to flex.

Along the arena wall, a line of archers lifted their longbows, aiming up into the dusky sky. The leader gestured for his bowmen to wait, then loosed his own arrow. The string snapped, and, with a hissing whine, the shaft arced through the dark air. It embedded in a toppled caravan some fifty feet short of the gate. Gritting his teeth in frustration, the leader motioned for his bowmen to hold their fire.

The Puppetmaster hadn't even looked up when the arrow struck. He tightened his hold on the gate, leaned back and pulled. The wrought iron squealed and moaned in complaint, bending ever so slightly. The Puppetmaster yanked harder, releasing a feral scream that echoed through the arena. The iron bolts of one gate pulled loose from the cement post. The gate crashed loose, falling into the carnival grounds with a raucous clang.

The young guard beside Marie muttered fearfully, "It's like the fire only made him stronger." He glanced toward his general, whose expression still had not changed. Swallowing hard, the soldier said, "Well, at least the estimate of five hundred men was right."

"No," Marie said calmly. "Look out to the east."

His brow furrowing quizzically, the guard craned his neck to see over the wall of the arena. He started.

There, moving without torches and without drums, was a black army, as large as the one on the road. They had come up, silent and dark, through the heath forest.

"There's another army positioning itself in the north," Marie added coldly.

"No." The guard squinted to make them out. "How do you know?"

"I can hear them," Marie replied, "and I can feel their souls. A thousand souls."

All three armies were moving. The Puppetmaster led his contingent through the gate, just out of longbow range, and formed them into a thick crescent that encompassed the southern and western edges of the arena; the armies that marched through the eastern forest spread out in similar arcs to the east and north. Only when all the warriors were positioned did the torches in the two dark armies blink to light. In a matter of moments, the arena was encircled by an unbroken ring of flickering fire. And the circle tightened.

The captain of the archers shouted for his crew of amateur longbowmen to nock and raise their weapons. The ring of soldiers outside the arena drew closer still. One by one, the archers raised their weapons toward the night sky. The captain held his hand aloft, preparing the signal. The armies were not quite in range.

A creaking clatter filled the air, followed by a shuddering boom. The army to the south had entered the fringes of the carnival and began toppling caravans to provide shelter for their archers. Again came the sound, and again, rattling through the stone arena. The first row of l'Morai's archers dropped to their knees behind the toppled wagons. On a silent cue, the drums that surrounded the arena broke into a thunderous roll.

"Damnit," cried the captain of the freak archers, pacing along the wall. Only the first rank of bowmen below were within range, and they already had cover. Fuming, he stepped onto a protuberance of the arena wall and dropped his hand. "Now!"

The twang of bowstrings and whistling whine of shafts overtopped the thunder of l'Morai's drums below. The captain of archers pivoted about on his promontory along the wall. He watched with fearful satisfaction as the arrows and bolts cut like black meteors through the night sky, streaking to the heart of the army below. The shafts descended in a humming mass. Most struck short, clanging on the cobbles or embedding themselves with dull thumps into packed earth. But a few of the rounds swept into the ranks of soldiers. Men cried out in gurgling gasps.

The captain whirled about, triumphant, and called, "Reload!" He watched joyously as the unskilled crossbowmen set their cranks to work and the ragged bowmen nocked arrows. They rose to shoot again. His amateur archers had gotten the upper hand on l'Morai's elite bowmen. The captain's smile faded, though, when he saw his own faint shadow, cast long and huge over the stands below.

Turning, he saw flaming arrows streak up from the ground in thick waves, like a thousand fiery falcons rising, soaring, converging on their prey. It was beautiful and horrible. The captain had no time to move, no time to scream. He heard the hiss of extinguished fire as a hot shaft sank into his throat. Off-balance, he lurched backward and fell soundlessly from the wall, crashing to the stone benches below.

To a man, the guards dropped flat when they saw the approaching storm of fire. Marie, hearing the shafts, shouted into the arena, "Down! Get under cover!" She fell flat, herself.

The arrows descended in a roaring holocaust, clattered and slid across the stone, jabbed into wood with shuddering thumps. From their burning heads, fire began to spread. The few freaks who rose to stamp out the flames were struck down in the rain of arrows. Screams of pain and shouts of fear added their clamor to the noise of the raining fire.

And, suddenly, in the midst of the clangor, a low, ominous voice was speaking. Though the sound was hushed, the voice spread through the burning arena. In the narrow corners and tight shanties, the words resounded. The words of the Puppetmaster.

"Surrender Marie to us, and we will let you live. . . ."

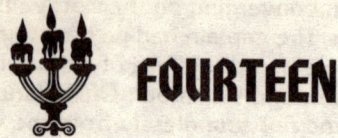 **FOURTEEN**

Even after the ominous pronouncement, the rain of fire neither ceased nor slowed. Marie huddled at the top of the arena, clinging behind the stone rail. The flaming shafts passed overhead with a hellish moan, descended, and sank, shuddering, into the sand. Into the freaks. From the center of the arena came screams of people struck by the burning shafts; the shouts were deafening.

"Into the stables! Everyone!" came a ragged cry.

Marie closed her eyes and nodded. "Yes, go into the stables."

Beside Marie crouched the young sentry who had described to her the enemy's approach. He examined the face of the woman general. Her sightless eyes were wide, but solemn determination showed on her lips. Wiping the sweat from his brow, the young sentry looked past Marie to the corpse of the archery captain. It lay amidst the stone seats, three arrows jutting from its back. Its face had already blackened from the fire.

Unable to bear the sight any longer, the young soldier gazed down to the arena floor below. Already the area was littered with bodies, burning or smoldering, still in death. A dozen freaks had died on their cots in the first wave of arrows. Of the folk that remained, some still darted amongst the burning wreckage, though most clustered at the stable entrance, pushing vainly to get inside.

Suddenly, the crowd shifted, folding in on itself. Out through the gap charged a piebald mare, its eyes ringed with white terror. Another horse bolted through, and another, adding the heavy thunder of their hooves to the thrumming red lightning that fell from the sky. A black stallion, a gray pony, a brown gelding, a white mare.

Swatting the beasts past them with frantic hands, the performers forced their way into the crowded stable.

The beasts charged out into the smoldering ruin of the arena, running beneath the blood-red rain. Wave upon wave of arrows fell, thick enough to obscure the opposite rim of the stadium. The horses galloped in a pointless circle about the inside of the seats, their wild eyes searching for some escape from the inferno. Neighs that were more like screams echoed through the stone walls, accompanied by the percussive pound of the charging feet.

Arrows plunged into the churning herd, sinking through hide into flesh and bone. The dumb beasts ran all the faster, their limping strides tearing up the ground. Some of their hides were on fire now, and the stink of burning hair roiled in smoky white trails behind them.

A black stallion reared, its bleeding eyes searching the smooth, white walls. With a scream from its foam-flecked muzzle, the charger spun about and clambered up the stony steps. Its hooves struck sparks on the rock as it surged upward. A panicked flux of horses followed behind.

Marie spun about, the crackling roar of their hundred hooves sounding like thunder as it split the air. She dropped to her stomach, pulling the young guard down to the ground as well. His crossbow pressed beneath him, the guard looked up with fearful eyes.

The black stallion, its satin coat bristling with burning

arrows, surged up, massive, before him. Then it lifted its ebony forelegs and soared for a moment overhead. Its rear hooves slid past the rim of the arena, bearing the steed into the blazing sky beyond. A final arrow struck with a shuddering thud in the beast's flank. And it was gone, over the wall.

The panicked beasts behind leaped as well, one by one cascading into empty air. A shrill horse-scream rose up over the walls as one creature plummeted, its impact on the ground below reverberating horribly through the arena.

Marie's small hand fastened on the young sentry's shoulder. "Let them go," she whispered, more to herself than to him. Marie's once-lovely voice was now low and ragged with fatigue. "Let them go. They think they will be free."

*   *   *   *   *

The flaming arrows fell in occasional, deadly storms throughout the night, burning to a cinder every scrap of wood—shelter, table, bucket—left exposed. Marie ordered all but a handful of the performers into the stables to wait out the night. Only she and a brave few remained on the walls, blindly shooting arrows and crossbow bolts, and hoping thereby to keep the army back.

On the north rim of the arena, a harlequin crazed by the first hour of flaming arrows recklessly strutted atop the wall, shooting his own arrows in a fevered, cocky show. His companions cheered him on for nearly an hour before he was struck through the ear by a fiery shaft. Jerking comically for a moment, he toppled to the stone floor. The night had seen many other freaks fall, but the loud, sloppy death of this one defiant soul cast a black pall over those left to fight.

The eastern horizon had grown blue-black: four hours

before dawn. The young sentry beside Marie hazarded a glance over the wall. "Looks like we've killed as many of them as they have of us."

"There are more of them," Marie noted flatly, slipping another bolt into the crossbow loader and beginning to crank.

"I'm glad for the stables," the youth noted. It was a weary hope—hope that she might send him there soon. "We'd've lost lots more."

She handed him the loaded crossbow. "We've lost enough."

One more rain of fire occurred before dawn. Then the assault slacked off to only a few, occasional shafts. Aside from the initial deaths, which numbered near fifty, Marie had lost only five men on the wall, each of whom was replaced from among the ranks in the stables. The performers' tenacious resistance, though, did not prevent the army of l'Morai from advancing within a hundred yards of the wall. The ring of siege had tightened.

The l'Morai troops had undoubtedly won the battle of morale: they hung on doggedly to each gain they made, gritting their teeth against the arrows and bolts that fell among them. The freaks, meanwhile, huddled like cattle in the stables.

Brushing off her blood- and grime-coated hands, Marie set off down the stairs.

"Where're you going?" the young warrior asked wearily.

"Going to get you a replacement," Marie said, "and to rally the crowd."

"I'll be waiting."

In the stables below, Hermos looked up as Marie entered the milling throng. Her eyes were sunken in black circles, and she wore a ragged field bandage around her right arm, which had been hit by one of the fiery brands. Her black hair was tangled and scorched, hanging in thick, clumped ribbons. Blood spattered her homespun shirt.

The mutterings and complaints that had echoed through the stables that night came to a quick halt as the tattered general entered. All eyes turned to her, and those who stood or sat in the passageways pulled back to let her through.

A warm, ironic smile crossed Marie's face as the people quieted. "Well," she blurted hoarsely, "we survived the night. And, thanks to the warriors on the wall, we probably killed more of the enemy than they of us."

Scattered applause rang out, dispirited at best.

"How many dead are there?" asked a dour dwarf. "Of ours, I mean." Those in front could see the young woman gather her strength to respond.

"The count is fifty-three," Marie responded, "fifty-three, and all the horses."

A rumble of fear and grief filled the packed stables.

"But they've nearly run out of arrows—flaming ones, at least. And we've got stores left, as well as the arrows of theirs that went out. Now *they'll* be forced to move forward under fire from *us*. The night may have been theirs, but the day is ours."

The responding cheer was weary, but heartfelt.

"How far from the walls are they?" a woman asked over the chorus of voices.

"They began the assault at about two hundred yards. Under cover of the firestorm, they've halved that distance. They're moving forward now by inches, rushing from cover to cover, sometimes trying to push caravans before them."

"We'll shoot their bleedin' legs off!" noted a man in blue tights.

"That's right," Marie laughed, for the first time that day. "They haven't reached the wall, and I don't plan to let them."

"What are our chances?" asked a small boy with a harelip.

Marie faced the child and smiled faintly. "Better. Our chances are better than they were last night, and better than the night before, or the one before that. If brave boys such as you can go out into the arena this morning to salvage any arrows worth saving, and brave adults like those around you can man the crossbows and kettles, I think we have a good chance."

Suddenly, the huge, whispered voice of the Puppet-master began to speak again. "You have seen how the horses died. You have seen how the slow ones among you died. The same will happen to each and every one of you, lest you surrender Marie to us. Once she is in our hands, we will leave you in peace."

Marie's face grew crimson. "That bastard," she muttered, whirling about and pushing her way from the crowd of performers. She stomped out into the sandy arena and faced the north and east, where the Puppet-master's army was entrenched. Seeing that no arrows fell around the blind woman, the crowd poured out of the stable entrance behind her. Marie felt her way along the arena wall to the stairs, and she climbed, her legs and arms pumping furiously. At the top, she approached the guardsman posted there, yanked a hollowed horn from his belt, and slumped down with her back to the wall. She curved the horn up over the rim of the wall and shouted into it.

"You stupid bastard! Only an idiot like you would attack a stone arena with fire! Especially an arena whose canvas cover has already burned down!"

The mob of freaks below, blinking up into the bright, morning air, laughed loudly, fearfully. Some even shouted their own defiant threats.

"You've been here a night and a morning, but I still don't hear you knocking on our door!"

As an angry roar rose up from the armies gathered beyond the arena, Marie gestured for the freaks to rush up the stairs and man the empty crossbows. The ragged multitude surged up the stone steps, and Marie shouted, "You've been shooting arrows the whole night and killed only a handful. But look how many of your folk lie dead." She smiled as the click and creak of loading crossbows filled the air. "Perhaps if you lifted your heads long enough to aim, you might hit something."

At that moment, she gestured for the archers to fire. The shudder and twang of discharging crossbows rang out, followed by strangled cries.

"It's your choice," Marie cried out as the archers slumped along the wall to reload. "Go home to your cheese shops, or go home to your graves."

Her voice was answered by the shriek of arrows, coming again over the wall.

* * * * *

The dead lay three deep along the inner wall of the arena that evening as Marie strode across the sandy pit.

Thooooom . . . Thooooom . . . Thooooom . . .

The Puppetmaster's ram had reached the wall. Freaks hurled stones down on the soldiers who worked it, poured boiling water onto their heads, filled them full of arrows. And for each one that fell, another rushed forward to take his post.

Thooooom . . . Thooooom . . . Thooooom . . .

The sound was relentless, dauntless, as though the arena had a giant, beating heart. Every smash of the ram was followed by a clattering cascade of stone from the bulwarks the freaks had so hastily built.

Thooooom . . . Thooooom . . . Thooooom . . .

Just as relentless were the Puppetmaster's whispered urgings for the folk to surrender Marie. After the tenth such offer, Marie left the arena rim, retiring to the stables. The place stunk of dung and urine, sweat and blood. The surviving sheep milled about in skittish clusters, and the folk leaned or sat or lay against the walls. Marie pushed past the wounded and weak who lingered there and felt her way along the rough-hewn planks that bordered each stall.

"Where is Oreaux the Oracle?" Marie asked one of the inmates.

The old man hacked, spat phlegm, and muttered, "He's down on the end, with his only surviving wife."

Marie nodded distractedly, squeezing the old man's gnarled hand in thanks. She pushed blindly on through the stable. The rumbling complaints of invalids and wounded dissipated as Marie moved past them. She had grown accustomed to this treatment. She was general of the outcasts, their savior when times looked hopeful, their oppressor when times turned grim.

At last Marie reached the spot where the oracle sat. She knew it by the satin veil draped over the doorway. As she drew back the veil with a tentative hand, Marie heard the jingle of small bells attached to its edges.

"Back! Get back!" came a sharp shout from a woman in the stall. "Get out of here!"

"I cannot," Marie began wryly as she stepped into the stall. "Your husband's sight is needed by your blind commander."

"Oh, my pardon, noble leader," said the woman in a musical, exotic voice. It was Satina. The woman approached Marie and dropped to her knees on the straw- and dung-strewn floor. "I thought you were a lamb nosing past the curtain."

"So did the Puppetmaster," Marie replied with an edge of derision.

Satina, crouched humbly on the floor, gestured toward the oracle, Oreaux. The man still sat in the wooden seat where he had been when Marie, Morcastle, and Hermos first visited him. His feet and hands were locked within their respective boxes, and his head in the wooden helm. The oval slit at the front of the helm showed that Oreaux's dark-skinned face had only grown more creased in the last few days. His eyes, too, looked weary: they spun about, as though following the erratic flight of a fly.

"I cannot come to fight for you," Satina said contritely to Marie. "I am the only wife left to him. If I were to die . . ."

"I need a seer, not a soldier." Marie stepped past the crouching woman. She approached the chair of Oreaux, dropped to one knee, and raised her face to the mad prophet. Her voice came in a low whisper, "I need a word from you, sir."

Satina struggled to her feet and set coaxing hands on Marie's shoulders. "Rise up, my general. It is not right for you to kneel here in this filth."

Marie turned toward the gentle woman. Her sightless eyes were brimming with tears. She inhaled deeply and her face became iron-hard. "If he is a true oracle and not a scam artist or a lunatic, I would kiss his feet to hear a word from him." She lowered her voice once again, her hands settling together on a dagger on her belt. "I'm not sure what to do now. It's always come to me before, but not now—I'd open my mouth, and the words would just come to me. Now there's just silence in my head. It sounds like . . . like death."

Satina set her slender, dark hand on the shackled arm of the oracle. "Forgive us, great Marie, but Oreaux hasn't uttered a single prophecy since the war began— since the night of the riot."

Marie's expression darkened. "Is he a fraud then? Is that what you're saying?"

"No," Satina replied, sudden anger in her voice. "Your war has drawn darkness over his mind, over his prophecies."

Marie edged nearer, her hand clutching the man's bony knee in a white-knuckled grip. "Tell him to walk through the darkness, to find out what lies beyond! I must know what to do!"

Before Satina could pry Marie's clenched hand from the man's knee, Oreaux began to convulse. His back arched, driving his shoulders against the chair. His head rattled back and forth in the wooden helm, spasms of pain gripping his face. He began rasping out words—gurgling, nonsensical phrases.

Satina's voice came with a cold finality. "He cannot walk through the darkness."

Marie's face grew quizzical. "Why?"

"Because the darkness is death," Satina replied heavily. "It descended when the riot began and has not lifted to this moment."

"Death?" Marie asked, the color draining from her smudged and bloodied face. "Whose death? His?"

Again Oreaux convulsed, and the spray from his lips struck Marie across the face. She winced and wiped the spittle from her cheek. The prophet's feet kicked furiously inside the boxes, and the throne began to pitch back and forth. Satina, listening to the unintelligible ravings of the man, steadied his tipping seat. In time, the spasms eased, and the stall grew quiet once again.

Satina said, "The oracle speaks of his death, and your death, and mine, and the deaths of every one of us who dwells here. When the riots started, the black curtain descended to cover the whole carnival. The curtain enfolds us all, here in the arena."

Marie shook her head in defeat. The screams of the past night and day echoed through her brain. She thought of Morcastle—dead because of this feud. And she thought of Hermos, the sweet, silent giant. He had such faith in his gods, fairy tales twisted into divinity by the Puppetmaster's tortures. Hermos had faith in Marie as well, and now she was proving as false a friend as Qin-sah. Yes, the man-giant, too, would be dead before the night was over.

"Is there no escape for us?"

The man blurted one, loud syllable, his breath billowing out into the fetid air of the stall.

Satina shook her head sadly, her eyes boring into the blind general. "No. We cannot escape."

Marie's small, white hands folded before her, and she began to wring them nervously. "That's it, then," she observed. "That's it. I can't do anything to save us now." Dusting her hands off, Marie rose. Her heart pulsed ponderously in her breast, and blood shone red in her features. "What should I do now? Hasten the death of the people? Forestall it longer?"

The whispered voice of the Puppetmaster once again echoed through the still air. "Surrender your general to me, all of you. Save yourselves. We only want her. It was she who sparked this war; it was she who pressed you into battle on her behalf; it should be she who pays the price."

Marie listened to the words. Her face had blanched but otherwise betrayed no emotion, as though she were oblivious to the meaning of the Puppetmaster's offer. Then, measuring her words, Marie said quietly, "Ask the oracle if the Puppetmaster's offer is good. Can the people really be saved if I surrender myself?"

Satina studied the face of the blind woman. Despite the bruises and cuts, despite the mud and blood and the blind eyes, a ragged nobility shone in Marie's features. "I cannot ask the prophet that question."

"Ask it!" Marie insisted.

The woman blinked in amazement, then kneeled down beside the oracle and whispered softly into his ear. Silence followed, broken only by the rhythmic boom of the ram outside. Then, abruptly, the prophet's macabre shuddering began again. A scream rose from his lips and pealed out through the crowded stables. Marie waited, her hand clutching the tattered neckline of her chemise.

At last, the oracle was still. Satina bowed in deference

to Marie and said, "If you surrender yourself for us to be saved, Oreaux still sees the black curtain around you."

Marie swallowed hard. "What about the others? What about everyone else? Will they be safe?"

Satina pressed her lips together. "He said he sees the black curtain around *you*."

A man's frantic shout came from the mouth of the stable. "Where is Marie? Where is she?"

"I'm here," Marie called back, her voice quavering slightly.

"Come quick. We need you at the rim right now."

Marie's face hardened. She reached out her small white hand to draw the satin curtain back from the stall entrance, and, in the moment before the bells jingled, she became once again the general of the freaks.

* * * * *

Thoooooom . . . Thoooooom . . . Thoooooom . . .

Hermos squinted into the nighttime air, peering beyond the ram and the soldiers swarming about it. His eyes settled on the distant battlefield, the windswept heath. "I don't see them."

The rotund man crouching beside him pointed to the darksome moorlands beyond. He reached into a grubby pocket on his tunic, drew forth a bit of foul weed, and packed it in his lower lip. "They're out there, they are. Another whole army." He punctuated the statement by spitting into a brackish puddle beside his feet.

Hermos paid no heed, blinking to clear his vision. Now he saw them, black forms moving on the black heath. On any other night, Hermos would have assumed their waggling heads were the tossing tips of the heath grasses. They spread out from the road in the west to the forest in the east, a black army double the size of the current forces of l'Morai. The first line trudged out of the shadowy heath, over the hedgerow, and onto the ruins of the carnival flat. Moonlight showed up a second row, and a third and fourth and fifth. . . . "Great Qin-sah."

"What's happening?" came the anxious voice of Marie, sliding into position beside Hermos.

The man-giant smiled as he peered down at Marie, then turned his attention again to the heath. "Another army."

Marie edged to the wall and leaned wearily against it. "Where are they from? Surely not another army from l'Morai?"

"Can't tell yet," Hermos replied evenly and mumbled a prayer.

The fat man spat another brown glob of the stuff and pointed with an arrow. "They're toppling caravans out there and smashing their way through stages."

Hermos nodded, watching a black mass of the soldiers swarm a shanty in their path and crush it beneath the weight of their tread. He clenched his jaw and looked toward Marie.

As though sensing the attention, Marie said, "Where could they have come from? L'Morai couldn't raise more troops. They've already got every man and boy in the city out there."

The pudgy man leaned closer to the rim and peered out suspiciously. "Dunno." His jaw worked through two or three compulsive chews before he spoke. "Wherever they're from, the l'Morai folk're pullin' back from the wall. That can't be bad news for us."

"Yes, it can," Hermos noted laconically.

Only now did the siege fires light up the faces of the arriving army. The man's mouth dropped open, the wad of weed falling from his lip. The new troops were skeletal—bones hung with rotting flesh and clotted earth. They wore tattered clothes, if any, and were smeared with mud or bloated with water. A breeze off the heath bore their stench up to the arena's rim.

Marie covered her nose, recoiling. "They've raised

the dead. The Puppetmaster still has strings on them. They've raised the dead of Carnival l'Morai."

The human army below retreated, leaving room for the advancing tide of dead. Onward they marched, what little was left of their flesh drooping in flaccid bands from their bones. Ghostly wails began drifting up over the rim of the arena. As the dead advanced, their glowing faces twisted into leering masks, and their laughter became hollow and hellish.

Hermos pulled Marie against him, more because of his own fear than because of hers. He peered narrowly over the rail. There, amongst the shambling multitude of moaning freaks, he saw one greenish figure lope away from the others. Its head was missing. As it lurched into the light, Hermos could see that the head was clutched by the hair in one tremulous hand while the other hand stroked the man's black, waxed mustache.

A moan of dread and sorrow escaped Hermos's lips.

"What is it?" Marie pushed away from the man-giant.

"Morcastle," Hermos replied. "He's with them."

Marie pulled back from Hermos and shouted, "Let me go! I have to stop this!"

"How?" he roared thickly, tightening his grip.

"Let me go!" She smashed her elbow into his side. With a grunt of pain, the man-giant released her. Marie pushed herself to her feet and began feeling her way down the wall. Hermos, too, rose, and scuttled in stooped fear after her.

"Stay down!" he roared.

Marie was heedless. Her hand dragged along the rubble-topped wall until she reached the blackened remains of a rope platform. Stooping, she found the rope coiled at her feet, one end knotted on a stone bench. She flung the other end over the railing and clambered atop the cold stone.

"Stop!" the man-giant shouted, angry now for the first time. "They'll kill you!"

Clutching the rope in her battered hand, Marie murmured, "Good-bye," and rolled from the rail. The rope slid in a burning spiral around her arm and across both palms, but she was oblivious. She little sensed the heart-tearing impact with the sandy ground below, little felt the brutal hands clamp about her arms. Her mind was filled with the mournful cries and prayers of the man-giant.

*   *   *   *   *

The guard slid his blunt fingers into Marie's hair and yanked her face up toward the Puppetmaster.

"As though I could see him," she rasped out sardonically, her throat straining against the cold iron shackle that bound her.

"Silence!" growled another soldier, yanking the chain on her ankles. Marie kicked the ground in response, sending a spray of sand into the guard's face. The warrior, gritting his teeth, drew his arms forward for another brutal yank. He stopped as a dry, croaking laugh began.

The Puppetmaster.

Maudit Sienne, Lord of Carnival l'Morai, stepped from a ring of dirty and weary soldiers and loomed gradually nearer to the captive. His swaying robes created the illusion that he floated above the ground. The smell of charred and rotting flesh swept in a slow wave in front of him, passing over Marie. She turned away in disgust. The Puppetmaster's dry chuckle died away into long, rasping breaths.

"At last," he sighed pleasurelessly. "Marie the Blind Juggler . . . Marie the Blind General. Your folk should be safer without you in charge."

"Call off your troops," Marie demanded vehemently, her raw voice cracking. "You have me now."

"They *are* called off," the man said in a somewhat

offended tone. "The soldiers have withdrawn from the wall and your . . . dead compatriots have dropped where they stood. Dead once more."

Marie shook her head. "But you're still alive."

The Puppetmaster sighed. "You will find, Marie my dear, that I am more your friend than your enemy."

"You murder freaks, you lead living *and* dead soldiers to kill my people, you drag me down here to be executed before them. . . . Forgive my distrust."

"They were my people before they were yours," the Puppetmaster said simply. "And don't worry, you will not be executed down here, before the arena gates. There must first be a trial, as you should know."

The Puppetmaster swooped forward, suddenly only inches away. He seized the sides of Marie's face in his scabrous, charred hands and bent down over her. She tried to break free, but his scaly fingers were strong as iron. She then felt a puffy, blistered harelip press onto her mouth. For one horrible moment, his jagged teeth fastened on her lower lip. Then, abruptly, he pulled away.

Marie spat blood into the man's face. He paused, then stepped farther back. His bony laugh echoed out again.

"Good luck in the Council Hall," the Puppetmaster said in a low, croaking voice.

"You can't win," Marie murmured back through gritted teeth. "You can kill me, but you can't win."

The soldiers jerked on her chain and prodded her with their swords. "Move along! Toward the road!"

Marie ignored the jabs, intent on the muttered commands the Puppetmaster was giving to another soldier.

"Pull all of the soldiers out except a force of two hundred. Set them in encampments about the perimeter of the carnival grounds. If any freaks leave the arena, close in and hunt them down."

Marie whirled about in her shackles and shouted, "You said you'd let them go free!"

The Puppetmaster's voice came in a growl. "I said I'd let them live."

* * * * *

The road to l'Morai was long and rocky, much more so than Marie remembered from her ride in the phaeton a week earlier. A week. She could little believe it herself. It was incredible that the apocalypse could come in a mere week.

As the sounds of the carnival died away behind them, Marie nearly stumbled to her knees, but she caught her balance before going down. Her neck was chained to the rear of the rolling ram, and with every jolt of the siege weapon Marie's collar yanked her forward. Twice already, she had fallen. Both times the stowed ram head, which bore a huge, partially flattened likeness of Marie, peered impassively back at her. After nearly falling a third time, Marie rested her head on the ram's massive chin, now cracked from its impact with the stone wall.

But the respite didn't last long. The soldier behind Marie saw to that. He began pulling her arm chain backward, bruising her wrists and straining her shoulders. The other soldiers responded in kind. They prodded and pinched her and traded filthy jokes about what a chained woman was good for.

By the time the military procession rolled into the city, dawn was reluctantly breaking behind a thick shelf of slate-gray clouds. Runners sent ahead of the army had reached l'Morai during the night and roused the folk to welcome their victorious forces . . . and to pelt the prisoner with mud, dung, and all manner of rotten vegetables.

Marie raised her head and kept it upright, unwilling to bow to the foul hail that fell upon her. With eyes closed, she strode solemnly through the streets.

"Freak," they shouted. "General of Freaks!"

After marching down each major thoroughfare, the parade—swelled by ranks of proud citizens—made its way up the hill toward the Council Hall. Ironically, talk of the hall comforted her: the cold, spare cell; the silence, the stillness; the chance to clear mud and spittle from her face and arms.

But that chance would have to wait. No doubt because of the swelling hatred of the crowd, the Puppet-master called for trial without delay. He flung wide the council doors and ushered the throng inside: "Come in! Come in, friends of l'Morai. Come hear the trial of she who killed your best sons and noblest brothers. The carnival witch stands accused."

 **FIFTEEN**

Two guardsmen forced Marie's right arm into the arm-well in the restraining chair. Gritting her teeth, she pulled and twisted, almost wrenching free. The captain of the guard, a muscled warrior with stubby fingers and foul breath, growled as he fought the arm back down and cinched it into the well with leather straps. He slid a thick plank over the top of the arm-well and clamped it down in its brackets. Marie's hand and forearm were sealed inside the chair. The guards then removed the shackles from her left arm and began wrestling it into place.

Snorting in satisfaction, the captain stepped away from the black wooden chair. He eyed the crowd that was filling the council chamber, then strode to the dark-ened back wall where the councilors' niches were. As he approached the Puppetmaster's seat—now the cen-tral niche, the chamber's seat of power—the smell of charred flesh and decay almost drove him back.

The captain slowed his pace and said, "The prisoner is latched into the restraining chair."

"Good," came the barely audible whisper. "We can-not have a madwoman break free in a crowded hall."

"The chamber should be filled momentarily," the guard said, bowing in accordance with etiquette and awaiting his dismissal.

For long moments, the Puppetmaster offered no response. The rasping sound of his lungs was gathered and focused by the stony arch above him. At last he spoke. "You don't like my odor, do you, Captain Castel?"

The muscular man looked up toward the dark, expressionless form in the niche. His black eyebrows bristled, and, inhaling, he said, "I cannot even detect an odor, sir."

"You are relieved from duty, Monsieur," the Puppetmaster said suddenly. "I have no use for captains who lie to me."

His eyes narrowing, the soldier executed a snapping turn and walked away.

The Puppetmaster rose to his feet and filled the archway around him. The hall was overflowing with citizens; the other councilors had taken their seats. "Good," he said to himself.

Marie was strapped into the chair now, like Oreaux the Oracle: her feet were locked into wooden boxes, her hands and elbows closed within the arms of the chair, her torso strapped to the backboard, and her head encased in a tight wooden helm with an oval opening for her face. The soldiers had only just finished the job when the voice of the Puppetmaster rang out through the chamber and echoed hollowly in Marie's helm.

"All rise and give heed."

The noisome murmurings of the spectators gave way to a rumble of shifting benches and chairs.

"So begins the trial of Marie the Blind Juggler, accused now of treason, riot-rousing, and murder. As the actions have been committed in full light of day before the witness of us all, the accusers in this trial shall be the warriors and citizens gathered herein. In the adjudication of these charges, let all citizens of l'Morai draw near in good faith, those with knowledge of this woman's deeds and misdeeds to testify, and those without to bring fair and impartial judgment unto this case."

"We hear," responded the crowd, their voices ringing as one in the high-vaulted chamber. Once again, the benches and chairs rattled as the folk found their seats.

The Puppetmaster moved from the darksome niche, stepping down the narrow ring of stairs. He drifted across the dais, emerging from the darkness behind it. His croaking voice rose up again. "As this case is unusual, so shall be this trial. Insofar as the accused is now known to every soul of the land, Marie would not be fairly represented by any counselor appointed by l'Morai, and therefore shall represent herself. Neither, I might add, shall the accusers have a counselor. In their stead, I shall present a case of accusation. Thereupon, we shall hear testimonies and see proofs from the gathered citizens."

A slight murmur circulated through the crowd, its watery echo playing among the shadowy frescoes on the vault above. The sound had almost died away when a woman near the front released a shocked gasp, and unsettled mutterings filled the room.

The Puppetmaster had revealed his face. Though his amorphous body was still wrapped in the black cloaks, he had drawn the hood from his head. A shaft of midday sunlight struck him.

He was horrifying. His head, twice the size that it should have been, was misshapen and covered with a mass of burns and half-scorched hair. The flames had destroyed the left side of his face. The skin that clung there was black and lined with oozing fluids. Other patches of skin had withered and burned away entirely, exposing a chalk-white cheekbone and a leathery eye unsupported in its socket. Most of the man's mouth had been spared destruction, along with the right side of his face. But the skin there was red and blistered, in some places scarred from more ancient wounds. The eye on that side was healthy, unlike its motionless twin. It peered sharply about, studying the gathered throng, and the blind woman who sat before them all.

Raising a near-skeletal hand into the light, the Puppetmaster drew his hood up again. His dry, crackling voice was quiet beneath the hood, but, in the silent chamber, it carried all the way to the doors. "As all of you know, even before being disfigured by fire, I rarely revealed my face to anyone. But I reveal it today. Those of you who will mock me may do so. The rest of you, look upon me as the symbol of this woman's evil deeds."

The Puppetmaster began to pace, his gait hobbled and pained. Again he spoke, his voice quieter still, and many of the citizens leaned forward and cupped hands behind their ears to hear. "She invaded my home on the carnival grounds, searching for something, I know not what. I found her there and, instead of bringing her to this court, let her go free. She repaid my kindness by plotting with fellow performers to start a riot, burn the top off the arena, drive the paying citizens out, and make my home a pyre around me."

He paused, staggering toward the blind woman in her restraining chair. He laid his long, knobby hand on her shoulder and said, "Have I spoken a lie, my dear?"

Marie was silent, her eyes closed and her lips pressed firm.

The Puppetmaster's hand settled onto the chair back and he shook it fiercely, shouting, "Do I lie?"

"No," came Marie's simple reply.

The Puppetmaster strode away from her, his steps wide and lurching. He toiled down the center aisle of the Council Hall, his crippled legs striking graceless, forceful steps. Halting suddenly, he lifted his arms into the air, tilted his head back, and cried out passionately:

"I am merely a manifestation in bone and blood of what she has done to us all! Her little rebellion has killed our best sons." Moving vaguely forward now, the Puppetmaster pointed into the crowd. "Madame Ferron, it was she who sent the arrows into your son, Phillipe. Monsieur Geisl, it was Marie the Blind Juggler who ordered the boiling water to be poured on the head of Francois." His voice softened and grew quiet, and he gestured to his side. "Mademoiselle Chardonneau, let me beg your forgiveness for sending your brave Hercio against this witch."

The Puppetmaster headed back toward the dais, the crowd murmuring in anger behind him. But his bellowing voice cut them short, coming in hammering phrases that increased in rhythm with each step he took. "All of you who lost your loves in this foul conflict, look now to me! Let *me* bear the image of the destruction that this woman has brought down on us all. Let my ruined face remind you of the horrors that she works on us, of the horrors that lie behind her beautiful visage and egglike eyes."

A stomping of feet and the rough rattle of affirming cries welled around the Puppetmaster as he gained the dais and reached Marie's chair. "But, to fully understand the perverse treacheries she has performed, we must remember what a friend to this state she once was. Staunch citizen, rigorous debater, heartbreaker of many a lad . . . Marie—before she was the freak, the blind, juggling misfit who began a war—was a young woman beloved and trusted by us all. But especially by her dear father, Francis Martinique, the cobbler."

The name sounded hollow and haunting in the wooden hood Marie wore. It grew louder, as if it were an insistent wind moaning through a tightly closed door. The name unsettled her, illuminating some long-dark, long-forgotten corner of memory in her mind. "No, not now," she whispered to herself, a minute tear threatening. "Not now."

The Puppetmaster's voice intruded into her thoughts, "She was not called Marie then. Her name was Yvette. . . ."

Images began to flash through the young woman's

mind, recollections from a time when she could see. A time before the supposed Fever. With a little moan of pain and fear, Marie stopped resisting the wind of memory, letting the door blow open wide. The tiny tear welled in her eye and fell.

*   *   *   *   *

Yvette was young, barely eighteen, that cool autumn morning as she sat with her father. Despite the chill wind in the quiet street beyond, the air within the sun-soaked brick courtyard was warm and comforting. Father's ebony rocking chair creaked gently, contentedly, beneath him.

"Why must you work today, Father?" Yvette asked, drawing a lock of her long, black hair behind her ear. The day was fine—a royal blue sky with thin, quicksilver clouds.

The man didn't look up from the thick piece of leather in his hands. He was carving out another shoe sole, his aged fingers guiding the curved blade of his knife. A tendril of sweet smoke rose up from his battered pipe. It twisted about his bristly gray mustache and eyebrows, lingering for a moment on his weathered skin, and then dissipated into the brisk air.

Yvette's brown eyes fixed unrelentingly on the old man. Straightening the embroidered hem of her black woolen dress, she leaned forward and touched his narrow knee. "Answer me, Papa."

He looked up a moment from his work, smoke wreathing his gray hair. "*You* are working today, too." His crescent eyes betrayed the smile that his mustache hid. Eyes the color of the sky.

"But I *must*, Papa. There is far too much to do to stay home," Yvette insisted, as she had a hundred times before. "But you, you have a shop full of shoes, with better prices and workmanship than any other cobbler in l'Morai. You deserve to rest one day per week."

Taking a last long draw from his pipe, the old man set it aside, along with the brown leather and his knife. He placed his hand on hers and patted it, smiling sweetly. "Why don't you give up your work? It's hard work, even for a man, and it frets away your soul. The money means nothing—I have a shop full of shoes, like you said. And the lads can never find you. The ghost of your mother would rest much easier—"

"If I stayed home," Yvette nodded with a smile. "I know, Papa. But Mother would also understand that I enjoy what I do. It doesn't take the soul out of me. It puts it in." She looked about at the crimson ivy that lined the courtyard and at the waving patches of late flowers. "Gardening was enough for Mama, and cobbling for you. But I want more."

"Well," the man said, the smile on his face fading, "it takes the soul out of me for you to do what you do." He again drew the leather toward him, placed his pipe in his mouth, and began to cut.

Yvette frowned, a pout she had perfected at age three and not given up since. She watched the old man's face; the sickle-shaped dimple in his cheek deepened. He was trying to pretend he didn't notice her pout—trying and failing. A twinkle of resignation appeared in his azure eyes.

Yvette smiled broadly, stood up, and stretched in the sunlight. The cool air felt wonderful against her skin, and the day's work beckoned.

"Dear Father," she said as she finished stretching, "though I hate to disappoint you, I must be going." She leaned down and kissed the side of his mouth that did not hold the pipe. Capriciously blowing smoke from the pipe bowl into his face, she stood up again and said, "Your daughter will be l'Morai's most famous woman by the time she returns this evening."

A sad expression hung beneath his white mustache.

"I hope she is still my daughter."

Refusing to acknowledge the thought, Yvette skipped from the warm cobbles of the courtyard into the dusty alley beyond.

It was in another alley, halfway across l'Morai, where she would find her fame. But fame came at a price, she knew, at the price of lives lost. She had not considered that the life would be her own.

"You two, go over there," Yvette snapped. She tapped the beige leather apron of the miller's son, one motley member of the brute squad assigned her. He turned dull, hazel eyes toward her, and she pointed down the alley. A leaning, two-story building stood opposite them, its bulk casting a blue-gray shadow on the rugged road. Black trails of soot covered the window tops of the building's half-timber walls, attesting to the fire that had gutted the inside. Most folk believed the burned-out inn was now only a dwelling for rats and vagrants. But Yvette knew otherwise.

"Get down," she hissed to the muscled bowyer as he walked past an open window. Marie shook her head, wondering whether the guardsmen assigned to her were getting worse, or she was getting more demanding. The other makeshift warriors—a gardener, woodsman, blacksmith, and a ploughman—stayed behind her, hugging the splintery wall of the fishmonger's. The suspicious reports had come from there.

She inspected the men behind her: four middle-aged townsfolk dressed in dowdy peasant garb and crouching with nervous grins on their faces. Only the woodsman wore the semblance of a uniform, though he had ceased to fit into it some ten years before. Yvette sighed, shaking her head. At least none of them had dropped his club or dagger yet.

Pointing at the gardener—a blond, thin-lipped man—Yvette said, "You—come with me. The other two of you, get on either side of that doorway with the bowyer.

And don't let anyone out."

They nodded nervously and dropped to their knees.
Scuttling away from her, they passed the guards at the
window and reached the charred door beyond. Seeing
them take their positions, Yvette motioned for the gardener to follow her. With quick, soundless strides, she
circled around the fire-gutted inn, past a fruit stand
loaded with rubescent apples, and into the street
beyond. The blond-haired gardener followed tight on
her heels, louder and more conspicuous than she.

"Watch your step," Marie complained, elbowing his
pudgy breadbasket. As he moved back a pace, she
said, "We've got the easy job. When we break in the
front door, the scamps'll run the other way. The brutes
in back will have to do the real fighting, but you'll need
to look scary enough that they don't challenge us. Do
you think you can do that?"

The man nodded wordlessly, having closed the gap
once again between them. His soil-blackened nails
clutched his club as though he held a garden hoe.

"Give me that," Yvette said, snatching the club from
his hand. She strode to the fire-charred door of the
burned-out inn and, with one rending blow, smashed it
into shards. She stepped through the rubble into the
darkness beyond, shouting, "No one move! You are all
under arrest by order of the Grand Council of l'Morai!"

The blond man behind her stumbled through the rubble-strewn passage and let out a vague roar to back up
Yvette's proclamation. It appeared the roar was unnecessary, though, for the twenty inhabitants of the
charred room sat motionless, staring up at her in mute
horror. Yvette smiled with satisfaction. The fugitives
were weaklings and cowards. Glancing toward the posturing gardener beside her, she commanded, "Get out
of the light," and batted him easily aside.

As dust-filled sunlight from the shattered door fell on
the creatures huddled in that dark, burned-out shelter,

Yvette felt her stomach turn. They were pitiable and grotesque. One woman had a green snake's head growing from her vast red belly. The tiny creature blinked myopically and hissed at the sudden light. Beside the woman sat a shriveled man, a blackened goiter drooping to his naval. There was a naked child at their feet, whose hindquarters were those of a short-haired dog. Beyond the jagged triangle of light, more freaks huddled, like rats in a dark hole. And the room stunk with their unhealthy, animalistic stench.

Approaching the woman with the snake in her stomach, Yvette positioned her club behind the woman's head. Faintly visible beneath the hairline lay the two tattoos. Yvette checked the necks of the next few freaks. They all had both tattoos: the red horse Quince with the spear through his back, which marked them as freaks, and the black Ear-Tied Hare, marking them for death.

Nodding grimly, Yvette said to the gardener, "No wonder they ran. They had nothing to lose. Well, at least they won't burden the citizens anymore.

"Come on inside," Yvette called to the brutes waiting in the alley, "and bring the chains." Crossing her arms and shaking her head in disgust, she muttered, "We'll have to use the wrist and neck shackles separately to chain all of them."

"Wait," came a weary voice from the dark back corner of the room. Yvette could just make out a man kneeling over a sprawled form. His hands moved in patient circles around a pitiful child with eyes the size of lemons. "Some of these people are injured."

Yvette stepped forward, her heart pounding and her lips wet with anticipation. They'd caught not only the escaped freaks, but the citizen who'd been hiding them out. The council would be pleased by this.

As the other brutes clambered into the room, Yvette pointed toward the dark corner and ordered, "Chain him first, and bring him to me. Then work on the others."

Nodding, two of the five brutes dragged a rusty length of chain across the ramshackle planking and gleefully fastened the shackles about the man's hands and neck. He resisted only long enough to finish wrapping the arm of the freak he was attending. The soldiers yanked him to his feet by the chains and thrust him across the crowded room toward Yvette.

Only then did the sunlight strike the old man's gray hair and bristling mustache.

"Father?" she whimpered.

It was the same sound—that whimper—that she would make a week later, when she saw him huddled in the musty cell.

"What are you doing?" asked the old man as his daughter appeared outside the bars. Lifting himself wearily from the wooden bed, he approached Yvette. She watched him, her piercing brown eyes studying his face. The darkness of the cellblock helped hide the deep-set lines and sleepless black rings she knew were there.

"I'm getting you out," she said, reaching into the pocket of her black woolen dress.

"What about the verdict?" the cobbler asked feebly, staring up to the stone ceiling. He could still hear the angry feet pounding the Council Hall floor above. "I'm not innocent, you know."

He said the words in his old teasing fashion, and Yvette averted her eyes from his. "I'm not innocent, either," she said, fitting the clanking key to the lock.

"I know," he said raggedly. His voice now was emptied of its spirit, its hope. He sighed. "I told you that being the hangman for the council would steal your soul."

The bars creaked open, and Yvette peered down the row of cells. "I'm getting some of my soul back today."

She gestured him out, but he hesitated, holding on to the rugged black bars. "Where am I to go? I can't return to my shop. I can't return to my life here. You've stolen it all, and my most precious daughter, too."

Her thin white hand clasped his, and she pulled him through the open cell door. "Don't you think I know that?"

"Wait," he said, withdrawing into the cell. "I forgot my pipe—my last true possession." Yvette released his hand, watching as the old man walked to the bed. "What about the others—the innocents you've rounded up and sent to mock trials? Can you get them out, too?"

Marie crossed her arms, refusing to reply. She pulled the door back wide, standing behind it. "Let's go. If they catch us, we'll both be dead."

Francis heard the footsteps before she did. With a wild scream, he leaped from the cell, slamming Yvette between the door and the wall, and shouted, "I'm free, you bitch!"

He ran into the arms of the approaching gendarme, and onto his drawn dagger. The blade pierced the old man's heart. With a faint groan of pain, he slumped forward, clinging to the gendarme's woolen uniform. As he slipped downward, his blood formed a curved cipher on the scratchy cloth. Sneering in disgust, the officer threw the old man off him.

Yvette staggered, dazed, from behind the door, just in time to see her father crumple to the rocky ground.

"Don't worry," the gendarme said, stooping to wipe the dagger on the back of the old man's tunic. "He didn't get away."

Yvette stood in shocked horror. She took slow steps forward, swallowing hard. Her father's ploy had bought her freedom, had bought her life. She dropped to her knees beside him. Even if her tears would cost her that freedom, that life, she wouldn't hold them back.

Her life was worthless now, anyway.

*   *   *   *   *

The Puppetmaster held up a scarred and withered hand to quiet the outraged shouts of the crowd. "Hold, hold!" he croaked. "Hold," he repeated a final time, "You have heard from her own lips of the idyllic life Marie had before she betrayed the city. You have heard how first she sought to cheat l'Morai of its justice by releasing her father, and second thought to destroy us all by raising up the freaks—outcasts and criminals—into an army to resist, and then invade us.

"But perhaps she has reserved some explanation for us," the Puppetmaster conjectured mockingly, treading a slow, limping circle about Marie. "Perhaps she can explain away her hundreds of crimes against the people of l'Morai." He turned to her, and an evil smile formed on his blistered lip. "Yvette," he said gently. "Yvette Martinique, daughter of Francis Martinique, cobbler to l'Morai—can you explain your crimes?"

Marie was silent—silent save for her heart, which labored madly beneath the leather straps. The images still flashed through her mind. The *images*—the former life of sight and citizenship and family and home. The life before she became a freak. Her past had suddenly returned to her, with its thousand smells and sights and sounds and fears and plans. It had eclipsed the world around her. It had silenced, for a time, the voice of the Puppetmaster and the angry roar of the crowd.

Francis Martinique was a name she had heard only moments before. But, with the return of her memories, he had become everything to her: loving father, guiding hand, patient teacher, city traitor, vain sacrifice. Preposterous as it all was, she even felt the old love return, more powerful than torture and magic and time. It was as if she had opened a long-forgotten traveling case to discover the familiar belongings locked within.

"Marie, I am speaking to you," came the Puppetmaster's whispered voice, intruding on her thoughts. "This is your chance to speak. Your chance to defend yourself against these indefensible charges."

A part of her mind heard him. A part of her mind screamed out for her to take up her own defense, to rail against the injustice of l'Morai. The false accusations, the blood sport of the Council Hall, the magical and material torture that created the freaks, the state-sanctioned freak show, the tattoos of life and death. . . . But to rail against it all would be to deny her part in it. To deny her guilt in her father's death, and Morcastle's, and perhaps even Hermos's. . . . The door of memory had been flung open, and she could not bear to swing it closed again.

"Marie," the Puppetmaster said, his rot-smelling breath curling in a cloud about her. He dropped to one knee, placing his hoary hand on the tattered hem of her skirt. "Have you no answer to these charges?"

A furtive tear broke over her eyelid and streaked down her cheek.

The Puppetmaster rose quietly. "Tears," he said to the hushed crowd. "Tears of guilt. Tears of regret. This is all she offers in her defense. Now, it shall be for the people to decide. Those who have testimony as regards this case of Marie the Blind Juggler, formerly Yvette Martinique, the cobbler's daughter, line up along the center aisle. One at a time present your name, line, and work for the scribe's record, then provide your testimony."

The resulting rumble was enormous as the crowd— almost everyone in the place—rose to their feet and shifted toward the center aisle. Still Marie sat in silence, tears streaming down her pale cheeks and dropping onto her slim collarbone. She listened as the testimonials began, listened in a blurred confusion of sensation and memory. As each citizen stepped forward, recounting some true or false grievance against Marie, she found her mind grasping at his or her words, pulling until it had drawn forth a new memory. Many of the attacks were vitriolic and false, and many more were passive and true. But all of them cut like razors into her heart. More than once, Marie gasped in remembered pain or sadness, or began shaking with the stress of facing the horrors long forgotten. For the first time that day, she was glad her feet and arms and head were locked away in the solid wood of the chair.

Finally, when it was all finished, Marie's clothes were wet with tears and cold sweat. She knew she was on the verge of losing her mind, and thoughts of the cold, quiet cell had grown all the more comforting.

"All listen now," came the clear call of a young council page, and Marie remembered that she had once occupied this same office, "to hear the verdict of the twelve Councilors of l'Morai concerning the guilt or innocence of Marie the Blind Juggler, once Yvette Martinique, daughter of the cobbler Francis Martinique— concerning the charges of treason, riot-rousing, and murder most heinous." The crowd, now seated, grew silent. "Those who say guilty call for sentencing of Mademoiselle Martinique while those who say innocent call for her release."

"Guilty," came a shout from a councilwoman on the far left of the wall.

And all the rest agreed.

"Twelve say guilty, none say innocent," the page pronounced. "Let the record read of the guilt of Marie the Blind Juggler of charges of treason, riot-rousing, and murder most heinous. I defer in the matter of sentencing to the noble council master, Monsieur Maudit Sienne."

From the Puppetmaster's niche came a raspy, growling voice that echoed through the council chamber. "Marie, in punishment for your guilt and by virtue of your status as a freak marked for death, I hereby

sentence you to scourging at the council post this
evening at the adjournment of this trial. Upon the post,
you shall be stripped bare to signify your state of
humiliation and to remove any impedance to the
whip's action. You shall receive thirty-nine lashes. If
you survive this, your wounds shall be salved and you
shall await execution by guillotine at dawn. The way to
the guillotine shall be a gauntlet lined with citizens of
l'Morai, who shall strike you with blunt instruments
until you are dead or have reached the guillotine.
Thereupon, your life shall be ended, and your head displayed upon the council gates as warning to all others
who might stray."

* * * * *

The golden blossoms in the courtyard garden glim-
mered in the evening sun; the bright heads of the flowers waved on their long stalks like the docile waves of a
placid sea. They were waving to her, the strong hand of
Mother, the gentle hand of Father. Yvette stooped and
plucked one of the wildflowers, drawing its faint and
mystic scent into her lungs. She spun about toward the
sunset and gasped at its deep hues: purple and crimson
and black.

The colors were profound and real, and she could
feel the smooth, clean brickwork beneath her feet, hear
the quiet creak of Father's rocking chair.

It almost masked the bite of the scourge.

SIXTEEN

The wooden blade of the shovel made a hollow slicing noise as it entered the sand. Leaning back on the handle, Anton the harlequin lifted a pile of sifting sand out of the hole and onto a growing mound beside it. He stopped for a moment and leaned the undersized shovel against his leg. The faded greasepaint on his face glistened with beading sweat. Straightening his weary, spasming back, he surveyed the darksome arena around him.

There were as many dead as alive, perhaps even more.

The living had worked throughout the day and now into the night, burying the bodies that lined the arena floor. Some of the corpses had begun to stink that afternoon beneath the sun. Despite weariness and desperation, the freaks doggedly dug, determined they would all have decent burials and marked graves. It was the only hope the survivors could cling to.

And so, in shifts they transformed the sandy floor of the arena into a graveyard. Anton watched the bone-weary workers as they shoveled sand from the arena floor and slid the limp bodies into place.

"You're digging too deep," came a resonant voice over Anton's shoulder.

He whirled and licked his lips nervously. It was

Hermos, Marie's man-giant friend. The harlequin eased off, rubbing a blister on his hand. "Too deep?"

"Not enough time," Hermos noted, straightening the sheet that draped his shoulder. "Too many bodies."

Anton's lip drew back, and he jabbed a thumb at his heart. "*I'm* the one digging."

Without a word, the man-giant headed away. His makeshift robes, fashioned from a set of sheets, rippled in the wind. He had become the self-appointed, surrogate priest of the rabble. In one narrow hand, he bore a torch, holding it high now as he approached a newly filled grave. The light shone on the moist sand, illuminating the feet of two mourners standing by. In Hermos's other hand, he carried a small bucket and a limp brush he had braided from horsehair left in the stalls. The bucket was rimmed in red—blood from the sheep they had slaughtered for the evening meal.

Hermos's voice rose thin and pure on the night air, singing a half-remembered hymn to Qin-sah. In his weariness, he wavered and dropped to one knee, letting the torch embed its butt in the sand beside him. Setting his bucket down, Hermos rubbed his forehead and muttered an improvised prayer. Then, he dipped the horsehair brush into the bucket and drew it out, dripping red.

"What's the name?" he asked hoarsely.

One of the mourners told him, and the man-giant leaned forward to paint the name on a small plate of limestone at the head of the grave. The blood would mark the grave until the stone carver could come by and set the letters indelibly. Reciting a prayer to Tidhare, least of the gods, Hermos set his brush in the bucket, fastened his hand on the pail's edge, and stood up.

"Hey, whoa, big fellow," came the small grating voice of a midget wearing an arm-sling.

"Valor," Hermos said huskily. "Got more prayers to say . . . more bodies."

"Could you come down for a moment?" Valor said, motioning with his free hand toward a loose pile of sand nearby. As Hermos dropped to his knees, the little man climbed atop the mound of sand. The man-giant sat, tucking the robe beneath him. Valor gestured for him to lean close.

"The council soldiers haven't let up all day, Hermos," he said seriously, his eyes pointing toward the edge of the carnival. "They're going to keep us here until we starve to death."

"Marie will come back," Hermos said, his voice ringing in his chest. "She'll come back."

The midget's expression darkened and, staring straight into the man-giant's eyes, he shook his head explicitly. "Hermos, you've got to understand: she's probably dead by now. They won't let her live. They're looking for someone to blame this on, and it's going to be her."

The man-giant's features were stoic as stone.

Latching on to one shoulder, Valor said, "Do you understand what I am saying to you?"

"Yes," the man-giant responded in a barely audible rumble.

"Good," said Valor, winking bleakly for a moment. "So, we've got to get out of here. If we stay here we'll starve to death. Do you understand?"

Again came the near-silent affirmation.

"I've been telling everybody we've got to break out, but they don't believe me. They're too tired of fighting and digging to even consider battling past the guards. They can't see beyond their own graves."

"We must escape," Hermos echoed. His mind returned for a moment to Marie's caravan, where they had decided the same.

"But nobody's willing to go if they don't know what's out there, what we're fleeing to," Valor said, "and they're right. We can't lead three hundred freaks and cripples across the heath to a cliff face. The soldiers would chase us and shoot us down."

The man-giant offered no comment, his enormous eyes glistening with tears.

"That's where you come in," Valor said, his voice straining with hushed excitement. "Your long legs can carry you faster than the guards out there. That's the most important thing. Also, you'll come back for the rest of us."

"What do I do?" Hermos asked.

"Find a passage for us, across the heath, through the woods, away from l'Morai. Find a route to some distant place," Valor said, his voice trembling. "You've got to find it soon, in the next two days. We'll be out of supplies afterward. But if you can find an escape, I can convince the other freaks to fight their way through the guards and follow you."

The man-giant's forehead furrowed, and he clenched his jaw. "How will *I* get through?"

"We'll create a diversion on the opposite side of the arena: a group of us midgets'll lower ourselves down the wall with a pulley contraption. While we're drawing the guards off, you slide quick down a rope and slip from the arena. Then head for the heath and find us a homeland."

The giant sat wordless, his long, bony hands sifting through the sand beside him. He sighed, looking up at the dying torches on the wall, and the scattered few freaks still guarding there.

"What if Marie returns?" he asked finally.

Valor only shook his head.

Hermos was already rising, pulling the priestly sheet from his shoulder. "Start the diversion."

The man-giant strode across the arena toward the stands. He passed Anton the harlequin, who was still shoveling the same grave.

"Start another," Hermos blurted without stopping.

"You start another," Anton snapped irritably. He tore the soiled and tattered ruff from his sweaty neck and mopped his brow with it. His black and white grease-paint was wearing very thin. Casting the ragged cloth to the sandy ground, Anton set his wooden spade in the hole and stepped down on it. The blade struck something hard. Gritting his teeth, he stepped down again. The shovel wouldn't sink.

"What's this?" he wondered aloud, standing his shovel in the mound of sand and reaching down into the deep hole. His ratty white glove fastened over a hard knob, which he drew out of the sand. It was a thigh bone, long and brown, devoid of flesh.

"Been diggin' too near another grave," came the weary voice of another harlequin, slapping him on the back.

"No," Anton said, blinking and staring blankly out over the arena floor. "Buried too deep, this one, and there's no skin left." He paused, his oversized shoe sliding across the sand. "Unless this arena's been used as a graveyard before."

* * * * *

The guardsmen laid Marie onto the battered wooden bed in her cell. Immediately the cracked planks began wicking the blood from her ribboned back. Her eyes, half-lidded in agony, fluttered as her lacerated back touched the wooden pallet. Staring down at her naked, limp form, the guardsmen pushed the blind woman farther onto the bed to make room for her pale arm, which trailed on the floor. After a few lingering looks, one of the guards retrieved her filthy bundle of clothes from a dark corner of the cell and laid them over her.

"Back away," the Puppetmaster growled from one corner of the cell. The soldiers complied, clearing an aisle between the looming carnival lord and the still woman. His one good eye twinkled beneath his hood in a vague, lascivious satisfaction as he watched the steady rise and fall of her chest. After a few labored breaths, the Puppetmaster turned to the guard standing beside him and struck his face with a skeletal hand.

"Get out! All of you!"

In wordless haste, the guards rushed from the cell, their hurried footfalls withdrawing into the passage beyond. The Puppetmaster listened as they passed over the iron-plated threshold of the prison, then he edged nearer to the almost lifeless form. He drew the ragged dress back from Marie and stared for long moments at her lily-white skin. She was, indeed, beautiful.

The Puppetmaster's good eye pivoted, drawn by a narrow rim of blood that was welling up about her shoulders and arms. With withered hands, he rolled her over. The skin of her back was furrowed like a field and ruby in hue.

"She'll not survive the night," the Puppetmaster noted to himself in a hoarse whisper. Easing her shoulders back down, the disfigured man drew the tattered dress back over her and stepped away. He stood there for a time, gazing at her, his charred features shadowed by the hood he wore. At last he muttered, "This will not do."

Wheeling, the Puppetmaster strode in quick, limping steps from the cell and swung the iron door closed with a creaking clang.

The sound roused Marie, though she had been vaguely awake through it all. She had known she was naked, known the ravenous eyes of the men lay on her—the shuffling guardsmen and the man who smelled of death. But she had remained motionless all the same, fearful that her wakefulness might bring further taunts and tortures.

After the sixteenth or seventeenth blow of the scourge, Marie's mind had descended into a humming, milky haze, removed from the pain. From that moment on, she had no longer felt the lash, only heard it as though it were biting into someone else's back. The screams of pain, too, had seemed to come from someone else. The few sensations that had filtered through the haze were odd: the fearful cry of a horse on a nearby street, a smooth stone beneath her bare feet, the smell of someone baking bread. And, just now, a whispered phrase: "She'll not survive the night." She knew it was true.

She was afraid. Suddenly she knew she didn't want to die. The iron-toothed tongues of the flail had driven the self-righteous anger from her. The lash had made her once again a freak—not a general of armies, not a prophet, not a revolutionary, but a freak. She was surprised at herself, at the panic that clutched her about the neck and thundered in her heart. Surprised and ashamed. After all, her death would be over soon enough, she told herself, and she was already beyond feeling the pain of it. There could be no cruelty to top what she had already felt. There could be no torture that would bring worse pain. In some ways, she was dead already.

She had died once when she betrayed her father to the council. She had died again when her attempted rescue of him ended in his death. She had died a third time when they blinded her. . . . How could this final death terrorize her so?

But it did. Death hovered thick and black before her like a patient phantom—capricious, malevolent, inevitable. No words could dismiss it. No hopes could dispel it. Its hot, chittering laughter had melted her mask of courage and dignity and power, revealing the frightened face of the blind girl beneath. Then it melted that face too, leaving only a cornered animal—fierce and feral and desperate to survive.

Marie knew she would do anything to escape.

She struggled to move, but her weary, sweat-soaked

body lay unresponsive. Tears pooled in her unseeing eyes as her life—hot and fluid—dripped away onto the cell floor.

She felt a touch on her shoulder—soft and fleshy fingers, the hand of a woman. A low voice cut through the cold air, sounding hollow and distant as though it came from the far-off heath. "I am Bethel. I am here to bind your wounds."

Marie murmured in response, struggling to speak to the woman. But her spent lips would only produce groans.

"There, there," the nursemaid said, rolling Marie onto her stomach. "I won't let you die."

"P-Please," Marie stammered, clenching her face with the effort of forming the words. "Help me . . . help me escape."

The woman patted her shoulder gently, concern rumpling her peasant brow. "There, there," she repeated. She began to apply a salve that burned in the lacerations like fire. At length, she said, "I practice healing, not treason."

The woman's hand settled on Marie's side, and Marie, spasming from the burn of the salve, clutched the warm fingers and clung to them tightly. "Y-You know," Marie gasped between shallow, raking breaths, "you're healing me . . . just to . . . be executed."

The woman's soft, broad fingers pressed back on Marie's hand. "I know."

* * * * *

Hermos panted, his body wet with sweat as he climbed the rocky face. Valor's plan had gone off without a hitch: the midgets had detained most of the soldiers, leaving only a thin reserve of distracted guards on the periphery. The man-giant had slid down a rope, rolled to cover behind an overturned caravan, and worked his way through the devastated maze of the carnival. Without alerting a single guard, he slipped into the tall grass and reached the gnarled forest that bordered the heath.

Throughout the long, black night that followed, Hermos pushed his way past dark brambles and slender stands of birch. He skirted the misty tarn and the peak beyond it, heading south until he entered a wild land of tossed boulders and scrubby trees. Noting landmarks, Hermos followed the lip of the basin before him. He reached a long, pitched shelf of rock and climbed it, rising toward the pink predawn sky. Before he gained the summit of the shelf, the white-hot sun pulled free from the horizon and cast enormous shadows across the lands. The man-giant rose to the crest of the hill.

Hermos dropped to his knees, his mouth falling open.

Before him, the land sloped away in a lush, green embankment, which was bordered on two sides by a glimmering sea. The hillside, dropping some half a mile, reached the ocean and extended into a narrow isthmus of rock between white, roaring waves. Hermos squinted, his eyes tracing out the long, fingerlike expanse. A mile or so across the ridge of stone, the isthmus widened into a broad landmass—a verdant continent, huge in the dappled light of patchwork clouds. On the land below, he saw a white form moving. He stared uncertainly for some moments before the beast raised its head, but as soon as it did, he knew it was a white horse.

"Qin-sah," Hermos said. "The bridge to freedom."

His heart catching in his throat, the man-giant knelt for a time, unable to move. Then, slowly, as though fearing to break the spell that lay over the land, Hermos rose and headed back toward the high heath and the mountain carnival. He had barely left the summit when his long, loping strides gave way to a hopeful run.

*   *   *   *   *

Marie sat up with a start, thinking she had heard her name rasped in the cold air. She clung to the thick, sticky wood beneath her and listened for the sound to repeat. Only the drumming of her heart answered. Easing herself back down onto the bed, Marie began to piece together where she was. The hard pallet, the bands of cloth that wrapped her chest and back, the dank odor, the telltale dripping of water in the distance. With settling dread, she remembered the prison cell, and remembered that this was the morning of her execution.

"Marie," came a ragged whisper.

She knew she hadn't imagined the voice. "Who is it?" she hissed, frightened, the words sibilant against the stony walls.

"Id's me," the voice answered, pathetic and low. It sounded as though the speaker's nose had been broken. "Reme'ber me? Karrig, de knife-man?"

Marie stiffened, sitting up despite the jabs of pain from her lacerated back. "Karrick?" She braced herself against the bed frame. "What . . . what do you want?"

"Dey're gonna hurt me some more, aren't dey? I'm afraid . . . I'm afraid," the man whimpered. "Whad are dey doing to me, Marie? I wanna excape."

"Where are you?" Marie asked fearfully, her knuckles whitening.

"I'm in de cell nexd to you," he said, snuffing the damp air. "Dey caught me before de war, afder de big fire in darena. Dey put me on trial, and I'm afraid."

"I'm sorry," Marie said. "Really, I am."

"Help me. Dey're gonna kill me. I know id," the man bleated.

Marie sat back on the bed and drew her knees up. "Can you use one of your knives to pick the lock or stab the guard or something?"

"Dey pulled dem all oud of me," the man moaned, beginning to sob. "Dey snapped dem from my bones and yanked dem oud ond de floor. And dey sold dem after de trial."

Pieces of a freak, Marie thought to herself. She shivered. "I'm sorry."

"Help me," the man repeated. "You can't let dem kill me. I dought we was friends."

Marie balled her fists beside her feet. "Is it light yet?"

Karrick muttered to himself for a moment. At length he said, "I see torches oudside." He paused, and Marie could feel his piercing gaze. "Dey're out dere to kill me. De night's not even over, and dey're out dere already."

The knife-man's mournful voice drove the last vestiges of sleep from Marie's body and awakened the pain once again. With the pain, the memories returned all the stronger.

"I don't want to talk anymore," Marie said. She slid to the edge of the bed and, hesitating as her bandaged back spasmed, stood up. Then, with cautious, painful steps, she staggered toward the back wall of the cell, as though hoping to escape the knife-man's voice.

"Help me," Karrick again cried. "Help me, help me . . ." The words dissolved away into a muttered litany of pain.

Marie didn't answer, raising her small white hands to clamp over her ears. She was truly sorry, but she could do nothing now—nothing for Karrick, for her father, or for herself.

Karrick began to shout, his words penetrating into her closed ears. "Help me! Help me!"

Marie approached the front of her cell. Her hands gripped the bars and wrenched futilely at them. "They're going to execute me, too, Karrick! They only healed me so I could run the gauntlet, so I could reach the guillotine alive!"

The silence that followed her words lasted for only a moment before the quiet, almost shamed cries began again.

Marie sat down facing a corner of her cell, her hands covering her ears. Karrick's voice grew louder, but Marie couldn't hear. She hummed a strange tune that she had not heard for years. A tune she had not heard since . . . Father had hummed it to her. Since she had been Yvette.

> O, pull the spear from Quince's back
> Though he be dead, my dear, my dear,
> For horses shouldn't die by blades
> But by the toilsome year.

The sound of the song comforted her, and she thought of Father, of his gray mustache and crescent eyes. Her tense muscles softened, and the pain of her torn skin began to ebb away. She could see him now, sitting there within the brick courtyard, carving leather and smoking his battered pipe. For a moment she was there with him, watching him with her deep brown eyes. All had been safe and warm and sane in his presence, in that little brick courtyard. How could such a lovely place still stand in this vast, cruel city?

Her daydreams dissipated. She smelled something foul: rot and ash and death. The Puppetmaster. He was coming. Down the long line of cells he was coming, coming to take her to the growing gauntlet, to the people gathered to kill her.

Karrick ceased ranting, and his furtive footfalls withdrew. In the sudden quiet, Marie could hear the Puppetmaster's approach. His feet thudded on the floor as though the prison were a giant drum. The somber rhythm of it was accompanied by the dull tamp of flails and scythes on the road outside.

The terror had returned. Marie painfully scrambled back from the iron bars. Don't beg him, she told herself, resisting the rising fear, don't beg for your life. She wished she could muster the anger that had driven her on before, but it was gone—gone like her eyes, and her father, and her childhood . . . her hope.

The Puppetmaster's key clanked as it slid into the aged lock, and he swung the moaning door open. Two heavy treads brought him into the cell, and the gate swung closed and locked behind him.

"Stay away from me," Marie murmured, more out of fear than anger. "Please . . . stay away."

The Puppetmaster halted, fixing Marie with his one good eye. The man's scent filled the stony cellblock. Marie bit her lip and backed to the rear wall of the cage as the Puppetmaster spoke. "The healer did well, I see."

Marie faced him mutely, her blind eyes wide.

"Her magic is limited," the lord of the carnival continued, his voice like stone on stone. He seated himself on the still-bloody bed. "But she knows about salves and bandages."

"If you're going to kill me, just do it," Marie proclaimed, mustering a bit of her former anger. "I'm not afraid to die."

"Then you are a greater fool than I imagined," the sepulchral man stated lightly. "Besides, I'm not going to kill you. The citizens are. Just like they always do."

Marie was about to ask what he meant, but held back. She would not be mouse to the Puppetmaster's cat.

"Just like the murders that started all this," the Puppetmaster offered, enscribing runic symbols into the sticky, brown blood where he sat. "You and your idealist friends chased a murderer for nearly a month, but couldn't find him because you looked for a solitary man." He paused, wiping the blood from his skeletal fingertip onto his woolen robe. He let the effect of his words sink in.

"Oh, we found him all right," Marie replied, calming her voice. "It's the whole damned city."

"I underestimated you—a common fault." The Puppetmaster swept toward Marie, grasped her hair, and pulled her head back so that her blind eyes were directed at his rotting face. "Yes, Yvette, the whole damned city. It's a sort of sport with them, you see—a necessary sport. That's why the crowd has gathered out there—for the sake of murder. That's why you loved working as my apprentice at the council—murder. It gets the blood going, it cleanses the brain, it cleans the stock of the city. We're a murderous race, Marie, building our houses on our fathers' graves. If the citizens didn't have you to kill, they'd turn on each other. L'Morai would devolve into factions, into civil war. But because of you, because there is a common, subhuman species of freaks that we can all hate and kill, the city coheres and evolves, and achieves heights of beauty."

Wrenching painfully, Marie pulled free from the man's bony grasp and scrambled away across the smooth floor. She stayed hunched on all fours like an animal, ready to spring for his throat or run for cover.

"How pathetic you look, my dear. We made you into a freak, then you made yourself into an animal, a rat—a subhuman, disease-bearing, child-killing monstrosity. In the eyes of l'Morai, you and your kind are the plague bringers, the pestilence bearers. Even a child would run a dagger into your heart."

Marie growled, "It's not true. My father wasn't that way."

"Your father was a rebel, perfect freak material," the Puppetmaster contradicted, stalking toward her. "If you hadn't caught him, he would have frayed away the fabric of our city. He would have proselytized, convinced others he was doing right, created a dangerous faction. But after he was captured and convicted, we would have made him a harmless performer, perhaps a juggler, like yourself."

Marie was trembling. The words of the Puppetmaster

made it all clear, undeniably so. "But we used to be citizens ourselves. We used to be neighbors and friends of
theirs."

"Yes," the Puppetmaster allowed, his voice growing
tight. "But now you are abominations: you are everything the citizens hate about themselves, every weakness and perversion they are afraid to discover within."

Marie scrambled past the swooping creature and
withdrew to a corner of the cell. "But why would they
create us if we are everything they despise?"

The Puppetmaster halted, staring with something
akin to pity in his bulging, scorched eye. "Because they
needed someone to hate. Someone to kill. Or they
would hate and kill each other." He plodded to the bed
again and sat down. "I'm not going to chase you about
the cage."

Marie reddened in shame. "If they need us, why do
they kill us?"

"You're an abomination," the man said simply.
"Morally, you must be stamped out, just like a murderer
must be executed. If it weren't for the tattoos, weren't
for restrictions against killing freaks that aren't marked
for death, the people would have destroyed the carnival
long ago."

Marie's already white face blanched, and her throat
constricted. "I have heard enough."

"No," the Puppetmaster answered dryly. "You've only
begun to hear. Come now, little Tidhare, it's time you
untied your ears."

*　*　*　*　*

An arrow struck the rock face of the arena as Hermos
frantically climbed. The arrowhead chipped and
sprayed stone into the man-giant's arm. He gritted his
teeth, his long, narrow fists wrapping tight about the
rope. If it weren't for the midgets above, grunting and

scrabbling to pull him up, he could make better head-way. Another arrow smashed into the stonework, this one embedding in a seam. Hauling on the rope, Hermos found slight purchase for his foot between the shaft and the stone. He moaned, pulling himself higher. His fingers were only inches from the top. With a muscle-tearing lunge, he snagged a handhold on the rim of the arena. That's when the arrow sank into his thigh.

The man-giant screamed, clawing at the top of the wall. The midgets fell back as he yanked himself up, draping his torso over the edge. Surging forward, his diminutive friends seized his ragged belt and flipped him over the rail onto the stone floor behind it. He landed with a thud on his back, the wind knocked from his lungs.

For a moment, all Hermos saw were scurrying feet and worried faces staring at his wounded leg. He leaned against the cold wall, fighting for air. At last, clutching the arrow that impaled his thigh, the man-giant spoke.

"I've seen it," he panted, "the bridge to freedom."

*   *   *   *   *

The Puppetmaster strode down the corridor of the cellblock, towing Marie on one chain and the whimpering Karrick on another. As they made their jangling way along, the knife-man's wide, fear-flecked eyes peered through the high windows in the rock wall. The sky beyond was fiercely blue and bright with morning. A cool, inviting breeze blew mockingly through the window onto the condemned pair, and Marie's mind returned to her former life.

The Puppetmaster nodded to the guardsmen that stood in the corridor ahead. The soldier drew back the prison's thick iron gates. Passing beneath them, the Puppetmaster reached a second set of guards, who fumbled to remove wooden beams from a set of doors.

The beams had barely cleared their brackets when the Puppetmaster kicked the doors dramatically open.

Karrick crumpled to his knees.

The cobbled way beyond the doors was thickly lined on both sides with a mob of citizens. Shovels, picks, flails, scythes, hammers, axes, clubs, and scores of other implements bristled in the crowd. Myriad metal edges glinted in the morning sun. "Hooray!" went up the hungry shout as the freaks appeared. A feverish light shone on the faces of those gathered.

At the far end of the gauntlet, on the crest of a hill where two roads met, stood a guillotine, black against the quicksilver sky. Beside it, a man with a dark hood hovered phantomlike, his hand resting on the switch of the raised blade.

"Greetings this fine morn, people of l'Morai," the Puppetmaster called out. "Are you prepared to execute these two enemies of the state?"

The mass responded with cheers and stomping feet and thumping weapons.

Karrick clutched the Puppetmaster's withered leg and pleaded tearfully for his release. Ignoring him, the massive man whispered to Marie. "You see how murderous they are?"

Biting back the fear, Marie snapped, "I can't see anything."

The Puppetmaster laughed and waved his cadaverous hand over her face. "This is something you *must* see."

Light jagged painfully into Marie's still-pupilless eyes. She blinked. She could see again. Her first sight . . . the black, moiling crowd, the buildings that huddled beyond the people's chanting, jeering faces, and the cold guillotine that waited for her. She trembled and clasped the Puppetmaster's hand.

The Puppetmaster said in a voice that was almost gentle, "I have the power to wipe away your sins, my

dear. The freaks have been delivered into my hands—
to guard, to guide, to kill, to raise from the dead."

Marie couldn't bear to listen, but her eyes, so long
blinded, refused to close. She remembered that street
from her childhood: hemmed in by cheery shops,
draped with banners, filled with street music. She
remembered walking by the cheese shop with her
father, rings of gray smoke fondly wreathing his silver
hair. She remembered a different day, standing along
the lane, shoulder to shoulder with the other citizens.
They were waiting hungrily, excitedly, for the first kill.
For one perverse moment, Marie was transported away
from the Puppetmaster's side to stand within the raging,
grinning mob.

The illusion was shattered, however, when the
Puppetmaster unchained Karrick and pushed him
toward the ravenous crowd.

SEVENTEEN

Shrieking pitiably, the knife-man stumbled forward.
He gained his footing and flinched back toward the
doors. The line of citizens converged on him, their flails
and clubs whirring in the charged air. A hollow, ringing
thud sounded as the first blow struck: the knobbed end
of a wooden staff bashed the man's shoulder blade and
sent him sprawling onto his hands. The wrinkled old
man that bore the staff followed up with another swing
that leveled the knife-man to the cobbles. The wall of
citizens encircled him, shouting and chanting like some
primordial pack of beasts.

"Kill him! Break his neck! Smash his brains!"

The frenetic shouts were accompanied by screams of
rage and odd explosions of laughter. The cudgels and
flails fell in a furious hail on the prone form, and the gathered knot of folk spat on his back and screamed obsceni-
ties. A boy, his ruddy face plastered with a fiendish leer,
pushed through the crowd and began kicking the man
vehemently. Seeing his young fervor, a buxom woman
stepped back and cheered him on.

Marie shaded her now-seeing eyes from the atrocities, but the horrible images did not disappear: Marie's
mind returned to former gauntlets—*many* former
gauntlets. She remembered standing at one such mass
execution with her silent, troubled father. She shouted

taunts at the stumbling captives, pushing forward to strike them with a stone she held.

Her father had forbidden any weapons in his house or the shop, and he attended the street executions only because the law compelled him to. But Yvette was different. She thrived in the surging, railing crowd. She loved the chants and screams, the heart-pounding, breath-gasping sport of it. With every bone she broke, every gash she tore, she felt she was striking a blow against evil itself. She was cleansing l'Morai of all that was dark and perverse, ridding it of its monsters in human flesh. The gauntlet wasn't so much an execution for her as an exorcism. Afterward, the streets were cleaner and kinder, more peaceful, more friendly. The killing somehow cleansed them all, as a violent storm purifies the air. Yvette always slept soundly the night afterward.

Lowering her hands from her face, Marie banished the memories. She looked up now through very different eyes. The crowd was drawing back from the thrashing body, pushed away by a meaty man who was nodding at someone down the street. Above the cries for blood and broken bones came shouts from those farther down.

"Save some for us! Don't break the legs!"

As the flails and clubs stopped falling, Karrick lay still, unwilling to move. His back was mottled in red and black and blue welts, some oozing blood thickly onto the cobbles. One of his arms lay in a boneless sprawl beside his still form, and his lungs heaved wearily. Seeing that he had no intention to move, the old man with the knobbed staff stepped toward Karrick and rammed the bottom end of his pole rudely onto his backside.

"Get up, you worthless fleck of filth," he shouted, punctuating the comment by leaning down and scraping his scabrous fingernails across the man's tattered back.

The crowd hooted in response. Their catcalls doubled as the knife-man scrambled awkwardly to his feet, stumbling once, then again, over the arm that drooped lifelessly by his side.

The old man with the staff swung its cudgel end one last time, glancing it off the fleeing man's calf and narrowly missing the crowd farther on. Heedless, the people descended again on the knife-man. With thudding swings and the snap of ribs, the beating began again.

"They hate us," Marie muttered, staring in pale disbelief at the crowd before her.

The Puppetmaster glanced down, studying her blank expression. "Hate is easier than love. That's why cities are built on it."

Seeing the knife-man's other arm crumple beneath a hammering club, Marie looked away again. She shuddered, and her hands, wet with cold sweat, were going numb. "I don't want to die."

The blistered and swollen skin of the Puppetmaster's mouth pulled back in a rictal grin. "You shall, my dear. So shall all the freaks at the carnival."

"What?" Marie gasped. "You said you'd let them live!"

"Oh, *I* won't kill them," the Puppetmaster replied casually. "But they'll die all the same. I can't let them go free, or they might attack the city in retribution. They'll starve in that arena, or go mad and kill each other."

"You are despicable," Marie replied flatly, her voice emptied of the hard-edged anger it once held.

"No." The Puppetmaster shook his head, and something like a consoling smile touched his features. "I am human."

"You can't let them die. It would be better if you'd just return to rule the carnival yourself. Set it up like it was before the fire, get the whole thing running again. . . . Do whatever you need to do to stop the carnage."

The man faced her squarely. "I'm glad you are finally thinking. Since you are, you surely realize the freaks would never accept me now. They'd never believe they were safe again." His voice trailed away, and he looked out toward the gauntlet beyond.

Karrick had tripped some hundred yards short of the guillotine, and a mob of citizens surrounded him, their cudgels falling in a sickening rhythm. Each time the weapons would rise up from the body, their tips were crimson, and a trailing spray of blood would sprinkle the crowds beyond.

"I have a much better idea than my returning," the Puppetmaster continued. "The freaks wouldn't trust me, but they *would* trust you."

A chill spread down her back, and Marie dropped, trembling, to her knees. She shook her head violently. "No! I can't betray them. I won't be part of this."

"You won't be betraying them. Remember, Marie, without you, they will starve to death in the arena. But you can save them. You can protect them," the Puppetmaster rasped. "You know what it is like to be a freak. You would guard them, speak up for them, keep them from the Council Hall and the gauntlet—like I tried to do for you."

"I can't do it," Marie interrupted, her voice cracking with the effort. "I can't be a puppetmaster."

"That's right, you can't," the hulking form wheezed. "I am, and shall always be, the Puppetmaster. It was my title before I took over the carnival, before I led a revolt to overthrow the corrupt lord who ruled it before me."

Marie blurted, "You? You took it over, just like . . . ?"

"Yes," the man replied simply, "just like you did. I was a revolutionary, too. I drove out the last carnival master some sixty years back, thinking I could free the freaks from their oppressors. I faced the same trial you faced, the same gauntlet, the same guillotine. And, when that man, that monster, told me I could die along

with my revolutionaries or I could return and govern
them, I chose—chose wisely. I've guarded my people
for sixty years as carnival master, Marie. Before I took
the role, the freaks were dying in scores. After, they
died one by one."

"I can't believe it," Marie murmured. "I can't believe
you did these same things."

"Believe it, Marie," the Puppetmaster assured her, his
voice for once devoid of malice, of deceit. "My friends,
my soul mates, are buried in the arena floor only feet
below your companions."

Marie doubled over at the Puppetmaster's feet, her
stomach knotted with sobs and her mind spinning furiously. Beyond the doors, the crowd was resignedly
withdrawing from the still corpse that lay, formless, in a
spreading pool of blood. Already they were shouting for
Marie to follow Karrick's bloody path. Already they
were wiping the crimson liquid from their weapons and
their hands.

"You'll be the Juggler, Carnival Master of l'Morai,"
the Puppetmaster said, breaking into her thoughts. He
drew a ruby pendant from the cord about his neck—the
pendant Hermos said he had seen in the Puppetmaster's hovel. The crimson gem spun in the harsh
morning light, its facets glinting with Qin-sah, God of
Horses, on one side, and Tidhare, God of Freaks, on the
other.

"Do not choose lightly, my dear. Though you can
protect your friends, you cannot lead them to rebel
again. For if you choose to become carnival master, I
will place this stone about your neck. From that
moment forward, you will be forever in the power of
l'Morai. You will channel its people's hatred and fear,
and you will never betray the citizens to your freaks.

"This pendant was worn by the very first carnival
master, and it has been worn by us all—every council
member of the city."

"The council?" Marie asked in less than a whisper.

"Yes." The Puppetmaster nodded. "Each member of the council is a former carnival master. None of us die the natural death of old age. Even the grandfather of us all still lives, the harelip Juron Cygne."

"Juron Cygne," Marie gasped. "I've heard a hundred people read that name off the cornerstone."

"Yes. He was the first carnival master. He buried his own brother in that cornerstone. Juron hated his brother, twin to him in all things save the childhood disease that disfigured him. André, you see, had worn the family's magical amulet, which warded him against the wasting illness that ruined Juron. It is this amulet I now offer to you."

He lowered the swinging necklace so that the ruby lay on Marie's trembling shoulder. Her breath came in uneven sobs as she sat up, feeling the cold, harsh weight of the ruby.

"Juron stole the pendant from his brother and buried him alive in the arena wall. As he died, André cursed Juron and the stolen amulet, channeling his tormented soul into the gem. He declared that whoever dons the pendant will be lord of the freaks, cast out by l'Morai but pawn of its hatred. Shortly afterward, the figure of Quince the Horse appeared on one side of the gem, and that of the Ear-Tied Hare on the other. It became the brand that magically tattoos citizens with the mark of freaks, and freaks with the mark of death. For, you see, the carnival master is the highest citizen, like Quince, and also the greatest freak, like the Ear-Tied Hare."

"Qin-sah," Marie muttered quietly, almost in prayer. "Tidhare."

Above the vicious chants of the throng, the Puppetmaster's voice rose. "So you see, Marie, if you don this pendant, you will become the next carnival master, saving yourself, and saving your friends from certain death." He shifted the chain, and the great red ruby slid down her breast like a giant drop of blood. "But you must choose, now. The pendant or the gauntlet."

*   *   *   *   *

Valor whistled once, dropping the friction-hot arrowhead from his hand and stamping in the pile of mortar powder on the sandy ground. Dismantling this wall would take forever. The stone he'd been trying to dislodge from the bulwark still hung there, clinging to its well of mortar. The midget harrumphed, resting his tired hand on the sling he wore. He looked askance at the other freaks gathered to each side of him in the dark entrance. They'd been working since Hermos had returned at midday, and still had removed only twenty-odd stones from their escape route.

Threading his way through the huddled workers, Valor reached Hermos, who kneeled beside the wall, clearing the last clumps of mortar from a particularly large stone. The midget tapped Hermos's side and asked wearily, "How far are we?"

The man-giant closed one eye and peered through a fracture that the ram had made during the siege. "Looks like almost."

Shaking his head sadly, Valor said, "I could've thought of a hundred better ways of getting us all out in a hurry. I could've thought of ten better ways alone of getting this wall down. We shouldn't wait till we're almost through to ram it. We should ram it now."

Hermos granted him a dubious look, then set his fingers around the loosened stone before him and started working it free.

"I know, I know. We don't want to alert the soldiers. Still, I say, what's the difference if they know?"

The midget's ramblings were cut short by a terse, whispered command that came from a harlequin at the mouth of the entrance. "Hermos, you'd better get up here."

The urgency in the lad's voice made the freaks stop working, though none could tell if the messenger was excited or afraid. Hermos, his eyes hard, strode with long paces across the sandy ground.

"What is it?" Valor called out impatiently.

"It's Marie," the lad said.

Hermos began to run as a shocked thrill passed through the crowd. Valor shot from the wall in fevered pursuit of the giant, and the others, a heartbeat later, dropped their rocks and arrowheads to follow.

Hermos vaulted up the stairs, taking ten in one stride. He passed the scrambling messenger a quarter of the way from the top and pressed on. The sound of twenty-some flapping feet filled the air behind him, mixed with the frustrated grunts of Valor. "Let me through! Out of my way! Hermos, wait!"

Hermos reached the rim of the arena and peered out across the ruined carnival grounds. His eyes followed the pointing finger of one of the freaks, out to the carnival gate. There, two guardsmen stood, well out of long-bow range, and they pointed down the heath road.

Scanning the dusty highway, Hermos spotted Marie. The man-giant's face brightened and something akin to a smile broke across his lips. She was walking alone down the trampled trail, a stick clutched in her hand. As she moved along the road's edge, the tapping stick guided her. Her tattered clothes had been replaced now with a thick gray robe, which wrapped her slight frame formlessly. The hood of the robe was thrown back from her midnight hair, revealing her elegant face and beautiful, lily-white eyes.

"Marie!" Hermos shouted in sudden joy, his voice ringing through the arena and filling the heath beyond. "Marie!" he cried again, but a swift fist in his calf silenced him before he could shout a third time. Looking down in sudden rage, he saw Valor pointing over the arena rim.

"The guards, you idiot!"

Hermos shot a glance out toward the thin line of soldiers that stood along the hedgerow at the periphery of the carnival. There was a gap in the line. Five of the warriors had broken from the ranks, their places being absorbed by the spreading line. Those five, swords in hand and crossbows on their backs, now rushed toward the gate. Toward Marie.

"No!" Hermos bellowed, pushing his way through the thick crowd that had gathered to gawk over the rail. In moments, he had reached a freak watchman. With one swift swipe, he wrenched the loaded crossbow from the man's arms. Then, with a growl, he bolted along the rim of the arena.

"What are you doing?" Valor screamed, his good hand raised imploringly. He jumped from the stone bench and followed in Hermos's wake, knocking the other performers out of the way.

The man-giant had already reached the rope he'd descended the night before. Grimacing with the effort, he slung the crossbow over his back and twined the hemp around his left arm. He paused for only a moment, checking to make sure the end was knotted about the stone bench and the guards were still out of bow range. Then he threw himself over the wall.

Cursing, Valor slid to a stop a moment too late. He slapped the rail in frustration and leaned over to watch the giant's descent.

Hermos was sliding down the rope, which spiraled in burning lines around his arm. The pain only deepened the fury on his face. His feet struck the ground at a run, spraying sand into the air behind him. He charged for the gate. With a moan of dread, Hermos saw that Marie had almost arrived, tapping her staff in apparent oblivion as she moved forward. He glanced the other way: the five guardsmen were converging on the gate, and the two gate sentries readied their swords. Hermos released a roaring scream that ripped through the air.

The guards flinched, and two of them broke off to engage the lunatic giant. As they ran, the soldiers reached back with practiced ease for their crossbows and brought them to bear.

In huge, leaping bounds, Hermos closed the distance to them, his face livid and a growl on his lips. He reached over his shoulder and grappled the stock of his crossbow, which bounced painfully against his back. He pulled the weapon awkwardly forward, hoping to shoot the first bolt. Too late. A metallic twang sounded from one of the soldiers' crossbows. Hermos felt a fiery jolt in his thigh: the quarrel ripped through it, coming out the other side.

He didn't slow.

With a white-faced gasp, the soldier ditched the empty weapon and drew his sword. The young warrior beside him frantically fiddled with his bow as he raised it for a shot. Another feral screech rang out from the man-giant, and the soldier triggered his quarrel into the sand.

Hermos descended on them. He was two paces from the swordsman when he discharged his bow. The quarrel buried itself in the soldier's chest, knocking him back off his feet. In the next instant, Hermos swung the empty crossbow about and raked it over the other man's face. The young soldier's neck snapped, and he flipped over like a limp doll.

Hermos didn't pause, his strides lengthening to bring him to the gate. Gasping in horror, the five warriors there whirled about to face him, sheathing their swords and scrambling to draw their crossbows. Marie stood surrounded by them now, small and helpless in their midst.

"Marie!" Hermos called again.

"Stop or die!" shouted one of the guards, hefting his crossbow and taking aim.

"Stop, Hermos!" came Marie's thin cry. Her voice had only a taint of its old anger. A new sadness filled it.

The man-giant staggered to a stop, more from the shock of what he heard in Marie's voice than from her command. Only then did he look down at the wound in his thigh, and the wide crimson line that ran from it down to his toes.

"The war is over," Marie called out, striking her staff on the ground for emphasis. She paused as though listening for the man-giant's footfalls. In the silence that followed, she said, "Drop your weapons, all of you."

The three remaining soldiers looked back dubiously at her, then at the gate guards. Marie handed them an elegant scroll, which she had produced from her pocket. The older of the two gate guards, a drawn man with a scarred cheek, took the document, unrolled it, and began to read. He blinked as he scanned the words, and his war-calloused thumb speculatively rubbed the seal at the scroll's base. Looking up from the document, he swallowed hard, and began to roll it up again. He handed the scroll back to Marie and nodded curtly to the soldiers standing there.

Quizzical looks crossed their faces, and a few reluctantly lowered their weapons.

"I said 'Drop them!'" Marie barked, striking the nearest soldier with her staff. The warriors complied, their swords and crossbows dully striking the sandy ground. When Marie spoke again, her voice was quieter, but it still carried to the man-giant. "You, drop yours too, Hermos."

Puzzled, the man-giant let his crossbow fall to the earth.

Marie pointed with her staff toward the captain of the guard and barked, "Tell them what the scroll said."

The captain looked at her, his lips drawing into a thin line. The younger soldiers around him regarded the man with confused expressions.

"Go ahead," Marie urged, pushing past the guards.

With steely eyes, the captain watched her go. "We're pulling out."

"What?" came the chorus of replies.

"You heard me! Spread the word. Get your things. We'll gather at the gate before marching out."

Marie nodded once. "Get going, unless you want to be dragged before the Council of l'Morai and charged with insurrection."

The men peered at her with angry, unbelieving eyes, then reluctantly dispersed from the gate.

Marie walked across the stony courtyard. She headed straight for the man-giant, her face down-turned and solemn as she tapped her cane on the rough rock.

Hermos stood before her, mouth agape, his hands clamped over the wound on his trembling leg. Straightening, the man-giant took a tentative step toward her, then another. "They let you go?"

"Of course," Marie snapped crossly. "They tried me. I was innocent." Her voice sounded odd, as though it were strained through metal teeth.

Hermos asked, "Are you . . . all right?"

"Yes," came the response, the edge in her voice softening.

With an uncertain smile, the man-giant took two short strides toward her and embraced her tightly. She felt stiff in his long bony arms, and, though she did not push away, she didn't return the embrace either.

"Praise Qin-sah you are back." Hermos lifted her and cradled her in his long, gaunt arms. Instead of trying to fight her way loose, Marie lay still in his grip. The man-giant's eyes narrowed, but, without comment, he carried her toward the arena. The pain in his thigh had disappeared and, despite the extra weight he carried, the giant limped only a little. He reached the wall, finding that someone had tied a loop at the end of the rope and lowered it for them. A crowd of smiling performers had gathered at the arena's rim, gripping the rope and motioning him to step into it.

Valor was at their front, sitting astride the rail and shouting, "Let's go! We can't wait for you to climb up here, you oaf!"

Nodding, Hermos stepped into the loop with his good leg and latched on to the rope with one arm.

"Heave!" cried the midget at the top, and the band of freaks one by one disappeared as they spread out down the stairs. The slack in the rope snapped taut, and suddenly, with frightening speed, Hermos and Marie were slung to the top. The loop yanked Hermos's leg over the rail, where his trailing leg snagged. The loop slipped from his foot, and the freaks, still pulling, tumbled backward in a laughing pile at the base of the stairs.

Hermos smiled at the giggling crew and set Marie down on her feet within the arena. She stood up, straightening her robes, and paced away from the man-giant. Struggling to draw his wounded leg over the rail, Hermos staggered after her.

Already, though, a cheering mob of about seventy performers stood in a thick ring around her. They tentatively reached out to touch her, as though fearing she might be a ghost, and poured out a torrent of questions:

"How did you escape?"

"What does that scroll say?"

"When are the soldiers leaving?"

"What happened in l'Morai?"

Valor wriggled his way through the pressing throng and tapped the walking stick she carried. "What's with this? I thought you didn't need one of these," he jibed happily.

Marie's face was stone-hard as she replied, "I do now."

Hermos pushed his companions aside to clear a path for himself. Reaching Marie, he fell to his knees and wrapped his arms about her.

She spun on him, her face very solemn and her sightless eyes boring into him. "Please, Hermos. No more." Her narrow fingers fiddled with a red gemstone that hung about her neck.

It was the ruby necklace, Hermos realized, the one that bore the emblem of Qin-sah. The one he had seen on the Puppetmaster.

"Come on, Marie," Valor urged. "Tell us what happened."

His request was answered by a chorus of cheers and prompts from performers all around.

Marie turned toward them, shivering as though she were very cold, and a single word emerged from her trembling lips. "Sit."

The crowd of freaks climbed over and onto the stone benches, eager to get as close as possible.

Hermos still kneeled on the stony ground beside Marie. "I don't understand," he breathed, his rumbling voice quiet on the tumultuous air.

She faced him, her eyes white as snow within the gray robes she wore. "Sit," she repeated, gesturing toward the rim of the arena. He rose, averting his eyes, feeling she could see right into his mind. Head bowed, he sat down on the stone rail.

The other performers, the seventy or so who were still able to move about without assistance, clustered on the seats below Marie. Their faces were grimy and lined from terror. Clothing hung in rags from their shoulders, the fabric marked by dirt and sweat and blood and soot. All the greasepaint was gone, all the masks, all the feathers and silks. They were no longer a troupe of exotic performers, but a swarm of dingy plague rats. Despite the dirt and despair, though, they stared hopefully, almost hungrily, at Marie.

Leaning her walking stick against the rail, Marie crossed her arms over her chest. The wind filled her midnight hair, blowing it playfully about her face as she gathered the nerve to speak. "We are free," she said, so softly that those farther than the first three rows leaned forward, cupping hands behind their ears. She began again, this time louder, "We are free. We must rebuild our carnival."

"What happened in l'Morai?" asked an enormous woman with small, in-turned eyes like a pig's.

"I went to trial," Marie answered, bowing her head for a moment. "I went to trial and told them about the carnival murderer. I told them what we had found, and they captured the man and killed him."

A murmur of amazement and disbelief rolled through the crowd. "Who was he?" came the shrill voice of the hostler.

Marie bit her lip and closed her eyes. "He was—he was—" her chin trembled for a moment, then her features hardened. "He was the cobbler. Francis Martinique was his name." Her face flushed, and, for a moment, she turned away from them.

"I thought he died ten years back," a dwarf interjected in his croaking voice.

"Why did they let you go?" Valor called out, his voice having lost its hopeful edge.

"I . . . I was innocent," Marie replied, "just defending my people, or that's what the council decided."

"So, now we build the city you talked about?" asked the dog-faced boy excitedly.

Marie shook her head, trying to form words on her lips. Sighing, she set her face toward the heath and said, "No. That was a foolish, foolish dream. That's why so many died in the war. I should have made you an army, not a city. We—" she inhaled deeply, apparently drawing the sweet smell of heath into her lungs "—we aren't farmers. We aren't laborers of any stripe. We are . . . performers—freaks—curiosities. We live for the show, and the show for us. . . . We've got to rebuild."

Valor shot a worried glance at the man-giant, who

was clutching his leg to stop the blood flow. Hermos's eyes were grave and sad.

"What do we do first?" called out the Clatch weakly. Hermos turned an amazed look at the midget. Big Boy had died during the first rain of fire, and the Clatch hadn't said a word since then.

"Yeah," Valor said, dropping from his seat and bowing before Marie. "We'll do anything. Anything you ask! Just say the word!"

Marie swallowed, and her head shook as she struggled to speak. "Tear down the bulwarks."

Valor rose and smiled broadly. "It's almost done already, thanks to me." He reached out and clasped her hand. It was cold as ice. "Let me lead you down there for the festivities."

Marie pulled back. "No. . . . I must tend Hermos's wound."

The midget stared up for a moment, then whirled about and shouted to the freaks, "You heard what the general said! Grab the picks and shovels, logs and ropes. We're gonna pull that wall down!" He motioned for a cheer, and the freaks responded raggedly. Glaring at them with stormy eyes, the midget gestured again. This time a rousing cheer met him. Gesturing for them to follow, he marched down the steps, and freaks fell in line behind him.

Marie eased, her shoulders dropping as the performers marched off. She stepped toward Hermos. One of the circus workers brought her a bundle of sheets and a small vial of salve. Receiving these, Marie said, "Thank you," and carried them to the man-giant.

Hermos's haunted eyes remained on her as she approached, but he said nothing, not even when her small hands settled on his leg to find the wound. She kept her face averted, offering no words of comfort. After locating the gouge, she tore the leg of Hermos's breeches away from it and gingerly examined the wound with her fingers. Apparently satisfied, Marie began ripping long strips from a sheet.

"What happened?" Hermos asked at last.

Marie hesitated for only a moment, then finished tearing the strips loose. She draped them over one arm while she opened the strong-smelling vial of salve.

"What have they done to you?" he pressed, his voice thick with concern.

Tilting the vial, she allowed the viscous stuff to seep onto the wound. She held it there, her hand trembling. "Nothing," she managed to rasp out.

A thunderous boom sounded as the performers ran a makeshift ram against the stone wall.

Hermos studied the blind woman's down-turned face. "Is it really you?" he blurted.

Marie paused in wrapping his leg. Another boom sounded, followed by the cascading sound of stone chips and debris. She resumed her wrapping.

Hermos drew his bloodied hand up to the back of her neck. "I missed you." He pulled her hair over her shoulder and gently smoothed down the hairline. She stiffened for a moment, as though she knew what he was doing. But already he had seen that the tattoos were gone.

Heedless, Marie finished wrapping his leg.

As Hermos stared, unbelieving, gooseflesh formed on the back of Marie's neck. He pulled the linen strip from her hands and sloppily tucked it into the bands wrapped on his leg. Then, grasping the sides of her head in his bloody hands, he turned her face up toward his. An expression that mixed fear and relief played across her features as the man-giant gazed into her searching, pupilless eyes.

Another massive *boom*.

"Can you see me?" Hermos whispered anxiously.

A tear streaked down Marie's cheek. She clamped her eyes shut. "Of course I can't."

The man-giant gathered her into his lanky arms. She did not resist, wrapping her small hands about his back and clinging to him. Hermos nodded mutely, the tears now streaming down his face, too. Lifting one long-fingered hand to cradle the back of her head, the man-giant gently removed the ruby pendant and uttered the last phrase that Marie the Blind Juggler would ever hear.

"May Tidhare forgive."

The quiet snap of her neck was drowned out by a shuddering thud and rumble from the bulwark below. A cheer went up in the tunnel as the stony wall tumbled and fragmented, spilling outward onto the sandy bed. Hermos gathered Marie's now limp body in his arms and rocked her slowly, as a father would rock his sleeping child.

"The wall is down!" came the ebullient cry of Valor from the arena floor below. "What is thy next bidding, O great general Marie?"

Hermos, gazing intently at the still form in his arms, almost didn't hear the question. The freaks, impatient for an answer, began rushing up the stairs. Hermos laid Marie down on the cold stone and lightly kissed her forehead.

"Good-bye."

He stood up and bellowed. "Run! Marie says run!" The freaks hesitated on the stair, gazing up wonderingly at the man-giant. "She says escape! Follow me to freedom!"

In five enormous bounds, the giant had reached the arena floor. Digging his feet into the thick sand, he shouted, "Freedom!"

It was Valor who next took up the cry, his eyes flashing knowingly at Hermos. "Freedom! Our only hope. Flee!"

The freaks echoed the call, and, like a fearful, bleating flock, they followed. Hermos bolted into the tunnel

that led from the arena. On his heels, the freaks rushed.
They clambered through the breach in the bulwark, following the manic man-giant out into the carnival
grounds.

   So they went, the ones who remained, running, walking, hobbling—on litters, on crutches and canes. The
line of freaks stretched out through the burnt and toppled carnival, out onto the heath, and into the forest of
a thousand graves. The soldiers sullenly watched them
go: the runners, the crawlers, the stragglers.

   Only the blind woman remained in the arena, the
cold of the stone floor slowly seeping into her body.

EPILOGUE

The carnival lay in ruins, ruins that made wonderful stomping grounds for boys. Black-haired Pierre, hiding beneath a burned-out caravan, released a squeal of delight as his friend Claude discovered him there. Claude reached under the caravan with a twisted stick, but Pierre rolled out the other side.

Claude shouted to the others, "I found him! I found him! Over here!"

Out of the wreckage, four other boys emerged. They were all older than Pierre; all had blond, sandy hair.

"Did you tag the little black-haired pus-bag?" shouted Bernard.

"Yeah," Claude lied, "got him with a stick."

"Did not!" Pierre protested as he ran. He shrieked again as the boys fell in line behind him. He dodged between a pair of torn-up sideshow stages and dropped to his hands and knees to slip through a tight opening. Skidding to a halt beside the small hole, Claude tried vainly to squeeze through. Failing that, he reached his long arms in to snag Pierre's foot. The younger boy pulled it back just in time, laughing in shrill excitement.

"We'll show you," Claude said, jumping onto the worn planks of the stage while Bernard circled around, looking for another opening. The other boys joined Claude, leaping up and down on the planks and making a deafening rumble.

Trembling nervously, Pierre scooted back to the opening and slid through. He ran down the alley, faded tarps rattling at his back as he went. Bernard sounded the alarm, and the other boys scampered off the stage and chased after Pierre.

As the boys closed on him, Pierre took a sharp turn and headed into the arena. Bernard was right behind, with Claude straining at his heels. Panting, Pierre tore through the echoing entrance and out into the lumpy sand of the arena floor. There he stopped and stared, wide-eyed.

The older boys piled into him, knocking him brutally to the sand. At any other time, Pierre might have started to cry, but he was too busy staring into the stands.

A man with the face of a cat sat there, his eyes slitted in hypnotic contentment as he gazed at the ruby pendant that dangled from his fingers.

Claude shoved Pierre hard, pushing him again to the sand. "Got you, you little worm."

"Wait," Pierre protested, rising up on his elbow. "Look at that man!"

Claude rose from the ground and glanced at the cat-faced man briefly, his eyes narrowing. "So what? We *got* you."

"But what's he doin' here?" Pierre asked.

"Who cares?" Claude replied, punching Pierre in the shoulder. Spotting a withered apple core on the sandy ground, the boy picked it up and chucked it at the freak. The core narrowly missed the man's face. Still the creature gazed at the boys imperturbably, his only response an enigmatic smile as he lifted the sparkling necklace and slipped it over his feline head. Turning his attention from the man, Claude said, "Come on. Let's go again. Who wants to be *it?* Stupid little black-hair ain't fast enough for me."

"Come on, just try to catch us," Bernard shouted at the younger boy.

"Wait," Pierre repeated, holding up his small hand and staring at the catman.

The other boys were already brushing the sand from their clothes. "Last one out is *it!*" Bernard said, running for the archway. The other boys, gritting their teeth, followed.

Pierre was last again.

BOOKS

I, Strahd

An Excerpt

by P. N. Elrod

PROLOGUE

Though it was a bright, hot dawn outside, there were no windows in this part of the castle. Van Richten had to provide his own light in the form of a small lantern, which he gripped with a white-knuckled fist. He paused on the last, rough-hewn step at the top of the spiral staircase, caught his breath, and held the lantern as high as his slight stature allowed. Its feeble glow only managed to push back the darkness for a scant few yards, just enough for him to see that the room was apparently empty of threatening occupants. That fact, of course, meant nothing in this place.

He glanced back the way he'd come. Cold stone walls curved sharply down into utter blackness, utter silence. The fingertips of his left hand, which had brushed against the walls as he'd gone up, were still numb from the chill, as if the rock itself had sucked the warmth right out of them. He flexed his stiff hand with a thin but rueful smile that tugged at only one corner of his mouth. *Like master, like castle*, he thought, then his smile vanished as he turned into the room.

If not the true heart of the place, the chamber was certainly a vital organ. Each high wall was covered with books—hundreds, thousands of them, more than Van Richten had seen in one place in his fifty-odd years of scholarly life. The yellow glow of his lantern picked up the sheen from well-oiled leather covers and gilt titles, the occasional flash of a gem, and the dull face of a tome so ancient that no amount of care or restoration could revitalize it. But the outer shell hardly mattered; what lay inside was important.

Van Richten breathed in the books' scent and felt his heart begin to race a little. If the monster had a weakness, and they all did in one form or another, perhaps it would be found here. As a man might be judged by the books he reads, so might a clue be revealed in the neat ranks of titles that marched up the walls. Van Richten suppressed another smile. Not by *any* stretch of fancy could Count Strahd Von Zarovich be considered a mere man anymore, though the local people seemed unaware of his true nature. He'd lost his allotted portion of humanity . . . how many centuries ago? And at what cost in lives and misery and agony of spirit for those hapless souls he'd touched in that time?

But I can't think about that now. Time is too short. Life *is too short.*

He had all the day ahead of him, midsummer day to be sure, the longest of the year, but brief enough now that he saw how much work lay before him. And where to start?

He moved quickly, lighting candles in their sconces as he found them. The black shadows grudgingly retreated. Though the room was cold like the rest of the castle, Van Richten decided to leave the great fireplace dormant. He was comfortable enough in the coat he'd thought to bring and two layers of sweaters. Besides, the telltale smoke would only let all and sundry know the place was occupied, and Van Richten had excellent reasons for keeping this visit as discreet as possible.

The gypsies knew about him, of course; one couldn't enter or leave the place without their help. He had paid them dearly for a guide to take him to the ring of poisonous fog that surrounded Castle Ravenloft. The potion they'd sold him to neutralize the poison had cost extra, but they'd only charged him half as much for the second dosage—macabre indication that they did not expect him to return. In the course of centuries, many bold explorers, well-armed and highly magicked, had gone in to deal with 'the devil Strahd,' as he was known locally. None had ever come out—at least not in the same condition as they'd gone in. What hope did a lone, middle-aged herbalist have?

None, he answered truthfully.

However, he did have knowledge, and upon *that* he was willing to gamble his life. Indeed, more than his life. If he was wrong . . . well, there were much worse things than dying, but he had a kind of escape prepared should it become an eventuality. Not pleasant, but better than the alternative.

So the gypsies had been more than willing to take his money and leave him to his fate. Van Richten had no doubt Strahd knew of his presence in the castle, but he was certain Strahd would do nothing against him. Correction, Strahd *could* do nothing against him.

It had taken Van Richten nearly a decade to guess the truth, and yet another five years of waiting to be sure, and this day, this one midsummer day, he'd proved it by simply walking unchallenged into Castle Ravenloft.

In those fifteen years the place had shown no sign of life. The merchants in the village that lay in its shadow had not received any orders for goods in all that time. The youngest of them even complained about the lack of custom. His father had known something of prosperity, but *these* days? The man had thrown up his hands in well-rehearsed despair for those lost profits. The others were silent or grimly amused by him.

In fifteen years, Lord Strahd had not collected the taxes, though the taxes had been dutifully compiled, the burgomaster proudly stated. There were many old wives' tales about burgomasters who had failed in this task and had come to very bad ends, indeed. Just wives' tales, to be sure, but sometimes there was truth to be found in such fancies. Anyway, none of the villagers, let alone the burgomaster, would risk complaint from their lord. The money, quite a lot of it by now, was stored in a special stone house in the center of town. Thieves? No. They had no fear of thieves. Even the gypsies would not dare to touch it.

Also in that time there had been few unexplained or unusual deaths, as had once been common. Young girls in the prime of their looks no longer disappeared without trace—unless they decided to elope with their lovers. Fifteen years of relative peace, fifteen years of nights that were not so dark as before, fifteen years that Strahd had . . . left them alone.

Some cautiously whispered that perhaps Death had caught up with him at last and taken him away. But if so, then why was the poisoned wall of mist still thick about the castle base? No one had an answer to that one, nor were any too curious to find out. One could ask the gypsies: they knew everything. Aye, and *told* everything. To Strahd. Best not to ask; you might not like the answer.

But Van Richten was sure he had the answer.

Strahd the Ancient, Strahd who was the Land, Strahd the great and awful Lord of Barovia—genius, necromancer, ruthless killer—was now at his most vulnerable.

Strahd Von Zarovich, the vampire, was in hibernation.

Van Richten, who knew as much about the undead as

any living man, was reasonably certain that for a few more years the master of the castle would be unable to stir from the sleep that was not sleep. The odd fact that the scholar stood where he stood—that he hadn't encountered Strahd's undead minions and necromantic guardians—seemed confirmation enough. Perhaps Strahd's dark magicks could not last through his years of quiescence.

But Van Richten was only reasonably certain, which was why he'd allowed himself only one day to investigate. Though he could have spent months poring through the rare books in this room alone, he did not believe in taking unnecessary risks. A single, isolated intrusion that would brush against the dimmed consciousness of the monster was as far as he planned to take it for now. Perhaps later—a year, maybe two, as the vampire settled back into his sluggish dreams—he would return . . . and then he would not be alone.

But for that future expedition Van Richten needed more knowledge. He needed facts, not rumors or folklore or tall tales.

Candles lighted, he looked around the room for a hint of where to start. Even without the implied wealth of the books, the place was a study in opulence. The richly stained wood trims, grass-thick carpet, and inviting couches and chairs all indicated that though Strahd was a monster, he valued his comfort.

Van Richten's brows lifted as he noticed one *objet d'art* in particular. Well. Von Zarovich certainly had excellent taste. Over the exquisitely carved mantlepiece hung an enormous portrait of a young woman. She was breathtakingly lovely, painted by an artist with the skill to capture not only her outer beauty, but the lively purity of her inner soul. There was no date on it, no signature to be seen, but the antique costume the woman wore indicated several centuries had passed since the paint had been wet.

She was mesmerizing, bewitching . . . and long dead. Possibly even one of the Count's early victims. If so, her fate had been a grim one, and Van Richten had no wish or time to speculate on it. His purpose now was to see that other young girls were spared from such horrors.

In the center of the room was a low and massive table, so highly polished that the multiple flames of the candles reflected from its surface as if it were a mirror. Smooth and bright, no speck of dust anywhere. . . .

Van Richten went very still as he regarded the implications of the missing dust. After a moment's thought, he swallowed and hoped his heart would return to its proper place in his chest. Though impossible to detect, it was logical to assume Strahd had placed some sort of magical spell on the room to preserve its contents while he slept. Who knows what damage could be done to the fragile volumes by the gentle onslaught of dust, worms, and nibbling rats? Strahd obviously did—and had allowed for it.

A great book and some sheaves of paper covered with writing lay on the table. Within easy reach was a pot of ink and some quill pens, all expertly cut to a proper point and ready for use. A chair was pulled away from this spot, as though the last occupant had only just walked out and not bothered to push it back into place.

As though at any moment he might return.

Van Richten firmly shrugged off *that* idea. If Strahd had been active, he would have done something by now. The master was asleep, and his castle, like one in some half-remembered child's tale, was in much the same condition. That was how the little herbalist from Mordentshire had been able to pass through the great gates, aware of the dangers, of the torpid guards living and . . . not living. It had been grim going to walk past the dragons that glared down at him from their stone perches and the gargoyles and all the other things that he'd sensed or imagined were lurking in the shadows around him, but he had done it. The traps still worked, but those could be avoided if one had the right skills. He'd gotten in, and, most importantly, he expected to get out again.

He moved toward the table and gently set his lantern down, using a stack of yellowing paper to keep its metal base from scratching the pristine wood.

You're a foolish old humbug, Rudolph, he chided himself. But he had an ingrained respect for workmanship, and the table was a beautiful piece of art, however terrible its owner.

Carefully and not a little nervously, he ran his fingers over the fine leather cover of the book. It had an odd texture to it, odd and repulsive, as if it were made from . . .

He yanked his hands away as he realized the source of the unusual leather.

Damn the creature. Damn the thing *that was capable of such an obscenity.*

After a moment's pause to offer a prayer for the soul of the book's victim, he inhaled a great breath, and reached out again, swiftly opening it.

It wasn't precisely a book, so much as a collection of various folios loosely bound together in such a way that more could be added or removed as needed. Some of the parchment pages were the color of cream, thick and substantial, made to last many, many lifetimes. Other pages were thin and desiccated, positively yellow from age, and crackled alarmingly as he turned them over. There were no ornate illuminations, no fussy borders, only lines of plain text in hard black ink. The flowing handwriting was a bit difficult to follow at first; the writer's style of calligraphy had not been in common use for three hundred years. No table of contents, but from the dates it looked to be some kind of history.

He turned to the first page and read:

I, Strahd, Lord of Barovia, well aware certain
events of my reign have been desperately
misunderstood by those who are better at garbling
history than recording it, hereby set down an exact
record of those events, that the *truth may at last
be known*. . . .

He caught his breath. By all the good gods, *a personal journal?*